"I don't believe I have ever seen so many women gathered in one place before. There must be thousands."

Tess tensed. "Wait. How will you find us again if we go inside without you?"

"I could probably spot you in the crowd by your pr… By your hair," Michael said.

"You were going to say pretty, weren't you?" She smiled, amused by the way his cheeks grew more ruddy.

"It would be wrong of me to mention such things, Miss Clark."

That made her laugh softly. "But I would find it delightful if you did. Does that embarrass you, Michael?"

"Of course not."

He brought the buggy to a halt, then quickly helped her alight. "I'll find you."

She knew that her eyes must be twinkling, because she was keenly amused when she shouted back, "And how will you do *that*, sir?"

Michael paused just long enough to lean down from his perch. "By your beautiful dark red hair." Then he flicked the reins and the horse took off.

USA TODAY Bestselling Author

Valerie Hansen
and
Sara Mitchell

Rescuing the Heiress
&
A Most Unusual Match

LOVE INSPIRED
INSPIRATIONAL ROMANCE

LOVE INSPIRED®

INSPIRATIONAL ROMANCE

ISBN-13: 978-1-335-45480-5

Rescuing the Heiress & A Most Unusual Match

Copyright © 2020 by Harlequin Books S.A.

Rescuing the Heiress
First published in 2011. This edition published in 2020.
Copyright © 2011 by Valerie Whisenand

A Most Unusual Match
First published in 2011. This edition published in 2020.
Copyright © 2011 by Sara Mitchell

Recycling programs
for this product may
not exist in your area.

This edition published by arrangement with Harlequin Books S.A.

For questions and comments about the quality of this book,
please contact us at CustomerService@Harlequin.com.

Love Inspired
22 Adelaide St. West, 40th Floor
Toronto, Ontario M5H 4E3, Canada
www.Harlequin.com

Printed in U.S.A.

CONTENTS

Valerie Hansen was thirty when she awoke to the presence of the Lord in her life and turned to Jesus. She now lives in a renovated farmhouse on the breathtakingly beautiful Ozark Plateau of Arkansas and is privileged to share her personal faith by telling the stories of her heart for Love Inspired. Life doesn't get much better than that!

Books by Valerie Hansen

Love Inspired Historical

Frontier Courtship
Wilderness Courtship
High Plains Bride
The Doctor's Newfound Family
Rescuing the Heiress
Her Cherokee Groom

Love Inspired Suspense

The Defenders

Nightwatch
Threat of Darkness
Standing Guard
A Trace of Memory
Small Town Justice

Visit the Author Profile page
at Harlequin.com for more titles.

RESCUING THE HEIRESS

Valerie Hansen

Though I walk in the midst of trouble,
you preserve my life.... With your right
hand you save me.
—*Psalms* 138:7

My husband was a firefighter, my son still is and my daughter also volunteered before she went into nursing.

The men and women in the fire service put their whole hearts into their work and no amount of praise or thanks for their efforts will ever be enough.

Chapter One

1906, San Francisco

"We can't ask Michael to do it. What would your father say if he found out?"

Tess Clark squared her shoulders, lifted her chin and smiled at the personal maid who had also become her friend and confidante. "Of course we can, Annie dear. Father would much rather we be escorted to the meeting by a gentleman than venture out unaccompanied, especially after dark. Besides, your mother's planning to attend, isn't she?"

"She said she might. But she lives down by the pavilion. She's used to being out and about in that neighborhood after dark." The slim young woman shivered. "It's no place for a society girl like you."

"Humph." Tess shook her head, making her dainty pearl earbobs swing. "Just because my family lives on Nob Hill doesn't mean I'm that different from other people. I want to support the cause of women's rights as much as you do." She pressed her lips into a thin line. "Maybe more so."

"But..."

Adamant, Tess stood firm. "No arguments. We're going to the meeting. I intend to hear Maud Younger speak before she goes back to New York, and we may never have a better opportunity."

"You're not afraid of what your father will do when he finds out?"

"I didn't say that," Tess admitted wryly. "Father can be very forceful at times. He'd certainly be irate if we made the journey alone. That's why we need a strapping escort like Michael Mahoney."

Annie covered her mouth with her hand and snickered. "And handsome, too."

Tess couldn't argue. She'd have had to be wearing blinders to have missed noticing how the family cook's son had matured, especially since he'd reached his mid-twenties. Truth to tell, Tess had done more than notice. She had dreamed of what her life might be like if she were a mere domestic like Annie rather than the daughter of wealthy banker Gerald Bell Clark. She might sometimes choose to view herself as a middle-class resident of the City by the Bay but that didn't mean she would be accepted as such by anyone who knew who she really was.

"I just had a thought," Tess said, eyeing her boon companion and beginning to smile. "I think it would be wise if we both attend the lecture incognito. I still have a few of my mother's old hats and wraps. It'll be like playing dress-up when we were children."

Annie rolled her blue eyes, eyes that matched Tess's as if they were trueborn sisters. "To listen to your papa talk, you'd think we were still babes instead of eighteen. Why, we're nearly old maids."

That made Tess laugh. "Hardly, dear. But I do see your point. Papa probably sees us as children because he's so prone to dwell on the past. He never talks about it but I don't think he's ever truly recovered from Mama's passing."

"I miss her, too," Annie said. "She was a lovely lady."

"And one who would want to march right along with us, arm in arm, if she were still alive," Tess said with conviction.

"March? Oh, dear. We aren't going to have to do that, are we? I mean, what will people say if we're seen as part of an unruly mob? Susan B. Anthony was arrested!"

"And she stood up for her rights just the same," Tess said with a lift of her chin. "According to the literature I've read, she never has paid the fines the courts levied."

"That's all well and good for a crusader like her. What about me? If your father finds out I went with you, he might fire me. You know my mother can't do enough sewing and mending to support me and herself. She barely gets by with what I manage to add to her income. If I lost this job…"

"You won't," Tess assured her.

"You can't be sure of that."

"I know that my father is a fair man. And he does love me—in his own way—so he'll listen if I find it necessary to defend you. I think sometimes that he's afraid to show much affection, perhaps because of Mama."

"You do resemble her. Same dark red hair, same sky-blue eyes, fair skin and sweet smile."

Tess began to blush. "Thank you. I always thought she was beautiful."

"So are you," Annie insisted. "The only real difference I can see is that you're so terribly stubborn and willful."

"That I get from my father," Tess said with a quiet chuckle, "and glad of it. Otherwise, how could I possibly hope to stand up to him, express my wishes and actually prevail?"

"When have you done that?"

"Well…" Tess's cheeks warmed even more. "I shall. Someday. When I have a cause, a reason that I feel warrants such boldness."

"Like woman suffrage, you mean?"

Tess sobered. "Yes. That's exactly what I mean. Now, go find Michael and tell him what we need. Look in the kitchen. It's Friday so he should be visiting his mother."

"You keep track of his schedule?"

"Of course not. I just happened to remember that he has every other Friday afternoon free, that's all, and I don't believe I noticed him being here last week." She looked away, taking a moment to compose herself and hoping Annie wouldn't press her for a better explanation.

"Come with me?"

Tess arched a slim eyebrow. "You're not afraid of him, are you?"

"No, I just get this funny, fluttery feeling in my stomach when I see him and I can hardly speak, let alone be convincing. It's as if my tongue is tied."

Unfortunately, Tess knew *exactly* what Annie meant. Between the mischievous twinkle in the man's dark eyes and his hint of an Irish brogue, he was truly captivating. "All right. We'll both go. He might be more likely to agree to accompany us if I asked him."

"Of course. He won't want to jeopardize his mother's job by refusing."

It bothered Tess to hear that rationale. She had hoped to persuade the attractive, twenty-four-year-old fireman to do her bidding by simply appealing to his gallantry. The suggestion that her family's importance, both at home on the Clark estate and in the city proper, might be a stronger influence was disheartening.

It was also true.

Michael Mahoney had come straight from work, shedding his brass-buttoned, dark wool uniform jacket and leather-beaked cap as soon as he entered the overly warm kitchen of the Clark estate.

He gave his mother a peck on the cheek, took a deep breath and sighed loudly for her benefit. "Mmm, something smells heavenly."

Clearly pleased, Mary grinned and chuckled. "Of course it does."

"Will you be wanting more apples peeled?" he asked, starting to turn back his shirt cuffs while eyeing a sugar-and-cinnamon-topped bowl of already prepared fruit. "I'll be glad to help, especially if I get to taste one of those pies you're making." He pulled a stool up to the table and sat down.

Hands dusted with flour, Mary was rolling circles of crust at the opposite end of the work-worn oak surface. "That's no job for an important man like you, Michael." She used the back of her wrist to brush a wispy curl away from her damp forehead. "You have a career now. You don't need to be helpin' me."

"Clark should have hired you a kitchen maid long

ago," Michael said flatly. "With all his money you'd think he'd be glad to lighten your burdens."

"I've had a few girls here. None lasted. They were too lazy. 'Twas easier for me to just jump in and do their chores than to wait."

"Still, I think I should have a talk with him."

"Don't you dare. I'd be mortified."

"Why?"

"Because Mr. Clark is a good man and a fine boss. I wouldn't want him thinkin' I wasn't grateful. He gave me a raise in salary you know."

"Over a year ago or longer. If Mrs. Clark was still in the household you'd have gotten more than just the one."

"I know. She was such a darling girl, poor thing. The mister's not been the same since she passed." Mary sighed deeply, noisily. "I know how he feels. Sometimes it seems like your da will walk in the door one day and greet me the way he did for so many wonderful years."

Michael chose not to respond. His father had been lost at sea while working as a seaman almost ten years ago, and before that had only come home on rare occasions. If they hadn't had a fading photograph of the man, Michael wondered if he'd have been able to picture him at all.

"It's been a long time," he said. "You're still a comely woman. Why not set your cap for a man who can take care of you?"

"Now, why would I be wantin' to do that when my lovin' son is goin' to look after me in me old age?"

Chuckling, Michael nodded. "All right. You've made your point. And I will, you know. I just have to work my way up in the department until I'm making enough money to feed us both and qualify for family housing."

He laughed more. "I don't suppose you'd be wantin' to live in the station house with all those rowdy boys and me."

"Might remind me of my brothers back in Eire, but, no, I have a nice room here. I'll wait till you're better set before I make my home with you."

He reached to steal a slice of cinnamon-flecked apple from the bowl and was rewarded by her "Tsk-tsk" and a playful swat in his direction.

"I always knew you were a wise woman," he said, popping the tangy bit into his mouth.

"And don't you be forgettin' it," Mary warned.

From the doorway came a softly spoken, "Forget what?"

Michael's head snapped around and he jumped to his feet. He knew that voice well, yet hearing it never ceased to give him a jolt. Whether it was a sense of joy or of tension, he had not been able to decide.

Licking his lips and dusting sugar granules off his hands, he nodded politely. "Miss Tess. Miss Annie. Good afternoon."

Annie giggled and followed Tess into the warm kitchen.

"Umm. That bread baking smells wonderful. I can hardly wait to butter a slab," Tess said.

Mary gave a slight curtsy and wiped her floury hands on her apron as she eyed the imposing gas stove. "Thank you, miss. It should be ready soon."

"Then perhaps we'll wait." Tess looked to Michael and gave him a slight smile. "How have you been?"

"Fine, thank you. I just dropped in to pay a call on my mother."

"As you should. Your employment is progressing satisfactorily, I presume?"

"Yes. I'm next in line to be promoted to captain of my fire company."

"How impressive. I wish you well."

He'd been studying Tess as she spoke and sensed that there was more on her mind than mere polite formalities. She and Annie had both been acting unduly uneasy, paying him close attention and fidgeting more than was normal for either of them.

"Thank you," Michael said with a lopsided, knowing smile. "Why am I getting the impression that you ladies have something else to say?"

"Perhaps because we do," Tess said. He saw her tighten the clasp of her hands at her waist and noticed that she was worrying a lace-edged handkerchief in her slim fingers.

"And what would that be?"

"I—we—are in sore need of an escort this evening and we were wondering if you would be so kind."

"An escort?" Michael's brow knit. "Don't you have a beau who can provide that service?"

Tess's cheeks flamed but she held her ground. "At the moment, sadly, no. However, Annie and I would be honored if you could find the time to accompany us. We can use one of father's carriages if you like."

His dark eyebrows arched. "Oh? And where would we be going?"

"Mechanics' Pavilion. There's going to be—"

"Whoa. I know what's going on there tonight. I won't be a party to your participation in such a folly."

"I beg your pardon?"

Well, now I've ruffled her feathers, Michael concluded, seeing her eyes widen and hearing the rancor in her tone. Nevertheless, he knew he was right. "The pardon you should be beggin' is your father's," he said flatly. "Mr. Clark has a reputation to maintain, for himself and for his bank. You can't be keepin' company with the likes of those crazy women."

"I can and I will," Tess insisted. "If you won't escort us, then we'll go alone."

His jaw gaped for a moment before he snapped it shut. "I almost believe you."

"You'd best do so, sir, because I mean every word."

Looking to his mother, Michael saw her struggling to subdue a smirk. That was a fine kettle of fish. His own ma was evidently siding with the younger women. What was this world coming to? Didn't they know their place? Hadn't men been taking good care of women like them for untold generations?

Sure there was the problem of widows and orphans, but there were benevolent societies to provide for those needs. The last thing San Francisco—or the entire nation—needed was to give women a say in politics. No telling where a mistake like that would eventually lead.

"I can't understand why you feel so strongly about this, Miss Tess. I've known you ever since my mother came to work here and I've never noticed such unreasonableness."

"It isn't unreasonable to want to hear the facts explained by one of the movement's leaders," Tess said.

Seeing the jut of her chin and the rigidity of her spine, he was convinced that she was serious so he tried another approach. "It could be dangerous. There have been riots as a result of such rabble-rousing."

"All the more reason why you should be delighted to look after us," she countered. "Well?"

Michael felt as stuck as a loaded freight wagon bogged down and sinking in quicksand. Slowly shaking his head, he nevertheless capitulated. "All right. I'm not scheduled to work tonight. If there are no fire alarms between now and then, I'll take you. What time do you want to leave?"

"The meeting commences at eight," Tess said. "I assume that's so wives and mothers will not have to neglect their families in order to attend. You may call for us at half past seven. I'll have the carriage ready."

With that she grabbed Annie's hand and quickly led her out of the room, their long, plaited skirts swishing around their ankles as they went.

Michael sank back onto the stool. When he glanced at his mother he noted that she was grinning from ear to ear.

"Well, well, if I hadn't seen it with me own eyes I'd not have believed it," Mary drawled. "My full-grown son was just steamrolled by a slip of a girl. 'Twas quite a sight."

"That it was," Michael said. "I can hardly believe it myself. What's happened to Tess? She used to be so levelheaded and obedient."

"You think she's not being sensible? Ha! If you ask me, she and others like her are going to come to the rescue of this wicked world. Imagine how those crooked politicians will squirm when they can't rely only on the good old boys who've been keeping them in office in spite of their evil shenanigans."

"Ma! Watch yourself. If Mr. Clark was to overhear

you, he might think you were responsible for Tess's crazy notions."

"More likely that girl's responsible for waking me up," his mother replied. "If I didn't have so many chores tonight, I might just be tempted to go listen to Miss Younger, too."

Tess had raided the attic with Annie and they had both come away with elaborately decorated dark hats and veils.

Annie's was silk with the brim rolled to one side and the crown bedecked with silk and muslin cup roses and a taffeta bow.

Tess chose the one she had always loved seeing her mother wear. It had two sweeping ostrich plumes anchored in a rosette of shiny black taffeta centered with a large jet ornament. That pin had been a gift from her father to her mother and Mama had always adored it.

Their shirtwaist blouses and lightweight, plaited skirts were their own but they had covered them with heavy wool coats. Tess's reached below her ankles. Annie's brushed the floor.

"I'm too short," the girl complained, lifting the hem. "I'll get it all dusty."

"Better dust than mud," Tess countered. "Just be thankful it isn't as wet out there as it usually is in the spring."

She glanced from the second-floor window of her bedroom where they were finishing their preparations. The garden below was bathed in a light mist, and beyond toward the Pacific, clouds lay low, obscuring the moon and much of the landscape, including the lights of the parts of the city nearest the shore.

"Hopefully it won't rain later tonight," Tess said. "Looks like the fog is going to be bad though."

"I know. Maybe we shouldn't go out."

"Nonsense. Did you order my mare harnessed to the buggy and tell them when to bring it around, as we'd planned?"

"Yes. But I don't know that we'll have a driver. The last I saw of Michael he was still with Mary. I thought surely he'd want to go home and change if he truly intended to take us."

"I suspect he was wishing he'd be called back to work so he wouldn't have to keep that promise," Tess said. "I sincerely hope he doesn't spend the entire evening lecturing us on the proper place of women in the home."

Annie grinned. "He can't really do that unless he goes inside and listens to Miss Younger."

"Which is highly unlikely," Tess added. "Wasn't he funny when he got so uppity? Imagine thinking he can tell us what to do."

"He sounded like your father may when he finds out what we've been up to tonight." Annie was shivering in spite of the warmth of her wool coat. "I'm not looking forward to that."

"Nor am I," Tess replied with a slight nod, "but I truly feel that this is a cause worth investigating. It's not as if you and I were planning to officially join the movement or anything like that. We're just curious. Think of it as a lark."

"Michael surely doesn't see it that way."

"No." Tess sobered. "But his opinion isn't our concern. As long as he lives up to his promise we'll have no trouble."

"I wish we'd asked someone else to escort us."

"I don't," Tess replied candidly. Truth to tell, she was looking forward to being driven into the heart of the city by the handsome fireman almost as much as she was looking forward to hearing the suffragette lecture.

She began to smile, then grin. There weren't many socially acceptable ways she could spend time with the cook's son. Not that she'd ever admit she was looking for any. Perish the thought. But this adventure would be fun. And perhaps in the long run, one more man would begin to understand why so many women were banding together to demand emancipation.

Annie's squeal startled her from her reverie. "The buggy's here!" She grabbed her hat to help hold it in place as she added another long pin. "It's time to go."

"All right, all right. Keep your voice down or Father will hear."

"Sorry." Annie pressed the fingertips of one hand to her lips while continuing to steady the large hat with her other. "Did you leave a note?"

"Yes," Tess whispered. "And I sincerely hope Father doesn't find reason to miss us and read it." She reached for the other young woman's gloved hand. "Come on. Our carriage awaits."

Chapter Two

Here they come, Michael thought. *Or do they?* He shook his head in disbelief. Except for the lightness of their steps, the approaching pair resembled stodgy matrons rather than the lithe, lovely young women he had expected. If this was their idea of a joke he was not amused.

While a groom steadied the horse, Michael circled the cabriolet to assist them. Frowning, he offered his hand.

"Good evening, Mr. Mahoney," Tess said, placing her small, gloved fingers in his and raising her hem just enough to place her dainty foot on the step leading to the rear seat.

"It'll be good only if your father doesn't find out what you're up to," Michael countered. "I can't believe you convinced me to be a party to this."

Stepping aboard, she laughed softly, her eyes twinkling behind the thin veil that she'd arranged to cover her face. "Neither can I."

"You two look like you're going to a funeral," he said with disdain. "I just hope it isn't mine."

Tess merely laughed. Michael was too troubled to comment further. Instead, he helped Annie up the same step, then vaulted easily into the driver's seat. "Ready?"

"Ready," they said in unison, sounding like two happy children headed for a romp in Golden Gate Park on a sunny afternoon.

Their carefree attitude irritated Michael. He'd spent enough time in the seamier parts of San Francisco to know that his chore of protecting these foolish young women might prove harder than either of them imagined. Yes, the city was more civilized than it had been right after the gold rush, but there were still plenty of ne'er-do-wells, drunks and just plain crooks out and about, especially after dark.

His fondest hope was that the crowd of women at Mechanics' Pavilion would act as an adequate buffer to help safeguard his charges. He couldn't hold off a mob single-handed, not even if he were armed, which he was not.

An aroma of salt water and rotting refuse from down by the wharves was borne on the fog, although it didn't seem quite as offensive as usual, probably because the evening was quite cool and there was no onshore wind to carry as much of the odor inland.

Michael flicked the reins lightly to encourage the horse to trot after he turned onto Powell Street. Driving over the cobblestones with the metal-rimmed carriage wheels gave their passage a rough, staccato cadence, although there was so much other traffic on the wide boulevard the sounds melded into a clatter that made it hard to differentiate one noise from the others.

Teamsters yelled at their teams, whipping the poor beasts to force them to haul overfilled wagons up the steep streets from the wharves. A herd of cattle was evidently being driven up Market Street because their combined bellowing and shouts of the drovers working them could be heard blocks away.

Add to that the occasional echoing pistol shot, probably coming from the seamier areas of the city, and Michael was decidedly uneasy. The sooner they reached the pavilion and he got these two innocents settled inside the hall, the happier he'd be.

A giggle came from behind him, tickling the fine hairs at the nape of his neck. It was Tess. Of course it was. Annie might be accompanying her but this so-called adventure had most certainly originated in Tess's active mind.

He glanced over his shoulder. "What's so funny?"

"Nothing," Tess replied, her voice still tinged with humor. "I was just thinking of how much more enjoyable this jaunt would be if we'd taken Papa's new motorcar."

"You'd need a different driver if you had," Michael told her flatly. "I've plenty of experience handling the lines but never an automobile."

"You drive them with a wheel or a steering lever, not reins," Tess teased. "Everybody knows that. Papa says the time will come when horses are unnecessary."

"I doubt that. Those machines will never catch on. Too noisy and complicated. Besides, you'd spend all your spare time stopping at pharmacies to buy jugs of fuel. Imagine the inconvenience."

"No more so than having to feed and water horses," she countered. "You should know all about that. Those fire horses you care for are beautiful animals. When they race through the streets as a team it's a thrilling sight."

"How would you know?"

She tittered behind her gloved hand. "I have seen them in action many times. And you driving them, if you must know."

"Have you, now? That's a bit of a surprise." When he turned slightly farther and smiled at her, he saw her gather herself and raise her chin.

"I can't understand why it should be. Station #4 is not too far from Father's bank and it is impossible to ignore that noisy, clanging bell and that steaming engine racing through the streets at such reckless speeds."

"It's only reckless if unheeding pedestrians step in front of us. The bell is meant to be enough warning for any sensible person."

To Michael's surprise, she agreed with him. "You're right, of course. I didn't mean to sound disparaging. I think your profession is most honorable."

One more quick glance showed him that she was smiling behind the veil and it was all he could do to keep from breaking into a face-splitting grin at her praise. There was something impish yet charming about the banker's daughter. Always had been, if he were totally honest with himself.

Someday, Michael vowed silently, he would find a suitable woman with a spirit like Tess's and give her a proper courting. He had no chance with Tess herself, of course. That went without saying. Still, she couldn't be the only appealing lass in San Francisco. When he was good and ready he'd begin to look around. There was plenty of time. Most men waited to wed until they could properly look after a wife and family.

If he'd been a rich man's son instead of the offspring of a lowly sailor, however, perhaps he'd have shown a personal interest in Miss Clark or one of her socialite friends already.

Would he really have? he asked himself. He doubted it. There was a part of Michael that was repelled by the affectations of the wealthy, by the way they lorded it over the likes of him and his widowed mother. He knew Tess couldn't help that she'd been born into a life of luxury, yet he still found her background off-putting.

Which is just as well, he reminded himself. It was bad enough that they were likely to be seen out and about on this particular evening. If the maid Annie Dugan hadn't been along for the ride, he knew he'd have had a lot more questions to answer; answers that could, if misinterpreted, lead to his ruination. His career with the fire department depended upon a sterling reputation as well as a Spartan lifestyle and strong work ethic.

Michael had labored too long and hard to let anything spoil his pending promotion to captain. He set his jaw and grasped the reins more tightly. Not even the prettiest, smartest, most persuasive girl in San Francisco was going to get away with doing that.

He sighed, realizing that Miss Tess Clark fit that flowery description to a *T.*

Tess settled back on the velvet tufted upholstery in the rear seat of the cabriolet and watched as they finally turned south on Van Ness and approached the center of the city. The streets in this district were well lit and broad enough to accommodate plenty of traffic, yet still seemed terribly crowded.

Parallel sets of trolley tracks with a power line buried

between them ran down the center of the thoroughfare. These lines sliced their way through the cobblestones in much the same way the cable for the cable cars did, except for the fact that the trolleys were driven by electric power. Traffic increased rapidly and included quite a few of the infernal motorcars that Michael had spoken so strongly against.

Tess leaned forward and placed one gloved hand on the low back of the seat near his elbow while pointing with her other. "There's an automobile. And two more. See? They seem to be much easier to maneuver, particularly over the ruts of the streetcar tracks, no matter how the driver approaches them."

"That's only because most buggy wheels are narrower," he argued, carefully maneuvering the cabriolet between a parked dray and one of the modern streetcars as it passed. "I can't believe how some people drive with no concern for anyone else. It's little wonder there are so many accidents these days."

"Father says the motorcars will put an end to that because there won't be any horses to get frightened and bolt." She noted how hard Michael was working to control her spirited mare in the presence of the unusual, sputtering vehicles. Some of the other teamsters were having similar difficulties. "See what I mean?"

"All I see is that there's probably not going to be a good place to leave this rig near the pavilion," he replied. "Would it be all right if I let you ladies off near the door and then looked for a spot around the corner? There should be more room on Market Street, as long as the drovers have their cattle rounded up and moved on by now."

"Of course," Tess said, hoping her inflection wouldn't

inadvertently reveal a desire to remain near the handsome fireman. "You can stop anywhere. I see the banner. This is where we belong."

"In your opinion." Michael huffed. "I don't believe I have ever seen so many women gathered in one place before. There must be thousands."

Tess tensed. "Wait. How will you find us again if we go inside without you?"

"I don't know. If you weren't wearing that enormous hat I could probably spot you in the crowd by your pr— By your hair."

"You were going to say pretty, weren't you?" She smiled, amused by the way his cheeks grew more ruddy in the light from the streetlamps surrounding the enormous meeting hall.

"It would be wrong of me to mention such things, Miss Clark."

That made her laugh softly. "But I would find it delightful if you did. Does that embarrass you, Michael?"

"Of course not."

He brought the buggy to a halt as close to the curb as possible, then quickly helped both young women alight and saw them to the curb before once again climbing into the driver's seat.

"Take off your hat after you get inside," he called over the din of the crowd. "I'll find you."

She knew that her eyes must be twinkling because she was keenly amused when she shouted back, "And how will you do *that,* sir?"

Michael paused just long enough to lean down from his perch and say more privately, "By your beautiful, dark red hair." Then he flicked the reins and the horse took off.

Beside her, Tess heard Annie sigh. "Oh, my. That man's smile could melt butter in the middle of winter." The shorter girl had clasped her hands over her heart and was clearly mooning.

For some reason Annie's overt interest in Michael needled Tess. She knew it was foolish to allow herself to be bothered, since the maid was a far more likely social choice for him to make than she was.

Nevertheless, Tess was surprised and a little saddened by a twinge of jealousy. What was wrong with her? Was she daft? Just because a man was stalwart and handsome and so glib-tongued that his very words sent shivers up her spine, it didn't mean that she should take his supposed interest seriously. After all, she was a Clark, a member of the San Francisco upper crust. And as such she did have a family reputation to uphold whether she thought it a silly pretense or not.

Standing tall and leading the way, Tess gathered a handful of skirt for ease of walking and crossed the lawn to the wide entry doors of the meeting hall. There were ladies from all walks of life proceeding with her in a flowing tide of gracious yet clearly animated womanhood, she noted, pleased and energized by the atmosphere.

Perhaps this suffragette movement would remove some of the social stigmas that had always set her apart from many of her good sister Christians like Annie, she mused. If it did nothing else, she would be forever grateful.

Michael worked his way slowly south on Van Ness Avenue and turned onto Market Street. As he had hoped, there was plenty of room there for the Clark buggy. He tipped a small boy in tattered knee britches and a slouchy cap to watch the rig for him while he was gone, then headed back for Mechanics' Pavilion at a trot.

He hadn't gone a hundred yards when a man grabbed his arm and stopped him. It was one of his fellow firemen.

"Hey, Michael, me boy. Where're you bound in such a hurry?"

Before thinking, he answered, "The pavilion."

That young man, and those with him, guffawed. "No wonder you're wearin' your uniform. If you're lookin' to use that badge to impress a good woman, you surely won't find one there. Where are you really goin'?"

"None of your business, O'Neill."

"Now, now, don't be trying to get above yourself, boyo." He laughed again, spewing the odor of strong drink on a cloud of his breath.

"Don't worry about me," Michael replied with disdain. "Just take care of yourself and don't end up in a bar fight again."

O'Neill's only reply was a hearty laugh and a slap on the back as he shared his amusement with most of the others gathered nearby.

Michael hurried away from the group of obviously inebriated men, hoping none of them decided to trail after him on a lark. It wasn't that he felt he couldn't handle himself well in any situation. He just didn't want his cronies to follow him all the way to Tess and continue their taunts, straining the difficult circumstances even further.

He needn't have worried. Getting past the crowd milling around in the street and on the sidewalks and lawn bordering the enormous Mechanics' Pavilion was so difficult, Michael doubted he'd be followed by anyone.

It was all he could do to work his way through to the meeting hall entrance. First he had to run the gauntlet of shouting, chanting, angry men carrying placards denouncing the women's movement, then convince the uniformed police officers posted at the doors that his intentions were peaceful and honorable.

"I escorted several young ladies," Michael shouted to the guards. "They're waiting for me inside. I promised to join them." He held up his right hand, palm out. "On my honor."

The burly doormen looked at each other and then back at him, clearly cognizant of his official fireman's attire. "All right," one of them said. "But any trouble from you and you're headed for the paddy wagon just like anybody else. We've got more'n one waitin' right out back."

"I promise I'm not going to be a problem," Michael vowed, still holding up his hand and doffing his hat as he sidled through the narrow space between the two broad-shouldered officers.

The door most of the women were using stood wide-open. That feminine multitude was sweeping through without being questioned, although many were casting sidelong glances at each other as if they were either worried or wary. Or both. He supposed, given that this kind of gathering was such an unusual occurrence, it was natural for some of them to be uneasy particularly if their husbands didn't know where they had gone.

On the other hand there were the stalwarts like Tess, who were obviously not intimidated by a crowd, especially not by one composed mainly of members of the fairer persuasion. How on earth could he hope to locate her among this mass of velvet and feathers, furs and veils? Surely she'd realize his dilemma and at least wave her hand in the air from time to time.

Straining with cap in hand, he stretched to his full six-foot height to peer at the seething mass of well-dressed women. Those who did not have fancy hats covered with flowers and feathers were in the minority, although there did seem to be a fair number of plainer bonnets or uncovered heads as well. That was where he'd made his mistake. By assuming that only Tess would be bareheaded, he'd become overconfident.

The press of the crowd was stifling. Various aromas of perfume assaulted him as they mixed and permeated the already overly warm inside air.

He raised his eyes to the vaulted ceiling and was in the midst of a short, silent prayer for guidance when he noticed a gallery.

As he headed for the stairway leading to the upper tier he continued to pray. "Father, I know there's no way I'll ever find Tess in this mess unless You help me." His heart skipped and hammered. "Please?"

Gaining the landing, he gripped the rail and gazed down at the rows and rows of benches facing a stage where several well-dressed but otherwise unremarkable ladies sat. If not for their position at the podium, he would have assumed they were merely a part of the audience.

Would Tess press closer to the stage so she could observe the speaker's expressions? He assumed so, given her earlier conversation and the determined way she had been behaving.

Starting at the center near the front, Michael began to systematically scan the crowd row by row. He had to force himself to take his time and study the back of each person's head carefully in spite of his burgeoning anxiety.

His "Where are you?" was spoken barely above a whisper. *There? No, that wasn't her. How about...? No.*

Jostled and pushed, he stubbornly clung to his place at the railing and prayed he wouldn't have to actually return to the ground floor and make a spectacle of himself in order to locate and be reunited with the two young women. Bringing them there in the first place was bad enough. Calling attention to such a folly would be a hundred times worse.

Michael took a sudden gulp of air. *There! Was that her?*

Maybe. Maybe not. His breathing was already ragged and his heart was pounding exactly the way it did every time he answered a fire alarm. His hands fisted on the rail. He wanted to shout out, to call to Tess. To see if it truly was her he was staring at.

Fear for her safety and well-being stopped him. There might be few folks in this particular crowd who would recognize wealthy Gerald Bell Clark's daughter on sight, but many knew her name only from the society pages of the *Chronicle*. It would be unwise to call attention to her in this unusual situation, especially since he was currently too far away to protect her if need be.

Watching and continuing to hold perfectly still, he willed the reddish-haired woman to turn her head just the slightest so he could be certain.

In moments she did better than that. Standing and swiveling while she removed her coat, she looked over the crowd behind her, eventually letting her gaze rise and come to rest on the balcony.

Michael tensed. His breath whooshed out with relief. There was no doubt. It *was* Tess.

He was about to leave his place to join her when he saw her raise her arm, grin broadly and wave to him as if she had just spotted the most important person present.

To his delight and equally strong sense of self-disgust, he was so thrilled by her candid reaction that he temporarily froze.

In all the time they had been acquainted, Tess had never looked at him that way before. *Or had she?* He blinked to clear his head and sort out his racing thoughts. No matter how hard he tried to deny it, he kept imagining that perhaps she *had* done so and he had been too blind, too dunderheaded to have noticed. Until tonight.

As he started back down the stairs to join her he corrected that supposition. It wasn't foolish to ignore Tess's apparent personal interest. In his case it was the only intelligent thing to do. Even considering her to be a mere friend could prove detrimental.

The idea that she might actually covet a deeper relationship with him was unthinkable. Ridiculous. Nothing good—for either of them—could ever come from entertaining such an outrageous folly. Not even in his dreams.

Chapter Three

The sight of Michael gazing down upon her sent a tingle of awareness singing up Tess's spine. There was no question that it was she whom he sought. The way his countenance lit up when he spotted her removed any possible doubt. And to her chagrin, she was just as thrilled to see him.

At her elbow, Annie gave a little shriek, "Up there! Is that Michael?"

Tess cast her a stern look. "Hush. You'll embarrass him. He sees us. He's coming."

"I know." Once again the maid's hands were clasped in front of her as if preparing to pray. "My knees are knocking something awful."

"Then sit down and get control of yourself," Tess told her. "We don't want to create a scene."

Tess, too, seated herself after managing to tear her gaze from the sight of Michael Mahoney zigzagging his way through the throng to join them. It wasn't easy to keep from peering over her shoulder in anticipation of his arrival. She kept herself busy by repositioning her hat and moving the pins that had held it firmly to her upswept hairdo.

Seconds ticked by. Tess was just about to stand and look for him anew when she sensed his presence.

"Is there room for me or shall I stand at the back of the room and wait?" he asked, bending to speak quietly into her ear.

Tess failed to suppress a shiver as his breath tickled her cheek and ruffled a tiny wisp of hair. She attempted to mask her reaction by gathering her skirts and scooting closer to Annie on her right.

"We'll make room," Tess said. "Please, join us." She had expected him to immediately comply. When he hesitated, she glanced up and noticed that he seemed uneasy. "What's wrong?"

"I don't know. I just got a funny feeling."

"Probably another little earthquake," Tess said with a sigh. "I've felt several since we arrived. At first I thought it was just the press of the crowd and all the perfumery making me a bit dizzy, but once I sat down, I decided it couldn't be that."

She folded her coat on her lap and patted the small section of bench that she had just cleared. "Come. Sit down. I think they're about to start the meeting."

As Michael eased himself into the narrow space and his shoulder pressed against hers, Tess was once again light-headed. She blinked and tried to concentrate, to gauge whether or not they were experiencing more earth tremors at that very moment.

It was impossible to tell. San Francisco was so prone to such things that few citizens paid them any heed. Unless the shaking was strong enough to cause actual damage, which was rare, the local newspapers gave the quakes short shrift as well. Feeling the earth move was no more unusual than the fog off the bay or the wind that preceded a storm.

Tess would have scooted closer to Annie if there had been a smidgen of room left. Unfortunately all the benches were packed, including theirs. That was a good omen for the suffragette movement but it certainly worsened her predicament.

If only she had had the presence of mind to keep her coat on as a buffer, she mused. Not only was she starting to sense an aura of warmth emanating from Michael, she was beginning to imagine that she could actually feel the man's muscles through the gathered sleeve of her blouse. That was impossible of course, yet she could not shake the unsettling sensation.

Leaning away a fraction of an inch, she noted that he shifted his position ever so slightly, too. Although he had obviously twisted to make more room for her, he had also placed himself so he could effortlessly slip his arm around her shoulders if he so desired!

That notion stole Tess's remaining breath. In her heart of hearts she wanted him to do exactly that. In the logical part of her brain, however, she knew he would never be so bold. Getting him to escort them to the lecture was already more than she had expected. Making this into a shared, pleasurable excursion was out of the question. The only reason Michael was even sitting with them was because he was trying to be gallant.

"You don't have to stay right here if you don't want to," Tess offered, hoping to gain a respite for her overtaxed senses and imagination without revealing her reasons for needing one. "We can meet you outside after the speaking is over."

Michael shook his head and cupped a hand around his mouth to speak as privately as possible. "I'd rather not. You are too vulnerable, Miss Clark. If anyone saw through your disguise it could pose a problem."

"I don't see how."

She noted his frown and the hoarseness of his voice as he replied, "You would be a valuable prize for anyone wanting to get back at your father or perhaps seeking a ransom."

"Me? That's preposterous."

"All the same, I'm not about to leave you. Either of you," he added, leaning farther forward to include Annie.

Just then, a portly matron in a copious cape and broad-brimmed hat paused in the aisle next to him and cleared her throat noisily.

When Michael didn't rise, she said, "I fear you have not noticed a lady in need of a seat, young man. I would think a member of a fire brigade, like yourself, would have better manners."

Although he set his jaw, he did stand, bow and reluctantly relinquish his place to the demanding woman.

If Tess had not been so relieved that he had been forced to give her some breathing space, she might have felt sorry for him.

"I'll be waiting for you right outside the south door, the one we came in," Michael had said in parting. "Keep an eye out for me."

It had eased his mind some when Tess had nodded but he was still nervous about leaving her. After all, she was naïve about the inherent dangers of gatherings such as this. At least he assumed she was.

He had occasionally seen her in the Clark family pew in church and was certain she had also attended fashionable soirees, but this kind of open meeting was totally different. Here, she might come across anyone from any walk of life. How she would handle such encounters was his main concern. If she exhibited the same high and mighty attitude he'd observed so far, she could wind up in serious trouble.

To Michael's chagrin, some of the same firemen he'd encountered earlier were gathered just outside the very door he had instructed Tess to use. That left him no option but to face them.

James O'Neill was puffing on a cigar. He began to grin wryly as soon as he spotted Michael. "Well, well. I see you were tellin' the truth. Have ye gone over to the ladies' side now?"

"Of course not. I'm just doing a favor for my mother's employer, that's all."

"Oh, and what would that be?"

Keeping his voice light and a smile in place so the other men wouldn't take offense, Michael changed the subject rather than answer directly. "Never mind that. What're all of you doing here? Did you follow me?"

"Naw. We're slumming," O'Neill replied, laughing raucously. "We decided to take a gander at the *lovely* girls." He roared with glee at his supposedly clever remark. "Have ye seen 'em? I'd sooner kiss me own sister."

"I wouldn't want to kiss your sister either—if you had one," Michael countered, joining in the laughter. "She'd look too much like you—and you are one ugly fellow."

"Well said," O'Neill shot back, clapping Michael on

the back and blowing smoke rings. "C'mon. Let's go find us a good pub and get some beer."

"Can't," Michael said. "I told you. I'm working."

"Moonlighting, eh? All right. Have it your way." He motioned to his cronies with a broad wave of his arm and a slight unsteadiness in his gait. "Let's go, boys."

Michael was relieved to see them walk away without further probing into his evening's plans. He wasn't ashamed of Tess—or of Annie. He just didn't want to take the chance of having his name linked by gossip with that of the young, beautiful socialite. It not only wasn't accurate, it wasn't seemly.

Although he was successfully climbing the promotion ladder within his chosen field, that didn't mean he considered himself worthy to court a highborn woman like Tess Clark. No matter how well he rose in the fire department ranks, some facts would never change. He was who he was. That he had accomplished as much as he already had was a testimony to his zeal for the job and honest hard work.

For that Michael was thankful, because it meant he'd had no unearned favors handed to him nor had he sought any. His rank and anticipated promotion were his responsibility and his reward.

"With the help of the good Lord," he added, casting a brief glance at the cloudy night sky beyond the streetlamps and remembering his spiritual roots. His father had not imparted any belief system but his mother had made up for it with a strong faith that never seemed to waver. As far as Michael was concerned, if he could become half the Christian his mother was, he'd be in good shape.

* * *

When the elderly, spry, white-haired president of the local society for the advancement of women stood, the crowd hushed. In a clear but reedy voice she introduced Maud Younger to a roar of applause and cheering.

Tess was surprised to note that Miss Younger didn't look nearly as old as she had imagined she'd be. Her clothing was a simple but fashionable white lawn waist with vertical tucks and a dark skirt, fitted by plaiting from waist to hip that accentuated her spare figure. Her grace and regal bearing reminded Tess a bit of her own mother, although this woman was barely old enough to have belonged to the same generation.

"Good evening," Miss Younger said, her voice carrying strongly. "As many of you know, I was born and raised right here in your fair city, and although I have been traveling the globe, I feel as though I've come home when I gaze upon the bay and wharves once again." She smiled. "They smell the same, too."

That brought a wave of laughter. She waited for it to subside before continuing. "Many of you come from a background of wealth. Others don't. That makes no difference in our movement. Here, we are all sisters, all equal in the eyes of God. Our goal is to make ourselves just as equal in the eyes of our fellow *men,* which brings me to the point. We have been treated as second-class citizens for countless generations. It is time for that unfair servitude to end."

As the cheers of the crowd rose and the entire audience stood to applaud, Tess felt a surge of pride for those present. Miss Younger was right. They *were* all equal. She had felt for a long time that she and Annie certainly were. Why, they had often shared the notion that they might as well be family. This movement was the affirmation of that idea, the answer to Tess's fervent prayers for understanding and equality.

Beside her, on the aisle, she heard a muttered yet clearly derogatory comment. Wide-eyed, she turned to the portly woman who had usurped Michael's place, studying her features closely for the first time. "I beg your pardon?"

"It's that evil harridan up there who should beg all our pardons," the matron said, frowning and pointing to the stage. "Does your father know you're here?"

"What?" Tess squinted at the round, jowly face. "Do I know you?"

"You certainly should. My husband and I see you every Sunday in church."

Recognition buzzed at the fringes of Tess's mind the way flies worried a horse's flanks in the summer. There was a fair chance that she had encountered this particular person in the past but she couldn't attach a name to that memory. "I'm so sorry, Mrs...."

"Blassingame. Mrs. Henry Blassingame. But never you mind," the woman said, gathering herself as if she were a mother hen with ruffled feathers. "You just watch your p's and q's, young lady. Mark my words, this whole movement will do nothing but cause trouble."

Tess faced her nemesis as the applause died down, determined to give as good as she got. "You don't see yourself as equal to me, Mrs. Blassingame? That's a pity."

"Well, I never..." The woman spun and shuffled up the aisle, her skirts swinging from side to side like a huge, clanging bell.

Tess felt a tug on her skirt from Annie and resumed her place on the bench.

"We should go before she tells your father," the maid said with unshed tears glistening. "The Blassingames are rich enough to have a telephone. If she rings him, he'll discover we're gone."

"I'm not afraid of Papa," Tess said, although she did feel an undeniable twinge of nervousness. She smiled for Annie's benefit. "If you're worried, then we'll go home now. I'm sure that will please Michael, too."

"There's another meeting tomorrow night and the night after," Annie offered. "Maybe you can get someone else to take you."

Starting down the aisle, Tess lightly grasped her friend's arm with one hand and carried her heavy coat draped over the other. "Don't you want to come with me, too?"

"Mercy, no."

"Why not?"

"Because it seems so wrong," Annie said, speaking quietly aside. "Look at all these women. They should be at home with their families. I know some must have husbands or children. That's where their duty lies."

"Can't they be individuals as well?" Tess asked. "I believe I am."

"Of course you are. You have all the money you'll ever need. But I don't. I never will. Neither will my poor mother, and if folks get all riled up about this suffragette movement, there's no telling how it will affect the likes of us."

"You're really afraid?"

Annie nodded vigorously. "Terrified is more like it."

"Then I apologize," Tess said tenderly. "I should

never have insisted we come. I'm just so used to the two of us doing things together, I never thought about how being here might feel to you. I certainly didn't mean to make you uncomfortable. How can I make it up to you?"

"Pray. Hard," Annie said. "That's what I've been doing ever since we left your estate."

"Good idea. Oh, dear. Look."

Pausing at the archway of the exit door, Tess peered out at the milling crowd that awaited them. She and Annie were the only ones leaving early and without the buffering presence of the other women inside the hall, they were going to have to run a gauntlet of angry husbands, fathers and brothers. Even those men who were merely standing there smoking and chatting with their cronies had begun staring as if she and her frightened maid were escaping criminals.

Tess had Annie help her don her bulky black coat before she turned and squared her shoulders. Facing such a show of strength and greater size, she felt minuscule but she was not about to let any shred of apprehension show.

Head high, she walked directly into the fray as if she expected the group to part the way the Red Sea had for Moses and grant her unhindered passage. To her surprise and delight, the closest men did just that.

Chapter Four

Michael saw Tess coming. Before he could reach her and Annie, however, they had been accosted by several of the angry men who'd been lurking amidst the crowd.

He had to push his way through to get to the women. Tess was standing her ground but poor Annie was cowering and weeping into her hands.

"Shame on you," Tess shouted at their nearest adversaries as she pulled the crying girl closer. "See what you've done? You're nothing but a bunch of nasty bullies."

Hearing that kind of talk made Michael cringe. He clenched his fists as he joined the young women and quickly placed himself between them and their antagonists. Surprise was on his side. Numbers were not. He was only one man and there were at least five of the others, two of whom looked able to defend themselves most adequately.

He slipped his arm around Tess's shoulders, including Annie in the embrace as best he could and said, "Sorry boys. My sisters need to be getting home. C'mon, girls. Papa's waiting."

It didn't surprise him one bit when Tess tried to twist out of his grip as he began to shepherd them away.

"Let go of us," she grumbled, loud enough to be heard by almost anyone within twenty or thirty feet.

Michael grinned over his shoulder at the other men and shrugged as if silently appealing for sympathy. The ruse worked. They started to chuckle and one of them gave him a thumbs-up.

Beside him Tess continued to make loud, intemperate statements as he hustled her along the sidewalk. "Stop this. I demand you release me, Michael Mahoney. Do you hear me? There is no need for strong-arm tactics. I can take care of myself."

"Oh, yeah?" He lowered his voice. "And how were you going to get away from that confrontation back there? *Talk* them out of it?"

"I was handling the situation quite adequately."

"That wasn't how it looked to me," he argued.

Deciding that they were out of danger, at least for the moment, he slackened his hold and Tess immediately shook him off.

She paused long enough to straighten her hat, withdraw one of the long pins that had held it in place and brandish the thin shaft like a sword. "See? I could have defended myself."

"For about two seconds, until one of those fellows disarmed you." He eyed the flimsy weapon. "Put that away before you hurt somebody."

"You mean like you?"

"Yeah, like me," Michael answered. "You seem to be having trouble telling your friends from your enemies these days and I'd just as soon be out of reach if you suddenly decide I'm one of the villains."

"According to Mrs. Blassingame, that woman who took your seat, it's Maud Younger who's evil. Imagine that."

"I can. Easily," he countered. "Almost any man out here would agree." He knew he'd spoken too candidly when he saw Tess's eyes narrow. Although she did stick the hat pin back where it belonged, her motions were abrupt and jerky, indicating that her temper was far from soothed.

She grabbed Annie's hand and forged ahead with the girl in tow. Rather than object, Michael fell into step in their wake. Their party was now far enough from the pavilion that they wouldn't automatically be connected with the ongoing suffrage lecture if they happened to be observed. That was a huge relief.

"Turn right at the corner of Market," he called. "The buggy is down about half a block. You can't miss it."

Although Tess didn't answer, he noted that she was heeding his instructions. *Fine.* Let her brood or fuss and fume or whatever else she wanted to do. As long as she went straight to the cabriolet without getting into any more trouble on the way, he'd be satisfied. It had been sheer folly to let himself be talked into making this trip in the first place. The sooner it was over, the happier he'd be.

Tess would have given a month's allowance to have had another handy mode of transportation. Oh, she knew she could hire a hack to deliver her and Annie to the top of Nob Hill or even take a streetcar part of the way. It wasn't that. The problem was, she had to see to it that her father's rig was returned promptly and in apple-pie order. He was rightly proud of the sleek black, covered buggy with its deep green trim and bloodred upholstery, as well as his fine stable.

The bay mare that they were driving tonight, however, was technically Tess's. It had been a birthday gift, although her father still acted as if he were lord and master over his entire domain, including all the horses, even hers.

Without waiting for assistance she approached the side of the cabriolet, hiked her skirts, placed a booted foot on the small step and reached for a handhold with which to pull herself aboard.

The oversize coat was a bother because it hampered her freedom of movement. Nevertheless, she did not intend to stand there and wait for a bossy man who obviously didn't think she could take care of herself.

She grasped the slim metal roof supports with gloved hands and pulled herself up. Or tried to. She did lift partway off the ground but that was as far as she got. Not only was she stopped abruptly when a portion of the hem of her coat was caught beneath her boot, that yanking action caused her to lose her grip.

Tess was badly off balance before she even realized she'd made an error. Arms cartwheeling like the blades of a misaligned windmill, her body stretched and began a slow motion, backward arc.

Annie screeched. "Look out!"

Tess gritted her teeth. In the split second it took her to realize what was happening, she barely had time to hope her fall wasn't going to harm her best friend.

Gasping once, Tess stifled a scream. She threw her arms back to try to catch herself, fully expecting to feel the impact of the cobblestones through her skirt and petticoats as she landed.

Then, suddenly, she was caught up in strong arms that swung her away from Annie and safeguarded them both.

"I've gotcha. You're okay," Michael said, sounding breathless.

Tess's instincts for self-preservation kicked in and she sensibly looped one arm around his neck to stabilize herself. That brought their faces closer together than they had ever been before.

Her eyes widened. The brim of her elaborately decorated hat was the only thing keeping them apart and she could feel his warm breath through the veil.

She wanted to speak in her own defense, perhaps even to chastise him for taking such liberties. But no suitable words came to her, nor could she seem to find enough fresh air to satisfy her needs.

Michael stared into her eyes. He was not smiling. "Are you all right, Miss Clark?"

Tess tried to take another usable breath, this time succeeding. "Yes." It was hardly more than a hoarse whisper.

She found it impossible to look away, to tear her gaze from Michael's. Eyes that she had always known were a rich brown had become bottomless pools of indescribable emotion. Their eddies whirled, drawing her further and further in until she was as lost in their depths as a hapless mariner abroad in a hurricane.

Still, Michael held her close. Neither of them moved. Neither spoke. Tess noticed for the first time that she was actually embracing him and she knew it was wrong to continue to do so. She was also unwilling to relax her hold even a smidgen.

It was Annie whose words finally brought Tess to

her senses. The girl grasped her sleeve. "Miss Tess! Are you all right? Are you faint?"

"No." The denial didn't sound nearly as firm as she'd intended. She began lean sideways and to push her rescuer away. "I'll thank you to put me down."

"Gladly." Michael set her on her feet so abruptly that Tess swayed for a moment. Although she knew instinctively that he was close enough to catch her again if she faltered, she was determined to thwart any such efforts.

Instead, she reached for Annie's hand to steady herself. "My coat was caught. I think I may have stepped on the hem. I'm fine, now."

"I know. I saw," Annie said. "I'm so sorry. If I'd realized sooner I'd have helped…"

Behind them Michael cleared his throat. "If you ladies are through making apologies, I suggest we be on our way. Once that lecture is over and the crowd disperses, we could be delayed a long time by traffic."

"I agree," Tess said.

She took the hand he offered, careful to keep from looking directly at him as she gracefully gained her seat and scooted over to make room for Annie.

What on earth had just happened between her and Michael? She could barely think, let alone recall everything that had transpired. He had caught her and kept her from falling, of that she was certain, but in the ensuing seconds something extraordinary had passed between them. Something she had never before felt with anyone, let alone an appealing man like him.

There had been a depth to their poignant bond that was inexpressible. And he had felt it, too. She knew he had. Chances were good that he'd be able to continue to mask his emotional involvement but she wasn't fooled.

She'd seen it in his eyes, had felt it in the way he'd held her close. Michael Mahoney had been every bit as touched as she had and no amount of rational thought was ever going to convince her otherwise.

Rational thought? Tess had to smile. There was nothing rational about the way she was beginning to feel about Michael. On the contrary, if she had been anyone but who she was, she might have been foolish enough to imagine she was falling in love with the handsome fireman.

That was impossible, of course. Tess's smile waned. She sighed. Some things might be changing in the way women perceived themselves but certain constraints of society could never be breached. One of them was the proper choice of a mate. She had standards to uphold. Duties to fulfill. She had already taken on some of the tasks inherent in running her father's home, such as acting as hostess when he entertained the hoi polloi of San Francisco. There was no way to continue to do that if she turned her back on her place in the normal scheme of things.

A sadness settled over Tess the way the fog often shrouded the bay. Why was it so easy for her to accept Annie and others like her, yet fail to fully accept the person she herself really was?

Michael didn't speak to his passengers again until he brought the buggy to a halt in front of the Clark estate. The way he viewed the situation, the less he tried to explain, the better. Besides, he hadn't had time to sort out his thoughts regarding the astounding way Tess had reacted when he'd raced to the rescue and caught her.

I couldn't stand back and let her fall, he insisted,

wondering if perhaps he should have done just that. He was beginning to see that his strong sense of chivalry might prove to be his undoing—unless he was very, very careful in the future.

It was going to be at least another year, maybe longer, before he'd be financially able to support his mother. If she lost her job at the Clarks' before that time, it would be a serious hardship. And if Gerald Clark had the slightest notion that his only daughter was being squired all over San Francisco by his cook's son, that was *exactly* what would happen.

Michael steeled himself for the berating he was certain Tess would deliver in parting. As long as he remained duly deferential, no matter how much it hurt his pride to do so, he figured the evening would end fairly well, considering.

As he prepared to help the ladies disembark, a young groom joined him and took hold of the mare's bridle.

Michael first helped Annie down, then offered his hand to Tess. So far, so good, he thought. Then he made the mistake of looking into those lovely eyes once again. They glistened like fresh drops of rain on a rose. And her cheeks reminded him of the velvety pink petals.

He blinked to clear his thoughts, to refocus on the task at hand without making a worse fool of himself than he already had. Unfortunately for him, Tess smiled and his heart sped as a direct result.

"Thank you," she said pleasantly as she stepped down. "It was good of you to agree to accompany us this evening."

Michael bowed slightly and released her hand, backing away as he did so. "My pleasure, ladies."

He heard Annie make a sound that reminded him of

wind whistling through a nearly closed window sash. Tess, on the other hand, laughed demurely.

He arched a brow. "Did I say something humorous?"

"Yes. But you did it in a very gentlemanly manner." She giggled behind her hand. "I'm sorry. It was just so plain that you didn't want to go, it tickled me to hear you claim it was your pleasure."

"Perhaps it was the good company I enjoyed rather than your destination." The instant Michael heard his words he rued them.

"Perhaps."

"Or perhaps I simply like driving a nice rig." He gestured at the mare. "That's a fine animal."

"Yes. She's mine."

"Really? If you chose her, you did well."

"Thank you." Instead of leaving him and going inside, she walked to the horse and began stroking its sleek neck with her gloved hand. "Actually, she was one of my father's but I asked for her for myself. He finally gave her to me on my sixteenth birthday."

"Nice gift," Michael said, thinking about how little he was able to afford to give his mother no matter how much he wanted to please and honor her. In contrast, the gift of such a magnificent horse only served to point up the difference between his and Tess's lives.

"I can have one of the stable boys drive you home, if you'd like," Tess offered.

Michael shook his head. "That won't be necessary. I'm used to walking."

"And it's almost all downhill from here."

Boy, is that the truth, he thought, biting his tongue to keep from speaking his mind. It would be downhill for him for sure if he did what his heart and mind kept suggesting. The mere idea of pulling Tess Clark into his arms and kissing her rosy cheek the way he wanted to was enough to make him blush as well as tie his gut in a knot.

It was also a clear warning. There were few things he could do that would be worse than acting the swain. As a matter of fact, right then he couldn't think of anything that would be more foolish. Or more appealing.

He touched the brim of his cap politely and backed farther away. "I'll be saying good night, then."

"Good night," Tess replied.

Michael knew he had to be imagining the tenderness in her tone and the personal interest in her charming gaze. If there was something unusual there it had to be that she was toying with him, pretending to care to lead him on so she could have a good laugh at his expense.

Well, that was never going to happen. He might be a tad smitten if he were totally honest with himself, but that feeling would pass. Tess would never know her flirting had affected him at all, let alone given him thoughts of courting. He was too smart to yield to such impossible yearnings. Too smart and too determined to triumph on his own. He didn't need anyone's influence or money to succeed. He was well on his way to becoming a captain. Nothing else was as important as that.

Not even love?

His jaw clenched. The clomp of his boots echoed hollowly on the sidewalk as he began to trot down the hill toward home, back to the reality that was his daily life. There was no way that he might care that much for Tess, nor she for him. Love was an overrated emotion, anyway. His mother had always insisted that his father had loved her, yet Michael had never seen him demonstrate anything but disrespect—when he was sober. When he was drunk, which was most of the time, he was just plain cruel.

That was another reason why Michael wanted to succeed. It was his fondest wish to provide well for his mother in her old age. She had worked tirelessly to raise him, practically alone, and she had earned a rest. Soon he'd be able to give it to her. Soon he'd get the promotion he'd been working so hard for.

He slowed his pace and began to whistle a tune. His life hadn't been easy but he'd come a long way since his upbringing as one of the immigrant children who were disparagingly called wharf rats. Someday, Lord willing, he'd be able to put that all behind him and never look back.

Chapter Five

Tess was barely inside the cavernous foyer of the family mansion and was standing in front of the mirrored hall tree removing her hat when she heard a familiar, attention-getting cough.

Annie immediately hiked her skirts and fled up the side stairs toward her own quarters.

Tess whirled to face the source of the cough. "Good evening, Father. How are you?"

"I might ask you the same thing," Gerald Clark said. He hooked one thumb in his vest pocket, took a puff of the fat cigar in his other hand and blew out a smoke ring as he eyed his daughter from head to toe.

"I'm fine, thank you," Tess replied. She would gladly have retreated to her room if her father had not placed himself directly in her path. To her chagrin, he was taking note of her meager disguise.

"Have you no decent wrap? I thought you had a much more suitable coat than that old one."

"It was mother's," Tess said.

"I'm well aware of that." His eyes narrowed in a

scowl while he took in the familiar hat with its special, jet pin as part of the decoration. "Are you mocking me?"

Tess's heart melted and she put aside her personal concerns in order to comfort him. "Oh, Father, it's nothing like that. Honestly." She stepped close enough to briefly pat his free hand. "We—Annie and I—just wanted something dark and unremarkable to wear into the city. I never intended for you to see us dressed like this. I would never do anything to hurt you. Surely, you know that."

"I had thought so, until now," Gerald answered. "Would you care to tell me why you chose to go out so late in the evening?"

There was nothing Tess could honorably do but answer truthfully. She busied herself removing her gloves so she wouldn't have to keep staring into his face, wouldn't see his disappointment when she confessed.

"It was all my idea. I wanted to hear Maud Younger speak at Mechanics' Pavilion and Annie was good enough to accompany me." She looked up in time to see a flush of color start rising in the older man's face.

"So I have been given to understand."

"Then you know I'm telling you the truth."

"Yes. I find your actions quite disappointing. What do you have to say for yourself?"

"Nothing. I didn't do anything wrong or unseemly. The crowd was very large and I'm sure my presence went unnoticed, at least for the most part."

"You will not go again," her father said flatly.

That was his normal manner of making his wishes known, yet this time it rankled Tess more than usual. "I cannot promise that," she replied, feeling a surge of power accompanied by an equal amount of foreboding.

"What?"

If Tess had thought his face flushed before, it was pale compared to the way it looked now. She could almost imagine jets of steam escaping from his ears. "I don't mean to be disrespectful, Father, but there is nothing bad about my attending meetings composed of genteel women, and I shall do so again if I choose."

"Bah." He bit down on the end of the cigar and kept it clamped between his teeth as he glared at her.

There had been many instances in the past when Tess had cowered under her father's powerfully intent stare. Not this time. Although she hadn't stayed for Miss Younger's entire lecture she had been impressed by the atmosphere of freedom within the hall. That and the suffragette pamphlets she had read and reread so many times that they were almost falling apart had given her inner strength.

Tess straightened her spine, nodded and took a few steps, sidling past her father to start up the spiral staircase. "I respect and admire you, Papa," she paused to say. "Please try to afford me the same."

She didn't look back and heard no comment in her wake. By the time she reached the sanctuary of her private suite and closed the outer door behind her, she was trembling at the thought of what she had just said and done. Still, she had succeeded. She had politely stood up to her father and he had not screamed or cursed at her the way he sometimes did the servants. As far as she was concerned, that had been a big, big step toward her eventual emancipation.

Sighing, Tess leaned her back against the door. *Praise God.* Not only had she managed to temper her father's expected wrath, she had done so without having to mention Michael Mahoney's participation in the evening's escapade. For that, she was most thankful of all.

Given the way her heart leaped at the mere thought of that attractive man, she was afraid her father—and anyone else who saw her—might discern that she was enamored with Michael to the point of idiocy. She could still imagine the sensation of being held in his strong arms, of feeling his breath on her cheek, of yearning to be near him every moment.

Heart pounding, breathing shallow and ragged, Tess fought to subdue her roiling emotions. What was wrong with her? Was she becoming unhinged? Scripture plainly warned against coveting and that was exactly what she was doing.

Is it wrong to merely daydream? she asked herself. Surely not. After all, if people had no lofty dreams and aspirations they would never accomplish anything of value.

"Yes, except this is an impossible dream," she whispered into her otherwise unoccupied boudoir.

She knew her conclusion was right. She also knew that she dared not confess her foolish imaginings to anyone. There were some things, some very personal things, that must remain private. Tess had shared many secrets with Annie Dugan, especially during the recent years after Mama's passing, but this ridiculous infatuation would not be one of them.

It occurred to Tess to wish that Michael would take serious notice of Annie instead, but she found she couldn't carry through with an actual prayer for such a thing. Seeing him courting the maid—or anyone else for that matter—would be like the thrust of a dagger through Tess's tender heart.

Breathless, she stood quietly and tried to understand why she was so overcome with unfathomable emotion. She had been acquainted with Michael for at least six years, ever since her father had hired Mary as their cook, yet she had never viewed him this way before.

She and Michael had talked and joked and had even engaged in innocent child's play as youngsters, such as the time they had been verbally sparring in the kitchen and she had blown a handful of flour onto his dark, wavy hair, then had laughed and run away.

Michael had chased and caught her in the rose garden, holding tight to her wrist so she couldn't have escaped no matter how hard she'd struggled.

"Let me go!" Tess had screeched, trying her best to twist free.

"Not on your life." He had been laughing, too, as he had shaken his hair and spread a dusting of the flour onto her blue frock. They had laughed, chased, played. Had a perfectly wonderful time until Mary had called out to them, stopped the tussle and scolded her fun-loving son.

Now, however, even the memory of those sweet, innocent times was enough to make Tess tremble anew and yearn to see him again even if he paid her no attention whatsoever. Truth to tell, she mused, the less special attention he paid to her, the better for all involved.

That was an unarguable fact. So why was she having such a hard time convincing herself to accept it as the most sensible choice?

When Tess awoke the following morning she was still reliving every wonderful event from the previous evening, especially the trip to and from the pavilion.

Pulling back the heavy drapes at her window, she stood for a moment to bask in the welcome rays of sun that had finally burned through the dreary fog. It was easy to compare that kind of contrast to the way she'd felt before and after she'd nearly taken a tumble and had spent those blissful few moments resting in Michael's arms. It was as if her whole life had been suddenly filled with a brightness so intense it was almost painful.

Dressing alone because she'd sent Annie back down the hill to visit her widowed mother, Tess descended the wide, sweeping staircase. First she'd breakfast with Father in the formal dining room the way she normally did. It might be trying to carry on a pleasant conversation after his negative reaction to her actions last night, but facing him this morning would help her discern whether or not he was still upset.

Entering the large, formal dining room she paused, puzzled. There was a floral centerpiece with unlit tapers standing tall and stately at each end of it. The handmade damask and lace cloth beneath was pristine, as always. However, the room was not occupied. Papa was not seated at the head of the table. Nor was there the usual silver coffee service waiting for him on the buffet.

Her breath whooshed out all at once when she realized what that meant. Papa had eaten early and left!

Immensely relieved to postpone facing the one person she never seemed able to fully please, Tess swept past the table with a lighter heart and lithe step and pushed the swinging door to enter the kitchen.

The cook looked up with a smile.

"Good morning, Mary."

"Morning, miss. You heard that Mister Gerald has already had his breakfast?"

"I saw he was gone, yes." Tess knew she was grinning foolishly but she couldn't help herself. She'd fretted for hours the night before, anticipating a confrontation with her banker father, and it looked as if he'd put aside his displeasure—at least enough to go about his normal business rather than dally to chastise her. Annie would be very glad to hear that, too.

"I believe I'll take my breakfast right here with you," Tess told the cook.

The woman's astonished expression made Tess giggle and ask, "What's wrong? Does it bother you?"

"No, miss. I'm just surprised, is all. You haven't been visiting me much since you got too big to beg sweets."

"I'll never be too old for that." Tess pulled up the same stool Michael had used the day before, sat down and leaned her elbows on the table in spite of knowing it was poor etiquette to do so. "I like it here. I can relax and not worry about how I sit or how I eat or anything else. Can you understand that?"

Mary smiled and her apple cheeks brought happy crinkles to the corners of her brown eyes. "Aye. I've often wondered how ladies like you can stand to be laced up so tight and sit so proper all the time. I'd think it would be a terrible trial."

"It is." Tess accepted the cup of hot coffee Mary placed before her with a pleasant "Thank you."

"You're welcome, miss."

Although Tess had always felt at ease in the kitchen, whether she was grabbing a cookie or maybe sampling the upcoming meals, she could tell she had just taken another step forward in her relationship with Mary Mahoney, especially judging by how the older woman was smiling down on her.

"Your dear departed mother used to visit me this way," Mary said. "Especially when…"

"When she knew she was about to pass?" Tess asked, her smile growing wistful.

"Aye. Mister Gerald didn't want to listen to how she really felt so she'd come out here sometimes and talk to me. She was a lovely person." The cook blinked back unshed tears. "And now that you're grown, you're the spitting image of her."

"That's what everyone says." Moved, Tess paused to sip her coffee and used the time to compose herself. "I do miss her. It's only been a little over four years, but there are times when I try to picture her face or recall the sound of her voice and I can't quite do it."

"That's all right," Mary said. "Remembering the love is all that counts. She loved you dearly."

"I don't know what I'd have done if I hadn't had my Annie to listen to me back then. It's no wonder we've grown so close."

"Where is Annie?" Mary looked past Tess toward the main part of the mansion. "Isn't she hungry, too?"

"If she is, her own mother will be fixing her something," Tess said. "She got so homesick after we'd been into the city last night, I sent her off to Mrs. Dugan's early this morning. We had hoped to see her mother at the lecture but the crowd was so huge there was little chance of finding anyone in that mass of humanity."

"Scrambled eggs all right?" Mary asked with her back to Tess.

"Yes, thank you. And in case you were wondering, Michael did a fine job as our chaperone."

"I didn't want to ask."

Tess chuckled. "I could tell. Actually, he ended up scolding me worse than Papa did when I got home."

"Oh, dear."

The cook's concern made Tess laugh more. "Don't worry. I didn't take offense." *And he also caught me when I almost fell. It was wonderful,* Tess added to herself, lowering her lashes to stare into her coffee cup rather than let her gaze meet Mary's and perhaps reveal too much.

"Good. I'm sure my son was only thinking of what was best for you."

"So he said." Tess felt her cheeks warming so much that she was certain it showed.

"Are you going back again tonight?" Mary asked.

That notion had already occurred to Tess. Her problem was not being able to count on Annie as a companion and proper chaperone. "I don't think so."

"'Tis a pity."

"Why?" Surely, Michael had not expressed any desire to repeat the previous evening, so Tess was at a loss to understand the underlying reason for Mary's question.

"Because I'd like to see what all the fuss is about," the cook said with a slight smile. "I wouldn't want to go alone, of course, but I thought…"

"I'd *love* to go with you," Tess said, beaming. "What a wonderful idea."

"Mister Gerald wouldn't mind?"

"I've already warned him that I might attend again. I know he'll approve of my choosing a sensible, mature woman like you for a companion."

"Then it's settled." The cook slid Tess's eggs onto

a plate, added a warm biscuit and delivered the meal to the table.

When she paused there, Tess looked up at her with a smile. "Is there a problem?"

"Only with me old coat and hat," Mary said. "'Tis good enough for church but I don't want to embarrass you."

"Anything that's good enough for the Lord is certainly good enough for me," Tess said. "If it really bothers you, though, I do have another coat and hat you may wear and then keep, if you like. They belonged to my mother."

"Oh, I couldn't."

"Nonsense. Annie wore them last night and they were too big for her so they should fit you perfectly. They're still up in my room. I know Mother would want you to have them in any case."

"It's a darlin' girl you are," Mary said. "Your mama would be very proud."

"I truly hope so," she answered wistfully. "I wish she were still here so I could ask for her advice."

"Could ye ask me?"

Tess almost choked. More warmth flowed into her already rosy complexion and she shook her head as she clasped her hands and bowed over her plate to ask the blessing.

Some of the most troubling elements in Tess's life were her errant, possibly sinful thoughts of Michael Mahoney. Confessing as much to the man's mother was *not* on her list of suitable ways to cope. Not even at the very bottom of that imaginary list.

When the telephone at Michael's fire station rang, the last person he was expecting to hear from was his mother. "What's wrong, Ma? Are you sick?"

"No."

"Then why are you calling? I didn't think you were allowed to use the Clarks' telephone."

"Miss Tess gave me permission and showed me what to do."

"Great. So, what's wrong?" He was imagining all sorts of terrible catastrophes, all beginning and ending with Tess Clark.

"Nothing. I just wanted you to know not to stop by tonight, in case you don't have to work, I mean. I won't be home after supper."

"Why not?"

"Because Miss Tess and I are going back to the Mechanics' Pavilion and…"

Michael couldn't contain his astonishment. "What? Are you daft, too?"

"Don't be silly. And don't be talkin' that way about Miss Tess."

"I suppose she's standing right there listening."

"Yes. And she's a fine lady."

"She's more like a spoiled brat," Michael argued, only half agreeing with himself.

"I'll pretend I didn't hear you say that, Michael Mahoney, and I certainly hope she didn't, either. Now put that Irish temper of yours back in your pocket and calm down."

Grumbling under his breath, Michael managed to control his gut-level response. If that impulsive young woman dragged his mother into trouble he'd never forgive her. Never.

"How are you getting to and from the pavilion?" he asked.

"I don't know. We'll be fine. Don't worry yourself one little bit."

He wanted to warn her to be careful, even toyed with the idea of ordering her to stay home. But he knew his mother. And he was beginning to know Tess a lot better than he'd planned to. Neither of them was the kind of woman who could easily be bossed around, although of the two, he figured his mother would be the more tractable.

"All right. Do as you please. Just stay together and don't talk to strangers. Hear?"

As she ended the conversation and hung up, Michael almost thought he heard giggling on the other end of the line. That was not a good sign. Not a good sign at all. It probably meant that his mother and Tess were sharing a laugh at his expense.

"O'Neill," he called up the narrow wooden stairs that led to the firemen's quarters on the second floor. "I'm going to need you to take part of my shift for me tonight."

There was a moan, followed by, "Aww, me head's splittin', Michael."

"It's your own fault if it is. Sleep it off till supper time. I'll wake you before I leave."

"What's so all-fired important? You got another moonlightin' job like last night?"

Michael huffed and answered under his breath, "No. This one's even worse."

Chapter Six

Since her father had objected to her wearing her late mother's favorite coat the evening before, Tess had replaced it in the attic chest. As she'd carefully folded the garment and prepared to lay it back in the trunk, she'd noticed a thin, linen-covered book tied with a satin ribbon. She hadn't seen that for years. It was Mama's journal.

Touched by nostalgia, Tess had intended to leave the precious book where it was, unread, but at the last moment she'd snatched it up, carried it to her room and slipped it under one of the feather pillows on her bed.

Now, dressed in her own elegant broadcloth coat with a velvet shawl collar and a much more demure chapeau bearing a few white feathers and small pink roses, she was ready for her evening adventure.

Michael had had so much trouble finding a place to leave the buggy the night before, Tess had decided it would be smarter to not use the cabriolet again that evening. She hoped her companion wouldn't object.

"I don't mind a bit," Mary said, buttoning the fitted,

hand-me-down woolen coat as she and Tess prepared to leave the house. "I walk into the city all the time."

"I wish I could say I did," Tess replied. "Father has always been too protective for that. I've never had the opportunity to explore much farther than the church over on Van Ness, at least not by myself." She smiled as she paused on the back porch and donned kid gloves. "I suppose you think that's odd."

"Not for the likes of you, it isn't. Mister Gerald is just looking out for you. He always has."

"It feels more like being a prisoner," Tess said with a sigh. "I know he means well, but…"

"Aye. They all do. It's the way they were raised, more's the pity. Take my Michael, for instance."

Tess's heart leaped in spite of her desire to keep from reacting to any mention of the man. "What about him?"

"He wasn't truly angry when I told him where you and I were going even if he did sound that way. He was just being bossy, like his father was, God rest his soul."

"I've never asked you about him. I'm sorry. Has your husband been gone long?"

"Long enough," Mary said with a soft sigh. "He wasn't gentle like my son but I know he did the best he could for us."

Hearing Michael referred to as *gentle* seemed odd to Tess. She thought of him as strong, stalwart and very masculine. Then again, she supposed a man's mother would view him in a different light than others did.

"I could hear the rise of Michael's voice when you told him where we were going tonight. He certainly didn't sound very happy."

That made Mary laugh. "I think they're all petrified that we women will stop takin' their orders. We won't, of course."

"Oh, I don't know," Tess said. "That notion does sound appealing."

She looped her arm through Mary's as they descended the sloping drive onto Clay Street and turned toward Van Ness. It seemed a bit strange to be on foot, let alone in the company of the estate cook, yet Tess's heart was light and her enthusiasm boundless.

The sun had set. A row of gaslights lined the upper portion of the avenue between the trees, illuminating their pathway. Fog was thin and patchy this evening which also lent an air of openness. Homes they passed were, for the most part, well-lit as well, thanks in part to the proliferation of Mr. Edison's electric lamps, especially in the wealthier parts of the city where the gas along the streets had also been replaced by electric lamps.

As an added plus, a warm breeze was blowing over the inland hills so the air was merely tinged with salty sweetness instead of bearing the unpleasant aroma that often rose from the docks, especially during the summer.

Tess sighed happily. This was true freedom. A simple change of habit had shown her a whole new world; a world where she could just be herself rather than Gerald Bell Clark's pampered daughter. It was an amazingly liberating feeling, one she found so exhilarating it nearly stole her breath away.

Michael had changed from his fireman's uniform into the black corduroy suit he wore when attending church, hoping to blend in better. If he'd had an Ulster overcoat such as his father had worn, he'd gladly have donned it, too, to ward off the evening's chill.

He joined the throngs of men once again milling in front of the pavilion. His dour mood fit the overall atmosphere perfectly. Hatless, with his thick, dark hair slicked straight back, he thrust his hands into the pockets of his suit coat as he paced, waiting and ruing the confrontation he knew was coming.

As before, the crowd was swelling with women from all walks of life, including society matrons, although he assumed that most of them were simply out for a lark rather than convinced that this crazy idea of equality for women had real merit.

Scanning the multitude, he spotted his mother before he saw Tess. Mary was taller in the first place, and since she was wearing an ornately flowered and beribboned hat that added nearly another foot to her height, she certainly did stand out above the crowd.

Elbowing his way toward her, Michael noted that Tess was at her side. He forced a smile and greeted them amiably. Or so he thought.

"Good evening, ladies."

Mary gasped.

Tess frowned before replying, "What are *you* doing here?"

"Looking out for the pair of you, if you must know," he said.

"We don't need looking after." Tess's chin lifted and she stared at him. "We are perfectly fine on our own."

"That's a matter of opinion."

"Yes, it is," Tess said. "Mary tells me she often walks about in the city. Alone. If you're not concerned about that, you certainly shouldn't worry about us when we're together."

Michael's jaw gaped. She was right. His mother did make a practice of strolling the city streets, at least some of them, unescorted.

"Not after dark, she doesn't," he countered.

Tess glanced at the well-lit pavilion and then gave him a self-satisfied smile. "It's hardly dark here, sir. Now, if you will excuse us, we'll be going inside."

Without thinking, Michael reached for her arm as she tried to pass.

Someone else tapped him on the shoulder from behind at the same instant.

As he turned to see who was interfering, he saw a flash of movement and felt a jolt to the side of his jaw.

Staggered, Michael released Tess. He blinked to clear his swimming head. A mustachioed dandy in a bowler hat and striped silk cravat was facing him with fists raised defensively, posing like a boxer in the ring. The man was jumping around on the balls of his feet as if there were swarms of biting ants inside his shoes.

"What the…" Michael began.

Tess raised her voice and interrupted with a sharp "No!" She stepped in front of him. "Are you all right?"

"Yes." Nevertheless, he rubbed his jaw and peered past her while Tess turned to face the attacker, her hands on her hips.

"Phineas Edgerton. What in the world do you think you're doing?"

"Defending your honor, Miss Clark." He stopped dancing around but didn't lower his fists. Nor did he take his eyes off Michael. "G.B. told me you might be here tonight."

"My *father* sent you?"

"In a manner of speaking."

"Well, go home. There's no need for you here. And certainly no call to go around punching innocent people."

In Michael's opinion, the man Tess had called Phineas was not planning to take her seriously. He was of a slighter build than most firemen and clearly not much of an adversary in a real fight. Still, he had delivered a hard enough blow to temporarily stun and Michael was not about to give him a chance to do it again.

When Phineas reached toward Tess, Michael acted. He pushed the thinner man away with more force than was needed and sent him reeling.

"Stop it. Both of you." Tess raised her arms and intervened as if attempting to keep two brawling little ruffians apart. "This is ridiculous."

Although Michael did give ground he remained ready to renew the battle if need be. "We'll see about that."

"No. You will see nothing." Calmly and deliberately, she nodded at the other man. "Phineas, may I present Michael Mahoney and his mother, Mary."

To Michael's dismay, he had temporarily forgotten that his mother was even present, let alone standing back and watching the whole confrontation.

"Mary, dear, this is Mr. Edgerton, one of Father's vice presidents," Tess continued.

The cook made a slight curtsy but did not offer her hand. Neither did Michael.

Tess went on, "I suggest we all go inside and find suitable seats before they're all gone." That said, she slipped her hand through the crook of the banker's elbow and motioned to Mary to do the same regarding Michael.

He offered his arm to his mother without hesitation. As long as Tess and that skinny fop were going into the lecture hall, he might as well accompany them.

Later, when he had a chance to speak to his mother in private, he intended to tell her exactly what he thought of her foolishness. Going to a controversial lecture like this was bad enough without joining forces with the boss's daughter to do so. There would be no way that Gerald Clark would not hear every juicy detail, thanks to his toady.

Michael clenched his fists. He wished he'd punched Phineas in the nose instead of merely giving him a shove.

He sawed his jaw from side to side to test it. Unless he missed his guess, he was going to be sporting a dandy bruise on his chin by tomorrow. That was what he got for letting himself be dragged into another of Tess's wild schemes.

Beside him, his mother tightened her grip. When he glanced down at her she peeked from beneath the brim of the fancy hat. "Your Irish is showin'," she said, giving him a sly grin. "You'd best mind your manners if you want to impress anyone."

"Only you, Ma," Michael said. "You know you're my best girl. Always will be."

Mary chuckled. "I surely do hope not. I have me eye on a houseful of grandbabies just as feisty and handsome as you are."

Tess was walking several paces ahead of mother and son and the crowd was creating a loud murmur that kept her from overhearing everything they said. The few words she had picked out, however, were enough to make her blush. Unlike Mary, Papa had never mentioned the next generation, nor had he pushed her to court more often than she had wished to. At least not yet.

Eyes downcast, she glanced at the expensively tailored coat sleeve where her gloved hand rested and recalled a few times when this man's name had come up in conversation. It was starting to look as if it was no accident that her father had chosen to send Phineas on this particular errand. He was young, single, well-born and a rising star in the banking business. Not only that, the Edgerton family was one of the richest clans on the west coast.

Tess shivered. Surely Papa wasn't trying to play matchmaker. Or was he? It would be just like him to try to manipulate her into joining two prominent families through matrimony, for the sake of increasing the influence and holdings of both.

Pulling her hand from the banker's sleeve, Tess eased away from him.

"Is something wrong, Miss Clark?" he asked, doffing his bowler and removing his gloves now that they were inside the hall.

"No. Nothing. It's just very crowded in here, don't you think?" She dropped back until she was beside Mary. "I see the front rows are already full. Shall we sit back here?"

"Fine with me."

To Tess's chagrin, the older woman immediately edged into the nearest row and led the way.

Both men stepped back politely, eyeing each other

like two feisty roosters in a barnyard. Tess balked. According to proper etiquette, she should follow Mary. That would place her between Michael and his mother, or, even worse, would leave poor Phineas sitting next to her on one side with the surly fireman on his other.

She glanced back and forth, unable to decide what was the best move. Michael looked ready to explode and Phineas was acting so proper and stuffy she wanted to shake him.

Her eyes locked with Michael's and she tried to will him to understand. It almost seemed as if he did comprehend her dilemma when he bowed slightly and said, "If you all will excuse me, I'll be waiting for you ladies outside like I did the last time."

Tess wanted to thank him, to let him know that she was grateful for his sensible choice. Unfortunately, she had no chance to speak before he quickly wheeled and stalked back up the aisle.

Phineas, however, seemed smugly satisfied, giving her further proof that he was far too much like her father to suit her. He gestured for her to follow Mary, then, hat and gloves in hand, joined her.

Having that man seated so close felt nothing like it had to have Michael beside her. There was no thrill, no warmth, no sense of strength or power. Phineas was simply there.

If she hadn't been with Mary, Tess would have left the lecture hall and abandoned the unpleasant man without a moment's hesitation. Her wish to do so doubled when Phineas leaned closer and whispered, "What did that ruffian mean by *the last time?*"

Tess merely folded her hands in her lap, faced forward and pretended she hadn't heard the question.

* * *

To Michael, standing idle outside, it seemed as if the meeting was lasting forever. He hoped his mother had gotten the women's movement out of her system by now. He'd certainly had enough of it.

The whole premise was crazy. Women had men to take care of them. They didn't need to be standing on a soapbox and yelling for more rights. It was bad enough that there were already a few female dentists and doctors practicing in the city. Why, a committee of misguided ladies had even petitioned the Board of Supervisors to allow women in the police department a few years back. Next thing he knew, they'd be wanting to join the fire brigades!

A stir near the wide sets of double doors drew his attention. They swung open and hoards of excitedly babbling women began to exit the hall.

Michael stepped up on the base of the monument to labor so he could peer over the heads of other men.

He spotted his mother, Tess and that despicable little banker in moments.

Shouldering his way through the crowd, Michael quickly joined them. If Tess was surprised to see him she gave to indication of it.

"I'll walk you home," he said.

"That won't be necessary but we do thank you." Tess smiled slightly. "Don't we, Mary?"

"Aye. We know the way. You can go back to work, son."

"I got O'Neill to cover for me," Michael explained. "I don't have to report back till morning."

Tess's smile spread. "Well, it won't take us *that* long to walk the few blocks home, even if it is mostly uphill."

Next to her, Phineas cleared his throat. "Ahem. I have a carriage waiting, Miss Clark." He fidgeted and ran a finger beneath his starched collar as if it was choking him. "I, um, well, I didn't know you'd be with anyone. It only seats two."

"Then I know there will surely be plenty of room for you to ride alone," Tess said, reaching to pat the cook's hand. "I shall walk with my friends."

It didn't escape Michael's notice that she had said *friends,* not *friend.* Good. The young woman might be capricious but she was definitely loyal. If she had gone off with that weasel of a banker and left his mother to trudge home alone, Michael would not have thought well of her. Not well at all.

To his delight, Phineas appeared to be struck dumb.

"Shove off, man," Michael told him. "You heard Miss Clark. She has no further need of you."

"Well, I never…"

"No, you probably haven't ever been talked to this plainly before. 'Tis high time you were."

In the background, Michael was certain he heard Tess's familiar giggle when the other man turned and stomped off. That laugh warmed his heart. Obviously she wasn't angry with him. What a relief.

Now, his biggest remaining concern was his mother's welfare. When her boss got wind of her nighttime outing with Tess, there was sure to be a blowup. He just hoped and prayed it wasn't going to cost her a job she loved and the rooms she occupied in the servants' wing of the estate.

When he offered his arm to Mary, Michael was astounded to feel Tess fall into step on his opposite side.

She was not only grasping his elbow as if they were promenading, she was grinning beneath her thin veil.

He chanced a smile in her direction. "I take it you weren't disappointed that your beau had no room for the likes of us."

"Oh, dear. I hadn't thought of it that way but you're probably right. Phineas is terribly snobbish." She huffed. "And he is certainly *not* my beau."

"I take it he believes he has your father's blessing to court you."

"Then Father is sadly mistaken," Tess replied. "I have no beau, nor do I seek one. The more I hear about women's rights, the more empowered I feel."

"You have no desire for home and hearth?" Michael asked, feeling his mother squeezing his arm as he spoke.

"I didn't say that, exactly." Tess gathered her skirts in her free hand to keep them out of her way as they began to ascend the steeply sloping avenue. "I simply see no pressing need to swoon at some gentleman's feet and pretend I am in need of sanctuary."

"I see." It was all Michael could do to keep from chuckling at her naïveté. She had grown up so cosseted by her father she saw herself as far more independent than she truly was. If Gerald Clark had not been exercising his control over her, he would not have bothered to send an emissary to the suffrage lecture to do his bidding and to squire Tess home.

Expanding upon that thought was sobering. G.B. had his fingers in plenty of political pies in city and county government, including the upper echelons of the fire and police departments. If he took a notion to sabotage a promotion within one of those organizations he would probably succeed.

When Mary asked that they rest for a few moments so she could catch her breath, Michael decided to use the opportunity to voice his concerns to Tess in the hope she would understand.

"I want to ask a favor," he said.

"Really?" Lifting the veil, she placed it atop the hat and looked directly at him. "All right. Ask away."

"I'd like you to make certain that your father doesn't blame me or my mother for your transgressions."

"And just what would those be?"

"This evening. And the one before," Michael said, gesturing at the pavilion that lay behind them at the foot of the hill. "He's a powerful man. If he thought we had led you astray he might not be very forgiving."

"Nonsense," Tess said flatly. "Annie said the same thing. You're all wrong. Father isn't vindictive. He may be stern but he's fair."

Although Michael nodded and dropped the subject he didn't stop wondering if Tess was fooling herself. G. B. Clark's reputation painted him as anything but evenhanded.

If he failed to be fair-minded, or if he refused to believe his daughter's claim that these nightly jaunts had been her idea, there was no telling how far the ripples of discontent would extend. Or who they would harm.

Chapter Seven

Tess would have loved to attend every lecture Maud Younger gave in the City by the Bay. What she didn't want to do was push her father too far, too fast. A week after her last trip to the pavilion she was still waiting for him to mention Phineas and chastise her for her behavior.

So far Papa hadn't said another word about the incident, not even when their pastor's Sunday sermon had dealt with forgiveness. Waiting for her father to finally get around to mentioning her transgressions was harder for Tess than being immediately scolded would have been.

As a result she had been unduly nervous when she entered the dining room each ensuing morning for breakfast.

Today, her father was dressed in a neatly tailored gray, pin-striped suit and vest that almost matched the color of his moustache. He sat at the far end of the massive, linen-covered table, his visage hidden behind a fresh copy of the *Chronicle*.

Tess skirted the table to pour herself a cup of hot

coffee from the silver service on the buffet rather than wait to be served. As she took her place at the opposite end of the long table she peeked around the floral arrangement and said, "Good morning, Father."

Gerald Clark merely grunted. That kind of reaction was far worse, in her estimation, than his angry words would have been. He had never been one to chat unless the subject of a conversation was finance or something else of equal interest to him, but his recent actions, particularly toward her, had seemed more off-putting than usual.

Looking for a way to draw him out and bring things to a head, Tess asked, "So, how is Phineas Edgerton doing these days? You haven't mentioned him much lately."

With that, the newspaper was partially lowered. Gerald peered over the top edge, his bushy gray brows knit. "If you must know, he is nursing a broken heart."

"Why?" Tess felt herself beginning to frown, too, and carefully schooled her features to eliminate any sign of negativity. "Surely he can't still be upset that I declined his offer to drive me home."

"He can and he is," her father replied. "That was cruel of you, Tess."

Astounded, she stared. "Cruel? Phineas intimated that I was welcome to ride with him but my companions were not. *That* was the cruel thing."

"What? You expected him to give way to servants? It's bad enough that you persist in treating Annie Dugan as an equal. The girl is your maid, Tess, not your friend, and it's time someone reminded you of your place as well as hers."

"Annie is a truer friend than any of the other young women I know."

"You see? That's what I've been trying to say. Your mind has been poisoned by that drivel you've been hearing at those idiotic lectures."

"I respectfully disagree."

Rising, her father crumpled the paper and his napkin next to his plate and faced her, his moustache twitching as his jaw clenched repeatedly. "There is nothing respectful about the way you speak to me, girl. I suggest you remember who supports you, who buys you those expensive gowns and pretty trinkets you love so much."

Tess fingered the dainty pearl earbobs that were her favorites. Other than those, the only jewelry she wore regularly was the cameo pinned at the high, ruffled neck of her blouse. That brooch had been her mother's.

"I do appreciate your generosity, Father," she said, struggling to sound normal in spite of wanting to shout, or weep, or both. "It was Mother who loved jewelry and furs. I ask for very little beyond my daily needs."

"Bah!" Muttering under his breath, Gerald Clark stalked from the room, leaving Tess to wonder if she should wait there for his possible return or if she dared head for the kitchen where she knew she'd find sanctuary with Mary.

She fidgeted, counted slowly to one hundred, then made up her mind. In a few quick steps she'd made good her escape.

"There may be extra duty to be had tonight," Michael told O'Neill. "We'll both need to be alert."

"Why? You plannin' to start some trouble I don't know about, boyo?"

"No. It's because of the crowds expected at the Grand Opera House. Caruso's singing."

"I'd lots rather hear a good *Irish* tenor," O'Neill said, grinning. "Those Italians are too full o' themselves to suit me."

That comment made Michael laugh. There were many immigrant populations in San Francisco and each thought it was the most important. He supposed that was normal, yet he wished they could all work together better for the common good. If the various factions weren't at odds with outsiders, they were busy squabbling amongst themselves. As far as he was concerned, it was wasted effort.

Stepping out onto Howard Street in front of Station #4, he looked at the Chinese laundry across the street, then turned and raised his gaze to encompass the expensive homes on Nob Hill to the north. It would be at least three more days before his usual visit to his mother and he'd had to miss last Sunday's services because of a small fire at Meigg's Wharf, so he hadn't seen Tess in over a week. Not even from a distance.

Would she be one of the opera patrons at the special performance tonight? he wondered. Perhaps. And if so, whose arm would she be on? If it happened to be that young banker's, as he suspected it might, Michael was not going to be pleased.

He snorted in self-derision. Who was he kidding? The only person he wanted to visualize standing beside Tess Clark was himself. He could easily imagine her lovely blue eyes twinkling at him; her lips curving gently in a smile that warmed him through and through no matter how cold the wind off the Pacific happened to be.

That dream was never going to come true, he concluded, so why waste time envisioning it?

Deep in thought, he circled the narrow, three-story fire station building and entered the ground-floor stables from the rear.

The behavior of the usually placid fire horses drew him back to reality. They seemed unduly agitated. Since there had been no recent alarm, there was no reason for them to be behaving as if they were about to be harnessed to one of the steam pumpers and race off to a fire.

Approaching the nearest gray gelding, Michael stroked its neck to calm it as he pictured Tess ministering to her mare the night he had driven her into the city. Her touch had been gentle but firm. She had the ways of a true horse lover and he admired that about her.

"As well as plenty of other things," Michael muttered, continuing to soothe the nervous animals as best he could. Several of them were prancing around in their stalls as if they were about to try to kick their way out. That was odd.

He raked his fingers through his thick, dark hair as he pondered the animals' unrest. They sometimes behaved this way after a slight earthquake and he assumed he had simply not been as aware of the shaking as the horses were. If so, they'd soon settle down. They always did.

Going about his chores, he fed and watered the teams, then sauntered back into the front portion of the station where the captain's scarred oak desk, a telephone and the red-enameled alarm box sat. Duty rosters were pinned to the walls next to a calendar from one of the banks G. B. Clark didn't happen to own. A pair of narrow windows flanked the front door. Because this room was so close to the stable and a live boiler also sat in the basement, it smelled more like a steamy barn than an office.

It wasn't much to covet. Nevertheless, it was Michael's goal to lay claim to it soon. Aspiring to the next rank made a suitable goal for the present. And maybe someday he'd be the kind of chief engineer who inspired his men to loyalty and valor the way Dennis Sullivan did.

The Sullivan family had their own private quarters over on Bush Street, Michael reminded himself. Quarters suitable for his mother and perhaps a family of his own, as well.

His only problem seemed to be an inability to picture any woman other than Tess Clark in the role of his wife.

"I wish I could take you with me to hear Caruso tonight," Tess told Annie. "But since I can't, I want you to go visit your mother again. You might as well stay over till morning."

"You'll need me to help you undress when you get home," Annie argued, shaking her head. "That gown is mighty tight."

"I can manage. If I get stuck I'll call Mary. Once I loosen this horrid corset I'll be fine." She tried to take a deep breath and failed. "If I don't swoon first."

"You look beautiful in that shade of green," Annie said. "The velvet shimmers when you move."

"I know. I love it." Tess patted her highly upswept hair and pivoted in front of the mirror so she could see the emerald and exotic-feather-decorated clip her maid had added at one side. "I just wish…"

Annie giggled. "I know. You wish you could show Michael Mahoney."

"I wish nothing of the kind!"

"Oh, then why are you blushing?"

Tess made a silly face and turned away. "I'm not. This outfit is simply constricting my breathing and I am a bit faint."

"Balderdash. You always blush terribly when anyone mentions that man. Admit it. You're fond of him."

"All right. I may care for him a bit. That doesn't mean I intend to get serious."

"Have it your way. You talk a good fight but you retreat the minute the tide turns against you."

"This tide has always run against me," Tess said sadly. "I am who I am. Nothing can ever change that."

"Maud Younger disagrees."

"Yes, but she has determined to remain single and dedicate herself to the cause of freedom and equality for all. I agree with her in principle. I just don't feel that strong a personal calling."

"Meaning?"

"Meaning, it would please me to someday marry and have a family," Tess said, staring out the window of her room without really seeing the city below.

Annie gasped, muting the reaction by pressing her fingertips to her lips. "You aren't considering that horrid Phineas person, are you?"

"No. Of course not. But until my father finds someone else, I've decided to make the best of it. Phineas will be meeting Father and me at the opera tonight." She made a face. "I've perfumed a lace hanky so I can breathe its lavender sweetness if I'm too overcome by his presence."

"I don't think a bucket of cologne would be enough to help me tolerate that man," Annie said. "You are much stronger than I am."

Tess shook her head gently, taking care to keep from dislodging her elegantly coiffed hair. "Not really. I pray all the time that the good Lord will spare me from having to marry such an odious man. There must be someone waiting for me, someone who will please God, my father *and* me."

"That's a tall order," the maid said, "but I will pray for it, too."

"Good." Tess reached for her white fur cape and the small, beaded bag containing her opera glasses. "And while you are praying, please ask that I will remain in control of my temper tonight. If Phineas tries to take liberties, I fear I might want to give him the same as he gave poor Michael the last time they met."

Annie gasped. "You wouldn't!"

"No, of course not." She smiled wryly. "But that doesn't mean I would not be sorely tempted."

It wasn't within Michael's jurisdiction to stand across from the opera house and watch the carriages and motorcars of the elite arrive to discharge their wealthy passengers. Instead, he had to be satisfied to position himself at the corner of Howard and Seventh streets so he could see all the way up to Mission.

He knew that unless the Clarks' driver was forced to circle the block there was little chance of catching even a glimpse of Tess. Nevertheless, he felt compelled to try.

Tess would be beautiful, of course. That was a given. And even if he failed to actually see her he could always imagine her loveliness the way he did nearly every waking moment, not to mention in his fondest dreams.

Michael no longer had any doubt he was smitten. Although he and Tess had been acquainted for years and had played like siblings when they were younger, he had only recently realized what an admirable woman she had become. It was undoubtedly just as well that he had moved into the fire station to live four years ago, before Tess had matured enough to catch his eye. If he had still lived under the Clark roof there was no telling how hard he would have had to struggle to keep his distance, especially if she had shown the least interest in him.

Was she interested now? He couldn't help but wonder. After she had asked him to be her escort to the lecture it seemed as if something important had changed between them. Was he imagining that she now looked at him fondly? Was he fooling himself that there was tenderness in those expressive, blue eyes when they met his? Surely not.

Michael shrugged. What difference did it make? He was a working man and she was an heiress. There was no chance, none at all, that he could ever hope to climb the ladder of success enough to be considered her peer, let alone earn enough to support her in the manner to which she was accustomed. And he would never accept money from her. Not under any circumstances. He had his pride.

Watching the slowly moving parade of elegant carriages and a smattering of automobiles turn onto Mission Street, he scanned them carefully, looking for the fancy cabriolet he had driven when he had been with Tess and Annie. When he finally spotted it, pulled by a brace of matched bays this time, he thought his heart might pound out of his chest.

The Clarks' driver was easing the sleekly polished rig between two smaller buggies when a motorcar passed in a sputtering, smoky roar, frightening several teams besides his and causing them to fight the harness traces.

Michael ran forward, leaped the tracks to dodge a clanging electric streetcar, and raced to Tess's rescue without a thought for his own safety.

He grabbed the horses' bridles and held on to the team for dear life, fighting against their desire to break free and run amok with the Clark carriage and its passengers.

Like the horses in the fire station, these animals seemed unduly fractious. "Easy, easy boys," Michael crooned. "Settle down now. Settle down."

Although the danger from the near accident was over in seconds, several nearby drivers continued to have trouble controlling their teams as well.

While Michael stood holding the horses, he saw Gerald Clark, in black tie, tails and shiny top hat, climbing down and offering his hand to the most beautiful vision of womanhood he had ever laid eyes on.

"We'd better walk from here or we'll be late for the opening curtain," the older man said, paying little attention to the uniformed fireman who had so gallantly come to their assistance.

Placing her hand in Gerald's, the woman gracefully disembarked. The flaring hem of her fitted emerald gown flowed around her ankles like sea foam on a beach after a storm. She wore elbow-length white gloves and a white fur cape that made her cheeks look like orchids nestled in the snow.

And her hair! Michael could hardly tear his gaze from that magnificent reddish hair. It glowed with inner fire and its curls and waves shimmered like polished brass. The jewels that adorned it accented her beautiful eyes, yet the glistening gems paled in comparison to Tess's natural beauty.

Instead of letting her father escort her all the way to the curb, she paused and faced Michael.

"Thank you for tending to the horses, sir," she said with a smile and a tilt of her head. "We could have been upset—or worse—if you hadn't stepped forward."

He nodded, touching the bill of his cap with his free hand. "My pleasure, ma'am. A lot of these horses seem hard to handle tonight."

"I had noticed." She lagged as her father began to urge her past. "Why do you think that is?"

"I don't know." Michael was so entranced he could barely think, let alone make polite conversation. This was the very chance he'd hoped and prayed for and there he stood, practically speechless.

"You're the prettiest girl in San Francisco tonight," he finally said aside, hoping that the street noise would keep his comment from being easily overheard, especially by her father.

Tess laughed gaily and glanced back over her shoulder at him as she walked off. There was a twinkle in her eyes. "Only tonight?"

Before Michael had a chance to answer, she was too far away to have heard him unless he had shouted. That would have been foolish. And highly improper. After all, what woman in Tess's position would want a passerby shouting to her about her beauty?

He waited until the Clarks' driver was ready, then released the team to him and returned to his former place on the sidewalk across the street. There was no need to stay away from the fire station premises any longer, although there was no current need for his services. He had seen what—who—he had been waiting for.

And he knew in his heart that he would never forget the way Tess had looked tonight. He'd meant every word he'd said. She was the most beautiful woman he'd ever laid eyes on, in San Francisco or anywhere else.

And when she had smiled at him with those dancing eyes and that impish expression that said far more than mere words ever could, he'd felt as if he were the only man in the world.

As far as he was concerned, Tess Clark might not be the only woman but she was the only one who mattered.

Chapter Eight

Gerald Clark, imposing as ever in his starched white ruffled shirt with diamond studs, pleated velvet cummerbund and tailcoat, greeted Phineas Edgerton in the lobby, as planned, making Tess's stomach lurch.

She accompanied her father up the stairway to his private box while trying her best to ignore the other man. They all waited while an attendant drew back the heavy, tasseled curtain that served as its door.

Following her father into the box, she was amazed by the garlands of real orchids, roses and narcissus that festooned the curved balcony of not only their box but all the others, as well as decorating the leading edges of the stage and orchestra pit. The embellishment made the opera house look like a beautiful garden and the scattered petals of fruit blossoms perfumed the air most deliciously.

Unbidden, Phineas cupped her elbow and guided her to a chair next to the larger one that was always reserved for her father. Once she was settled, the younger banker collapsed his top hat and placed his silver-handled cane

across the closest seat at her other hand, clearly appro-
priating it for himself.

"Are you comfortable, my dear?" Phineas asked,
hovering as he helped her off with her cape and draped
it carefully over the back of an empty chair.

Tess merely nodded, feeling so trapped she was ready
to scream and seeing no way to escape, gracefully or
otherwise. As far as she was concerned, being sand-
wiched between her father and Phineas Edgerton was
akin to being laced into her corset. The sooner she could
be free of all of them, the happier she'd be and the better she'd be able to breathe.

Withdrawing her ebony and silver, engraved opera
glasses from the beaded bag, she raised them and con-
centrated on watching the stage as the orchestra finished tuning up and the overture began.

"I was delighted when G.B. asked me to accompany
you this evening," Phineas leaned closer to say.

All Tess did was lift a gloved finger to her lips in
a plea for silence. To her relief, he settled back in his
seat and stopped trying to engage her in conversation.

Watching the performance, Tess imagined herself as
the gypsy, Carmen, with Michael as Don Jose. Except
that she would never lead the man she loved astray like
that, nor would she turn from him to another man the
way she knew Carmen eventually would.

At intermission, Tess politely excused herself and
left Phineas and her father behind in the box, insisting
with a demure blush that she had no need of an escort
to the powder room.

Her thin satin slippers made no sound on the thick
carpet as she hurried quickly, gracefully, to the multi-
paned window at the end of the hallway. That alcove

was located close to the ladies' room door so she figured she could always duck in there if anyone happened to question why she was prowling the halls alone.

She'd gone to that window specifically to look down on San Francisco. To seek another glimpse of her personal Don Jose. The city below was well-lit and bustling with activity, as expected. Would Michael still be lingering on the corner where she had last seen him? Probably not. Nevertheless, she had to look.

Shading her eyes from the dancing flashes of light from the crystal prisms on the electric lamps behind her, she studied the street. It was no use. If Michael was still among the pedestrians she was unable to pick him out from so far away.

Tess folded her gloved hands and closed her eyes to pray, "Father, please tell me what to do. How can I let Michael know that I care?"

Unshed tears gathered behind her lashes as she pictured the gallant fireman. "And keep him safe, Lord. Please? He's in danger all the time and I would die if anything happened to him."

That heartfelt, honest prayer became her answer. She loved Michael. Period. If only she could run to him right now, throw herself into his arms and tell him... *Tell him what?*

Behind her the house lights flashed, then began to dim. It was time to return to her seat—to her father and Phineas—for the rest of the performance. For the betrayal of poor Don Jose and the eventual death of Carmen.

Tess had to force herself to take the necessary steps. She sighed as she reentered the Clark box and resumed her place. This was not the right time to act on her revelation and go in search of Michael. She had a duty to Papa to remain with him for the rest of the evening. It would cause him great worry and consternation if she left the opera house without explanation, and trying to sensibly voice what was on her heart was beyond impossible.

Not only would he have been livid as a result, she herself wasn't sure how she felt or what she might say with regard to the yearnings she was experiencing.

Enrico Caruso's continuing portrayal of Don Jose was magnificent and beautifully tragic as she'd known it would be, yet all Tess could think about was how dashing Michael had looked when he'd raced to her rescue and grabbed the bridles of the frightened horses.

As the famous tenor sang and her mind drifted with the music, she was able to couple her memories of the real hero in her life with the romantic images created onstage. Tears gathered behind her lashes once again and she tried to blink them away without letting either of her companions see that she was so moved.

Her heart soared, then plummeted, then rose again on wings of hope as the orchestra played and the magnificent voices lifted together to tingle her nerves and leave her enthralled.

Every note, every crescendo, reminded her of Michael. If this was what true love did to a person's emotions, she didn't like it one bit. How could she possibly have been foolish enough to have fallen for that man?

A lump in her throat and a shiver singing up her spine provided absolute proof. She not only could have, she had. The question was no longer what had happened, it was what she should do about it to avoid the kind of tragedy being portrayed in the final act of the Bizet opera.

By the time the curtain fell and the performers were taking their bows, Tess was no closer to a sensible conclusion than she had been before. That was the basic problem, of course. There was nothing logical about her dilemma so there could be no rational decision.

Mostly, she wanted to speak privately with Michael, although how she might accomplish that—or what she would say to him if she did—remained a puzzle. It was only Tuesday. By her reckoning it would be at least a week and a half before he revisited the estate, assuming he stuck to his usual schedule. And anything could happen to alter that.

Tess's vivid imagination pictured him meeting and falling in love with someone else in that short space of time, just the way Carmen had ultimately chosen the toreador over the soldier who had given up everything for her love.

That vivid notion pained her deeply. Not that she had any claim on Michael Mahoney. Yet, in the back of her mind she kept hoping that something would alter their circumstances enough that they could face their attraction to each other and at least discuss it sensibly.

Women clad in furs, satin and diamonds had gathered at the base of the stage and were showering a proud Caruso with roses and effusive praise.

Yawning, Gerald Clark led the way out of the box before the applause had fully died, leaving Phineas to help Tess don her fur wrap.

San Francisco's mayor, Eugene Schmitz, a former orchestra leader himself, encountered the group in the teeming upper hallway and struck up a lively conversation with the banker.

"If you gentlemen will excuse me," Tess said with a slight smile and careful incline of her head so she wouldn't disturb her highly decorative coif, "I'll be waiting in the lobby." She fanned herself with a gloved hand for emphasis. "I must have some fresh air."

To her dismay, Phineas immediately offered his arm and stepped forward to escort her. She had no choice but to allow him to do so. Moving slowly amid the press of the crowd, they descended the staircase from the private box to the immense, vaulted lobby with its gilded fixtures, Raphaelesque murals and crystal chandeliers.

She paid little attention to anyone other than to return their polite nods or brief greetings. Traversing the plush Oriental-patterned carpeting of the staircase, Tess had to admit that briefly touching Phineas was better than possibly slipping in her new shoes and causing a scene. The last thing she wanted was to give her father more reason to chastise her.

The lobby was teeming with opera aficionados, all praising Caruso's performance. Tess knew it was a coup to get the famous New York Metropolitan Opera Company to appear at their opera house and she was proud that her city had managed to do so for the second time.

"Wait here while I go shout for the carriage," Phineas said, patting her hand in parting after they reached the lobby level. "G.B. should be down to join you in a moment."

Tess nodded amiably. She wasn't afraid to be left alone in the midst of the milling multitude, even though a few of the attendees' outfits were not up to the elegant standards of hers and her father's. In Tess's opinion, that was a good thing. The more people who could appreciate the fine arts, the better for the city as a whole.

Spotting a sleek carriage that she assumed was hers, she clasped her cape at her neck with one gloved hand and lifted her gossamer hem slightly, proceeding out the door. When she drew closer to the street, however, she realized that she had been mistaken so she stepped out of the way to let others pass.

The foyer of the opera house was too crowded to comfortably reenter and the night's weather was fairly pleasant for a change, so she decided to remain outside to wait for Phineas and her father.

Bejeweled women swept past like the outgoing tide, most prattling excitedly about how they'd found Caruso such an enthralling hero figure. Tess smiled to herself. She'd enjoyed the opera, of course, but in her eyes there was only one true hero.

Still picturing Michael, she imagined she saw his familiar, broad-shouldered figure crossing the street and coming toward her.

Her breath caught. She pressed her hand to her throat. Disbelief was quickly replaced with delight. It *was* Michael! And he had clearly noticed her, too.

Nervous and unsure of what course to take, she edged to the fringe of the mass of exiting opera lovers and waited for him.

He rushed directly to her. The sight of him was so thrilling, so dear, she immediately offered her hand. He grasped and held it without hesitation.

"Michael," Tess whispered, knowing that there was much unsaid in her tone, in her gaze. "How did you find me in this terrible crowd?"

"I don't know," he replied softly. "I can only stay a moment. I have to get back to the station soon."

"You shouldn't have come again. I don't want you to risk losing your job."

"I won't. A friend is covering for me. I just had to see you again, to tell you how beautiful you are."

"I want to meet where we can talk more freely," Tess said quietly aside, squeezing his fingers for emphasis. "Not at the house, though. Perhaps you could send word through Mary and I could meet you some afternoon in Golden Gate Park."

"I'd like that," he said.

Before she could reply he lifted her hand to his lips and kissed the backs of her fingers through the glove, exactly the way she had seen many fine gentlemen express affection.

Tess was glad Michael was still holding her hand because she felt woozy. Her eyes widened. Then she began to smile broadly. "I wish you were the one escorting me home again this evening."

His eyebrows arched and he gave a soft laugh. "So do I, Miss Clark. So do I."

"You should call me Tess, you know."

"Should I? I wonder."

She saw his smile fade and his focus narrow as he glanced past her shoulder, then dropped her hand.

"Here comes your father. I have to go."

"Meet me? Promise?" Tess called after him as he whirled and jogged back across the street.

Although he didn't answer or even wave, she knew he would be getting in touch with her to set up their rendezvous. What she would say to him, or he to her, when they finally did meet in private was another matter altogether. She only knew that the prayer she'd said for Michael during the intermission was already being answered. The rest of her many concerns she would also try to release and leave the results up to God.

She turned to greet her father. To her great relief he was showing no sign that he had seen who had just kissed her hand and had won her heart long before that.

For the time being, keeping her father in the dark was exactly what Tess wanted. If and when the time came to tell him of her errant heart's desire, then she would pray for the wisdom to do so prudently.

In retrospect, it was easy to imagine that God had brought her and Michael together for His divine purposes. She wasn't about to deny a providential nudge like that. She simply wasn't ready to beard the lion in his own den and confess anything to her father before she was sure it would be necessary.

Suppose Michael rejected her profession of love? she asked herself. The very thought of such a thing made her tremble but it also provided a caution against blurting out her feelings without making certain that they were returned in kind.

Michael was so engrossed in thoughts of Tess and her plea for a private meeting with him that he was back on Howard Street in front of Station #4 before he even realized he'd arrived.

What had he done? Had he inadvertently led her on?

Michael made a guttural sound of self-disgust. Of course he had. And he had no one to blame but himself. He'd given in to his desire to see Tess again and by approaching her tonight he had made her believe that his interest was too personal.

Who was he kidding? It *was* personal. And kicking himself for displaying his fondness for her so openly would do no good.

The sensible course of action was to meet Tess as she'd asked, then explain to her why they could never declare any shared affection. He could do that. He *would* do that. It was the only honorable choice.

Clenching his jaw, he entered the rear of the fire station and noticed that the horses were still snorting, shuffling and acting decidedly uneasy. When he spotted O'Neill trying to comfort them he joined him.

"What's wrong with all these animals tonight?" Michael asked.

"Beats me. I thought maybe you'd given them an extra ration of grain."

"Not me. Must be some other reason. A lot of the horses out on the streets are acting the same way."

His fellow fireman began to scowl. "That doesn't sound good. You know what usually happens when they get this upset."

"Sure." Michael shrugged off the concern. "Don't worry though. The city may shake a little from time to time but it never amounts to much. Any serious trouble we were going to have has already happened years ago." He eyed the steam pipes leading up from the boiler in the basement that they kept heated in preparation for charging the mobile pumpers with hot water. "It's not like it was in the old days before the fire brigades formed. We're ready for anything now."

O'Neill nodded. "Aye. That we are. I'll just feel better about it when these horses tell me it's safe again."

Chuckling, Michael agreed. "Me, too. In the meantime, how's your hangover? Do you want to take the watch tonight or shall I?"

"Since you let me nap away me big head all afternoon, I think you should have the whole night to sleep, if you want," O'Neill said with a wry grin. "Callahan and I can listen for any alarms and wake you if we need you."

Michael figured he wouldn't sleep a wink because of his constant thoughts of Tess but he nevertheless accepted the offer of an entire night off. His quarters were upstairs in the station, along with those of many of the other firemen, so he wasn't far away if he was needed.

He clapped his friend on the shoulder. "All right. It's a bargain. I'm such a light sleeper I usually hear the alarm going off anyway."

"Why do you think I drink?" O'Neill asked with a grin. "Can't hardly sleep without a little medicine to calm the old nerves."

"I wish we could give some to these poor nags," Michael said with a snort of derision. "If they don't settle down pretty soon they'll be too worn-out to pull the engines."

"I know. I'll stick with 'em for a bit. Might even make me a pallet out here so I can tell if they get worse."

"You sure you don't want company?"

"Naw. I owe you. Besides, horses don't care if there's a bit of the grog on a man's breath."

"You haven't been drinking again, have you?"

"No. Not yet," O'Neill said. "But I may be sorely tempted by the time this night is over, and that's a fact."

"Well, if you do hit the bottle don't tell me about it," Michael warned, "or I'll have to report you."

"Yeah, yeah, I know. That's why you'd make a better captain than I ever would. Have ye heard anything more about your promotion?"

"No." He felt a twinge of foreboding. If he declared his fondness for Tess Clark and her father was as upset about it as Michael expected him to be, he could kiss any thoughts of rising in the fire department's ranks goodbye.

That, however, was not the basic reason why he intended to disabuse her of any notions that they belonged together. The insufficiency was his and his alone. He could never hope to attain the high station in life to which Tess belonged. And he would never presume to ask her to lower herself to his class among the more common folk. She deserved better.

"But not a man like that odious Edgerton," he muttered to himself.

Climbing the narrow wooden stairway to the common bunk area on the second story, Michael kept shaking his head in disgust. There was no way a man like him could hope to influence Gerald Clark one way or the other, so why concern himself with the possible choice of suitors for Tess?

Troubled as well as frustrated, Michael stripped off his uniform coat and boots and threw himself onto his narrow cot without bothering to finish undressing or turning down the covers. He laid his arm over his eyes to try to blot out the image of Tess being courted by anyone but him.

On either side of his bed, sleeping firemen snored loudly. The racket wasn't enough to distract Michael's thoughts or keep him from recalling every nuance of Tess's image and every inflection of her voice when she'd begged for a meeting.

Yes, Michael concluded sadly, *I'll meet her. And I'll tell her that no matter how either of us may feel, there is absolutely no chance we can ever find mutual happiness.*

In his heart of hearts he knew that was true. But deeper, in the part of him that he suspected was his soul, he was still able to visualize putting his arms around Tess and seeing her gaze up at him with the same tenderness she'd displayed outside the opera house that very evening.

She was a vision of pure loveliness coupled with an intelligence and wit equal to any man he'd ever met, himself included. And her eyes! When she'd looked at him with such intensity, such affection, he'd had to struggle to keep from kissing her in spite of the hundreds of witnesses milling around.

Nurturing that image and letting his sleeve blot up the sparse moisture that kept gathering in his eyes, Michael finally dozed off.

Chapter Nine

April 18, 5:13 a.m.

Tess was dreaming. She was wearing her emerald-green gown again and being escorted to the opera by a tall, handsome, well-dressed man who could only be Michael Mahoney. Everyone was deliriously happy, especially her. Even Papa was smiling and holding out his hand as if accepting her choice of a beau.

Then, suddenly, the whole opera house began to quiver. When Tess tried to scream, she was mute.

Awakening abruptly, she was confused. She blinked rapidly to help clear her head and try to focus.

This was no dream. It was a true nightmare. The room was actually rocking and there was a loud, ominous rumble echoing throughout the house, as if the very walls and floors were groaning in agony.

Tess shouted, "Annie," at the top of her lungs before she remembered that she had sent the girl into the city to visit her mother, Rose, the evening before.

Fisting the sheets, Tess held on to her bedding and peered through the narrow openings between the drapes at her windows. Night was still upon them, although a waning moon illuminated the swaying trees in the formal garden and there was a glow to the east above Mount Diablo. Dawn was very near.

The ground continued to shift. It was less of a jerking motion now and more like riding the waves at sea.

Scooting to the edge of her mattress, Tess grasped the carved mahogany bedpost and hung on for dear life. The great, stone house on Nob Hill was built on firmer ground than much of San Francisco was but it still felt as if it was about to be shaken apart.

"Father!" she shouted above the roar and creaking. "Father. Are you all right?"

Gerald Clark's gruff "Yes" gave her relief in spite of its harshness. "Stay where you are," he ordered.

Tess could tell by the changing direction of his voice that he was not taking his own advice. And if he could move about, so could she.

Swinging her bare feet to the floor, she continued to cling to the bedpost, hoping to keep her balance. She reached one hand for a robe she'd left lying on a nearby fainting couch and lurched toward the door as she slipped her arms into the robe's belled sleeves.

Her left shoulder slammed into the doorjamb. Hitting that frame and leaning against it was the only thing that kept her on her feet.

After pausing to tie the sash of the pale silk dressing gown, she made her way awkwardly to the spiral staircase that lead to the main floor and grabbed the top railing with both hands. A flurry of activity was taking place below.

"Father!"

"I told you to stay in your room."

Someone had lit a few of the old gas lamps to illuminate the foyer and she could see Gerald's deep scowl in shadow as he glared up at her. His thick gray brows were knit, his grimace clearly visible.

"I'm safer down there with you," Tess argued.

"Not if this ceiling caves in."

She could see the continuing sway of the crystal chandelier above the entry hall. The heavy, ornate fixture seemed securely anchored to its carved medallion, yet there was no way to predict whether or not it was going to stay that way.

"I think the shaking is almost over," Tess said, starting to inch her way down the stairs while keeping a tight hold on the banister. "It's not nearly as bad as it was when I awoke."

"That doesn't mean the first shock is all there will be," her father insisted. "If you must be up and about, I suggest you dress properly. And tell Annie to get down to the kitchen and help Mary prepare extra meals. We may have to feed refugees."

That notion chilled Tess to the bone. Refugees? In her home? Surely the destruction of the city could not be that extensive. Plenty of previous quakes had damaged buildings here and there and had started a few fires which were quickly extinguished. That kind of repeated event, though troublesome, was easy for a city the size of San Francisco to handle, especially given the marvelously efficient fire brigades that had been organized, particularly after the mid to late 1800s.

Her breath caught. Fires and destruction meant danger for Michael! Her heart raced at the mere notion. She wheeled and started back to her room, keeping a steadying palm pressed to the hallway walls for support as she went.

Although she could dress without Annie, the usual elaborate upsweep of her hair would have to wait. Under these horrible circumstances, such trivialities hardly mattered.

"Dear Lord, watch over the firemen and all the others who are trying to help," Tess prayed, adding a silent, special word for dear Michael.

Continuing to brace herself as a different, more circular manner of shaking commenced, she staggered back to the window in her room and clung to the edges of the heavy drapes as she threw them open.

What she beheld made her tremble nearly as badly as the earthquake. Multiple small fires were already scattered across the panorama between her home and the shiny, copper dome of the new city hall. Since there was more than one blaze, she assumed the fire department's resources would be sorely taxed.

Once again the movement of the ground abated, although for how long only God knew. Grabbing the first ensemble she saw in her armoire, Tess threw on her clothing. She was buttoning the jacket to her favorite afternoon ensemble and smoothing its gray, gored skirt when she once again looked down at the city.

"Praise the Lord, some of the fires are already out," she whispered, immensely relieved. Everything was going to be all right. And as soon as Annie arrived home from her mother's, they'd both lend a hand in the kitchen, just in case Father happened to be right about refugees.

It was not beneath Tess to volunteer to do housework. She was far from the helpless female her father assumed her to be and she didn't mind proving it, especially lately. Though Mama had been frail all her life, her only daughter was a strong woman just like Maud Younger and the other suffragettes she admired so.

Someday Father would have to admit that he had raised a child who was more like himself than he'd ever imagined, Tess mused. And when that happened, she was going to be tickled pink.

The first inkling Michael had that something was very wrong was the rocking of his narrow, metal-frame cot. He'd been dreaming of being aboard a ship and had thought at first that the movement was part of that dream.

Then he opened his eyes and saw the truth painted in the dim glow of sunrise. He sat bolt upright, staring in wide-eyed disbelief.

The lanternlike lamp hanging from the center of the ceiling was swinging as if a giant hand were pushing it to and fro. He heard glass falling, windows cracking. Tiny pieces of white-painted plaster began to rain down on him and the other firemen.

He instinctively raised his arms for protection, shouting, "Look out, boys. Take cover!"

A distant roar filled his ears, as if a hundred hissing, chugging steam locomotives were racing to converge in that very room. The sound built until it was deafening, and as it increased so did the strength, lift and drop of the tremors.

The beds began to lurch like bucking horses. Empty ones bounced higher than the others as the floor heaved, then subsided, only to do it again and again. Michael's cot inched all the way across the room before it hit an interior wall and stopped traveling.

"Dear God, help us," he shouted, noticing that many of the others were also calling out to the Almighty. And well they should. This was nothing like the other quakes he'd experienced. This one was massive. Catastrophic beyond description.

He'd just begun to think the worst was over when the movement altered and changed course, causing even worse damage. Bricks began to shake loose and fall from the outer walls into the street below.

Outside, shrill cries of injured and dying animals rose to join the cacophony of human terror. Grown men and women could be heard shrieking like terrified children.

The ground continued to tremble. The entire fire house swayed and shuddered. The nearest window popped out of its frame and disappeared in a hail of mortar, stone and brick.

Michael attempted to stand. Instead, he hit the floor on all fours. Crawling along the buckling boards, he braced his back against a wall and wriggled into his boots as best he could from a horizontal position.

Time seemed to be standing still, yet he knew several minutes must have passed since the initial shock had awakened him. This was no normal quake. This was *big*. And their problems wouldn't be over just because the trembling eventually stopped. If it ever did!

His already racing heart leaped into his throat and he breathed a name that made his gut clench. "Tess."

There wasn't a thing he could do for her—or for anyone else—until he had learned the worst and seen if he was needed on the job immediately. If he was to be held in reserve for later assignment, as he hoped he would be, the first thing he was going to do was head for the Clark estate and check on the two most important women in his life.

He suddenly remembered the telephone his mother had used to call him. As soon as he could, he'd ring the Clarks' house. He had to know for sure that she and Tess were all right.

"Father," he prayed as he staggered to his feet and lurched toward the door, hoping against hope that the stairs would still support his weight, "please look after them. Both of them."

Michael was through arguing with himself. Miss Tess Clark was a vitally important part of his life. She always would be, whether he ever chose to admit it to her, or not.

Tess held tight to the banister, worried about another aftershock, as she made her way to the staircase and started down for the second time that morning. Father and the other male servants were no longer gathered below so she paused there to look for damage. Other than a few spidery cracks in the walls, everything looked secure.

A rising sun was peeking over the tops of the trees and beginning to brightly illuminate the east windows, making the need for artificial light unnecessary. That was good. Apparently, there was no electricity to power the chandeliers or Father would not have bothered to light the gas wall sconces.

While Tess watched, one of the closest flames fluttered as if starved for fuel. Then, the next in line began to do the same, a clear sign of danger.

Working her way cautiously from room to room, she checked to be certain that each valve was tightly closed and each switch for the electric lights was also turned off. Their house seemed to have weathered the earthquake without too much destruction but that didn't mean that the gas mains and electric lines from the city below had not suffered plenty of damage.

According to her father and his outspoken friends including Mayor Schmitz, the land under the wharves and Chinatown and even much of the downtown business district, was terribly unstable when shaken. That explained why the areas nearest the bay were always affected the most when the ground shifted.

"It must be dreadful this morning," Tess muttered to herself as she worked her way through the house, carefully skirting shattered remains of porcelain bric-a-brac and imported glassware that had once been so dear to her mother.

Keepsakes no longer held the importance they had even yesterday, Tess realized. Although the loss of such lovely trinkets saddened her, it was the other citizens whose welfare was uppermost in her mind.

Over and over she prayed, "Dear Lord, please, please help the poor people in the lowlands."

When she reached the kitchen she saw Mary peering with concern at the tall, blackened stove pipe that had been the outlet for smoke from the wood cookstove before it had been replaced by a more modern, gas model.

"Are you all right?" Tess asked, slightly surprised to note a tremulous quality to her voice.

Mary gasped, whirled and rushed to her, enfolding her in a mutual embrace of support and commiseration. "Yes. Are you?" She sniffled.

"Yes," Tess answered. "That was terrible. I thought it was never going to end."

"Aye." The older woman nodded and stepped back, looking chagrined. "I'm sorry. I shouldn't have hugged you like that. I just…"

"Nonsense. We both needed it. There's nothing like a disaster to make everyone equal." She swiped at a stray tear sliding down her cheek. "Is everything still in working order? I saw you looking up at the flue."

"Just giving thanks that Mister Gerald installed gas for cooking, even if it was hard for me to get used to," Mary said. "That pipe shook loose. You can see the soot on the wall. I suspect we'd best not use any of the chimneys till they're checked for damage."

Tess had not thought of that kind of problem. "You're right. How clever of you."

"Just repeatin' what Michael always says," Mary explained. "He's more worried about what might cause fires than he is about earthquakes, at least he used to be. After this mornin', who knows?" She sank heavily into one of the kitchen chairs and blinked back tears of her own. "I'm fair troubled about him."

"So am I," Tess said without embarrassment. At a time like this she saw little reason to hide her true feelings. Joining Mary, she reached for the cook's hands and clasped them tightly atop the table. "I saw him last night, at the opera."

"My Michael? He was there? How? Why?"

"I was hoping you might be able to tell me," Tess said. "Has he confided in you?"

"About what?"

Here was the moment of truth, the instant when she could have made excuses and kept her opinion to herself, as before. This time she chose not to. "About how he might feel regarding me."

"No." The older woman's eyes widened. "Of course not. Why would he be tellin' me anything about you?"

"Because we have developed strong feelings for each other," Tess said. "Oh, he might deny it but I know better. I saw it in the way he looked at me last night."

Mary was shaking her head. "You were beautiful, all dressed up formal-like. Any young man would have looked on you with admiration."

"Not the way Michael did," Tess insisted. "I shall never forget the way he took my hand and kissed it."

Astonished, Mary jerked free and jumped to her feet. "He did no such thing."

It was more a question than a statement, at least that was the way Tess interpreted it. "Yes, he did. And he was so handsome and charming I wanted to forget everything else and run away with him then and there."

"Such nonsense," Mary muttered. "'Tis a terrible, terrible thing."

In spite of the recent disaster, Tess managed to smile and reply, "*Terrible* is not at all the way I would describe it. As a matter of fact, it was so wonderful I can't find words that are magnificent enough to half do it justice."

Chapter Ten

Havoc reigned in the center of the city. When Michael ventured forth he realized he wouldn't need the stairs to reach street level. He was already down there. Portions of the upper floor had fallen onto the lower one and all he had to do was step through the remains of the doorway and climb over a pile of loose bricks to reach the street!

Stunned, he stepped out and turned slowly in a circle, staring in disbelief. It was gone. The station was *gone*. The American Hotel, next door, lay in a heap, too. Its upper floors were askew and the lower ones had vanished, just as the office in the fire station had. Nearly the entire block had been flattened and the few partial walls that were still upright looked fragile enough to be toppled by a mere zephyr.

He knew at a glance that there was little difference any one man's efforts could make. Even if every able-bodied soul in San Francisco tried his best, it wouldn't be enough to alleviate this much suffering or save even half the lives he knew were presently being snuffed out like candles in a wintry gale.

His intent had been to report for duty. He would have, had there been anything left of the office at his station. The collapse of the second floor had buried the alarm system as well as the telephone he had hoped to use—not that there was even a remote chance either was still operable.

Coughing from the dust, eyes smarting, he picked his way through the rubble toward what had once been the stables, dreading what he might see and expecting the worst.

That was exactly what he found. Although all but one of the horses seemed to have broken free and escaped the carnage, the lifeless body of James O'Neill lay half buried by tons of wood and masonry. So did every single piece of their expensive fire equipment.

There was also a gaping hole over the standby boiler in the basement and Michael could see its pipes hissing and spitting streams of hot water. The only good thing about that was the moisture dribbling down and quenching the hot coals before flames could escape the firebox and cause more destruction. If more destruction was even possible.

Stunned, Michael dropped to one knee beside his friend's body and automatically checked for signs of life.

"Ah, James," he murmured. "'Tis a sad, sad day. I'm so sorry." Touching the man's exposed wrist, he felt for the pulse he knew would not be there. Tears gathered in his already smarting eyes and he heaved a sigh.

"Father, take my friend to be with You," Michael said. "He had his faults, as we all do, but he was Your child."

Rising after a quick "Amen," he did the only thing he

could. He left and went to look for the rest of his comrades, continuing to ask God's favor and mercy upon them as he picked his way over and between piles of fallen bricks and stone.

To his relief, he found most of the other men gathered in the middle of Howard Street, gaping at the building that had been the pride of Company #4 only minutes ago. There, they were being formed into a loosely knit workforce by a junior officer who had assumed temporary command since their captain didn't seem to be thinking clearly.

"I just came from the stable. We've lost O'Neill," Michael announced, managing to keep his voice strong and steady for the sake of the others. "Looks like most of the horses ran off but the engines are good and buried. There's nothing left to work with. All we can do is concentrate on helping the living."

The officer gestured toward a pile of splintered wood on the corner that had been the American Hotel. "Michael's right." He pointed to individuals. "You three start digging over there where you hear cries."

Although the firemen were clearly in shock, they complied.

"What about me?" Michael asked.

"I was going to go try to find Chief Sullivan," he said, "but I'm sending you, instead. Tell him we need to know if he wants us to join another company or stay and work here, on our own."

"Do you really think it matters?" Michael asked, staring at the destruction and shaking his head as he tried to accept all he was seeing. "What if I can't find him?"

"Then do whatever you feel is right. I won't be holding my breath waiting for you to come back. At this point, we're all pretty much on our own."

"I agree."

Michael turned and started off. Stone facades of notable buildings that were now unrecognizable extended in drifts into the street. Miles of flat paving stones were buckled like crumpled paper and there was a rift in the street as if the land had been split apart by the hand of an angry giant.

The sight of water gushing from ruptured pipes within the chasm made Michael shiver. If the main supply lines had fractured, as he now believed they had, firemen would have to tap cisterns that were strategically placed throughout the city in order to get enough water to quench the fires.

Suddenly a disheveled, gray-dirt-covered young woman lurched toward him and grabbed his arm, forcing him to stop and pay attention to her. He started to explain his mission and shake her off, then caught his breath. "Annie? Is that you?"

She was muttering unintelligibly. All Michael could make out was, "Tess…"

His heart nearly stopped. He grabbed Annie by the shoulders. "Tess is here? Where?"

"She, she…"

As he watched, Annie's eyes rolled back in her head and she swooned.

He knew he couldn't abandon the helpless young woman to the milling crowds that were beginning to fill the streets. Nor did he dare place her inside one of the already tottering buildings. There were sure to be deadly aftershocks and more buildings would collapse. That was a certainty.

Just then, another, lesser quake rumbled. The land beneath Michael's feet vibrated like a bowl of warm gruel. He crouched over Annie, using his back to try to shield her from additional falling debris.

Dust rose in roiling clouds that choked lungs and burned eyes even more than before. In the distance, he could hear the rapid clanging of bells, meaning that some fire equipment was still in service and gallant crews were responding to the columns of smoke he could see starting to rise at all four points of the compass.

"Dear God, what do You want me to do?" Michael prayed fervently. "It'll take too long to carry her up Nob Hill through all this."

Casting around for answers, he noticed a group of loose horses. Five heavy-bodied work animals were congregated around one of the bubbling waterholes that had so recently appeared in the middle of the street. One of those horses, a huge gelding with a roached mane and braided tail, was wearing a harness that bore the fire department insignia.

Michael whistled. The dappled gray's ears perked up. It turned toward the shrill sound, then slowly began to approach, head down, the damp, dusty hide of its withers quivering.

The escaped fire horse was far too tall to mount while bearing his semiconscious burden, so Michael took hold of its halter and led it over to a fallen column. He wouldn't have tried to ride most other horses without a proper saddle but he knew this one, and as far as he was concerned it might as well have been heaven-sent.

Climbing up on the fluted edges of the stonework, Michael eased a groggy Annie onto the horse first, then swung a leg over so he could sit behind and keep her from sliding off. She moaned without totally regaining her senses.

Michael paused, his loyalties torn. Since his station had no teams and no usable equipment, there was little he could do other than proceed to try to ascertain where he and his fellows would be needed, as he'd originally been ordered. However, he'd also been told that he was free to use his own discretion so he would first ride to the Clark estate, deliver Annie and inquire about his mother and Tess.

If they were safe there, as he hoped, he'd be able to relax and return to try to find the chief or to simply concentrate on rescue work. If Tess was missing amid all this terrible wreckage, however, he wouldn't stop searching until he found her.

His heart would not let him.

Tess was passing the bay windows in the parlor when she caught a flash of movement out of the corner of her eye and saw a figure on horseback drawing nearer.

Far from prepared, she nevertheless hurried to the front door and threw it open, expecting to welcome the first of the refugees. Her jaw gaped when she recognized who had actually arrived.

Tess's hand flew to her throat where she felt her pulse fluttering madly. It was *Michael!* And he'd brought Annie home. *Praise God!*

"I'm glad to see that this house stood," he said by way of terse greeting. "Are you all right?" His voice sounded so hoarse Tess barely recognized it.

"Yes. Fine. And so is your mother. I just left her." She hurriedly approached. "What's happened to Annie?"

"I don't know. She's been pretty groggy." He scooted back so he could lift the young woman more easily and lower her to the ground. "Come and take her. I have to be getting back."

Tess held out both hands.

Michael eased his burden down.

Annie immediately recovered enough to begin to cling to Tess, sobbing quietly as if she were an injured child seeking comfort in the arms of its mother.

"Where did you find her?" Tess asked him.

He slid to the ground beside the horse and grasped its bridle as he answered, "She found me. Near Union Square. She fainted before she could tell me if you had been with her."

"Why would I be with her? You knew I was going home after the opera last night."

"I assumed so, yes, but I'd heard that a lot of nabobs did stay late to party at the Palace with Caruso. If she hadn't called your name before she fainted, I wouldn't have been confused."

"I sent her visiting in the city last night because I wasn't going to need her here. Her mother's house is on Geary Street, not far from where you say you found her." Tess managed a smile. "*Your* mother is busy cooking up a storm in case we need to take people in."

He took a few steps closer. "Good. I'm surprised to hear you still have enough gas for the stove. Don't count on it for long, or telephones or electricity, either. And guard your use of water till we see how bad that damage was. I suspect most of the mains are gone."

"All right." She continued to gaze at him with affection, hoping he would understand how much she cared. "Be careful? Please?"

"I will." The way his penetrating gaze met hers reminded her of the night before, only with even more empathy and concern. She yearned to reach for his hand but managed to restrain herself. Barely. "How bad is it down there?"

"Worst I've ever seen or ever hope to see," Michael said soberly. "A lot of buildings are either already down or soon will be. I know there can't be much left of Chinatown or the shacks along the waterfront, either."

"That's terrible. Wait. Why aren't you fighting fires?"

Averting his face, he seemed to concentrate unduly on patting the horse's neck. When he did speak again, Tess understood why he had looked away. He'd been hiding the depth of his emotions.

"I was off duty, sleeping, when the quake hit," Michael said. "It's a wonder I survived. The whole station is in ruins."

"What about the other men?" Her heart ached for him, especially after he told her about finding his fellow fireman in the collapsed stable.

"I could just as easily have been the one staying down there with the horses," he added. "O'Neill made the choice to work all night because I'd let him sleep off a hangover earlier in the day."

That was more poignancy than Tess could resist. Keeping one arm around the still-weeping Annie, she grasped Michael's hand. "I'm so sorry."

"Thanks." He gave her fingers a quick squeeze before releasing them and starting to back the horse away. "I'm going to stop by the kitchen before I go. I want Ma to see for herself that I'm okay, in case she hears rumors about the station."

"Of course. Have her give you food and water. Take

more than you think you'll need," she called after him as he walked away. "I'll tend to Annie."

Before Tess could finish shepherding her maid through the front door, however, the young woman dug in her heels. "No! I have to go back."

"Whatever for? It's dangerous down there. You heard what Michael said."

Annie was adamant. "I don't care. I couldn't find my mother anywhere. The whole house fell down on top of us." Half sobbing, half hysterical, she gasped for breath. "You have to help me, Tess. We can't just leave her there. What if she's still alive and waiting for me to dig her out?"

Tess was ashamed that she hadn't thought that far ahead, hadn't considered Rose Dugan's welfare. Of course Annie was frantic. Any good daughter would be. Apparently, the disaster had rattled Tess's brain more than she'd first imagined or she would have remembered to ask about Annie's mother immediately.

"Do you think you can manage another trip this soon?" Tess asked, her heart aching for her friend.

"I can do anything for Mama."

"Then we'll go. Together. Just let me gather some supplies." She guided Annie into the house with an arm around her shoulders. "You go tell Mary to pack us a big basket of food, then have one of the men harness my mare to the smallest buggy. I'll go upstairs and collect sheets for bandages."

"I looked and looked and called for her as soon as I crawled out," the young woman insisted with a tremulous voice. "She didn't answer me. I couldn't find her anywhere. Not anywhere."

"Don't worry. We'll find her," Tess promised boldly.

In her heart, she was praying fervently that Annie's beloved mother was still alive. Judging by the indications she'd had so far, a great many people were not going to survive to see today's sunset over the Pacific.

Michael was just bidding his mother a fond farewell when Annie burst into the kitchen. Her hair was still ratted and her face streaked with dirt and tears. To his chagrin she was behaving irrationally, hurrying around the room and throwing food into a basket without bothering to even wrap it in a napkin.

He was about to tell her that he already had all the supplies he needed when she suddenly froze, covered her face with her hands and began to sob.

"There, there," Mary said soothingly, taking the young woman in her arms and patting her back. "You'll be all right. Sit down while I make you a nice cup of tea."

"No!" Annie pushed her away. "I have to go back to my mama's. I have to help her."

"Oh, darlin'," Mary crooned. "You can't be goin' down there all alone again. It's too dangerous."

Sniffling, the maid swiped at her tears and shook her head. "I'm not going alone. Tess is going with me. I have to get the buggy ready." She broke away and dashed toward the back door, brushing past Michael as if he were invisible.

Watching through the open door, Michael saw her race toward the carriage house. His heart sank. Until a moment ago, he had thought the situation couldn't possibly get any worse. Now, he knew better.

Giving his mother a peck on the cheek, he turned to leave.

"Are ye goin' back to work?" Mary asked.

"In a manner of speaking. The first thing I need to do is stop Tess."

Mary snorted. "Oh? And how do ye propose to do that?"

"I'll reason with her. Tell her how bad it is down below. She'll have to listen."

"Will she now? I'd like to see that."

"What else can I do? It's bedlam out there."

"I don't know. But giving that hardheaded girl orders isn't the way to go about it. You'd have a better chance of standin' on the tracks in front of a steam engine and expecting to hold back the train with your bare hands."

That opinion was so accurate it made Michael smile. He nodded. "I'll think of something."

By the time Tess reached the stables and joined Annie, there was a horse hitched to a buggy all right, but it wasn't her faithful mare.

She stopped, hands fisted on her hips, and stared at Michael. "What do you think you're doing?"

"Helping you get back to Annie's mother's safely," he replied, standing tall and showing no sign of being cowed by her display of righteous indignation.

"I'm taking my own horse," Tess insisted. "Unhitch your animal immediately."

Michael was slowly shaking his head as he held the gray gelding's bridle and led it a few paces, then fiddled with the length of the trace chains before he looked back at her. "No," he said flatly. "This horse is used to noise and strange smells. He's far less likely to bolt."

"My mare is fine."

"Here, she may be. And even that's not certain. Drive

her by the worst of the damage and she's bound to smell death or fire and start to act up."

"Don't be ridiculous." In the back of Tess's mind she could see Michael's point but a rebellious tendency kept her from admitting as much. She stood her ground. "Well? I'm waiting. Remove your horse this instant."

"If I do—and I don't promise I will—how long do you think it will take you and Annie to get your mare into harness in his place? Do you have that much time to waste? Or should you stop arguing and get in the buggy so we can all be on our way?"

Tess felt Annie grab her arm and hold so tight it pained her.

"Please," the maid pleaded, "let's just go. You can argue with Michael all you want after we find my mama."

Although it went against her personal preference, Tess had to agree. "All right. Get in. I'm driving."

Instead of offering his hand and assisting her to climb into the buggy as he had in the past, Michael leaped into the driver's seat and took up the lines.

Tess pulled herself up and tried to shove him aside with no success. "Move over, sir."

"I think not," he said, giving her one of those grins that always used to curl her toes.

In this case, however, Tess seemed immune to his Irish charms. Disgusted, she plunked down on the seat next to him while Annie climbed into the back to ride amid their provisions.

Tess kept her arms crossed and her spine rigid until they pulled out onto the road and started down the hill. She had to give up and grab hold when the buggy began to zigzag around piles of fallen masonry and bump over ridges of buckled cobblestones.

Thankful that Michael was driving, she watched him expertly squeeze the rig through newly narrowed passages and past hazard after hazard as they traversed the normally broad, open streets.

What she beheld was horrendous beyond words. Horses lay on their sides, unmoving though still in harness. Buggies and wagons were smashed. Whole city blocks of row houses had been reduced to matchsticks or were leaning so precariously they looked as if the slightest push would send them tumbling down one after the other.

Then, as Tess observed more and more of the damage and heard survivors keening over the bodies of the dead and dying, she wilted. Tears blurred her vision. Awe and fear filled her heart.

One hand gripped the side of the seat, her knuckles white from the sheer force of her grasp.

When she opened her mouth to speak, her voice was tremulous. "Oh, dear God," she said prayerfully, "help these poor people."

Beside her, she sensed the intensity emanating from Michael. It wasn't only the muscle power he was employing to handle the nervous horse amid such chaos, it was far more. His entire persona was as tight as a drum, his large, capable hands fisting the reins as if they were about to be snatched from him by a malevolence beyond imagining.

Tess could finally understand what he had been trying to tell her back at the house. This devastation was beyond human comprehension. Looking at what was left of the once-familiar streets and neighborhoods, Tess wondered how anyone, anywhere, could have survived.

Chapter Eleven

Michael would have done almost anything to keep Tess and her maid from having to view all this carnage but since they had insisted on coming, he figured it was best if he stayed with them as long as possible.

He had originally thought that the screaming during and immediately after the quake had been the worst part. Now that he was back in the thick of it, however, he realized that the murmuring, moaning and pockets of eerie silence could be just as bad.

Some men, women and children roamed the littered streets as if in a daze, barely cognizant of their surroundings while others were already lugging trunks and other belongings down the streets toward the railway station, the docks or the ferry terminals.

"You should have turned back there," Tess said, pointing. "Mrs. Dugan lives on Geary Street."

"We can't get through that way," Michael replied. "I tried earlier. Whole teams and wagons are buried under deep piles of rubble. The drivers are probably trapped beneath tons of bricks, too."

"Oh, my."

"That's not all," Michael went on. "Look over there. See all those loose wires hanging down?"

"Yes. Why?"

"Because they may be very dangerous, depending on whether they're electric, telegraph or telephone lines." He cast her a sober glance, meaning it to serve as a warning. Instead, she grasped his arm and held tight.

"Then you will be in terrible danger. How will all the rescuers manage?"

"I don't know. Let's take one crisis at a time," Michael said. It was his fervent hope that they'd quickly locate Annie's mother so he could be on his way again. He wasn't ready to think further ahead than that. The prospects were too demoralizing.

He carefully maneuvered the buggy through the rubble as far as possible, then stopped and climbed down. "Come with me. We'll go the rest of the way on foot."

"But what about Father's rig? If I abandon it he'll be furious."

"Suit yourself." Michael was already starting to unhitch his horse. "If I were him, I'd be more concerned about my family. Where was he this morning, anyway? I didn't notice him when I was at the house."

"Your mother said he took some of the servants and went to check his bank. He takes that responsibility very seriously."

"Ah, so that's why he wasn't underfoot giving orders. I wondered why we didn't hear him bellowing when you decided to make this trek."

"He would have understood. He might even have come along to help us."

Although Michael strongly doubted that Gerald Bell Clark was that altruistic he chose to keep his opinion to himself. So far Tess seemed to be going along with his sensible suggestions pretty amiably and the last thing he wanted to do was antagonize her.

Continuing to unhitch while his passengers retrieved cargo, Michael quickly led the horse out from between the shafts and tied up the long driving reins so they wouldn't foul or drag. He fastened a few bundles of their meager supplies to the horse's harness as Tess handed them to him.

"Are you sure Father's rig will be all right here?" she asked, hefting one of the picnic baskets Mary had prepared for them and leaning to one side for balance as she carried it.

Michael almost laughed at her naïveté. "Look around you. Do you think something like that really matters?"

"No," she said, sighing poignantly. "I suppose it doesn't." She looked to Annie. "I can't quite tell where we are. Is your mother's house close by?"

"Yes. Follow me," Annie said, taking the lead by stepping over more rubble in the street and wending her way west.

Finally, she paused and pointed. "There it is. See? The gray house with the porch that's fallen into the street."

Foreboding gripped Michael. Could anyone have lived through the crashing force of that building's collapse? Sure, Annie had survived—and so had most of the other firemen who'd been asleep in the station house with him this morning, so he figured anything was possible. It just wasn't very likely.

"Where were you when it happened?" Tess asked Annie.

"Sleeping. Mama made me a pallet in the parlor."

That was apparently the portion of the home that was partially propped up on broken, misplaced rafters, Michael noted. The rear section, however, lay nearly flat on the ground.

He led the horse as close as he could, then hitched it to a lamppost, hoping it wouldn't run off if more tremors occurred.

Tess and Annie were already approaching the tumbledown house. Michael caught up to them.

"I was right there," Annie said, pointing with a trembling finger. "See? There's the corner of the gray blanket I was sleeping on."

"Where was your mother's room?" he asked.

Annie stared, wide-eyed. "Over there. Under the part of the roof that's on the ground."

"All right. We'll move as much loose lumber as we can and see if we can tell anything. If we still can't, we'll hitch the horse to the main rafters to pull them off. There's no other way we can possibly budge anything that big ourselves."

"But what if Mrs. Dugan is trapped under there?" Tess asked, grabbing his arm and halting him. "We can't move too much until we're sure we won't be hurting her."

It was an effort for him to ignore Tess's touch even though the sleeve of his shirt lay between them. "One decision at a time," Michael said, pulling away. "You two start over there nearer the street. I'll take this section because of the heavier timbers."

To his relief, both women hiked their long skirts to their boot tops and waded into the debris without further questioning of his authority.

When he heard Tess say, "Come on, Annie. I'll pass

the pieces to you and you can toss them into the street," he wondered if she knew why he had assigned the tasks the way he had. Perhaps. He wanted to be the one to clear this section because he was relatively certain that Annie's mother lay beneath it. He couldn't protect the poor girl from the loss of a loved one but he could at least soften the initial blow by not letting Annie be the one to uncover the remains.

Tess was giving him a telling, sidelong glance and she nodded slightly when he looked over at her. She *did* know. And she, too, was trying to protect Annie. In spite of the dire circumstances, that conclusion warmed Michael's heart and made him proud. Not everyone who preached equality practiced it. Tess did both.

Tess's long, loose tresses were not only getting caught on the refuse as she labored, the hair that lay draped over her neck and shoulders was making her beastly hot. She drew the back of her wrist across her forehead to sweep away perspiration, hoping her face wasn't half as gritty as it felt.

Straightening to stretch her aching back, she sniffed something odd on the air. There was the usual scent of the ocean, as well as odors from countless other unpleasant sources, but this was different. This was far worse.

She glanced at Annie and saw that the girl was also wide-eyed with concern. What about Michael?

"Hey!" Tess shouted over at him. "Do you smell smoke?"

He whirled. "Yes. Get out of here."

Instead, Tess hurried to his side by stepping on what was left of the porch roof. "No. Let us help you."

"You can't do anything. Look." He pointed to puffs of smoke starting to rise from what was left of a nearby building. "It's liable to be too late in a few minutes. That fire's close and the wind's blowing this way."

Annie covered her face with her apron and began to sob hysterically while Tess tore at the remaining broken boards that still covered the area where Rose Dugan had lain.

"Go get my horse and back him in here," Michael shouted, grabbing Tess's shoulders and giving her a turn and a push to start her in the right direction. "We can't delay any longer."

"What if Annie's mother is alive under there?"

"Then we'll get her out, God willing. We can't leave her to burn to death."

"Where's the fire department? Why don't they come?"

"The stations that weren't destroyed have to be fighting as many fires as they can handle already," Michael said, gritting his teeth and grabbing another armload of splintered wood. "Hurry up with that horse."

Tess couldn't fault the overwhelmed and undersupplied professional firemen who were risking their lives to try to save what was left of the city. She simply hoped and prayed that her meager efforts would be sufficient to help rescue the tiny sliver of suffering humanity that was currently relying upon the three of them.

"Dear God," she murmured, directing her plea heavenward as she tugged on the bridle of the stalwart fire horse and urged it to enter the field of splintered boards, "Show us where to look? Where to pull? Please?"

No booming, divine voice echoed from the sky but Tess nevertheless felt a sudden sense of peace and surety. She turned the animal, gathered the harness traces and passed them to Michael, then watched as he fastened the ends around the nearest heavy beam.

The makeshift rig was ready in seconds. It was now or never.

Michael signaled and shouted, "Pull!"

Tess gritted her teeth, hiked a handful of skirt, grasped the horse's reins just below the bit and pulled as she shouted, "Git up! Go!"

The big gray leaned into the task, his muscles bunching, the leading edges of his wide front hooves digging in.

At first, nothing budged. Then she felt the load he was hauling give way and shift. He edged forward.

Afraid to look back, almost afraid to breathe, Tess continued to lead him slowly away, step by cautious step.

When she heard Michael shout, "Stop! I see her!" with such evident passion and exuberance, she whirled and stared. "Is she…?"

"She's alive," he yelled. "She's moving!"

Overcome, Tess leaned against the horse's neck and began to silently thank God.

Annie helped her mother crawl out from under her bed and Michael swung Rose into his arms so she wouldn't have to try to walk through the rubble.

"Are you all right?" he asked.

The older woman was both weeping and grinning as she clung to her daughter's hand. "Fine, fine." She cast a fond look at Annie. "I knew you'd find me."

"Tess helped," Annie said. "And Michael. I couldn't have done it without them."

"Then thank you. All of you," Rose said, half sobbing.

Michael was pleased to see that the older woman

seemed to be in good condition, especially considering the fact that she'd had half a house sitting on her for several hours.

Tess was apparently just as surprised as he was because she quickly joined them to share a hug with Annie and ask, "What happened? How did she survive?"

Michael answered, "The old, solid oak bed she slept in supported the rafters enough that they didn't bear down on her. She's scratched and bruised but otherwise every bit as well as she claims to be."

"Prayers were answered," Tess said.

"Amen to that." They had reached the horse and he paused with his burden while Tess took its bridle to lead. "We'll hitch up the wagon again. I want you all to go to a refugee center and get checked out," Michael said, concentrating on Tess. "Mrs. Dugan needs to see a doctor and you may have injured your hands when you were digging."

"I agree about the doctor for Rose," Tess said. "But Annie and I are fine." Her brow knit. "I don't suppose she'll want to leave her mother, though. I can understand that. If my own were still alive I'd want to be with her."

"Good. Then it's settled. I'll carry Mrs. Dugan back to the buggy so she can ride while you lead the horse to keep him calm. Can you manage that?"

"Yes, but I should be getting home," Tess said.

To Michael's ears she didn't sound nearly as convinced as she usually did when she made a declaration like that. "Why? Your father may not come back for days. Not if he's as worried about the money in his bank as you think he is. Besides, my mother knows where you went and why. If Mr. Clark asks, she can assure him that you're fine."

"Am I fine?" Tess asked softly.

It concerned him to hear less and less strength in her speech, to see the sparkle leave her beautiful green eyes. Clearly, she was exhausted yet unwilling to admit how weary she was.

"You will be," Michael told her. He was relieved to note that the Clarks' buggy was right where they'd abandoned it. The only things missing were a few household items from the back that they hadn't taken with them.

He placed Rose Dugan gently on the seat and assisted Annie aboard so she could sit close to her mother and steady her. Tess had already backed the horse between the shafts and was starting to hitch it to the tugs and breeching straps when he finished getting the others settled.

"Here, let me do that," Michael said, rushing to her aid. "You're tired."

"I may be tired but I'm not helpless," Tess insisted.

He might have backed off then, if he hadn't seen her trembling and sensed how close she was to losing control of her emotions.

Instead, he took those dainty hands in his and gently held them still. "I will never think that of you. This ordeal has been a terrible strain on everyone. If you won't rest for your own sake, do it for Annie and Rose. You need to be strong to look after them."

"I'll manage."

"I know you will." He turned slightly so Tess could see past him. "Look at their house. Even if Rose isn't badly injured she may be too upset to function. They'll need someone who is both intelligent and levelheaded. They'll need you."

He smiled, wishing their circumstances were differ-

ent so he could take Tess in his arms and comfort her
the way Annie and Rose were comforting each other.

To Michael's delight, a wan smile began to lift the
corners of Tess's mouth. She nodded. "I do understand.
You're saying that this is only the beginning of our trials, aren't you?"

"Yes."

When she raised tear-filled eyes to him, sighed and
took a step closer, he gave in and opened his arms to
embrace her.

Tess slipped her arms around his waist and laid her
cheek against his chest.

There they stood, out in the open in full view of what
was left of San Francisco, and Michael didn't care a
whit what anyone else thought. The only thing he really dreaded was the next few moments when he knew
he'd have to force himself to leave her. How could he
act nonchalant when he was dying inside at the mere
thought of it?

Tess seemed to sense his emotional withdrawal because she leaned away enough to look up at him. "What
will you do now? You said your station was destroyed.
Where will you go to work?"

"I'm not sure yet," Michael replied. "I was on my
way to find Chief Sullivan and get new orders for Station #4 when Annie waylaid me. He's a good man. If
anyone can coordinate this fight and win it, Dennis
Sullivan can."

"I saw a lot of water running down the streets," Tess
said. "Will there be enough left in the main lines to put
out the fires?"

"I don't know." Michael gazed into her lovely face,

ignoring the smudges on her cheeks and the tangles in her flyaway hair.

Sadly, he understood far more about what was happening than Tess did. He might never see her again. Might never have another chance to bend lower and kiss her.

Even if she slapped his face for taking such liberties it would be worth it to try, he decided. Then if he had to enter eternity this very day, he could do so remembering the sweet taste of her lips.

He gently threaded his fingers through her long hair and cradled the back of her head. She was staring at him as if she yearned for what he was about to do. At least he thought so.

Slowly, as if handling fragile porcelain, Michael canted his head to the side and felt her arms tightening around his waist.

The brush of her warm, soft lips against his sent a shock wave through him like lightning arcing over the bay during a violent storm. His emotions became the ocean waves, his heart the pounding surf.

He sensed Tess rising on tiptoe to prolong their kiss, deepening and intensifying it until they were both left breathless.

When he finally set her away by grasping her shoulders, he could tell that she was every bit as staggered, as overcome with emotion, as he was. "I'm…"

Tess reached up and pressed her fingertips over his mouth to silence him. "Don't spoil it by saying you're sorry, Michael. Please don't."

He kissed the fingers caressing his lips then grasped her wrist and placed a second kiss in her palm before closing her hand. "There. Keep that one for whenever you feel lonely."

"I am always lonely when you're not with me," Tess said, unshed tears glistening.

Afraid to reply for fear he might disgrace himself by weeping openly, he put an arm around her shoulders and ushered her closer to where the horse waited.

He bunched the reins before handing them to her. "There was quite a gathering of refugees in Union Square but I think it would be wiser for you to press on as far as Golden Gate Park to be farther from danger. Wait for me there. I'll find you."

"When?" Tess whispered. "How soon?"

"I don't know."

Placing one more quick kiss on her lips, he whirled and loped off, dreading the incontrovertible fact that his life might be required of him that very day and he might never again lay eyes on the woman he loved.

He already ached for her, for the precious moment they had just shared and for the days and years that lay ahead. If God took him in the line of duty, how would she cope with that loss? For that matter if something happened to Tess while he was otherwise occupied fighting fires or taking part in rescue operations, how could he ever forgive himself?

His eyes burned. His throat was raw. With tears coursing down his cheeks and clouds of smothering smoke making him cough and gasp for air, he increased his pace.

At that instant, he wasn't sure whether he was running toward his duty or away from the overwhelming urge to give in and return to Tess while he still could.

Chapter Twelve

If Tess had not kept thinking about Michael and their all-too-brief kiss, she might have found it harder to cope with the sights and sounds and smells surrounding her.

Seated in the buggy, Annie and Rose clung to each other while Tess led the horse carefully, slowly through the ruins of the city and headed toward the enormous, rectangular park that lay between Fulton Street and Lincoln Way.

A pall still hung over the populace, although many people seemed to be snapping out of it. Here and there she actually heard laughter and spied children running and playing despite what had occurred. Youngsters were the most resilient survivors, of course, because they didn't truly comprehend the enormity of such a widespread disaster.

Tess could understand the intense emotional conflict the adults were experiencing. Part of her wanted to break down and sob while another part urged her to smile and perhaps even celebrate life.

There were many unfortunate souls who could not rejoice in their circumstances the way she and her companions could, and those people were to be pitied. However, even the worst losses couldn't negate the thankfulness of personal endurance and survival. To deny being grateful for that would be like questioning God's sovereignty.

There was a newly built decorative stone wall around the northeast corner of Golden Gate Park. Bypassing that, Tess worked her way into the park proper and stopped the buggy beneath the arching branches of a slim eucalyptus.

Quite a few larger, more substantial trees, such as cypress and pines, had actually been toppled by the quake, making her glad she hadn't been parked under any of them then. Nor would she take such a chance with those that remained upright—or with the monuments honoring President Garfield, Francis Scott Key and others.

Tying the reins loosely around the trunk of the sapling, she gave the trusty horse a pat and returned to her passengers.

"I think we'd better use the buggy to stake out our space," Tess said, "before so many others arrive that we're all jammed in together and have no privacy." Studying the gathering multitude and fearing the worst, she pressed her lips together.

"Will we be safe here?" Annie asked as she jumped to the ground and reached back with Tess to assist her mother.

"I think so. If there are too many more shocks we can always move over to the tennis courts. Since we have no idea how long we'll have to stay here, I think grass will make the best carpet."

"What about finding a doctor for Mama?" the maid asked.

"I'll see to that. You two stay here and guard our supplies while I scout around."

"Alone?" Annie's eyes widened. "You can't just go wandering off by yourself. What would your papa say?"

"Hopefully, he'd realize that I have a brain of my own and know how to use it," Tess replied, managing a smile. Now that they were ensconced among survivors and no longer had to keep looking upon the death and mayhem that lay beyond the boundaries of the park, she was feeling a definite sense of relief.

Little wonder that sounds of happy conversation and more playful children were so prevalent here, Tess thought. Although this situation was no cause for celebration it was, nonetheless, plenty of reason to give thanks. They were alive and well. And many thousands of other citizens were sharing that blessing, as well.

Given the alternative, it was perfectly natural to be joyous. After all, the worst was probably over and as soon as the firemen doused the fires they could all begin to restore life as it had been mere hours before.

Looking around her, Tess was struck by the uplifting sense of camaraderie and shared experience. Praise be to God they had found and rescued Annie's mother and knew that Michael's was safe and sound atop Nob Hill.

Other than Michael, whom she would always worry about no matter what, that left only her father to cause her a bit of concern. It was foolish to worry much about her father. Gerald Clark knew most of the important men in town as well as in state government, thanks to his financial status. If he had a problem, he could always call upon the mayor or even the troops that were stationed at the Presidio.

But Michael? Now that was a different story. Pausing, Tess scanned her surroundings, shaded her eyes and peered into the distance. Little smoke was visible to the north where the sea entered the bay. The Pacific shore lay down the hill, directly to the west, and the bulk of the bay was east, past the city proper.

What's left of the city, that is, she reflected, once again lamenting the terrible loss of life.

Papa would be more concerned with damage to property, of course, and she could see marvelous chances for him to eventually put some of his money to good use rebuilding the city he loved.

They could even open their home to refugees the way he'd suggested, she added, pondering possible ways to provide hot meals without endangering the house by lighting cooking fires before the chimneys were properly inspected.

Dodging wagons and pedestrians, Tess quickened her steps. She would first check the nearby clubhouse to see if there was medical assistance available inside. If not, perhaps someone there would be able to direct her to a doctor for Rose.

Thinking of the older woman's narrow escape made bile rise in Tess's throat. If they had been a few minutes later, Annie's mother would surely have burned to death in the splintered ruins of her home.

"And if I hadn't listened to Michael and let him use *his* horse, we would probably have arrived too late to save the poor woman."

That sobering thought settled in Tess's heart and mind like a boulder. Michael again. Always Michael.

A sudden yearning to be with the gallant fireman filled her so thoroughly she felt dizzy. A nearby slatted wooden bench offered temporary respite and she quickly availed herself of it.

Seated with her elbows on her knees, her hands pressed over her face, she closed her eyes and began to pray for the man she loved, focusing more than she'd ever thought possible and shedding silent tears for the life she feared they might never have a chance to share.

For Michael, the trek to the fire station on Bush Street seemed to take forever. When he arrived and saw the pile of bricks from the collapsed chimney of the California Hotel lying atop the smashed firehouse, he gaped, then grabbed the arm of the nearest passing fireman and insisted on being informed of the station's status.

"There ain't no station, if that's what you're meanin'."

"What about the chief engineer? Where's he?"

"On his way to the hospital, if any of 'em are still standing. Sullivan's quarters collapsed with him and his wife inside. She's okay but the chief fell all the way through to the basement and ended up scalded by a ruptured steam pipe from the boiler. He's alive but it don't look good."

"Then who's in charge?"

"Beats me. Battalion Chief Walters said that we should just stand by till he decides what to do. He said he was gonna drive around and see what was going on if he could get his buggy through these streets. And I ain't seen hide nor hair of acting Chief Dougherty since before the quake."

"What about survivors? Who's helping them?"

"Don't know. You volunteerin'?"

"Could be. I know where there's a spare horse and

buggy we could use." Michael hesitated and clapped the young man on the shoulder. "Will you be all right?"

"I ain't never gonna be all right again and that's a fact." The dusty fireman shook his head and wiped his sooty eyes. "Maybe this is Armageddon."

"I don't think so," Michael said, "but time will tell. If we get more shakes, be sure you and the others are in the clear." He eyed what was left of the once-thriving California Hotel. "There are still enough bricks hanging on up there to do plenty more harm if they fall."

"Don't know that I care much at this point," the young man said. "Seems unfair for the best chief we ever had to die right when we need him the most."

"I thought you said he was still alive."

"I did. But I saw the burns and I wouldn't wish sufferin' like that on my worst enemy. He ain't gonna make it. No way."

"That's up to the Almighty," Michael said.

Snorting, he wiped his nose with his sleeve. "This shouldn't of happened. No, sir."

Michael had no ready rebuttal because he didn't understand, either. No one could. If the earth had trembled a few hours earlier he would have been the one tending to the horses and he might easily have been killed instead of poor O'Neill.

His breath caught. What if the quake had come while Tess was still at the opera? He hadn't seen the edifice himself but he'd heard that it was in shambles. The loss of life the evening before, when Caruso had been performing for a packed house, would have been catastrophic. Those who had not been killed outright would probably have been trampled to death by others who were trying to escape.

The notion that Tess could have been caught in that tempest of human agony cut him to the core.

"But she wasn't. She's safe," he reminded himself firmly. "And I have work to do."

His mind was spinning. Where to begin without proper leadership? Who was going to take over and manage the manpower and equipment the various departments had left? He didn't have the rank or authority to do so no matter how much he wished he could.

Until Battalion Chief Walters returned or acting Chief Dougherty instituted some kind of overall battle plan, it looked as if he was as much on his own as the gangs of men who were wandering the streets and stopping to pull survivors from the wreckage at random.

That was a worthy goal, at least for now, Michael decided. Speaking to the fireman he'd just encouraged, he explained, "Union Square is filled to overflowing. I'm going to go get a wagon and start hauling the injured and elderly over to Golden Gate Park. When Walters or Dougherty get here, tell them Company D only lost one man that we know of, but we have no usable equipment. We'll need a new assignment."

"All right. If I see 'em I will. Who knows whether Walters'll even make it back?"

"He has to," Michael insisted, looking into the distance and seeing clouds of billowing smoke and a telltale reddish glow. "If somebody doesn't take charge soon we could lose the whole city."

The other man gave a guttural laugh. "If you ask me, she's already a goner. We got no communication, no alarm system, and half the hydrants are dry. Cisterns the same way. The ones that've got water are so full of garbage they're 'bout useless, or so I hear."

"All we can do is make the best of whatever we have," Michael said. "I'll stop by later and see if there's any plan of action yet."

And in the meantime, he told himself as he turned and started to jog toward the park, *I'll be able to check on Tess again when I commandeer her rig.*

He knew there were plenty of other conveyances he could appropriate but he wasn't about to do so. No, sir. Not when this plan included seeing his beloved Tess once more.

Chapter Thirteen

By the time Gerald Bell Clark reached his still-erect bank building, Phineas Edgerton was already there looking after things.

"Phineas! Good man. How bad is it?"

"Bad enough, G.B. Have you seen the crowds in the streets? Rabble. Pure rabble. No telling what they'll do in these circumstances. Maybe even storm the vault."

"My thoughts exactly," Gerald said, patting the younger man on his slim shoulder. "I brought extra men with me and stationed them outside to act as guards. And we have plenty of ammunition. I think we can hold off a small army, if it comes to that."

"What about your house, your daughter?"

"Tess will be fine. I ordered her to stay home."

Phineas huffed. "What makes you think she will abide by your wishes when she's been filling her head with all that woman suffrage nonsense?"

"My daughter is a reasonable person. She'll do as I say. And she'll eventually agree that you are the best choice for a husband, too. Just give me time. I'll bring her around."

As Gerald watched, he saw the other man's expression harden. Not that he could blame him. Tess was a headstrong woman, one worthy of being a Clark, yet difficult to handle.

Gerald was certain that his choice of Phineas as his future son-in-law would prevail, even if it took Tess a little time to accept the idea. The man was a gem, unfortunately not too muscular or particularly comely but with the intelligence and shrewd instincts a successful banker needed. And once Tess became his wife, the Clarks and the Edgertons could merge their fortunes and create a banking dynasty that was unrivaled. It was a perfect plan.

Eyeing Phineas, Gerald stifled a grimace. His grandchildren might turn out to be gaunt-looking with long, hooked noses if they didn't happen to favor Tess's side of the family tree, but that was the least of his concerns. Once he got her married off and properly settled, he could stop losing sleep over the possibility of her making a poor choice of a husband and start fully concentrating on his business again.

Gaining that kind of peace of mind was worth any sacrifice. He should know. He'd made a similar one when he'd married the sickly but wealthy wife who had borne him a headstrong, troublesome daughter instead of the strapping son he'd always wanted.

As Tess wended her way through the mass of refugees she was both amazed and befuddled. Many were sooty and weary but others seemed so nonchalant about the circumstances that had forced them out of their homes it was incomprehensible.

Well-dressed women in fancy frocks, coats and the

kind of elaborate hats she and Annie had worn to the suffragette lectures were chatting, laughing and holding sway as if they were about to serve tea in their own drawing rooms. Many had apparently had some of their finest furniture transported to the park so they would be comfortable there, acting as if they considered the outing a mere lark. Didn't they know about all the poor souls who had perished? Didn't they care?

"All right," a man shouted just to her right. "Everybody smile. Let's show those hoity-toity easterners that nothing bothers us here in Frisco."

Tess paused and scowled at him. He had a tripod and small camera set up and was actually taking photographs in the park, apparently bent on taking full advantage of the disaster to fill his pockets with filthy lucre. And he wasn't the only one. There were pushcarts brimming with fruit and baked goods making the rounds. Even the Chinese had come, apparently for safety as well as to peddle their wares, and were freely mingling with residents of the city who would normally have treated them with disdain.

Still, wasn't this the kind of equality and freedom Maud Younger had espoused? Tess wondered. *Perhaps,* she answered, *but what a shame it took such carnage to bring it about.*

Reaching the small clubhouse where she had expected to find some semblance of organization, Tess was greeted by a group of rowdies instead of the refined gentlemen she had expected. The crudely clad young men had taken over the main room as if they belonged there and were in various states of repose. Some had even propped their muddy boots on the manager's desk with no apparent qualms.

Tess hesitated briefly before deciding that she was being too quick to judge. After all, she was anything but pristine-looking herself, having dressed without much thought and having later employed her bare hands to dig through the wreckage of Rose's house.

She nervously brushed her palms over her skirt, tossed locks of her long hair back over her shoulders and cleared her throat. "Excuse me. Can any of you tell me where I might find a doctor?"

The raucous laughter that ensued told her she had been right to prejudge these men, fair or not.

"You want *what?*" one of them asked, shouting to be heard above his cronies' catcalls.

"A doctor. I have a friend who may be injured."

He snorted and spat onto the already filthy floor. "Lady, are you crazy? There ain't no docs here and there ain't gonna be. Go on now. Leave us in peace."

"But…"

One of the other men lobbed a juicy apple core toward the doorway. It splatted on the floor, just missing the hem of Tess's skirt.

Startled, she jumped away, to the amusement of the entire group, then whirled and began to run back toward the spot where she'd left the horse and buggy.

Why had she let Michael convince her to come here? They should have gone home, to the house on Nob Hill, where they'd at least have had a roof over their heads and sufficient food and water.

Suddenly realizing she'd become disoriented, Tess stopped and turned in a circle. Everything looked different than it had just minutes ago. Tides of people were entering the open grounds in a never-ending flow of humanity, evidently bringing with them as many of their worldly goods as they could carry. A few were even towing chairs with bundles lashed to their seats in lieu of a suitable wagon or cart.

Seeking to find a landmark and get her bearings again she stood on tiptoe. All she could see in the distance was the same surging, jostling, pushing, determined kind of horde that surrounded her.

Outside the park boundaries a steady procession of erstwhile evacuees rushed by, headed for the docks or to the railway station although Tess couldn't imagine that those tracks were in any better shape than the buckled remains of the trolley routes that had been thrust out of the ground like so many twisted jackstraws.

As she turned back to scan the park grounds, the head of a familiar-looking gray horse rose above the hats of men and women in the distance. Tess's jaw gaped. She stared. Someone was driving her buggy toward her, against the main flow of pedestrian traffic. No one had permission to take her rig. Therefore, a thief must be making off with their only means of transportation!

Hiking her skirt to her shoe tops, she began to elbow, shoulder and zigzag her way through the crowd as best she could. "Excuse me. Let me through. Please, move aside. I must get past."

Time slowed. She felt as if she were taking one step back for every two she took forward. People pushed her. Blocked her without seeming to even notice. Impeded her progress until she was ready to scream.

She refused to give up. Surrounded closely by the swarm of people, she could no longer actually see the horse's approach but she remembered that it had been headed for the gateway she had finally reached. *Praise God.*

Panting to catch her breath and coughing from the smoky air, she waited while trying again to peek over the heads and hats that kept interfering with her view.

The horse suddenly burst through as the crowd parted and gave ground. Tess lunged for its bridle and grabbed a fistful of reins below its bit, shouting, "Stop! Thief!"

Startled, the animal tossed its head, nearly lifting her off the ground. She held tight. Her sharp cry of, "Stop this buggy this instant," seemed to have the desired effect because the command was obeyed.

Ready to shout for a policeman or at least appeal to passersby to assist her in exacting justice, Tess gritted her teeth, stepped to one side of the heavily muscled horse's chest and looked up, ready to give the driver a good scolding.

Her jaw dropped. *Michael?*

The fight went out of her as quickly as her breath had and she sagged against the animal's neck, overcome with gratitude to her heavenly Father for bringing them together again in spite of the turmoil.

Michael was beside her in a heartbeat, taking her in his arms and consoling her. "Calm down. It's just me. You're all right."

All right? Oh, yes. She was more than all right. She was superb.

Her own arms slipped around his waist. She knew she should say something, do something, but for those few precious moments all she wanted was to stay precisely where she was. With him. With her Michael. As long as he was willing to hold her close and comfort her, she was more than delighted to let him do so.

"I have to borrow the horse and buggy," he said, lightly kissing the top of her head and noting how satiny her lovely hair felt in spite of its tangles. "I knew you wouldn't mind. Most of the buildings in the city aren't safe. I'm going to be bringing in the folks who want to come here and can't make it on their own." His grip tightened for a moment before he released her. "Can you get back to Annie and Mrs. Dugan by yourself?"

He could tell Tess wanted to say no, but she nodded affirmatively instead. That was like her. She might be barely able to drag one foot after the other, yet she'd insist she was fine.

"I'll make sure I come by to check on you as often as I can," he said. "I promise."

She gazed up at him. "What about the fires? They must be bad. We can see a lot of smoke from here. Look at this air. I hurts to take a deep breath."

"I know." Michael wasn't sure how much to tell her, then decided that knowing the truth was better than believing the wild rumors that were undoubtedly circulating.

"Chief Dennis Sullivan, the man I was counting on to manage this battle, was mortally injured in the quake," he said, watching her reaction and seeing the empathy he knew she'd express.

"I'm so sorry."

"We all are. It's my understanding that some of the alarms are being repaired but so far there's no real organization. Fires are burning around Market and Kearney, and of course on Geary Street where the Dugans' house was."

"There must be more than that," Tess said, gripping his forearm and blinking back tears. "I know I see signs in other places."

He noted the passage of the bright silk robes of a group of Chinese: men, women and children as well as two-wheeled carts of trade goods and personal possessions. "Aye. I expect Chinatown to be leveled, if it isn't already. Those shacks are like a tinderbox just waiting for the strike of a match."

Michael knew it was wrong to delay any longer when he was sorely needed for the rescue efforts. Tearing himself away from Tess was going to be one of the hardest things he'd ever had to do.

"I have to go," he said tenderly as he pried her fingers from his arm. "I have work to do."

"I know." Wide-eyed, she stared up at him. "I can't just sit here and bide my time when I may be able to help, too. Take me with you."

"That's out of the question." He was about to turn away when she grabbed his shoulder.

"No! Wait. I have a wonderful idea. There are more horses and buggies in our stables. If we head that direction I can hitch up a much bigger rig and we can either each drive one or I can ride with you. What do you say?"

His initial reaction was denial. Then he gave her idea more thought and had to agree that portions of it had merit, though it was also fraught with danger.

"How do you propose to get a larger buggy like the cabriolet through these streets?" he asked. "Chances are good it will break down before we've gone a block. What then?"

Facing him, Tess fisted her hands on her hips. "That rig you're driving is the most fragile of them all and you know it. Papa has an old freight wagon at home. It's sturdy oak, with wire-rimmed wheels. If we hitch a four horse team and put your sensible, strong one in the wheel position for stopping power on the hills, we should be fine. And we'll be able to haul a lot more, too."

"That makes sense," Michael finally said. "Give me a note so your grooms know I have permission and I'll do it." He could tell before he'd finished speaking that his alteration of her proposal was not going to meet with her approval. Not even slightly.

"Oh, no, you don't," Tess said with a lopsided smile. "I'm not going to make it easy for you to get away from me this time. If you get orders to go fight fires I won't argue, but until that time I'm going to become your shadow."

"You are a stubborn, willful woman, Miss Clark. Do you know that?"

"I certainly do," Tess replied. Her grin spread. "Now, are you going to stand there and debate or are you going to drive me back to see Annie so I can tell her where I'm going?"

Without ceremony he hustled her to the buggy, spanned her small waist with his hands and lifted her high enough to place her feet inside while she shrieked the way she used to when they had played and teased as children.

Her eyes were bright, her cheeks flaming when she

plopped down onto the seat, slid over and watched him climb aboard.

Michael took up the reins. So far, he'd had no problem with anyone trying to usurp their transportation but he knew that was probably only because those fleeing the city were not yet desperate enough to begin acting like an unruly mob. That kind of behavior would start soon, he feared. Which was another reason why he'd have preferred that Tess stay with the Dugans and that everyone remain inside the park. There they'd be safe from possible aftershocks, spreading fires and anticipated threats of violence.

He cast her a sidelong glance and found himself admiring her fortitude immensely. She was an extraordinary person, one he was privileged to know. That she was a comely *woman,* even with her long hair hanging loose and her cheeks smudged, did not escape him either. Nor would it escape the notice of the city's criminals when the usual rule of law was overturned due to a lack of ready enforcers.

Once they reached the Clark estate, Michael vowed, he was going to do more than change wagons. He was going to arm himself so he could defend Tess's honor. That was an added reason to keep her close by, he rationalized. As long as she was with him she'd be even safer than if he'd left her alone with the others in the park.

His justification wasn't really logical. He knew that. He also knew he considered it providential that he had encountered Tess at all. If it hadn't been for the tall, stalwart fire horse standing out above most of the crowd he'd have had a terrible time locating Annie and Rose in the first place. His disappointment when Tess had not been with them had been palpable.

That was when he'd begun praying to see her again. And soon after that she'd run up to him and accused him of theft. Given the slim chances of that meeting amidst all this chaos, he had to assume that his fervent prayers had been answered.

Transferring both driving lines to his left, he took her hand in his right and held it gently. "It will be worse out there every time you go. People are hurt and dying. So are animals. Are you sure you're up to this?"

When she threaded her slim fingers between his, smiled and said, "I can do anything if I'm with you," Michael was immediately so filled with joy he felt shamefaced. It seemed wrong to experience happiness when so many were suffering. Yet when Tess was by his side, how could he possibly feel otherwise?

Chapter Fourteen

During the tortuous drive back to Nob Hill, Tess tried to focus on how she'd help others rather than dwell on the dire situations she couldn't hope to alleviate. So much misery. So much loss. If she opened her mind to the vast hopelessness all around her she was afraid she wouldn't be able to function at all, let alone make herself useful.

Michael guided the buggy past the impressive Crocker and Huntington estates, then turned up the drive of the house she had called home for her entire life. It was good to see how little damage the stone-clad mansion had sustained, although it did show thin cracks radiating out from the corners of a few of the tallest windows gracing the drawing room and her father's library.

Mary was waiting on the stoop next to the kitchen door, wiping her hands on her apron, when Tess climbed down and embraced her.

"You brought her back." Mary looked lovingly at her son. "Bless you."

"We're not staying," Michael said. "Tess will explain. I'm going to the stables to water this horse and change rigs. While I do that, you two start packing up more bandages and supplies."

"Of course."

Tess could see unshed tears brimming in the older woman's eyes and she realized there was moisture in hers, too. She normally wasn't one to weep so easily. Apparently, the sight of so much suffering had brought many people to the edge of their endurance, including her.

She whisked the telltale dampness off her cheeks as she led the way into the kitchen. Mary had managed to lay out a grand spread of food on the table as if expecting guests.

"Have many people stopped by to eat?" Tess asked.

"Only your father and a few of the servants, so far. Mister Gerald said he left some of the men watching his bank and was going to drive around in his motorcar looking for more to hire as guards."

"You did tell him where I'd gone, didn't you?"

The look of pity on the cook's face told Tess what had happened. Regardless, she chose to ask, "He didn't even miss me, did he?"

"He was just preoccupied with other things," Mary alibied. "I'm sure he figured you were right here with me, like you are now."

"Well, I'm not staying," Tess said firmly. "I'm going back down the hill with Michael."

"Mercy, no!" Mary's hands worried the apron into a knot. "You can't be doin' that. Not with everybody in such a tizzy. 'Tis safer here."

"Nevertheless, I intend to help all I can. Michael needs me. I'm going to be there for him."

"Is he daft?" She grasped Tess's shoulders. "Think, girl. What if you're attacked? There's always a bad element by those docks. No tellin' what they'll get up to once they see there's no law."

"I've thought of that. So has Michael. I promised to fetch Father's pistols and a box of bullets. We won't be going back unarmed."

Mary began to wring her hands and weep. "You can't do that. I've heard shooting. And terrible explosions."

"That's just the authorities clearing a path so the fire can't progress. Michael heard that Mayor Schmitz and General Funston decided to use dynamite to make a firebreak around the mint."

"What about all the gunshots? How can you hope to hold your own if there's so much lawlessness?"

"Most of that firing was probably from the army," Tess said. "The mayor himself told the soldiers to shoot looters on sight." She patted the cook's hands. "Don't worry on our account. Michael knows all the firemen and most of the police by sight, if not by name. We'll be fine."

Squaring her shoulders and wiping her eyes with the corner of her apron, Mary regained control. "Well, then, don't just stand there, girl. Go fetch those pistols while I pack you some more food."

Tess paused just long enough to plant a kiss on the older woman's damp cheek, then turned and raced up the stairs to her boudoir. She grabbed a carpet bag from the armoire and quickly stuffed it with extra articles of clothing and toiletries she thought she might need.

Pausing to scan her room and think, she was about to head down to the library to raid her father's gun cabinet when she remembered her mother's journal.

Before she could change her mind, she slid a hand beneath her bed pillows and retrieved the slim, ribbon-tied volume. It went into the carpetbag with her clothes. Then, she wheeled and ran.

With no handy helpers left at the Clark estate, it took Michael nearly fifteen minutes to find suitable harnessing for the rest of the team he was assembling. He was finishing preparing the fourth horse when Tess joined him.

"Good choices," she said, tossing her bag and some bedding into the wagon bed while Mary added sacks of food before returning to the kitchen for more.

"Put big Jake, the roan, in the other wheel position," Tess said, "and I'll hitch my mare in front of him."

"I couldn't find any tack here that would begin to span the girth of the gray," Michael replied. "It's a good thing he already had most of his fire department rig on when I found him running loose."

"Father prefers lighter, faster teams, as you can tell."

"Where is he?" Michael asked, dreading the possibility that Gerald Clark might venture outside and accost them.

Tess's sharp "Ha!" told him otherwise. "Papa is off tending his money, as usual," she said. "He's so concerned about me he didn't even remember to ask after my welfare when he came home to get his automobile."

"Just as well." Michael chanced a grin in the hopes it would lift her spirits. "I'd hate to have to explain why I was making off with his horses, his wagon *and* his daughter." To his relief, Tess smiled.

"Plus the brace of ivory-handled pistols in my carpet-bag," she said. "I think he'd be more concerned about getting those guns and his rig back, especially if we were taking the cabriolet. I seriously doubt he'll miss this wagon. Or me."

"That's another good reason to stay with me. I missed you so badly this morning I almost gave up my job just to come looking for you."

"I know you'd never really do that," she said, gazing at him so sweetly his heart nearly melted. "But I do thank you for the kind thought."

Quickly convincing himself that he needed to double-check the traces on her side, Michael ducked under the chins of the two leading horses to bring himself closer to Tess before he spoke from the heart. "What you said when I saw you after the opera was right. We do need to have a private talk. When this is all over there are some important things to discuss." Emboldened by the tender look in her eyes he grasped both her hands.

Without any comment other than a slight smile, Tess tilted up her face, closed her eyes, stood on tiptoe and brushed a kiss across his lips.

It was barely a breath, like the warm summer breezes that sometimes drifted over the hills toward the sea, yet it touched him so deeply he could hardly think, let alone find the rest of the words he wanted to speak.

He knew this was not the right time to confess his love for Tess, no matter how badly he wanted to. Delaying their return to the city for any reason could cost innocent lives. Thinking only of themselves was not the proper way for good Christians—or anyone else, for that matter—to behave.

Michael bent to return her kiss and lingered mere moments before he steeled himself to face his duty and whispered, "We need to go."

* * *

It seemed to Tess that the more needy people they stopped and picked up, the more they encountered waiting by the side of the road and begging for a lift. The wagon bed was already filled to overflowing, plus there were able-bodied men walking alongside while their women and children rode.

Tess was thankful that Michael's temporary assignment was to rescue and gather the living because they had passed many other wagons, and even a few automobiles, that were being used to haul away the dead. Those sights were so ghastly and shocking they turned her stomach.

He halted the team when they came upon another fireman in uniform. The man was bending over his buggy. Judging by the way its body was canted, the axel had snapped.

Michael called to him. "Chief Walters? Is that you?"

The man straightened. "Aye. Mahoney?"

"Yes, sir." Michael saluted. "I've been looking for you. Any orders?"

"Not yet. I've checked on all the stations. It's bad. Don't know what we'll do without Sullivan."

"Is he still alive?"

"Yes. They transferred him to the Presidio but it doesn't look good."

Tess noted that the older fireman was eyeing their loaded wagon. "Looks like you found a way to make yourself useful. Keep it up for now. By tomorrow morning we should have a better idea about what we'll need. If you can get to Union Square and it's still open, report to me there at eight. If not, go down to the ferry terminal. We've got men and equipment coming over from Oakland and San Mateo then, too."

"Why wait till morning?" Michael asked.

Walters's shoulders sagged and he sighed. "Because they've got their own problems over there. It's the same all up and down the coast. Only they don't have nearly the fires we do." He shook his head. "Never thought I'd see the likes of this day."

"How many men have we lost?" Michael asked. "The only one I know about is O'Neill, from my station."

"A couple of others, far as I know. And some police officers. I haven't even tried to get an accurate count yet."

When he took out a handkerchief and blew his nose, Tess could tell it was mostly to mask his raw emotions.

While Michael bid the chief goodbye, Tess spotted two barefoot children standing across the littered street. She hailed them. "Do you two want a ride to the park so you don't hurt your feet on all this glass and trash? That's where we're going."

Their grimy faces brightened and they headed for the wagon as if they had just been offered a piece of cake.

Tess scooted as close to Michael as she possibly could to make room for the slim, dark-haired girl and her little brother on the driver's seat and greeted each of them with a hug. "Are your parents nearby? Might they need a lift, too?"

Both children lowered their heads and stopped looking at her. The girl murmured, "No, ma'am," and began to weep as she pointed to an immense pile of rubble.

"I'm so sorry," Tess said. "You can stay with me and my friends for now, if you want. We have a nice place saved in the park." She paused and smiled. "My name is Tess. What's yours?"

The girl was the only one who looked up. "I'm Rachel and this is my brother, David."

"Pleased to meet you." Tess turned to Michael. "I think it's time we headed for the park and unloaded these folks so we can come back and start again, don't you?"

"Yes. I just hate to leave anyone behind."

She saw him eyeing the horizons and assumed he was sizing up the conflagrations that still threatened the heart of the city as well as some outlying areas. Every direction she looked there was more smoke, more ominous glow, more signs that the situation was growing worse.

Distant explosions continued to startle her as well as the horses, and although Michael seemed as stalwart as ever, he had nevertheless armed himself with one of her father's pistols, leaving the second one for her.

Resting her hand lightly on the back of his, she sought to reassure him. "You're doing all you can right now. The chief just said so."

"I know. But that doesn't make it any easier to wait patiently when I've been trained to fight fires."

Pondering what else she could say that might ease Michael's mind, Tess was distracted by a tiny movement beneath the edge of a broken board at the side of the road. It might be nothing, yet she was positive she'd spied something odd.

An intense compulsion to investigate made her grasp Michael's arm and shout, "Stop!"

He tensed. "What's wrong?"

"Over there. I thought I saw something."

"What?"

"I'm not sure." She was already clambering past the youngsters and climbing down from the wagon on her own. "I'll be right back."

Her initial loud exclamation had startled the horses and Michael was still having to work to control the team, so she knew he wouldn't dare follow. That was just as well. With all the horrible things they'd come upon already, there was a fair chance her imagination was playing tricks on her. She almost hoped that was the case.

Tess slowly, warily, approached the pile of wreckage that had drawn her attention. Whatever had originally caught her eye wasn't visible from this angle. Pausing, she listened intently. A soft mewling was coming from beneath a nearby splintered board. A kitten, perhaps?

Taking cautious steps, she bent to lift the slab of wood and was astonished to uncover a pudgy little blonde girl. The child looked barely old enough to walk. Her blue eyes blinked open. The moment she saw Tess hovering over her she puckered up and began to wail.

Tess waved to the crowd at the wagon. "Over here! Somebody help me look."

She quickly scooped up the wailing toddler, held her close and stood back while several of the men from the wagon and a few hearty passersby began to throw aside heavier wreckage in that immediate vicinity.

It took only seconds to uncover two bodies. One was a young woman who was clutching a baby blanket as if she had been trying to flee to safety with her child. Next to her lay a once-handsome man who had likely died assisting his wife and baby.

Saddened, Tess carried the probable orphan back

to the wagon where helping hands pulled them both aboard. Women crowded around to coo and sympathize and admire her newfound treasure. So did Rachel and little David.

"Is the baby okay?" Michael asked.

"I don't see any injuries. I think she's upset because I scared her, that's all."

"Well, there's sure nothing wrong with her lungs."

The men who had left the group of refugees to help Tess search were returning to their families. Someone in the rear of the wagon passed forward a small quilt and Tess wrapped the tiny girl in it, cradling and rocking her in spite of her loud lamenting.

"Hush, baby, hush," she cooed. "We'll take good care of you. I promise." She rocked more. "Hush, now. That's a good girl."

When she finally raised her gaze from the child to look at Michael again, the expression on his face was so touching, so heartrending, it brought unshed tears to her eyes.

She assumed he was thinking the same thing she was. If only they had driven through this particular area sooner, had thought to look here before the baby's parents had succumbed, perhaps they could have saved the whole family. But they had not.

Tess kept reminding herself that the waif she was cuddling and trying to comfort had survived the collapse of an entire apartment house. That alone was a wonderment. Finding her parents alive and well, amid all that horrible wreckage, would have been next to impossible no matter how soon they or anyone else had begun to search.

She followed Michael's line of sight past her shoul-

der and watched as other men continued to pull bodies
from the rubble of the tenement and lay them out in the
street. All over the city, piles of the dead were growing. How many there would be when the final tally was
made was beyond imagining.

Moved beyond words, Tess pressed the child closer
and continued to rock her. The little girl's sobbing lessened. She chanced a peek by lifting a corner of the
coverlet and saw that the precious, exhausted little one
had not only fallen asleep, her breathing had grown
more natural.

Closing her own eyes, Tess prayed wordlessly for the
child's lost parents and for all the others who had gone
to glory already. How long would it be before rescuers
like Michael and his comrades had the opportunity to
rest, let alone sleep? The way things looked at present,
it was going to be a long, long time.

Michael halted the loaded wagon in an open area
near where the Dugan women were camped. "Okay," he
announced to his passengers. "This is as far as I go. Be
sure you take all your things with you when you leave."

He paused by the front wheel to lift the brother and
sister down. He tousled the boy's mop of hair, then
pointed the children to the Dugan camp before helping Tess disembark.

"I'm going to take this baby to Rose and Annie for
temporary safekeeping," she said. "They'll know how
best to care for her." A slight smile lifted the corners
of her mouth. "I'm afraid my education as a nurse for
children is sadly lacking."

"Looks to me like you're doing fine. Is she still
asleep?"

"Yes. I keep checking her because I can't help but worry. I'll feel better when Rose has had a good look at her, too."

"Okay. Hurry back. We'll need to be heading out again as soon as possible."

"I will. Don't leave without me."

The sight of Tess cradling the tiny tot as she turned and started to walk away reminded Michael of a Christmas crèche. She'd make a wonderful mother some day. Experienced or not, she was nurturing and loving the same way his mother was. Tess's strong will and decisiveness, in addition to those other sterling qualities, would stand her in good stead no matter what trials life presented.

Trials such as these, Michael concluded, taking in the multitude that had already begun to raise makeshift tents in the park and settle into a semblance of routine and order.

There were myriad kettles warming over small fires or portable kerosene stoves and the like. Families were resting together on pallets composed of blankets and whatever other suitable materials they could assemble. If it hadn't been for the foggy air, the smell of smoke and the booming of dynamite that shook the ground as badly as some of the aftershocks had, the encampment would have seemed like nothing more than a bunch of city folks enjoying leisurely afternoon picnics in the park.

Frowning as he finished emptying the wagon of passengers and their household goods, Michael started to look around for Tess. Why hadn't she returned? What was taking her so long?

Concerned, he climbed aboard the wagon for added elevation and scanned the crowd, starting with the eucalyptus sapling which marked the Dugan encampment. There was Annie. And her mother was bending and talking to the two youngsters they'd just delivered.

In the extra moments it took him to also locate Tess, Michael's heart began to pound. Perspiration dotted his brow. Then, he spotted her reddish hair and his breath whooshed out audibly.

Relief was short-lived. Tess wasn't alone with Annie, Rose and the children. Someone else was with them. Even from that distance, the man's bowler, cane, tailored suit and foppish mannerisms looked decidedly familiar. And most unwelcome.

Rather than leave the wagon to approach on foot and chance actually losing their only means of transportation to thieves the way Tess had imagined, Michael maneuvered the team closer.

He halted them directly behind the dandy in the black bowler hat and wrapped the driving lines around the brake handle.

Judging by the man's uneasy stance and the way Tess was facing him with her hands on her hips, Michael was fairly certain she was not pleased. Then he heard her order, "Go away, Phineas," and was positive.

Jumping down, fists clenched, Michael came at the other man from the rear. Tess's glance and quick smile telegraphed his approach, however, and he lost the element of surprise.

The banker whirled and raised his silver-handled cane defensively. Instant recognition registered in his narrowed eyes. "What do *you* want?"

Michael stood his ground. "I should be asking you the same question."

"I've come to escort Miss Clark out of this disgusting

muddle, not that it's any of your business," Phineas said with a jut of his chin that emphasized disdain.

"I'm making it my business," Michael countered. "Miss Clark has chosen to stay here with me, and I'll thank you to stop bothering her."

If the situation hadn't been so serious he would have laughed aloud at the air of dismay and astonishment on the banker's weasel-like face.

The man looked to Tess, apparently realized she was in full agreement and snapped his jaw shut.

She began to grin. "There you have it, Mr. Edgerton. Now, if you'll excuse us, we have work to do. Please assure my father that I am in very good hands."

Circling Phineas while he stood there looking at her as if she had just fed him unsweetened lemonade and then punched him in the stomach besides, Tess offered her hand to Michael and let him help her climb back aboard the freight wagon.

As Michael joined her, took up the lines and urged the team forward, she slipped her hand through the crook of his elbow and snuggled closer, much to his delight.

Tess giggled softly, privately. "At least you didn't have to threaten to shoot him, although a good scare like that might have served him right."

"Don't tempt me."

He knew his grin was far too satisfied to be respectful but he couldn't help himself. These trying circumstances were painful in many ways, yet they had also brought him closer to Tess than he'd ever hoped to be. Even after the danger was past and the city returned to normal, he'd remember these hours with both sadness and jubilation.

Every person they rescued was one more sign that life went on; and every loss, like the tot's parents, was a reminder of how precious each day should be.

It wasn't that Michael didn't realize how desperate their overall situation was or how much worse it could still become before it was over. He was simply doing the only sensible thing by taking one minute, one hour, one day at a time.

What the future might bring was more than unknown. It was almost too frightening to ponder.

Casting a sidelong glance at his lovely companion as they drove out of the park, he prayed, *No matter what becomes of me, Father, please look after Tess. She is the dearest thing in the world. I know I don't deserve her. Please take care of her and help her find the kind of happiness she's earned.*

The idea that he might not be a part of Tess's future, might not be granted further blessings regarding the woman he loved so intensely, so completely, haunted Michael's thoughts.

Wisely, he refused to dwell on such a possibility. Right now they both had vitally important work to do. If Tess had not been with him on the last trip, that poor babe might not have been discovered, might not have been rescued in time. That alone was proof he should let her continue to accompany him, at least for as long as he deemed it safe to do so.

The traffic in the damaged streets had lessened measurably, probably because many citizens had already fled. He imagined they didn't much care where they went as long as they were far from the shaking, although as Chief Walters had said, the earthquake had caused severe damage many, many miles away as well.

Thankfully, the electrical power plants had been shut down for safety's sake. So had the gas. Night would soon be upon them, leaving little light other than that from an occasional lantern and from the fires still raging in the distance.

"At dusk I'm going to take you back to the Dugans' and leave you there," he told Tess. When she stared at him and opened her mouth he quickly added, "Don't argue. I plan to go check in with Chief Walters again, assuming I can locate him in all this chaos, and see if I can persuade him to give me an assignment right away instead of waiting for morning."

"Meaning, you don't want me underfoot?"

"I wouldn't have put it quite that bluntly, but yes. It's my job."

"And you need to do it. I know how badly you want to."

Michael nodded and smiled wryly as he looked down at the backs of the team. He and that big gray horse were a lot alike in their instincts, weren't they? Every time they heard the clanging of an engine in the distance or saw flames, they both tensed, both acted as if they wanted to forget everything else and race to the fire, which, of course, was exactly how they did feel.

It was Michael's most fervent wish that he could make Tess understand that fact when he finally had to leave her. This brief time they'd managed to spend together had already lasted longer than he'd dared hope. Sooner or later, they were going to have to part.

There was no other option.

Chapter Fifteen

Tess spent the bulk of that night dreaming she was still beside Michael, still thrilling to the sound of his voice, still safe and secure because of him and only him.

As she began to stir she found herself picturing his handsome, rugged face and remembering his expression when he'd finally bid her goodbye.

Tess could tell he hadn't wanted to leave. When he'd put his arms around her she'd simply stood within his embrace and relished every moment. Then, she'd lifted her face and he'd kissed her.

Seconds later, breathless, he had stepped back and apologized. "I'm sorry. I had no right to do that. Especially not in front of all these people."

Tess remembered smiling while also being afraid she might burst into tears. That was the last thing she wanted to do, particularly since an open expression of sorrow might have made their parting even harder on Michael.

"I suppose we could have hidden away behind a bush or something to spoon, but don't you think that would have raised even more eyebrows?"

To her relief, he'd then began to give her the tilted,

Irish grin that was his trademark. "Are you inviting me to misbehave, Miss Clark?"

"Not yet," she'd replied. "But don't lose hope. I soon may."

Michael had grasped both her hands then and held them tightly, forming both a barrier and a bridge between them as he'd said, "I look forward to it."

That was the moment Tess now remembered with the most fondness. It wasn't their actual parting that gave her shivers of nervous delight, it was the promise of a bright future. With Michael.

She sat up and rubbed her eyes. Explosions in the distance continued to shake the ground. Around her, much of the camp was stirring and she could smell the pleasant aromas of coffee and frying bacon.

Yawning, Tess saw Rose and Annie fussing over the baby while Rachel and David devoured enormous bowls of oatmeal as if they'd missed many meals and were trying to make up for it all at once.

She joined the other women. "How is our baby this morning?"

"Hungry," Rose said. "I was worried that she might be a finicky eater but that's not going to be a problem."

"Do we have enough food?" Tess asked, glancing at the older children. "If not, I can go home and get more from Mary."

"There's plenty," Annie said. "You should rest. You worked too hard yesterday."

"I can't argue with that," Tess said with a smile as she raised both arms over her head and tried to stretch some of the pain out of her muscles. "I am definitely not used to doing that much physical labor."

"I'd fetch you a cup of coffee but I don't want to stop tending the baby," Rose said. "Maybe Annie…?"

"Nonsense. I'm certainly capable of doing things like that myself." Tess tossed her head to swing her long hair back over her shoulders and leaned carefully over the fire to reach the pot. It wasn't familiar. "Where did you get this, anyway?"

"Scavenged it, right out in the street over there," Annie said proudly. "You'd be amazed at how much stuff is being thrown away as people head for the ferry. The streets are lined with piles of precious things."

"That was very smart of you," Tess said. "I was all over town yesterday and it never occurred to me to pick up a thing."

"It's not like I was looting," the maid insisted, coloring. "The pot and these cups were just lying there, abandoned on the ground. I rinsed them down by the lake before I brought them to Mama."

"And we're all glad you did."

Settling down and sipping her hot coffee, Tess gave thanks for many things, including the baby's health. The only clue anyone had to the child's name or family was of the tiny locket she wore and the approximate location in which she'd been found. It was hard to make out the faces in the pictures but Tess had high hopes those images would nevertheless help identify the child's surviving relatives and return her to what was left of her family once a proper system for doing so had been established. The same was true of the older children, although they were capable of giving their names so there would be no doubt.

Calling to Annie, she asked, "Is there anything I can do to help either of you?"

Since both women were quick to assure her there was not, Tess decided to try to make herself presentable, just in case Michael had a chance to return before reporting for fire duty.

She reached into the carpet bag for her hairbrush and felt its smooth tortoiseshell handle. At the same time her fingertips brushed the journal she'd grabbed on a whim. It had been wise to preserve it because it had belonged to her late mother, she assured herself, handling the slim volume as if it were a precious relic and wishing she'd thought to rescue the family Bible as well.

Should she untie the narrow pink satin ribbon and read her mother's private musings? Tess wondered. Surely, there was no reason not to. Not now. Not when Mama was gone to glory.

Tess cradled the book in her arms, pressing it against her chest, her heart. In the midst of this crisis she wished mightily that her mother was still beside her, still able to offer comfort and counsel. Since she was not, however, perhaps she had left behind some wise words which would help at a time like this.

Seating herself atop a pile of folded blankets, Tess untied the ribbon clasp and opened the book, laying it across her lap to peruse while she worked the tangles out of her long hair at the same time.

Mama's early years seemed pretty mundane, Tess noted, leafing through them quickly. Then as her mother adjusted to marriage and tried to please her husband, the mood subtly changed.

The rhythmic movement of the hairbrush stilled. Tess stared at the page she had just turned.

I have had a lovely baby girl, she read. *My Gerald is upset, of course, but he'll soften toward her eventually. I know he will. And I have promised that we shall try again for the son he covets so.*

Tess knew she shouldn't have been surprised to read such a plain truth because she had often heard her father say practically the same thing, yet it hurt to read that Mama had agonized over it, too.

There was more to follow, special mentions of Tess's babyhood accomplishments and her ensuing youth. The pages were filled with love and appreciation for her daughter but continued to lament the fact that there had been no additional son.

Flipping to the back of the book, Tess swept aside the blank pages until she reached one of the final entries.

I fear I shall not go to heaven, her mother wrote. *I harbor too much unforgiveness in my heart. I want to love my husband the way I used to but I cannot. I have tried to bear the son he wants and have failed him. Now it is too late. May God forgive me.*

Through her tears, Tess read one more line, its words directing her to turn the page. There, she saw a notation addressed to her!

My darling Tess, I hope you may someday see this. Don't weep for me. Weep for your father. He is a bitter, unhappy man and surely will remain so for as long as he lives. You were my best and only joy and I always loved you dearly. I pray that you will find the happiness I missed and that you will live the life of your dreams, not try to mold yourself to anyone else's desires.

Follow your heart. Read the scriptures as I taught you. And remember that I loved you more than life itself. It was signed, *Your loving Mama.*

A tear dropped, dampening the paper and causing the ink to start to bleed.

Tess quickly closed the book and dabbed at her eyes. "Poor Mama. And poor Papa, too," she added, realizing how her parents' lives had been at hopeless odds for so many years.

In retrospect she ached for her mother. Yet she could also see how that attitude of daily martyrdom might have caused her father to withdraw. Papa liked his world well-ordered. Within his control. Managed to the hilt. To have a wife who was not only ill but clearly disappointed in her entire existence when there wasn't a thing he could do about it must have driven him to distraction.

Sighing, Tess got to her feet and slipped the journal back into her carpet bag with the hairbrush. She tugged at the hem of the jacket of her wool dress and smoothed the outfit over her hips, dusting the skirt with her hands and shaking out the hem.

When this turmoil was past and they were back at home, she'd talk to her father, she vowed, and let him know she understood why he'd always seemed so gruff. That might not change anything between them but she felt beholden to try.

Beginning to smile wistfully, she looked out at the crowd and thought of Michael. There was no sign of him or of the team and wagon this morning so she assumed he had already reported to Chief Walters. That was the most likely scenario, although she couldn't help hoping he was currently on his way to the park with one last load of refugees, instead.

No matter what, Tess vowed to be ready. She ran her fingers over her hair to smooth it carefully, then once again patted at her dusty skirt.

She couldn't imagine anything else, now or ever, that would mean more to her than catching sight of Michael Mahoney and she wanted him to be just as pleased when he saw her even if she hadn't been able to change her clothing or have her long hair properly dressed.

She smiled, remembering the way he'd threaded his fingers through her loose tresses when he'd kissed her. Truth to tell, if there was the slightest chance he'd repeat that loving act she might never, ever, pile her hair atop her head again.

The sun shone bloodred as it began to peek through the smoke-filled atmosphere and add another kind of glow to the eastern sky. Michael had checked Union Square the night before and had seen nothing to indicate it would be a usable gathering place. Therefore, he planned to report to the ferry terminal. He had time for only one more task before he went on duty.

Walters's and Dougherty's decision to hold some able-bodied men in reserve made sense; he just kept wishing his station hadn't been destroyed in the initial earthquake so he and the others of his company could have gone to work immediately.

In the next hour or so, Michael intended to make certain his mother was safe no matter what. Judging by the position of the rising sun, it was still early, though the haze and smoke made it impossible to be certain of the time.

A strong wind had arisen at daybreak, made worse by the circular updraft the fires themselves were generating. Flames rose in death-dealing tornados, bearing millions of hot embers aloft then showering them over the roofs and other remains of previously unscathed buildings.

His jaw clenched. Crumbled relics of total destruction lay everywhere and buried among them many poor souls who had been unable to save themselves. Those were people he and his fellows should have been able to rescue. Somehow. That was what they'd trained for, stood ready for. Who could have imagined that the fire brigades would fall victim to so much devastation before they had a chance to even act?

The view from Nob Hill, once he reached it, was also disturbing. Michael called out to his mother as he stopped the team outside the mansion and was relieved when she burst out and ran straight into his arms.

"Oh, God be praised," Mary keened. "I didn't know what to do. The fire…"

"You're still safe here, at least for the time being. But I want you to pack up so I can take you down to the park to stay with Tess and the others."

"Why? Surely the firemen will stop this soon."

Michael shook his head slowly, considering the carnage he'd just passed. "I don't know when. None of us do. Mayor Schmitz has ordered blocks of buildings close to the fires blown to bits instead of trying to cut a firebreak farther away. That system doesn't seem to be working."

Mary gazed up at him, tears welling. "I promised Mister Gerald I'd stay and watch the house even if all the other servants left."

"Have you seen hide nor hair of him?"

"Nobody's been here since yesterday. Mr. Clark swore he was going to look after the money at his bank no matter what."

"That figures." Michael glanced up at the shimmering half disk of light peeking over Mount Diablo. "I have about an hour, by my reckoning, before I have to report to the ferry terminal. Go get your things and load all the food you can carry into sacks or pillowcases while I see if there's a decent horse left for you to ride." He gestured at the team. "These animals have done more than enough."

"But…"

Michael stood firm. "No buts, Ma. There's no time to argue."

As Mary turned away she paused long enough to ask, "Is Miss Tess all right? And our Annie and her ma?"

"They're fine. Now hurry."

It hadn't taken his mother's mention of Tess to bring her to Michael's mind. She'd never left his thoughts, his prayers. The aura of her natural beauty and her tender smile would dwell with him, in his heart and mind, forever and always.

And, God willing, he'd see her once more, at Golden Gate Park this very morning.

Tess was pacing and beginning to get terribly anxious when a slim dirt-dusted young man burst through the passing crowd and accosted her.

"Miss Clark!"

She frowned, puzzled, before recognizing him as a messenger boy her father had often employed. "Jimmy?"

"Aye. It's me." He snatched his soft tweed cap off his head and clutched it in grimy fingers.

"Did Papa send you?"

"No, ma'am. I come myself. He told us all to go away but he won't leave."

Tess touched his arm through the sleeve of his sooty shirt. "Is fire threatening the bank?"

The boy shook his head, his tousled hair scattering bits of ash and dirt. "Worse. It's the dynamite. A soldier said they was gonna blow up the whole block and we should clear out, but Mr. Clark, he won't budge."

Eyes wide, Tess scanned the distance. Smoke hid details of the city so well it was impossible to tell how close the danger might already be to her father.

"All right, Jimmy. You've done your duty. Now either go find your family, if you can, or stay here with us. Rose and Annie will give you something to eat and drink."

The youth looked worried. "Yes, ma'am. Thank you, Miss Clark." He squinted up at her. "You gonna go talk some sense into your papa?"

"If I can," Tess said. She pulled a shawl around her and stood tall, shoulders pinned back by determination. "Tell the others where I've gone. As soon as I've seen Father I'll come right back, one way or the other."

She heard him answer, "Yes, ma'am," as she strode off. It would have pleased her mightily to have Michael's moral and physical support at this moment but since he was probably already working, as he should be, she'd handle Papa alone.

Michael would be proud of her for taking initiative, she reasoned, and once she'd joined her father she'd also have the opportunity to convince him he truly was loved by poor Mama and also by the daughter he had never fully accepted.

That was one of the main reasons Tess felt she must make the trek to the bank. The Lord had used the journal to show her what she needed to do and say with regard to her father. If she tarried she might never get the chance to make things right between them.

Less than half an hour had passed when Michael arrived at Golden Gate Park with his mother. He'd asked a man with a pocket watch for the correct time and had been relieved to learn he was running ahead of schedule. That pleased him no end because it meant he'd be able to steal a few minutes of precious time with Tess before he had to leave her again.

Helping Mary dismount and shepherding her to the lean-to Annie had strung up from a bedsheet, he started to unload the sacks of provisions they'd had tied behind the saddle, handing them to the older children while he watched the women share mutual hugs and weep for joy.

The unloading completed, he placed the final bag on the ground and frowned. "Where's Tess?"

"She—she's gone," Annie said, clearly upset. "I would of stopped her if I'd known what she was planning. She was gone by the time the boy told me."

"Gone? Where? What boy?" Michael knew his tone was harsh and demanding but he didn't have time waste.

"To Mister Gerald's bank," the maid said. "A messenger told her the army was going to blow it up. She went to fetch her papa."

"Into *that?*" Michael swept his arm in a gesture that encompassed the destruction outside the park. "What was she thinking?"

Annie's compassionate tears and soft, sobbing reply failed to reach his ears or touch his heart. Turning on his heel, he mounted the fresh horse and made sure the pistol in his belt was secure. Then he yanked the reins to spin the horse in a tight circle, aimed it toward the gate and kicked it. Hard.

By his calculations he had little time left in which to locate Tess and see that she returned to the park, with or without the idiotically stubborn father who had caused her to leave the place of sanctuary.

"That's a laugh," Michael muttered in self-disgust. "Gerald Clark's hardheadedness can't hold a candle to his daughter's."

Chapter Sixteen

Panting and coughing, Tess wiped her smarting eyes in a futile attempt to stop them from burning. She blinked rapidly, hardly believing what lay before her. The street was not only eerily deserted by every single citizen, there wasn't an armed guard or a soldier apparent, either.

The only nearby action seemed to be taking place directly in front of Papa's bank. A familiar-looking figure was loading bulging canvas sacks into the back of what looked like a greengrocer's wagon and covering them with loose hay.

She approached with a frown. "Phineas?"

He didn't even deign to glance her way. "What do you want?"

"My father," Tess said. She looked in the direction of the bank's double doors, half expecting to see her predictable papa lugging more sacks of money toward the wagon. There was no one else in sight.

"Where is he?" Tess asked.

"How should I know? When I got back from running errands for him he was gone." Snorting in obvious derision, Phineas began to cough and wheeze. "This smoke's about to kill us all. I suggest you leave."

"Not until I find my father."

"Have it your way," the younger banker said snidely. "Just stay out of my way."

"What are you doing?"

The look he shot her was clearly derisive and demeaning. "I should think that would be obvious, even to you. I'm preserving your family fortune for you while your dear father runs away to save his own skin."

Hardly, Tess thought, perusing her surroundings in more detail and immediately spotting proof she was right. Papa would never have left without taking the fancy new automobile that was parked thirty feet away. There were not enough of those expensive contraptions around for her to be mistaken, particularly since he'd had it painted a deep maroon instead of settling for the usual black color.

Realizing that Phineas had been lying, she saw no reason to stand around and argue, particularly since she'd left the park in such a hurry she'd forgotten to bring one of Papa's pistols along.

Tess quickly gathered her dusty skirts and lifted them so she could more easily scale the piles of building stone and decorative carving that had fallen from the façade of the once-impressive building.

The bank's mahogany-framed doors, with gilded lettering on their glass inserts, were standing ajar. She stepped through the portal and stared, hardly able to believe her eyes.

Plaster had fallen from the ceiling and pieces of it were scattered across the previously highly polished marble floor of the lobby. More white flecks also dusted the bars enclosing the now-empty teller cages, making them look as if a snowstorm had recently occurred inside the bank.

"Papa?" Tess cupped her hands around her mouth and called again, louder. "Papa, where are you?"

Suddenly, the fine hairs on the back of her neck prickled and her skin began to crawl.

In an instant she knew why. A sinister voice vibrated in the stillness. "I told you he left. You should have listened to me."

Shivers shot up and down her spine. She held her breath. Phineas was standing directly behind her, so close his breath was palpable. His presence was not only frightening, it was clearly menacing.

Before she had a chance to whirl and confront him, he caught her upper arm in a painful grip and began to propel her toward the door to her father's private office.

Tess pummeled him with the fist of her free arm and tried to break free. "Let me go! What are you doing?"

"Just taking care of business like I told you," he replied. Jerking open the door to the office, he shoved her through.

She stumbled forward, nearly losing her balance. The immediate slam of the door made more plaster rain down. The ominous clicking of the lock gave her chills.

Recovering and growing angry, Tess peered into the dusty gloom, afraid of what she might see. There was a strange-looking dark shape lying at the far end of the oriental rug.

"Papa!" She ran to him. Fell to her knees at his side. Touched his shoulder. He didn't move.

Lather whitened the neck of Michael's horse. He thanked God he'd saddled a fresh mount from the Clark stables when he'd fed and watered the weary team and turned them out into a paddock.

The horse's shod hooves clattered on the cobblestones while Michael prayed the beast was as agile as it looked. This kind of speed was not only impulsive it was just plain reckless even on a good day, which this certainly was not.

As he neared the bank he could see something happening out in front. Although he wasn't particularly surprised to spy the dislikable dandy who pleased Gerald Clark so much, he wondered where the older man had gone. His fondest hope was that Tess had joined her father and that they were both safely away from the danger. Then he noticed Clark's abandoned motorcar and his heart sank.

Leaping off the horse before it had slid to a full stop, Michael grabbed Phineas by the shirtfront. "Where's Tess?"

"You're the one who said you were taking care of her. What's the matter? Did you lose her?"

"She said she was coming here," Michael shouted. "Now where is she?"

The wiry man didn't answer. Michael saw his beady eyes dart first to the bank doorway, then aside to the street where the automobile sat, then back to the bank. That was his answer! Tess was in the bank.

Michael flinched and ducked as an explosion less than a block away shook the ground and loosened even more of the bricks and stone that had not fallen in the original earthquake or its aftermath.

Casting his odious captive aside like useless rubbish, he raced into the bank. "Tess! Where are you? Answer me!"

A second explosion drowned out any reply there might have been and brought down a fresh rain of plaster.

Before that echo had died, Michael was already twisting the knob on the door that displayed her father's name and title. It didn't open.

"Tess!" He banged with his fists. "Tess, are you in there?"

"Yes! Look out for Phineas," she shouted. "He locked us up."

Michael whirled, expecting an attack. Instead, he saw the loaded wagon driving away with Phineas Edgerton holding the reins and cracking a whip over the backs of the team.

"Stand away from the door," Michael yelled, pausing only a second before he added, "Are you back?"

"Yes. Hurry!"

One swift kick with the flat of his boot was all it took to spring the latch and free the prisoners.

Tess immediately threw herself into his arms and clung tightly while her groggy father leaned against the jamb for support and mopped his brow.

The older man's head was bleeding slightly and he looked ashen but Michael was satisfied all would be well—until he heard G.B. order, "Get your hands off my daughter."

"No, Father, no." Tess continued to hold fast to her heroic fireman. "Michael is rescuing us. It was Phineas who locked us in."

"That's impossible. The Edgertons have impeccable breeding. One of theirs would never do such a thing.

You've misunderstood. Phineas is merely helping me preserve the bank's funds."

Pointing to the now-empty street, Michael disagreed. "Oh, really? Then where is your wonderful vice president and where is your money?"

It should have gratified Michael to see the older man's shoulders droop as reality dawned. Instead, he actually felt sorry for him.

Gerald rubbed his sore scalp, noticed traces of blood and used the handkerchief to tend to the wound. "I thought another earthquake had knocked me out but now I wonder. I don't remember a thing after I walked into my office."

"He must have hit you from behind." Tess released her hold on Michael enough to give her father's arm a brief pat. "Come with us. I have a tidy little camp set up in the park. We'll look after you."

It was clear to Michael from the narrowing of the banker's eyes and the way he was staring into the street that he had no intention of letting Edgerton escape. In this terrible confusion, however, successfully following anyone would be next to impossible.

Placing a light kiss on the top of Tess's head, Michael sighed and delivered his own bad news. "I can't go with you, remember? I have to report this morning." He looked to the older man. "Will you take Tess back to the park?"

Although Clark's reply was neither quick nor firm, he finally nodded and said, "Yes."

Satisfied, Michael cupped Tess's face in his hands and tilted it up for one last kiss. He didn't care if her father had an apoplectic fit over it, he was going to bid the love of his life a proper goodbye.

His mouth was tender yet demanding, almost desperate, she noted, as if he feared that this might be their last touch, last kiss.

The emotional turmoil bubbling inside Tess brought to mind words she had not intended to speak—at least not until she and Michael had calmly discussed their mutual feelings. Her lips parted. Trembled. Looking directly into his eyes, she whispered, "I love you."

Moisture sparkled in the depths of his dark gaze. He froze and stared at her. "I…"

To Tess's dismay he never finished the sentence, never told her he loved her in return. Instead, he whirled and strode away.

Michael's abrupt departure left her totally confused. How could he just walk off like that? Hadn't he heard what she'd said? Didn't he care? In her deepest heart she was certain he loved her, so why hadn't he spoken the words?

She felt her father's hand at her elbow. Blinking back tears, she managed a wan smile for his benefit.

"Come on," Gerald said. "I'll drive you back to the park in my automobile."

Tess could tell from his tone and posture that that was not at all what he wanted to do. "If I weren't here, would you go after Phineas instead?"

The older man shrugged, clearly disheartened. "I don't know. Perhaps."

"Then let's."

"Don't be ridiculous. You don't belong out on the

streets in the middle of all this. Don't worry. I'll look after you." He smiled slightly. "After all, I did promise your young man."

"He is, you know. My young man, I mean," Tess said, blushing. "I know he's not highborn or rich, the way you wanted, but I love him dearly."

Blowing out a noisy sigh, Gerald nodded. "Well, I guess we can forget about you marrying Edgerton in any case." He wiped his brow and blotted his eyes with the crumpled handkerchief. "I can't believe how fooled I was. Thank goodness you didn't take to him the way I'd hoped you would."

Tess huffed. "I loathed that odious man from the first moment I met him."

"You did?"

"Yes. The things I learned at the suffragette meetings have helped me stand up for myself." She smiled when she saw her father's bewildered expression. "Don't look so shocked, Papa. All I mean is that I now trust in myself, know my own mind and stick to what I feel is right. That leaves Phineas out in the cold."

She laughed softly at the imagined image of the skinny, supercilious fop literally shivering from the cold shoulders she'd already given him. There was no man for her except Michael Mahoney and she knew it—all the way from the top of her head to her toes.

"Besides," Tess said, growing dreamy eyed as she pictured Michael, "I prefer gallant firemen."

"Is that what the young man does for a living?" Gerald asked. He cupped her elbow, gestured at the door and started to escort her toward his waiting motorcar. "He's Mary Mahoney's son, too, isn't he?"

"Yes, and I can't think of anyone I'd rather have for a mother-in-law."

"You two have discussed matrimony, then?"

Tess sobered. "No. Not yet. But we shall." She colored slightly. "I'm sure Michael will do the right thing and ask you for my hand."

"Let's hope so." Gerald brushed soot and ash off the upholstery on the automobile's passenger seat before assisting her into it, then walked to the front of the car to crank the starter.

Before he could bend to begin, Tess stopped him by adding, "I want to marry for love, Father. I don't want to count on it developing later, the way it did for you and Mama."

It was immediately clear, judging by the befuddled look on his face, that her conclusions had been correct. Her poor father had never viewed his marriage as a love match. She saw his lower lip quiver.

"It's true," Tess insisted before he could argue. "Mama loved you dearly. I read all about it in her journal."

He stared. Blinked rapidly. Took a deep, shuddering breath, then said simply, "Thank you."

This was the perfect moment to speak her mind, to tell him the rest of the things she'd planned to say. Nevertheless, Tess's pride and the memories of his past rejection almost stopped her—until she thought of how Jesus had always taught his followers to forgive.

Emboldened by her faith and the knowledge that what she was about to do and say was right, she added, "And *I* love you, too, Papa."

The changing expression on her father's lined, weary

face was a combination of tenderness and awe. He was clearly thunderstruck, so much so that his jaw dropped.

Like Michael, he didn't choose to return her profession of affection but in this instance Tess was satisfied. Papa had loved Mama and he loved her, too, in his own way. Although he had never been a demonstrative man, he harbored deep feelings, feelings that now shone in his countenance.

That will do, she concluded, basking in a sense of familial belonging that she had never known before. Both her parents had done their best. The only truly sad thing was that Mama had passed on without knowing how much Papa had cared for her.

Tess vowed she would never allow that to happen with Michael. She would tell him every day how much she adored him. And he would hold her in his arms the way he had a few moments ago and...

A lump in her throat and a rapid pulse signaled the rise of the lingering fear she'd kept denying. Her last glimpse of Michael Mahoney might have been the final one she'd ever have. He was about to enter the belly of the beast, to stand and fight a fire that had already consumed a third of the city or more.

Given the terrible ongoing danger and the lack of proper tools with which to wage that battle in spite of the influx of engines and men from Oakland and other cities, he might not survive long enough to become her husband.

Chapter Seventeen

A portion of the fire had jumped Van Ness at California and Powell streets and was climbing the side of Nob Hill by the time Michael joined his fresh crew. They all donned leather helmets and heavy canvas coats.

"You're in charge of this team, Mahoney," Chief Walters ordered, gesturing at the horses hitched three abreast in front of the steam-powered pumper. "We don't know if there's any water left east of Van Ness but the navy has fireboats working the docks so I'm sending you and some of the others up Powell. Do the best you can. And God help you."

Michael nodded, his mouth dry, his nerves taut. He'd definitely done the right thing when he'd moved his mother out of the Clark mansion. It sounded as though they might soon lose their battle to preserve the expensive homes of the city's most affluent residents.

"That's no different than losing Rose Dugan's house," he muttered to himself, knowing he was right. Any person's home and possessions were valuable to them, no matter how little monetary investment was involved. Perhaps if the fire departments had had more ready equipment and manpower to wage war on this disaster in all areas of the city in the first place, the conflagration wouldn't have spread so far and gotten so out of hand. Then again, no one could possibly have foreseen a battle like this.

He climbed aboard the engine, set a booted foot on the brake and threaded the pairs of reins between his fingers so he could control each individual horse. The snorting, pawing, sweaty team was more than eager to be off.

"Ready, men?" Michael shouted back at his crew.

When he was answered with a chorus of affirmative shouts he snapped the reins, gave the horses their heads and braced himself as they lunged ahead, blowing hard and straining to get the heavy engine rolling.

Michael had little chance to do more than skillfully guide the team but he did manage to see, as they drew nearer to Nob Hill, that several mansions had already been reduced to smoldering ruins.

Above them the newly built but never opened Fairmont Hotel, which had been billed as the jewel of the city, was starting to look as if every window was brightly curtained in dancing, deadly orange and red.

He shouted to the horses. They kept up the frantic pace, the pumper careening left and right as they dodged debris littering the streets.

For the first time in the past few days Michael's mind was too occupied by the task at hand to return to thoughts of Tess more than occasionally. He was approaching a staging area where other engines and crews had massed to make a stand against the fire's progress.

"Whoa," he shouted to the team. "Whoa, boys. That's it. Easy, now."

Bringing his rig to a stop at the edge of the group, he called down, "Where do you want us?"

The chilling answer wasn't long in coming. A sooty, sweaty fireman looked up at him and shook his head sadly, somberly, his shoulders slumping as if he were on his last legs.

"I wish I knew," the man called back. "You boys might as well spit on that fire. We just ran out of water in the last cistern."

Tess sat beside her father as he drove cautiously toward the park. She could tell he was pondering something important because now and then his brow would furrow or his lips would form a grimace.

"Are you angry at me, Father?" she finally asked.

"What?" He looked astonished. "Of course not. What gave you that idea?"

"The look on your face," she explained. "I was afraid you might be blaming me for the fact that Phineas got away."

"Don't be silly. It's not your fault. If I'd heeded your opinion in the first place he might not have fooled me so completely."

"You shouldn't blame yourself," Tess said tenderly. "After all, you only know what you learned growing up." That comment made her father snort derisively, much to her surprise and puzzlement.

He glanced at her. "You really don't know the whole story, do you?"

"Story of what?"

"The struggles of my youth. I didn't have a dime to my name until I married your mother. She brought her fortune into our family. All I did was invest it wisely and make it grow."

"You—you mean you weren't born rich?"

"Hardly. We were dirt poor when I was a boy. Why do you think I cared so much that you had all the best of everything? I didn't want you to struggle the way I had."

"What about your parents?"

"They died when I was in my teens, just as I always told you. What I didn't say was that I apprenticed myself to my future father-in-law at his bank in Philadelphia. That was how I learned the business and eventually met and married your mother."

"You were like Phineas! No wonder you thought he'd be perfect for me."

Gerald made a sour face. "I hadn't thought of it quite that way but I suspect you may be right."

"We shouldn't let him get away, you know." Tess had been checking side streets as they drove and although she had not seen any sign of the grocery wagon she was still hopeful. "What if we drove around a little before we headed for the park? There's always a chance we might catch a glimpse of him. I don't have a pistol with me but I don't think he was armed, either."

The astonishment on her father's face quickly became thoughtful. "I suppose there would be no particular danger as long as we stayed in the car and stuck to areas that have already burned."

"Exactly. Do you have enough fuel?"

"I poured in another gallon when I stopped at the bank. We should be fine for a while."

Tess began to grin. "In that case, let's go find that wagon and see that Phineas gets what's coming to him.

"What about your young man? We promised…"

"You promised. I didn't," Tess said, grinning. "Besides, Michael has his hands full right now. If we decide to take a little detour it won't matter to him. Not as long as we eventually end up at the park as planned."

Gerald gave her a look that was almost respectful, although Tess was sorry it had taken a series of tragedies to bring it about. She might physically resemble her late mother but that was where the similarities ended. She was smart and strong-willed, just like her father, and it was high time he gave her credit for having backbone.

Michael had helped his fellows stretch a hose line all the way from the bay. His engine and others like it had been hooked in tandem to pump the seawater up the hills but he knew the breakdown of even one engine in the line would mean failure of the entire operation.

Now he could see flames licking the sides of the Huntington mansion. Crocker's place was next. Worse, the streets around Nob Hill were once again teeming with evacuees, folks who had not seen fit to leave earlier when their passage to safety would have been relatively easy.

"Hey! Slow down. You can't race through there," Michael yelled.

He waved his arms to no avail as wagon after wagon rolled through the intersection and crossed their canvas hoses at a pace that was nearly rapid enough to rupture them. Didn't those drivers know how fragile the heavy fabric could be when it was wet? Didn't they care that those metal-rimmed wheels were likely to cause leaks that couldn't be repaired?

Frantic, he kept trying to divert oncoming wagons. The wealthy were finally realizing that the disaster was going to reach their sanctuaries and were hurriedly attempting to rescue their expensive possessions. As far as he was concerned there was nothing on this earth as valuable as human life, yet those people continued to defy the orders of the very men who were sworn to save them.

Michael bent his back with the others who were hauling some of the heavy hose to the side of the road. Wet paving stones were slick. Hazardous. Sweat and sprays of seawater dripped from his leather helmet and stung his eyes till he could barely see.

"There goes another one," someone shouted, pointing. "Look."

Michael raised his head, blinked and wiped his smarting eyes with a kerchief. His heart plummeted. The mansion directly next door to the Clarks' was catching fire and beginning to burn as if some malevolent force had just doused it with kerosene and touched a match to the base.

Behind him, a horn honked. He whirled, ready to block the way of whoever else intended to pass. To his horror, the automobile belonging to Gerald Clark was approaching. And Tess was still aboard.

Michael lunged toward the car and grabbed the edge of the door on the driver's side. Staring past her father, he shouted directly at Tess, almost losing control of his temper enough to curse. "What are you doing here?"

"The horses," Tess cried, pointing.

"Forget it. It's too late. You can't go up there." Michael was adamant as well as terrified for her. He grabbed her father's arm. "Go back. Can't you see what's happening?"

The car shuddered and its engine died. Gerald looked

surprised. "Sorry. We saw the smoke and thought we could be of assistance. Can we do something? Anything?"

"No. If you can get this thing started again you need to turn around and leave. Otherwise you'll need to push it out of the way and walk. You can't stay here. It's too dangerous."

"All right," the older man said. "You take care of yourself—son. My daughter expects you to come out of this mess in one piece."

A brief glance at Tess confirmed how much she cared. Michael managed a conciliatory smile for her benefit. "Don't worry. I'll find you when this is over."

Although their gazes locked he said no more. There was nothing else to say, nor was there enough time in which to say it properly. He had a duty not only to his own crew but to the other engines in the pumping line. The fire beneath each boiler had to be stoked and the buildup of steam efficiently managed in order to push every last drop of water through those long lines.

Backing away, Michael headed for his pumper as the older man climbed out of the car. At least Tess would still have an escort back to the park, even if it wasn't him. He checked the gauges on his instrument panel and saw with satisfaction that the steam pressure was holding steady. *Good.* Running this equipment was an art as much as a science and, modesty aside, he was one of the best engineers in all of San Francisco.

Another glance told him that Gerald had failed to get the car started. He and several other men were pushing it backward while Tess sat behind the wheel.

Michael gritted his teeth. He wanted to be angry with her and her father, yet he was so relieved to have seen that they were all right he couldn't manage to stir up much ire. Perhaps he'd feel differently later but right now, right here, he was simply thankful.

Tess slid from behind the wheel and climbed down as soon as she felt the rear tires contact the curb. The high color in her father's face worried her. She quickly took his hand and led him aside. "Are you all right?"

"Yes. I just need to sit and rest a bit. It's that confounded starter. I shouldn't have cranked it so much."

"I thought we had plenty of gas?"

"We should have had," Gerald replied, mopping his brow and perching on the rear bumper of the automobile. "We may have broken a fuel line during our rough travels." His eyes misted. "I should have listened to your young man and taken you straight to the park."

"Nonsense. We might have come across Phineas. It's not your fault that we didn't."

As Tess sat beside him and watched, her father looked as if he were about to weep. "It's not that. It's the money. I put it first."

"You were just thinking of your depositors."

Gerald shook his head. "No. I was thinking of the money. That was all that mattered to me. That was all that's ever mattered. Oh, I told myself I was working for the good of my family but it always came back to the same thing. The bottom line." A few tears began to streak his cheeks. "I let life pass me by."

"It's not too late, Father," Tess told him tenderly. "You still have me. We can do wonderful things together. I had thought of turning the house into a refugee center, for a short while, at least until some of these places are rebuilt and people can go home again. Or maybe it can be an orphanage for children like that poor little tyke I found in the rubble yesterday. You should see her. She's adorable."

He arched and eyebrow. "You were out on the streets?"

"Aiding the needy. With Michael." Seeking to distract her father and keep him from drawing inappropriate conclusions, she added, "You can use your influence to help the cause of woman suffrage, too, if you wish. There are some extraordinary ladies involved in that movement."

He patted her hand. "Nonc as extraordinary as you, I'm sure. You are truly a treasure, Tess. I wouldn't have thought we'd ever talk to each other this way and now here we are."

"I suspect we will still have our differences," she replied, smiling knowingly. "But we must always remember this day, no matter what."

Looking past him, she let her gaze wander up the hill. Her jaw dropped. The firemen had not halted the fire the way she'd assumed they would. Flames were now leaping from the roofs of the Crocker and Stanford mansions and being blown ahead like the unstoppable gale that preceded a hurricane. And her home stood next in line!

Chapter Eighteen

Michael had assumed Tess and her father had left the area because he no longer saw either of them. Smoke billowed, whirled and eddied, sometimes thick, sometimes mere wisps. Always it burned eyes and lungs. And always it filled in just when he thought he was about to see through and discern more about what was going on in the distance.

It didn't matter to him directly, of course. He didn't dare leave his post. He merely wanted to see how the nozzle men were faring and tell if his ongoing prayers for their success were being answered.

A gust of wind off the ocean caught beneath the wide, back brim of his hat and lifted it off his neck to the extent allowed by the chin strap. Michael pivoted to brace himself. The smoke ahead parted momentarily.

Far up the hill he thought he caught a glimpse of movement, of a denser gray merging with the smoke. The flash of reddish tresses and the whipping of a woman's skirt disappeared rapidly into the cloud. Could it be her? Would she be that foolish?

Taking the chance that his conclusion was right, Michael shouted, "Tess! No."

Every instinct within him was screaming that he must chase after the woman, must somehow bring her back even if she wasn't Tess. He knew he didn't dare. His specific skills were not only invaluable, they needed every hand they already had on scene and more if they hoped to make any difference in the progress of the fire. He had sworn allegiance to the fire brigade. He could not turn away. If he did, hundreds more might die as a result.

Cupping his hands around his mouth, he shouted, "Tess!" at the top of his lungs. "Tess! Come back."

The smoke darkened as if night had fallen and closed like a malevolent fist around the retreating figure, hiding even the most basic shadows as if they had never been there. As if he'd only imagined witnessing the love of his life disappear into the bowels of the inferno.

Michael moaned. His heart and soul cried out. He began to weep, silently but openly, until he was barely able to focus on the crucial gauges positioned right in front of his face.

Tess trusted her intuition to guide her through to her goal. It did. By the time she reached the estate grounds she was coughing so badly she couldn't catch her breath. Her eyes were red, swollen and burning.

Shooting pains in her ribs, caused by the intense exertion, doubled her over. She refused to give up or turn back. Clutching her waist, she wrapped both arms around her torso and staggered on toward the stables.

The roof above the main part of the structure was already cresting with flames. Horses snorted. Whinnied in fright. Tess followed the sounds to locate her mare and the others she'd come to rescue.

She was overcome with relief to discover them all outside in a paddock instead of locked away in their stalls. *Hallelujah!* She wasn't going to have to brave fire in the barn to rescue any others.

She shut her eyes for an instant and breathed a heartfelt "Praise God."

The frantic animals were galloping in circles in the paddock, moving as a herd in hope of escape the oncoming flames. She could certainly understand their fear. Hers was palpable. And growing to the point where she was nearly beside herself.

"Easy, easy," she said, struggling to control her trembling, dampen her wheezing cough and speak to them calmly.

It was readily apparent that tone didn't matter. Those horses were not about to listen to anyone. Clearly none were calm enough for her to catch and bridle either, let alone hope to ride. She might as well have tried to throw a saddle on a wild mustang.

There was only one sensible thing to do. She unlatched the gate to offer the animals their freedom, praying that their survival instincts would be strong enough to carry them to safety.

"Here! Look!" she yelled before breaking into paroxysms of coughing and grabbing her ribs again with her free arm.

She waggled the open wooden gate back and forth to help them spot it through the haze. Her mare was the first to dash through. The others followed.

When the last horse had raced past, Tess came to her senses and took stock of the situation. The stable building was already a total loss and the house was about to join it. Fire was consuming the eucalyptus foliage above the lawn as if it was part of a line of oil-soaked torches rather than the beautiful green-and-gray shade trees she remembered.

Paroxysms of coughing shook her till she could hardly stand, let alone think of fleeing.

She fell to her knees in the dirt.

"God, help me," she muttered as smoke burned her eyes and stole the last of her sight. "What have I done?"

A hand clamped firmly on Michael's shoulder gave him a start. He wheeled. It was Chief Walters.

"It's over," the chief said. "We're shutting down and falling back. We've lost two of the pumps in the line and there are no replacements."

Rubbing his face against the sleeve of his heavy coat, Michael hoped his despondency didn't show. Truth to tell, he felt as dead as the earthquake and fire victims he'd seen lying in the streets. He'd stayed at his post and done his duty no matter what. So had the others. But it hadn't been enough. All their pride in the fire brigades had been for naught. San Francisco lay in ashes. And so, he feared, did his heart.

Walters peered at him. "You look awful."

Trying to subdue a shudder, Michael pointed. "I—I saw a woman run into the smoke a few minutes ago. It looked like Tess Clark."

"Are you sure?"

"No," he answered honestly.

"You think it was her though, don't you?"

"Yes." Pointing to the automobile, he saw that Gerald Clark was still resting beside it, apparently ill, while several passersby tended to him. "She and her father drove up together. Their car stalled. The last I saw of her she was over there with him."

"She's the woman I saw riding with you on the rescue wagon yesterday, isn't she?"

Michael nodded, fighting to control his emotions and barely succeeding.

To his surprise, Walters choked back a sob. "I haven't told anyone else this. I lost my wife in the quake."

Clapping a hand on the chief's shoulder, Michael said, "I'm so sorry," identifying with the man's grief far more than he liked.

"Go," Walters ordered suddenly. He gestured with one arm and gave Michael a push with the other. "Go find her if you can. I'll take care of shutting down your engine."

The enormity of the other man's selflessness in the wake of his own deep personal loss touched Michael to the core. God might not have dispatched a guardian angel to answer his prayers but He had certainly acted when He'd sent the chief.

"Thanks," Michael shouted, beginning to race up the hill as if all his weariness had suddenly been replaced with an unending supply of strength and stamina.

He knew where he'd last seen the shadowy figure. And he knew the basic layout of the Clark estate. If it had been Tess who had disappeared into the smoke he'd find her. Or die trying.

Tess's basic instincts told her to get away from the buildings so she began to crawl, feeling her way along the ground. It was impossible to tell in which direction she was heading so she simply tried to locate enough air to sustain life.

It wasn't easy. Every time she thought she was in the clear, the wind shifted and bore down on her, as if it were a ruthless pursuer, intent on stealing her last breath and rendering her helpless.

Prayer, as she'd always practiced it, was impossible. She could barely breathe, let alone whisper a suitable appeal, so she let her thoughts cry out to God for her.

Mostly, she repeated, "Father, help me," over and over, with a few pauses for uncontrolled fits of coughing and vows of repentance. Could she expect an answer? Did she dare beg God for rescue after recklessly putting herself in such an untenable position?

Tears of sadness and physical pain bathed her eyes and wet her lashes. They dripped into the dust, sometimes landing atop the backs of her hands as she felt her way along inch by inch. At least she'd saved the horses. Or at least she thought she had. Releasing them had been the most logical option. If she'd had more time she might have tried to climb aboard her mare and let it choose a route of escape for them both. Now, it was too late.

Closing her eyes, Tess bent forward to rest her forehead on her clasped hands. Everything was becoming blurred, surreal, even the roar from the flames that were devouring the house. All she wanted to do was rest. Sleep. Let her weary mind carry her away from all this.

Suddenly, something stung the back of her neck. It felt as if a hot poker had been shoved into her hair!

Pain jolted her into alertness. Grabbing at her head to beat out the smoldering embers, she inhaled. Got a good breath. And let out a piercing scream.

* * *

Michael heard her screech and his blood chilled. It *was* Tess he'd seen walking into the smoke and she was hurt.

He braced himself, cupped his hands and answered with, "Tess! Where are you?"

No answer came. Peering in the direction he thought the noise had originated, he forged ahead.

Filling his lungs was impossible. He managed to barely gulp enough air to shout out from time to time. He stretched his arms ahead of him, feeling his way and nearly blinded by the stinging smoke.

Knowing Tess, she would have headed for the stables, he reasoned. The first thing she'd said when she and her father had arrived was "The horses."

"Tess! Answer me."

Heavyhearted, totally spent, Michael tripped. Stumbled. One hand touched the ground. The other...

He'd found her!

Grabbing the slim shoulder where his hand had landed, he gave it a shake. "Tess! Wake up."

Unspoken prayers rose from the depths of his soul. *Please, God. Let her be all right.*

Still, she didn't stir. Didn't respond.

A flicker of fire caught his eye. There was a glowing ember in her hair!

Michael closed his hand over the fire, ignoring the singeing of his own flesh. Water. Where was the closest water?

Squinting into the drifting smoke, he spotted what he thought was the large trough he'd used when tending the team. That would more than suffice.

He had to temporarily let go of her hair in order to

stand and gather her into his arms. In three long strides he'd reached the side of the wooden trough.

Without further thought he plunged Tess's whole body into the water, then briefly pushed her head under, too.

Tess popped up out of the water flailing, sputtering, dripping and gasping. Her words were hoarse and unintelligible but they were still the most wonderful sounds Michael had ever heard.

He reached for her. Pulled her partially into his arms without letting her leave the trough. "Easy. Easy. You were on fire," he said brokenly. "I had to dunk you. Thankfully, it also brought you to your senses."

She threw her arms around his neck and began to sob with an intensity beyond anything Michael had ever experienced.

His emotions were no more stable. Holding her close, he wept against her dripping hair and thanked God they'd been reunited. In moments, he realized that they were not yet safe. Far from it.

"We have to go," he said, recovering his senses enough to begin to assess the situation. "Can you tell which way the street lies?"

Tess shook her head. "No. I got terribly turned around. Then I fell and..." Clinging tighter, she was wracked with renewed sobs and coughing.

"Pull yourself together," Michael ordered. "Think. After you let the horses loose, which way did they run?"

"I—I—I don't know."

"Yes, you do. You're sitting in their watering trough. Use that to get your bearings."

Straightening, she peered into the thick air. "I can't see a thing."

"Neither could those horses but I'd trust their judgment over mine any day." He got to his feet and helped her climb out of the water. Her clothing and hair were soaked and dripping, which was exactly the way he wanted her to be. "Now, which way?"

Tess sagged against him. He knew she was nearly spent but he needed her advice if they hoped to find sanctuary.

He tightened his grip around her shoulder and insisted, "Tess. Come on. You can do this. Which way did they go?"

Slowly lifting her arm as if it weighed tons, she pointed. "That way."

Michael stopped himself from asking if she was certain. At this juncture there was no use delaying. If she was mistaken and they fled into a worse conflagration instead of a safe zone, they would meet death together.

His jaw clenched. No. That would not happen. They would get through, somehow. God had brought them this far. He would not abandon them now.

Tess's head was swimming. She still wasn't sure whether Michael's presence was a figment of her imagination or if he was truly there. She even doubted the chill of her wet clothing at first. The last thing she recalled clearly was falling to her knees and folding her hands in preparation for meeting her Maker.

The rest of the time was a blur. Her legs felt as limp as the ribbons that bound her mother's journal. If this was all imaginary, then perhaps she would soon see Mama face-to-face in heaven.

At her side, she sensed the strength that was Michael. Blinking, she looked up and saw the beard stubble on his chin. This could *not* be a dream. It was far too real. There was fire and smoke all around them. She could barely see him, let alone discern their path. Where were they going?

Coughing, she managed to say his name, "Michael?"

"I've got you. We'll make it," he replied.

"I'm so sorry."

His hold tightened. "Let's get out of this mess first. We can talk about other things later."

"I love you," Tess said before breaking into more paroxysms of coughing.

"Yeah," he answered gruffly. "I know. And I love you, too, even if you are crazy brave."

That was enough to satisfy Tess. If this was a dream it was turning out exactly the way she'd always envisioned. And if it was real, as she hoped, she had just heard the man she planned to spend the rest of her life with say he returned her love.

"Thank You, Jesus," she whispered, feeling a surprising surge of energy and a renewed lightness of her steps.

She gazed lovingly up at her gallant fireman. "You'll get us out of this. I know you will."

"I'm sorry about your house."

"It was just a building," Tess said. Eyes inflamed and streaming tears in reaction to the constant irritation, she peered ahead. "Look! I think the smoke is clearing."

Although he didn't immediately say he agreed, he did pick up their pace. When she had trouble moving fast enough to keep up with him, he swung her into his arms and carried her.

Tess wrapped her arm around his neck and hung on tightly, placing her cheek against his shoulder as he began to trot. A sound rumbled deep in Michael's chest and at first she thought he might be crying.

Then, as they broke into the open and were able to see that they were truly safe, she realized he was laughing.

Bearing his wondrous burden into the center of the street where they'd be clear of any threat from either fire or collapsing structures, Michael set Tess on her feet and doubled over, hands on his knees, trying to catch his breath.

"Where are we?"

He rose and scanned their surroundings. "Columbia Street, I think." Laughter continued to bubble up in spite of his breathlessness. "I can't believe it. We made it!"

"Only because of you."

When she grasped his hand he realized he hadn't escaped unscathed. Although he tried not to show pain, she noticed his flinch and turned his palm up.

"What happened? When were you burned?"

He knew all too well and, given their shared elation, he figured this was a good time to tell her. "I think I did it putting out the fire in the back of your hair."

Tess looked so astonished he had to assume she didn't remember.

"That was the main reason I dunked you in the horse trough. You do recall that, don't you?"

"Oh, yes." She made a face as she glanced at her sopping skirt and jacket. "I thought you were trying to drown me."

"Never," Michael said, grinning so widely his cheeks ached. "I might consider spanking you if you tried anything that reckless again, though."

She stepped back, hands fisted on her hips. "You wouldn't dare!"

Chuckling, smiling and shaking his head, he said, "You're right. I wouldn't. But not because I'm afraid of you, Miss Clark. I'd never lay a hand on you because I love you. I saw what that kind of rough treatment did to my mother and I want you to always trust me. I'd never harm you."

Spreading his arms, he wordlessly invited her back into his embrace. As soon as she was snuggled against him he broke the news that he'd have to be getting back to duty.

Tess's hug tightened. "Must you?"

"Yes. Chief Walters released me to go after you but I owe him as much more work as I'm capable of. You have to understand that."

"Of course," Tess said, although she didn't sound very convinced.

"We can cut around to Powell and probably get through there, now that that part of the fire has burned out. When you rejoin your father and head for the park, remember that and try to travel where it's already burned. Just stay away from those idiots with the dynamite."

"Blowing up things is not working very well, is it?"

Michael sighed, disgusted and discouraged. "It might have, in the right hands. Most of the men who were given the job of placing the charges had no experience. I suspect they did more harm than good."

As he drew her to his side and began to escort her toward their destination he realized how fatigued he was. Not only had he spent several a night without sleeping, he'd worked at top capacity since morning.

Smiling to himself, he glanced down at the precious woman beside him. He had vowed to give his life to save her if necessary and he would have kept that promise if it had come to that.

Now, however, his heart was overflowing with gratitude for the privilege of remaining with her. Their chances of mutual survival had been slim to none. Yet here they were. Together.

He bent to place a kiss atop her head, not minding the dampness of her hair or the perfume of smoke.

"I hope I didn't lose too much when it burned," Tess said, patting the back of her neck to investigate. "I have a notion you like my hair."

"I love *everything* about you and I always will, with or without your beautiful hair," he said honestly.

She giggled. "Does that include my stubborn streak?"

"Let's just say I'm working on accepting that." His laughter melded with hers. "I suspect it may take me a while longer, especially if you keep exercising it the way you did today."

"I really am sorry I did such a stupid thing."

"I know you are. Hopefully you're a lot smarter now."

"I was smart enough to fall in love with you in spite of my father." She laughed softly, then went on. "You aren't going to believe the secrets I learned about him today. He and I are a lot more alike than I'd thought."

"As long as he accepts me as I am and doesn't try to put me to work in his bank, I'll be satisfied," Michael said.

"Oh, what a marvelous idea!"

He stiffened. His eyes widened and he stared at her. Then she followed her statement with another giggle and eased his mind. "Don't scare me like that. I thought you were serious."

"Never," Tess told him. "I love you just as you are. And I absolutely *adore* firemen."

Chapter Nineteen

Tess was astounded at the visible change of the whole area by the time she and Michael arrived at the spot where she'd left her father. The street was as wet as it would have been after a rain. Gangs of firemen had been uncoupling the hoses, breaking them into shorter lengths and rolling them up. Most of the steam pumpers had already left.

Michael took her hand, led her over to Chief Walters, and proudly announced, "I found her!"

When Tess saw the pathos in the other man's expression she was more than touched.

He and Michael had been sharing an exuberant handshake. As soon as they stopped, she also offered her hand. The chief took it. Like her, he was smiling through unshed tears.

"Thank you," Tess said. "Thank you for letting Michael come after me."

"Rules are made to be broken, especially in times like these," Walters replied. He eyed her from head to toe. "Are you all right?"

"I will be." Another coughing fit made her pause.

"It can take a long time to get over breathing in that much smoke," he cautioned. "Be sure you take it real easy for a while."

"I will." Thinking of Michael having to go back to work and fight fire when he'd been exposed to as much flying soot and ash as she had, she was crestfallen. Part of that harm to his lungs was her fault. So was the burn on his hand.

She saw both men glance toward the idle automobile so she asked, "Is my father still around?"

"No," Walters said. "He was acting ill so I sent him down the hill on one of the other engines."

"Ill? Oh, dear!"

"Don't worry, miss. I doubt there was anything wrong with him that one look at you won't cure. He was so beside himself after he lost sight of you, he started raving and shouting but not making a bit of sense. He refused to listen to reason. I had to have some men force him aboard the pumper and hold him there to get him to leave."

She felt Michael's arm tighten around her shoulders, offering the same moral support on which she had grown so reliant.

"How about letting me drive Tess?" he asked. "At least as far as my next assignment?"

To her relief and joy, the chief nodded immediately. "That's what I figured to do." He began to smile. "I didn't see much point in your risking your life to get her this far and then making her walk all the way to the park."

"Is that where you sent Papa?" she asked.

"Yes. Nurses and doctors who had to evacuate from the emergency center in the basement of city hall are set up in Golden Gate Park." He nodded at Michael. "Our hose wagons will handle the rest of this mess. Drive the young lady as far as the park, then rendezvous at the ferry terminal again for new orders."

Michael saluted. "Yes, sir."

In parting, Tess once again reached for the chief's hand. "God bless you," she said. To her amazement he nodded brusquely, then turned on his heel and strode away.

When she looked up at Michael there was shared sorrow on his face. He bent to whisper, "Chief Walters's wife was killed in the earthquake."

"Oh, no." Her hand went to her throat, her heart breaking for the poor man's loss. "No wonder he was so willing to let you come after me."

"Yeah. I'd thought of that, too."

Michael checked the harness on his team while she waited, then helped her climb onto the driver's seat before joining her.

She slipped her hand through the crook of his elbow, marveling at how natural that action had become. It seemed as if she and Michael were already one in the eyes of God, the way they truly would be after they were married.

She sighed, basking in his nearness and drinking in the blessings of their time together as though it might yet be limited. Her heart was torn between peace and trepidation, happiness and grief, aspirations of a bright future and lingering dread.

Tightening her hold, she smiled at him. He mirrored the gesture. They were both still coughing at times but the hacking hoarseness seemed to be lessening. It hurt her to breathe deeply and her throat felt raw so she assumed Michael was also experiencing those detrimental aftereffects.

And he was headed back to face even more.

"I want you to promise me something," he said, concentrating primarily on driving the team instead of watching Tess. He was afraid if he said what was on his mind and saw her start to cry he might not be able to keep his own emotions in check. The last thing he wanted to do was let her see him weep. Especially since he couldn't blame his tears on the effects of the smoke the way he had before.

"Of course. Anything." She laughed lightly, nervously. "Well, almost anything."

"Good girl."

"I may be good, but I'm no longer a girl," Tess argued genially. "I guess you noticed that."

"Oh, yes." Chancing a quick smile at her, he was amazed by how lovely she was, even in such a bedraggled condition. He chuckled. "You don't look quite up to snuff right now but I have an excellent memory. I remember you at your best."

"I am a sight, aren't I?" Making a silly face at him, she started rubbing at the dirt streaking her soggy skirt. "It's all your fault. This used to be a lovely afternoon outfit."

"That's the problem, then," he joked back. "There was nothing *lovely* about this afternoon. You wore the wrong dress to the party."

"I must have. It's certainly ruined." Shaking her head slowly, pensively, she stopped trying to spruce up her clothing. "Given what I went through while wearing it,

I'm glad it can't be salvaged. I'd certainly not want to put it on again. Too many bad memories."

That was the perfect opening for Michael to speak. No matter how hard it was to voice these thoughts, he knew it must be done. Soon.

"Speaking of memories," he said, fighting to keep his tone even and his voice strong, "I want you to promise me that if anything should happen to me, today or any day, you'll go on with your life and keep trusting the Lord."

"Don't be silly. Nothing's going to happen to you."

"Just the same, I want your promise."

"Oh, Michael. How can you ask that of me? I don't even want to think about what my life might be like without you."

He held firm. "Promise, Tess. Say it. I need to hear it from you."

"It's that important to you?"

"Yes. It's that important."

Waiting, he could feel her trembling, even through the sleeve of his heavy coat. She had a tender heart, a woman's heart, despite all her bravado and the outlandish emancipation ideas she'd adopted.

"All right," she finally said. "I promise that if anything happens to you to keep us from getting married I will go on with my life."

He would have felt a lot better about her vow if she had not followed it with, "But if you think you're going to weasel out of marrying me, Michael Mahoney, you'd better think again."

It would have pleased Tess to have arrived at the family camp aboard the fire engine and been able to show it off to the children, at least. Unfortunately, Michael stopped outside the park perimeter.

"You'll need to walk from here," he said. "Can you manage?"

"Yes." Every fiber of her being kept insisting that she could not possibly leave him, yet she knew she must. When he kept hold of the reins instead of climbing down to assist her, she was puzzled.

Michael gave her his trademark Irish grin and wound the three pair of lines around the brake lever before opening his arms. "Come here, darlin'. Kiss your future husband goodbye."

"That's more like it," Tess said, throwing herself into his embrace. "You had me a little worried."

"Never worry about my love for you, no matter what," he whispered against her cheek, his breath tickling her ear. "I'll love you forever."

That was almost more than Tess's fragile frame of mind could bear. He sounded as though he was bidding her a final farewell because he didn't expect to return. The mere thought of that happening made her heart clench.

Leaning away just far enough to cup his beard-roughened cheeks in her hands, she held his face still and gazed into his eyes, willing him to share her belief. "You are coming back to me, do you hear? I am not going to take no for an answer. You know how stubborn I am, right? Well, this is how it's going to be."

To her relief, he didn't look angry. On the contrary, his smile spread. "Are you finished?"

"Yes," Tess said, "providing you've been listening to me."

"I've been listening."

"Then don't even think of arguing."

"Yes, ma'am."

She knew he was teasing her by making fun of her seriousness but she didn't care. This was the note on which she wanted them to part—happy, smiling and sharing a kiss that would carry them both through to the end of this crisis.

Pulling him closer, her hands still holding his cheeks, she placed her lips on his and felt his tender response. She knew they both looked a fright and that neither cared one iota. All that mattered was this expression of love and the promise of a bright future.

Tess held on even after Michael started to ease her away. Her eyes were closed, her heart open.

"We're drawing a crowd, darlin'," Michael drawled. "I think I'd best let you jump down and be on my way. Don't want the good citizens of San Francisco complaining about misuse of fire department equipment."

Her eyes popped open. He was right! "Oh, my! We do have an audience, don't we?"

"Afraid so." Taking her hand, he helped her step past his booted feet to the edge of the platform, then carefully lowered her over the side of the pumper till she gained her footing.

That was when the applause and cheering began. Tess's cheeks flamed. Unsure of what to do, she simply curtsied as if answering a curtain call from the stage of the opera.

Atop the engine Michael removed his hat and took his own bow, much to the added delight of passersby, before calling to the team and starting to pull slowly away.

Stepping back, Tess waved gaily after him, hoping

he hadn't spied her misty eyes. She was not going to cry. Especially not in front of him. He *would* come back to her.

He must. Because if he didn't there was no way she'd be able to keep her promise and go on with her life. Whether he realized it or not, Michael Mahoney *was* her life.

The route Tess followed to wend her way through the masses of tents was, by necessity, meandering. The actual distance from the gate to their camp, however, was short. Tess was more than glad of that since her legs ached from running almost as much as her ribs and chest did from coughing.

She would have liked to make herself more presentable before returning to friends and family but if what the chief had said was true, poor Papa wouldn't care how dreadful she looked.

Ducking around a clothesline that some optimistic soul had hung between two trees to dry laundry, she burst into the clearing with a light heart and heavy limbs. Weariness threatened to overcome her at any moment.

Annie was the first to give an ecstatic shriek and alert everyone. In seconds Tess was surrounded by the other women and the two older children, all hugging her, babbling and shouting questions that were so overlapped none were clear.

"Wait. Please," Tess said, holding up her hands. "I'll tell you everything soon." She scanned the campsite. "But first I need to see Papa. Is he here?"

"Sleeping," Mary said. "Rose got a powder from one of the nurses and we put it in his coffee. He's finally resting. He was in a sorry state. Near hysterical, he was. Such a pity."

"I know. I heard," Tess replied. "They told me it was all because of me. I must see him."

Edging past the children and giving them each a pat on the head, she was relieved that neither they nor the adults insisted on following her.

Shadows inside the shelter were made deeper by the layer of soot that had accumulated on the outside. She paused. The still form of Gerald Clark lay on a pallet in the midst of what few household goods they had managed to gather.

Tess's hand went to her throat. Her jaw dropped open. She stared and whispered prayerfully, "Thank You, Jesus."

It made sense to want to weep for joy when she and her father were finally reunited. What she had not expected was to be so shocked by his appearance. Papa had always seemed invincible. Strong. Competent. Now, lying there with his back to her he looked frail, his gray hair mussed and his clothing rumpled and grimy.

She approached him slowly, quietly, giving thanks that his breathing was even and his rest apparently untroubled.

Pausing behind him and looking down, she spied a second surprise. There, cradled in the sanctuary provided by the curve of her father's sleeping form, lay the darling orphan child she had rescued. The baby's fingers were curled around Papa's hand and she, too, was fast asleep.

Unembarrassed and astonished, Tess just stood there and gazed at the unexpected sight. After everything that had happened to them and to the whole city she knew she was being given a special gift. Seeing Papa—her papa—showing tenderness to a child that wasn't even his own was more than unforeseen. It was unbelievable.

Rare blessings like this one might be occurring all over the city, she realized. Even terrible catastrophes could result in changes for the good.

The babe stirred. Tess saw her father gently stroke its curly, blond hair and heard him whisper, "Hush."

Rather than startle him by announcing her presence and perhaps frighten the little child as well, Tess quietly fell to her knees beside the pallet, rested her hand on his shirtsleeve and merely said, "Papa."

Gerald sat bolt upright, jaw gaping, and clamped her in an embrace that was so tight it hurt. "Tess! I thought…"

"I know," she said, patting his back. "I got lost in the smoke. I would probably have died if Michael hadn't come after me."

"I didn't see where you went," Gerald managed to say before breaking down. "I looked away for a minute and when I turned around you were just *gone*."

"Michael saw me, praise the Lord, and his chief let him follow. I went up the hill to save the horses."

"*Horses?* You risked your life for animals?"

"I know it was foolish," she admitted. "But all I could think about was doing something—anything. It seemed as if everybody was failing no matter how hard they fought." She eased herself away from him to watch his face when she said, "The fire took the house. Everything is gone. Ashes."

Gerald was adamant. "Who cares? It's just a house. And the funds Phineas took aren't important either. I never should have driven you up there where you could get hurt."

"It's okay," Tess said soothingly. "I'm here now. There's lots of help coming in on the ferries and the army has been mobilized, too. This terrible peril can't last forever."

Even as she said the words, Tess wondered if she was right. Logic said she was. The experiences of the past couple of days, however, demonstrated that this trial would not end quickly or without even more loss of life.

Picturing Michael, she once again said a silent prayer for his deliverance. She wanted to trust God. Wanted to rest in the promises of scripture. Really, she did.

Then in a flash she remembered the collapse of building after building, the cries of the injured, the relentless march of the inferno, and her assurance fled like the smoke that was covering the city and its shores.

Gerald Clark lifted the dozing babe and started to hand her to Tess before he took note of her sooty clothing.

He stopped abruptly and smiled. "Look at you. I suspect I'd better take charge of this little one for a while longer." Struggling stiffly to his feet, he led the way out of the shelter. "I want you to tell me everything, even the bad parts, and I'm sure the others would like to hear all about your adventures, too. Shall we go sit with them?"

"Of course." A wide grin lit her face, too. "I am *very* glad to see you—to see everyone, Papa." Amused, she eyed the babe he was cradling. "I must admit, you are not the same man I thought you were."

"No one is the same after this," her father said, joining the others and handing the babe to Rose. "Now, sit down and tell us your story."

Just then the ground shook again and all over the park people froze in midmotion, waiting and hoping the tremors would stop rather than worsen.

How many earthquakes did this make since the big one? Tess wondered. She doubted anyone was still trying to keep track of the number of aftershocks. Truth to tell, she was beyond caring. There was no sensible course but to face one day at a time.

There was one thing she did intend to count, however. The hours and days until she and Michael Mahoney were together again.

Chapter Twenty

The next few days passed so quickly Tess was amazed. By Saturday morning, most of the fires had burned themselves out and those that were still smoldering were doused by most welcome showers that also helped clear the air.

Occasional rain complicated life in the park little. Most of the campers stayed warm and dry because the army had provided thousands of tents as well as the manpower to help erect them. Trainloads of other necessities had started arriving from as far away as New York to the east and Oregon and Washington to the north. Boats also continued to ferry supplies and workers over via ports in Oakland.

Tess had taken Rachel and David to the rail depot with her several times, ostensibly to help her tote an allotment of bread and milk. The little boy hadn't been much actual help but she knew he needed to feel useful to fend off melancholy.

She was the same way. Each hour that passed she grew more anxious to see Michael again, and if she dared let herself dwell on her emotions she got worse.

Thankfully Annie had been able to dress her hair in a way that hid the burned-off place and she'd found a nice black skirt and white blouse to wear after she'd scrubbed herself clean. The only other thing she yearned to show Michael was how well she'd recovered.

Thanks to their newly erected tent, Rose and Mary had arranged comfortable quarters for everyone, even setting aside a special private corner for her father while the women and children bunked together. The sight of the usually stuffy banker snoring peacefully atop a quilt spread on the ground was truly a wonder to behold.

Tess supposed, given the fact that Papa was the senior member of their group and was still recovering from all the smoke he'd breathed, he did deserve individual consideration. It seemed to her that the older women were fussing over him too much though. Rose in particular.

Keeping as busy as possible, Tess had sent David to one of the lakes that lay inside the park boundaries to fetch a bucket of wash water. By the time he staggered back to their tent he'd spilled most of it. Nevertheless, she greeted his efforts with praise.

"Thank you so much," she said, relieving him of the pail. "Why don't you go ask Mrs. Dugan for a cookie?"

Shaking his head and staring at the ground, he scuffed his toes through the trampled grass.

"Why not? You've earned a reward." Reaching out, she put one finger beneath his chin and tilted up his face. There were tears in his eyes. "What's wrong?"

"I want my mama to bake me cookies."

"Oh, honey." Crouching and pulling him closer, she rubbed his bony back through the fabric of his shirt to soothe him while she tried to think of a suitable distraction.

"Tell you what," Tess said brightly, keeping one arm around his shoulders and combing his thick hair off his forehead with the fingers of her other hand. "Why don't you and I both go back for more water? Then we can carry twice as much."

David sniffled and wiped his nose on his sleeve. "Okay."

Comforting words failed her so she merely acted the part of the boy's boon companion. His sister, Rachel, being older, understood that their parents were missing and probably deceased. But poor little David was still hoping, still looking up expectantly at every passing lady as if one of them might turn out to be his mother.

If Tess had known what the woman looked like she would gladly have continued to search the thousand-plus acres of the park long after the children had grown too weary to go on. All Rachel thought she remembered was that her mother had been wearing a light blue dress right before the earthquake had leveled their home. Considering the number of refugees packed into the sea of tents and still wandering the streets, finding one particular woman in a blue dress was like looking for a needle in a haystack. And that was assuming the woman was still wearing the same clothing.

Message boards had sprung up in the most unlikely places. Unfortunately, recent downpours had destroyed many of the scrawled messages soon after they'd been posted and there was a shortage of paper and pencil with which to communicate further.

Walking beside her, David tentatively put his small hand in Tess's. She was touched. He might not understand how deeply she grieved for him but he was apparently sensing her concern, her empathy.

Only seconds had stood between her and death. She knew that now. If Michael had not come after her, she would have died just as so many others had. Although she was grateful for life, she also felt guilty for having survived when so many other worthy souls had been lost.

Beside her, the boy tensed and tugged on her hand.

"What is it, honey?"

He pointed down a row of tents. "Is that my mama?"

Tess bent next to him to follow his line of sight so she'd be sure she was looking in the right place. "I don't know. Do you think it may be?"

Shoulders slumping with dejection, he finally shook his head and said, "No. That lady's too old. My mama's prettier, too."

Tess was about to ask if he wanted to go take a closer look just in case, when she spotted something she had certainly not expected. The bowler, the cane, the prim way of almost strutting when he walked. It was him. There was no mistake. It was Phineas Edgerton!

Eyes wide, she cast around for landmarks, finding few. She and David were walking along the main concourse but where exactly were they? If she left there to go back to get help she might never be able to locate this place again. Not only that, Phineas might decide to flee while she was gone.

Crouching, she took the boy by the shoulders, held him still to look him in the eyes and spoke seriously. "I have a very special job for you, David. Do you think you can do it?"

"Uh-huh."

"Okay. Give me your bucket to hold. I want you to run back to our tent and fetch my papa as fast as you can. You know who I mean?"

Because the child appeared apprehensive, Tess added, "He's really a nice man but he's been kind of sick so he sometimes sounds cross. He'll be very happy when you tell him what I want."

She paused, making sure the child was still paying close attention, then continued, "Tell him I found the man who stole the money. And tell him to bring a gun with him when he comes to meet me. I'm going to wait right here so we don't get confused and look in the wrong place. Do you understand all that?"

"Uh-huh."

"Okay. Go. Hurry. Run."

Watching the spry little boy race back the way they'd come, Tess was torn. She wanted to stomp up to Phineas, slap his smug face and tell him exactly what she thought of him. A few days ago she might have done exactly that, even though she'd known better. Now, however, she was going to force herself to wait. Running headlong into danger had almost gotten her killed. She owed it to Michael—and to herself—to listen to her brain, not her heart, for a change.

Mopping up after a blaze was one of the hardest parts of firefighting. It was not only tedious, it was boring. There was no excitement, just smoldering ashes, the stench of burned wood and the flotsam that was all that remained of people's hopes and dreams.

Michael hadn't seen Tess or his mother or any of the others in longer than he liked. Soon that separation would be over. He wasn't particularly keen on facing Tess's father again until he'd had a chance to speak privately with her but he wanted to see her so badly he'd have faced a cage full of hungry lions to do so.

That thought made him smile. Gerald Clark did roar like a lion at times, although there was a good possibility that the banker was little more than a pussycat once he dropped all the bluster. Time would tell.

Picturing Tess, his lovely Tess, brought a grin to Michael's face. He needed sleep. And a shave. And above all a bath. He knew he should at least try to make himself more presentable before he called on her, even in the park. By now, she would have had plenty of chances to spruce up and he felt he needed to do the same in order to show his respect.

The army had set up a facility in which all the men could refresh themselves, both citizen volunteers and those who had been laboring in an official capacity like him. If he hadn't been near the Presidio when he was finally released from duty he might have thrown good manners aside and hurried to the park just as he was. However, given the ideal circumstances, he decided to tarry just long enough to bathe, shave and try to find a decent, clean change of clothes.

Then he would answer the calling of his heart and rejoin Tess. He didn't care how weary he was or how much his whole being insisted he must have rest. There would be no sleep for him until he had found Tess. Until he knew she was all right and showed her that he was fine, too.

Michael began to smile again as he visualized their glad reunion. If she missed him half as much as he missed her, there was going to be a lot more opportunity for the groups of survivors to ogle them and cheer.

Tess was pacing, off to one side of the walkway, while keeping an eagle eye on the last place she'd seen Phineas. If it looked as if he was going to escape before Papa got there she'd have to do something. But what? She didn't dare accost the weasel of a man, regardless of how appealing that move sounded. She was not only unarmed, she'd promised David that she'd wait right there for him.

Standing on tiptoe and straining to peer into the distance, she kept watching for some sign that her father was on his way. There was plenty of activity all around her, in and out of the park, but no sign of Papa.

Tess turned back. She could see Phineas doing something. Was he moving away or merely gesturing to someone? It was impossible to tell anything from this great a distance.

"Heavenly Father, help," she prayed in a whisper. Surely, God had not brought her onto this particular path at this exact moment to show her the evil person she sought, then snatch him away again?

She fisted her hands, barely noticing the slight soreness left on her palms after having felt her way along the ground during the fire at the estate.

Her heart leaped at the vivid memory. She'd been ready to give up. Resigned to her fate. And then Michael had arrived and had saved her.

Michael. That was who she needed this time, too, she reasoned. He could make short work of Phineas and see that he didn't get away with anything else. Reflecting on the past, Tess wished she'd let the two men duke it out when they'd had their confrontation in front of the pavilion. Then perhaps Phineas wouldn't have taken his ire out on her father.

That notion brought her up short. Was *that* what this was all about? Instead of being a simple robbery, could Edgerton's actions have been more of a prideful vendetta against her family? It was possible, even probable, given the way her father had tried to engineer their courtship and she had refused to even consider it.

Staring into the distance, deep in reminiscences, Tess almost missed seeing Phineas mount a horse and prepare to depart.

The instant she came to her senses and realized what she was seeing, her heart began to pound. The option of easily confronting him had just been removed. Neither she nor Papa would be able to catch a running horse and they had none of their own to ride in pursuit. Not yet. He had sent word for his cohorts to keep an eye out for the horses she'd released, especially her mare, but so far there had been no word on their whereabouts.

Freezing in place, feeling as if her feet were rooted to the ground more solidly than the tree under which she stood, Tess saw a change in the rider's position. Not only was he reining his mount around, he looked as if he was about to charge in her direction!

"Papa, where are you?" she moaned, quickly checking the course to their camp. She didn't see any sign of either her father or the boy.

What she did see, however, was Phineas cantering toward her, riding casually as if he hadn't a care in the world.

The closer he drew, the angrier she became. He was going to pass right by her as though she didn't even exist.

Tess steeled herself. No, he wasn't. Fate had brought him into her sphere of influence and she intended to act.

Raising her arms and waving them with the express intention of frightening his horse, she stepped into his path and managed to scream, "Stop, thief!" once before breaking into the uncontrollable, racking cough that still plagued her.

Chapter Twenty-One

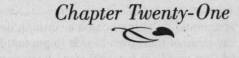

Striding purposefully into Golden Gate Park, his energy amazingly restored by a bath and the thought of seeing Tess again, Michael made straight for the camping area she had been occupying. Everything looked different since the addition of real tents and he prayed that she and the others hadn't decided to move to another location. If that were the case, there was no telling how long it might take to find them.

He rounded a corner. Something lightweight and short crashed into his knee, nearly knocking him over. He made a grab and came up with a handful of shirt and collar. Inside the shirt was a wriggling, dark-haired little boy.

When Michael recognized him as the one he and Tess had rescued, he smiled. "Hello, there. Take it easy, okay? Don't be runnin' around like that."

The child twisted to get away. "Let me go."

"I will, I will. Settle down. I'm not going to hurt you. Your name is David, right?"

Still the boy thrashed, adding swift though thankfully wildly inaccurate kicks to his efforts. "Let go!"

"All right, all right." Shaking his head, Michael loosened his grip and watched the frantic child speed straight for a large tent that now occupied the space where Tess and Annie had first camped.

As far as Michael was concerned, bumping into that particular boy had been the answer to his prayers. If this was where the child was staying, Tess was probably there, too.

Michael squared his shoulders, took a shaky breath and prepared himself for the blessed reunion he had feared they might never share. He was home. Moments away from seeing the only woman he had ever loved and taking her in his arms.

He got within several yards of the front flap of the tent before the boy burst out, followed by a wild-eyed version of G. B. Clark. The man was wielding one of the pistols Tess had liberated from the estate prior to its destruction by fire. The pistol's mate was stuck through Michael's belt.

Making a grab at Clark as he passed, Michael was astonished to see the barrel of the gun swing around and point right at his midsection.

He threw his hands into the air and stepped back. "Whoa! Don't shoot. It's me. What's going on?"

The look of frenzy in the older man's eyes didn't lessen but he did lower the weapon to his side. He was already gasping for air and hardly able to speak clearly enough to make himself understood.

"Run," he ordered, shoving the pistol's grip into Michael's hand. "Follow the boy."

"Why?"

All the older man had to say in addition was "Tess," for Michael to spring into action. He didn't care what the problem was. If it involved Tess, which was certainly the way things looked, nothing in the world was going to keep him from catching that fleet-footed child.

Tess wasn't convinced that Phineas's galloping horse would be able to stop before it crashed into her. Calling upon her knowledge of horses, she held her ground in the center of the path, praying she was right about equine instincts and capabilities. Not every horse had a lot of horse sense, which had always made her question how that odd saying had gained such common usage.

Standing firm, she braced herself, feet apart, preparing to dodge in the opposite direction of whatever course the horse ultimately chose.

Wild-eyed and snorting, it not only spied and heeded her, it did its best to react in a sensible, timely manner by putting on the brakes. If Tess had been asked how she would have preferred to see this encounter end, especially in view of her untenable position, she knew she could not have imagined a more perfect result.

Then, it got even better. Instead of merely sliding to a halt by squatting on its haunches and bracing itself, the horse began rearing on its hind legs and giving voice to its fears with a piercing whinny.

"Whoa!" Phineas shouted.

Tess echoed his cry. Still holding her arms aloft, she jumped up and down and yelled, "Whoa. Whoa. Easy, boy."

There must have been something soothing about her voice or perhaps her self-assurance, she concluded, because the horse gave one last leap, then stopped, snorted and came to her with its head lowered as if reporting for duty to a new master.

The poor thing was quivering. So was she. Taking hold of its bridle, she ducked, fully expecting Phineas to try to apply his quirt and begin whipping either the horse or her. Or both.

That didn't happen. Nothing else did. Puzzled, she glanced at the saddle. It was empty. Looking behind, she saw the odious little man lying flat on his back in one of the mud puddles that had been left after the rain.

He was moving his arms and legs and cursing, so he probably wasn't hurt too badly, Tess decided, stifling a grin. She refused to agree when her naughty side urged her to be glad he'd fallen. Instead, she settled for rejoicing over the fact that he had not escaped for a second time.

Suddenly, strong arms grabbed her from behind. Had Phineas had cohorts? Were they going to harm her because she'd thwarted his flight?

Tess released her hold on the horse's bridle and screeched, "No!" at the top of her voice, causing the animal to rear again and almost hit her with its flying front hooves when it came back down.

She was quickly swung out of imminent danger. Twisting and writhing, she struggled to break free. Those arms held her like iron bands, pinning her own upper arms to her side so she couldn't fight back and lifting her feet off the ground to deprive her of traction.

She kicked. Screamed. Gasped to draw breath against the tightness of the hold. Fought until she was so spent she wondered if she might swoon.

Then, out of the blue, she thought she heard her captor say, "Tess," and froze to listen.

Again it came, echoing in her ears and settling in her heart. "Tess."

She went limp, barely able to stand let alone support herself. Cradling her gently, Michael turned her to face him and accept his embrace.

Speechless, she clung to him. Nothing else mattered. Nothing else registered in her consciousness. All she could do was wrap her arms around his waist and hug him with every ounce of love and gladness she possessed.

He began kissing her hair, the top of her head, then bent to brush his lips across her cheek before pulling her close again. Time stopped. The only thing Tess could hear was the beating of their hearts in rapid unison.

She would gladly have stood there basking in Michael's presence for the rest of her life.

Then her father's voice and the sound of his deep cough stirred her senses and she remembered what she had been doing before Michael had arrived.

Keeping her arms around his waist she nevertheless looked over at the older man. He was red-faced and obviously laboring to breathe.

"I did it! I found him, Papa." She pointed to where the thief had landed. "Look. I stopped Phineas."

To her chagrin, Michael eased his hold. When she lifted her glance to him she saw anger where she had expected to find undying love. His mouth was firm. His eyes had narrowed. And there was a definite frown on his face that had not been there before.

"I didn't go looking for trouble, if that's what you're thinking," Tess explained. "David and I were on our way to fetch wash water and I happened to spot Phineas down one of the side roads."

Although Michael was definitely listening, it was evident he had not yet put aside his ire.

"What would you have had me do?" Tess asked, stepping back and fisting her hands on her hips. "I sent David to fetch Papa and a pistol. I waited out of sight." She rolled her eyes. "I didn't want to just stand there but I did. For you."

"For me?" One dark eyebrow twitched.

"Yes, for you. I didn't want you—or anyone—to have to come to my rescue again because I'd acted stupidly, so I was behaving myself."

"That'll be the day," Michael said.

Studying his expression, Tess was positive she'd seen one corner of his mouth lift slightly. His forehead was beginning to smooth out, too. And happily, there was more twinkle and less anger reflected in his eyes.

She took the chance that he was softening and let herself smile slightly as she said, "I suppose you will insist that you have just saved me again, in spite of my own considerable valor in this instance."

"I might."

Her smile grew at the sight of his lopsided effort to mirror her expression. "Okay. Have it your way. If you insist on keeping track, we'll count this as your second heroic rescue." Continuing to tease in the hopes it would lift his spirits even more, she made an exaggerated curtsy. "I thank you, kind sir."

"You're welcome." Michael offered the pistol back to Gerald after using its barrel to gesture toward Phineas. "One of us needs to see to *that*."

Tess looked, too. The wiry banker was starting to crawl out of the mud and although he wasn't moving very fast, he nonetheless would bear close watching.

"Don't shoot him, Papa," she warned, seeing the fervor in Gerald's eyes as he accepted the gun. "I didn't see any sign of the wagon he was driving so we don't know where all the money went." She laughed lightly. "And don't tell me it doesn't matter. We need to find it. If not for you, at least for the sake of the depositors."

"You're right," her father said. Although he was shaking his head at her, Tess could tell he was pleased. Perhaps all these challenging events had helped him see that she was a capable person rather than a helpless woman.

Now, if she could just convince Michael of the same thing, she figured she'd be in good shape.

"Am I forgiven yet?" Tess asked him.

"I'm thinking about it."

"Well, don't dally too long," she quipped, glancing at Phineas as her father poked him into action with the gun barrel at his back. "I do have one other suitor, you know."

Hearing that, Michael began laughing so riotously that he eventually started coughing, and at times it was hard to tell one noise from the other.

Tess stayed right with him, both in mood and by the unwanted complaints from her irritated lungs. Everybody in the city had been affected by the bad air to some degree, even those who had arrived after the fires had been quenched. Such things were to be expected, they'd been told, but that didn't make it easier to tolerate, particularly when it hampered normal activity as well as speech.

Rubbing Michael's back through his cotton shirt to soothe him, she fought her own urge to continue coughing. "Are you okay?"

"Sure," he managed. "Just got carried away."

"You shouldn't laugh at poor Phineas," Tess said,

smiling. "After all, he's probably going to spend the rest of his life in jail." The smile widened. "While you get to spend yours with me."

"Well..."

She gave him a playful punch on the shoulder and saw him break into the endearing Irish grin she had always loved seeing. Then he enfolded her in his embrace once again and Tess knew all was right with her little corner of the world.

Michael watched Gerald Clark start to march Phineas toward one of the guardhouses that had been set up to help maintain order in the refugee camp. There weren't many soldiers stationed there, nor were there a lot of police on duty inside the park. Some of their officers had been killed by falling bricks and the able-bodied remaining ones were needed far more to patrol the streets. Looting was still going on, although not nearly as much as it had been several days ago. Even the criminal element seemed cowed by the disaster, as well they should have been.

Keeping Tess close by his side as they walked, Michael and she followed her father. They could hear Phineas whining and begging for Gerald's mercy but judging by the older man's stiff stature and apparently unsympathetic attitude, his former vice president was wasting his breath.

"What do you think will really happen to Phineas? I mean, what if he gives all the money back?" Tess asked Michael.

"Why? Are you plannin' on waitin' for him to get out of prison instead of marrying me, darlin'?"

"Not on your life, mister. I already told you. You're stuck with me."

"Good. Then why worry about anybody else?"

"Because I feel sort of responsible," she said. "I was the one who rejected Phineas. I wonder if he would have stepped outside the law if that hadn't happened?"

"The best way to tell the good people from the bad is to offer an easy opportunity to do wrong and see what happens," Michael told her. "God does that all the time, especially when He gives us the choice whether or not to believe in Him."

"I suppose you're right."

"You only *suppose?*" He gave her a quick squeeze. "Don't you know that the husband is always right and the wife is duty-bound to abide by his every decision?"

"Oh? Where does it say that?"

He considered telling her he'd read it in the Bible, then thought better of it. Tess was an extraordinary woman, his mental equal without question, and no easy argument was going to influence her much. Living the rest of his life with her was going to be a true adventure, whether she continued to participate in woman suffrage or not.

Purposely changing the subject to reflect his thoughts, he asked, "So, are you planning to settle down and be a normal married woman soon or do you intend to continue dragging my mother to emancipation lectures with you till you're both impossible to live with?"

"I'm already impossible if you ask Papa," Tess quipped. "Besides, I don't know how long it will be before there's even a decent place to hold our meetings. According to rumor, the pavilion burned down."

"Aye. It did."

"See? That gives you a reprieve, at least until some of San Francisco is rebuilt. Papa is already planning to replace his bank right where it used to be."

"Good. I understand a lot of folks are already drawing up plans for bigger and better buildings. I just hope they follow the rules and use steel the way some of the newer places did."

"That didn't help the city hall."

Michael disagreed. "It did as far as loss of life was concerned. The masonry fell but the dome is still standing. They were able to operate a temporary hospital in the basement, too, until the fire got too close and they had to move over here."

Eyeing her father, Michael asked, "How is he doing, anyway? His cough sounds terrible."

"So does yours," Tess replied. "I think he's getting better, though, as long as he takes it easy. Running to get to me is what set him off this time."

"How does he feel about your suffragette interest?"

Laughing, Tess gave Michael a hug as they paused and watched Gerald Clark usher his prisoner into the guardhouse and close the door behind them.

"He hates the whole idea," she said. "The funniest thing is how Rose Dugan keeps trying to convince him he should change his mind and throw his support behind the movement. So does your mother, only she does it from a distance."

Michael arched an eyebrow. "Are you saying what I think you're saying? Has Rose set her cap for him?"

"Sure looks like it to me. Time will tell. They're both lonely and homeless so that puts them on a more equal plane than ever before." She giggled behind her fingertips. "You should see them together. It's really sweet."

"*Sweet* will be when you and I are wed," Michael reminded her. "I have no idea where we'll live or how I'll support you and my mother both, but I'll manage somehow."

"You'd better," Tess gibed. "Not only am I stubborn, I can be very impatient."

"Are there any more of your sterling qualities you think I should know about?"

"If there were, I doubt I'd tell you," Tess said. She cuddled closer and Michael wrapped her in his embrace.

"Are you ready to give another laudable performance for the spectators?" he asked, speaking more quietly and using one hand to cradle her cheek and tilt her face up.

"I thought you'd never ask," Tess said.

As Michael began to kiss her he was so happy, so sure that theirs was the right match he could barely keep from shouting for joy. Tess Clark was going to become his wife. The details of their life together would fall into place later, perhaps after the city was back on its feet. Whatever trials lay ahead he knew they could face and conquer them as long as they had each other.

He sensed Tess's willingness and deepened their kiss. Knowing that she was eager in spite of the fact that her father might open the guardhouse door and accost them at any moment gave Michael intense reassurance.

Truthfully he was glad his future bride was as hard-headed as she was or she might have listened to her father and married the wrong man just to please her family. Now, that would never happen.

Tess was his.

And he was most definitely all hers.

Epilogue

Tess smiled wistfully as she stood next to the small paddock behind her modest new San Francisco home and watched her mare pace. The horse was clearly approaching the time when she would foal.

One of Tess's hands rested on the top rail of the fence, the other on her own expanded waistline. She briefly closed her eyes and tilted her face up. It felt wonderful to bask in the warmth of the early June sun after so many prior days of fog.

The mare snorted and stamped her feet, restless and demanding attention. Tess put out her hand to stroke the horse's velvety nose. She knew exactly how the poor thing felt, at least she thought she did.

Giving birth was going to be a new experience for them both and one that she, at least, was looking forward to, particularly since her experience helping care for the three darling orphans they'd rescued after the quake. Thankfully all of them had been adopted by their distant relatives just as she'd hoped, and Rachel had even written a few times to tell Tess how happy she and David were with their new family.

Tess sensed rather than heard her husband's approach, looked over her shoulder and smiled. The moment Michael put his arms around her she leaned back, sighed with contentment and gladly let him help support her.

"How are you feeling today?" he asked tenderly.

Tess smiled. "Wonderful, if you like fat women."

"I love this one," he said, kissing her hair.

"I think the mare is close to foaling."

"Are you two having a race?"

Laughing softly, Tess said, "Uh-huh. But I'm not sure who's going to win."

"That's partly why I came home early. The chief was more than happy to switch a few schedules when I explained why I needed a little time off."

He began to massage her shoulders the way he often had lately and she felt the tension easing.

"Did you tell him you were afraid I couldn't handle things by myself? Your mother's right there in the house, you know. I could always call her if I needed help."

"Aye, but you probably wouldn't," Michael said knowingly. "And the last thing we need is to have you trying to pull a foal when you should be resting."

"I know. I just thought my being here would help the mare feel better. She and I have a lot in common."

"I'm far more worried about you than I am about her," Michael said.

Turning, Tess wrapped her arms around her husband's waist as best she could and laid her cheek on his chest. "As your mother would say, 'Don't you be worryin' now. The good Lord's watchin' over us.'"

"I know. I just love you so much I can't help it."

"Good. See that you stay that way." Her tone remained light but her thoughts had sobered. "And thank you again for agreeing to live up here. I know it wasn't easy for you to accept a loan from Papa." She touched the badge pinned to his coat. "I'm so proud that you got your promotion. You deserved it. And now we'll be able to pay him back much faster, too."

Michael nodded agreement. "If he'd insisted we build a mansion the likes of the one where you grew up, I don't think I could have ever gotten used to it. This size house is much more to my liking." He chuckled. "I suspect I'd like it even better if it wasn't built right next door to your father's new place."

"I know what you mean. I was worried about that to begin with, too, but Rose has been keeping him so well occupied he has little time to bother us."

Lifting her face, Tess displayed a satisfied grin and arched her brows, pausing until she was sure Michael had noticed. "I told you they would eventually become a couple. Papa got to know Rose very well when we were all camping in the park. By the time the new houses were finished, there was no way he could have denied that they belonged together, even if he'd wanted to. And she makes a wonderful stepmother. Now Annie and I really *are* sisters."

"I know, I know. That's one more time when you were right. I've already lost count. It sure surprised me when your father and Rose were finally wed, though, especially since she's still so involved with giving women the vote."

"So is Papa. Now. At least in a monetary way. I can't wait till Rose convinces him to march in the streets carrying an emancipation sign!"

"Neither can I." A chuckle rose from deep in Michael's chest. "No doubt Gerald Clark's society friends are in a terrible tizzy over his marriage. And our wedding, too, although we've given everybody a year longer to get used to you being Mrs. Mahoney."

"It still takes me by surprise occasionally," Tess confessed. "Being your wife is such a blessing it's hard for me to believe all my dreams have come true."

Her vision misted with contentment and joy as she caressed her husband's cheek, smiled and asked, "Are you going to kiss me right now, right here, Michael Mahoney, or do you want to go stand in the middle of Golden Gate Park again so we can draw a crowd?"

"Any place is fine with me, darlin'," he drawled, smiling and bending to begin to answer her request.

Tess thoroughly agreed. She closed her eyes. Right there, right now, she had never been happier.

Just then their unborn baby gave her a swift kick in the ribs, bringing a vivid reminder of the way life was finding new meaning since the devastation.

A bright promise awaited her family, her friends and the rebuilt city of San Francisco. She could hardly wait to see the future begin to unfold.

* * * * *

A popular and highly acclaimed author in the Christian market, **Sara Mitchell** aims to depict the struggle between the challenges of everyday life and the values to which our faith would have us aspire. She is the author of contemporary romance, historical suspense and historical novels, and her work has been published by many inspirational book publishers.

Having lived in diverse locations from Georgia to California to Great Britain, Sara uses her extensive travel experience to help her create authentic settings for her books. A lifelong music lover, Sara has also written several musical dramas and has long been active in the music miniseries of the churches wherever she and her husband, a retired career air force officer, have lived. The parents of two daughters, Sara and her husband now live in Virginia.

Books by Sara Mitchell

Love Inspired Historical

Legacy of Secrets
The Widow's Secret
Mistletoe Courtship
A Most Unusual Match

Love Inspired

Night Music
Shelter of His Arms

Visit the Author Profile page
at Harlequin.com for more titles.

A MOST UNUSUAL MATCH

Sara Mitchell

Do not say, "I'll pay you back for this wrong!"
Wait for the Lord, and he will avenge you.
—*Proverbs* 20:22, NIV

He hath sent me to heal the brokenhearted, to preach
deliverance to the captives, and recovering of sight to
the blind, to set at liberty them that are bruised.
—*Luke* 4:18, KJV

To Melissa Endlich, my dear editor, for her consummate editorial skill, and her faith in me. Thanks for everything.

Acknowledgments

Profound thanks to the following, all of whom were gracious with their time and generous with their information. Any historical errors are *entirely* the author's doing.

Once again to the staff members in the US Secret Service Office of Government and Public Affairs, and the staff of the US Secret Service Archives, for their courtesy and invaluable assistance.

Saratoga Springs, New York

Mary Ann Fitzgerald, City Historian, Saratoga Springs

Allan Carter, Historian, Saratoga Racing Museum

...and all the other wonderful individuals up in Saratoga Springs I spoke to a time or two, or exchanged emails with.

Jekyl Island

Gretchen Greminger, Curator, Jekyl Island— spelled "Jekyll" from the twentieth century onward! (So nobody would be confused...)

Clint and the rest of the staff at the Jekyll Island Museum.

Gretchen, many, many thanks for helping me perfect the plot and make it work! You're a perfect example of a peach of a Georgia gal!

God's blessings to one and all.

Chapter One

Theodora Langston watched Edgar Fane stroll across the lobby of the Grand Union Hotel. A half smile lurked at the corners of his mouth, while a swelling crowd—mostly ladies—clustered about him. His gray fedora tipped forward jauntily and one pale hand lightly swung a brass-handled walking stick, tapping the marble foyer with each step. Mr. Fane epitomized a gentleman out to enjoy his season at Saratoga Springs. He had the right, seeing he was a son of one of the richest men in the country.

Thea watched him, and her heart burned with hatred.

As he passed the marbled pillar where she stood, the indifferent gaze passed over her as though Thea were part of the pillar. Edgar Fane, she had discovered over the past ten days, preferred his female admirers long and willowy and adoring, or dainty and luscious and adoring. She could feign adoration, but since her unextraordinary face and physique failed to capture the scoundrel's interest, Thea would have to try a different strategy. She had spent the last of her deceased grandmother's trust fund on this crusade, and would not abandon her quest until Edgar Fane was behind bars, where he belonged.

Her troubled glance fell upon Grandmother's ruby ring, snug on Thea's engagement finger. She was accustomed to ink from a printing press, not fancy rings. Still, the facade of wealth was necessary to gain access to the higher echelons of Saratoga Springs society. Justice did not come cheaply. The ring might be real, all the lavish gowns she'd purchased from Bloomingdale's with the rest of the trust money might be the latest fashion, but she was living a lie.

She could hear her grandfather's voice as though she were standing in their library on that rainy afternoon a month earlier. *Thea, you mustn't think such things about him.* He had sounded so gentle. Gentle, and defeated. *Mr. Fane proclaimed his innocence with equal vehemence. No proof of malfeasance on his part has surfaced.*

You are innocent, but you're the one they arrested, you're the one those awful Secret Service operatives treated like a common criminal!

I was the one who tried to deposit counterfeit funds.

But it was Edgar Fane who had paid Charles Langston with those bogus funds.

The burning hatred inside Thea seethed, cauterizing her heart. No use to pray for forgiveness, or ask for divine help. Her grandfather could pray all he wanted to, but Thea doubted God would oblige Charles Langston with an answer. Because of Edgar Fane, her grandfather's faith had dimmed to the stub of a barely flickering candle. As for Thea, life had finally forced her to swallow an unpalatable truth: She could not trust anyone—God or man—to see justice served. If she wanted Edgar Fane to be punished for his crimes, she'd have to do it herself.

For all her life she'd played a part—the good child, the grateful girl, the admirable woman—while inside, insecurity and anxiety clawed with razor-stropped spikes. Now she was about to embark on her most ambitious role. She did not enjoy the risk and the public nature of the charade, but she was confident of her success.

The crowded hotel parlor seemed to lurch, and Thea braced herself against the grooved pillar until the sensation dissipated. She never should have used her mother's maiden name, a constant reminder that no matter whether her present life be truth or lie, she remained the abandoned daughter of a wayward youngest son and a vaudeville singer from the Bowery. No surprise that for most of her childhood she struggled with dizzy spells.

As for faith, life had finally forced Thea to swallow an unpalatable truth: something was lacking in her, something missing from birth that made her unlovable to everyone but her grandfather.

Despite Charles Langston's attempts to give her the life of a privileged young lady, perhaps she was Hetty Pickford's daughter after all.

The high-pitched whinny of an alarmed horse cut through the noisy road traffic on the Saratoga Springs Broadway. Moments earlier Devlin Stone had emerged from the Indian encampment arcade, where he'd spent the past two hours shadowing a suspect. Scarborough disappeared into one of the sidewalk eateries, and Devlin let him go, instead searching the street until he spotted a foam-flecked bay hitched to a surrey in front of the Columbian Hotel. Hooves clattered on the cobblestones by the curb and the horse's head strained against the checkrein. The driver, stupid man, yanked on the reins while shouting an unending barrage of abuse.

Anger flaring, Dev approached just as the terrified horse reared in the traces and plunged forward straight toward a pair of young boys on bicycles. Dev leaped in front of them. "Move!" he ordered, whipping off his jacket.

The two boys scrambled for safety but the horse swung his head around, ears flat and teeth bared. Devlin grabbed the driving reins just behind the bit, then flung his jacket over the blinkers to completely blind the horse.

"Easy, boy…calm down, you're all right. Nobody's going to hurt you now."

"Hey! Whadaya think you're doing?" the driver yelled, sawing on the reins in a vain attempt to regain control.

With his free hand Dev reached for his pocketknife. "Probably saving this animal's life, and unfortunately yours," he responded in the same soothing tone as he lifted the knife, slicing both reins twelve inches from the bit. "There you are, fella. No more pressure on your mouth. That's it…just relax."

He dropped the knife back in his trouser pocket, unlatched the checkrein. The driver's complexion had gone from the boiling flush of rage to dirty-sheet gray. Good. Devlin held his palm in front of the horse's nostrils, waiting until a hot fluttering breath gently blew over his fingers before he slowly removed his jacket. A single quiver rolled through the flanks, but the horse stood still, watching Devlin.

"Good boy. You're all right." He applied light forward pressure and the horse docilely allowed Dev to lead him across Broadway onto a calm side street.

Devlin turned to the driver. "Get out of the buggy."

"I'm not paying for the harness you ruined," the man complained, climbing stiffly down from the surrey.

"How about you shut up and hand me the rest of the reins?" Before Devlin pummeled the bounder himself.

The lash of temper did the trick, for without further argument the man complied. In seconds Dev formed a makeshift hackamore, and secured the end to a hitching post.

"You know horses well enough," the driver observed grudgingly. "Guess I owe you. Don't know what spooked the stupid animal."

"Try having a piece of metal crammed in your mouth, then have someone yank on it until it bleeds." Devlin eyed the other man with disfavor.

"Yeah...well, I don't usually do my own driving." He glanced at the now-quiet horse, a flicker of admiration warring with the sneer. "Anytime you want a job as coachman, look me up." He reached into his vest pocket and tugged out an ivory calling card.

"No, thanks. I'd have to be around you." Devlin rummaged for a fifty-cent piece, flicked it so the coin fell with a soft thud onto the packed dirt inches from the man's shiny shoes. "Enjoy a cup of coffee at the Congress Spring Pavilion. I'll return this animal. Where'd you rent him? The livery on Henry Street? By the way, you are right about one thing." He waited a moment before continuing, "I strongly suggest you do hire a driver. Because if I catch you mistreating a horse again, rest assured you'll feel a lot worse than the animal."

The driver bristled anew. Then, jaw muscles working, with his heel he ground the coin into the dirt, swiveled and stalked off down the street.

An hour later, mostly recovered, Devlin stood on the piazza of the Grand Union Hotel, surrounded by a herd of chattering humanity instead of a spooked horse in a herd of Broadway traffic. He wished, not for the first time, that he was back in Virginia, surrounded by his own horses, none of which had ever known the cruelty that poor livery hack endured. The pasture would be lush and green, and if he looked up he would see the ancient Blue Ridge Mountains against a summer sky instead of rows of massive white marble columns supporting a structure billed as the largest hotel in the world.

Over the aroma of ladies' French perfume and men's sweat he caught a whiff of popcorn. Maneuvering his way between a cluster of ladies debating on whether to visit Tiffany's before or after a promenade along Broadway, Devlin shouldered his way over to the vendor to buy a bag of popcorn.

Bright summer sunshine poured over Saratoga, onto the twenty-plus thousand tourists enjoying a season at the place touted as "America's Resort." An ironic smile hovered at the corners of Devlin's mouth. How many of the guests would scramble for the first train leaving the depot if they knew an operative for the U.S. Secret Service prowled among them?

Perhaps he should have flashed his badge at that lout earlier—except Dev was here undercover, the badge and credentials safely hidden in his own hotel room.

Of course few operatives—if any—could spend an entire season playing the part of a wealthy gentleman of leisure. In the first place, Congress would never approve the funds. To Devlin's way of thinking, such short-sightedness plagued a lot of government officials. He'd only been with the Service for two years, and at the moment did not feel adequate to match wits with the Hotel Hustler.

In only three years, the invisible thief had cost un-suspecting dupes somewhere in the neighborhood of fifty million dollars—and nobody could figure out how he managed it.

The previous autumn, Service hopes had soared when a call came in from the chief of the New York City office; they'd arrested a man at the bank where he tried to pass bills matching the Hustler's work. Infuri-atingly, the man denied all knowledge of counterfeit-ing, claiming the false bills had come from Edgar Fane. Corroborating evidence could not be found either to support his claims or prove his guilt, and they'd been forced to release Charles Langston. Edgar Fane hadn't even been arrested, much less charged. Another dead end in this impenetrable maze.

Counterfeiters were a despicable bunch. Pervasive as flies, they swarmed the country, mostly in cities, under-mining the national currency. A few of them had com-mitted murder. Over the last decade, for the most part the Service had done a crackerjack job closing down the worst of the gangs.

But the Hotel Hustler had them stumped.

Devlin accepted that pride as well as a dose of cuss-edness had concocted this present undercover infil-tration scheme. Chief Hazen reluctantly sanctioned it, telling Devlin he certainly wouldn't look a gift horse in the mouth.

He'd laughed when he said it.

Dev shook his head and resumed watching the front of the Grand Union Hotel. Six weeks earlier, a reliable snitch had informed another operative that the Hustler would be at Saratoga, but as always no other information, such as a description, had surfaced. Three guests, one of them Edgar Fane, warranted surveillance, based upon these scraps of evidence tirelessly gleaned over the past twenty months.

Some ten minutes later patience was rewarded. Dev watched the impeccably clad Edgar Fane emerge onto the piazza, surrounded by his throng of hangers-on. Dev had been shadowing the cultured, congenial fellow for three days, and the man did not fit the usual profile of a criminal. Privileged son of the owner of exclusive emporiums all over the country, Fane scattered money and bonhomie wherever he traveled. The money thus far was genuine. Dev wasn't convinced about the rest. Edgar Fane reminded him of a Thoroughbred he and his uncle once reluctantly agreed to train for the owner. Flashy specimen of horseflesh, conformation of champions—but not an animal to turn your back on.

Edgar Fane paused, lifted his hand. Several women approached, and Devlin watched in some amusement as they jockeyed for position—the buxom redhead boldly thrust her arm through Fane's, while a regal blonde offered a narrow white hand adorned with several rings, which Fane adroitly kissed even as his other hand patted the redhead's arm. The trio merged into the crowd, easy enough to follow since the redhead sported a gigantic hat the size of a saddle.

Devlin shouldered away from the column, then paused, his gaze returning to the third woman, the one Fane had barely seemed to notice as the other two women led him away. She stood very still, and in this chattering, gesticulating, endlessly restless crowd that stillness piqued Dev's interest. Without fuss, he tucked his hands in the waistband of his trousers and sauntered down the steps, pretending to scan the crowd while he memorized the young woman.

Unremarkable height and build in comparison to the luscious redhead and slender blonde. Like most society women, she styled her mass of honey-colored hair in the current Gibson girl fashion. Creamy magnolia complexion and a soft mouth, large dark brown eyes gazing after Edgar Fane with an expression of—Devlin's eyebrows shot up. Was that anger, or fear?

He wasn't to know, because the woman abruptly turned in a graceful swirl of skirts and hurried off in the opposite direction.

Chapter Two

Thinking fast was one of the Service's unwritten requirements: intrigued, Dev followed the spurned woman instead of shadowing Fane, keeping at least a dozen people between them. When a potential masher approached her, his manner a trifle too familiar, Devlin's fingers twitched with the need to intervene.

Wasn't necessary. The young woman laughed, said something; the vanquished masher tipped his hat and moved away. So. The lady knew how to dismiss louts without causing offense.

Perhaps she'd had a lot of practice.

For several more moments Devlin followed her, automatically memorizing traits, from the slight tilt of her head to the firm assurance in her steps, the swanlike neck and softly rounded shoulders. A fine figure of a woman, perhaps. But he needed to see that face again. Moving quickly, he wound his way along the teeming walkway until he was some twenty feet ahead of the woman. He bought a frankfurter from a sweating vendor, absently munching while he chewed over his response to this particular female.

With an internal jolt he realized his acute interest bordered on personal rather than professional. He needed to see her face not only to jot down an accurate description in his nightly notes, but to discover if that blaze of emotion in her eyes had been a trick of the sunlight, rather than a revelation of her character. In his experience, women didn't always feel like they acted, or acted like they felt.

Devlin might begrudge the instant attraction this particular female had tweaked to life, but he'd be foolish to discount its power. Last time he succumbed, his heart was kicked, stomped and tromped. The Blue Ridge Mountains would be flat as the Plains out west before he'd trust his heart to another woman. Yet without any effort on her part—she didn't know he existed, after all—this one touched a crusted-over piece of it. Annoyed with himself, Dev moved closer, assessing her like an operative instead of a calf-eyed rube.

She'd make a useful shover, flirting her way through the stores that fronted Grand Union Hotel, handing over bogus bills to cashiers too dazzled to notice they'd just been bamboozled. After stealing thousands of dollars in purchases, she and the cur who supplied the counterfeit goods would turn around and sell everything the deceitful little shover had bought. The game had been played with various permutations throughout the country.

Not this time, Devlin muttered beneath his breath, despising those who preyed upon the innocent, the weak, the gullible. He bit off a tasty chunk of hot frankfurter.

Less than three paces away, a matronly woman draped in deep pink lace lifted her arm and waved to someone. "Miss Pickford?" she called out. "Theodora? Is that you?"

Amazingly, the woman Dev was following started, then offered a smile only someone watching her closely—such as himself—would recognize as strained. For a moment she wavered. Then she blinked and the smile warmed into cordiality. "Mrs. Van Eyck. I'm sorry, I didn't see you. The crowds…"

Dev took another bite, and eavesdropped without a qualm.

"How lovely you look today, dear," Mrs. Van Eyck gushed. "Have you heard from your darling fiancé this week? Do tell me, you know how much I adore those dashing British aristocrats. You must join me—I was just on my way to the springs for a healthful dose of the waters. I must say, the practice of charging for a drink these days is depressingly crass…. Where is your chaperone, Theodora? Mrs….oh, dear, I can't seem to recall her name."

"Mrs. Chudd. She doesn't care for crowds, or heat, so I've left her reading a book in one of the hotel's parlors."

So Miss Theodora Pickford conveniently ditched her chaperone, and had already snagged herself a man. One who doubtless loved her in blissful ignorance of her interest in the son of one of the richest men in the country. Like a cloud passing across the sun, disillusionment shadowed Devlin's mind. His successes with the Service might satisfy an inchoate longing to serve his country, but the scope of human greed continued to catch him off guard.

"Where is Mr. Van Eyck today?" the two-timing flirt inquired.

Well-modulated voice, Devlin noted grudgingly. Warm, with a dash of humor. She smiled with her eyes as well as her mouth, and nobody would believe her to be anything other than genuine. Nobody except an undercover Secret Service operative whose belief in humanity had just endured another drubbing.

"Oh, you know Mr. Van Eyck. Playing cards at the Casino," Mrs. Van Eyck babbled along. "Annoying, when the weather is fine, isn't it? My dear friend Esmeralda—I introduced you the other day, did I not? Her husband's second cousin is distantly related to Queen Victoria, you know. I was quite mystified to learn your fiancé was unacquainted with him. You did tell me your intended is an earl?"

"I did, but you may have forgotten that dear Neville feels tremendous responsibility for all his family properties. They're scattered all over the British Isles, not to mention a villa in Italy, so he's rarely in London."

Why, the minx was lying! The slightly elevated voice, restless movement of her hands, dilated pupils—subtle signs but clear indications all the same.

More likely her absent fiancé was a butcher from Cleveland, or some gout-riddled banker twice her age. She might even be lying about having an intended at all. The particulars could be supplied with time. All that mattered for the moment was that Miss Pickford had an association with one of the suspects on Devlin's list, that she felt no qualms in wandering about without escort or chaperone and that she was a liar.

Too bad for you, darling, Dev thought. He detested liars, personally as well as professionally.

Unless the liar happened to be himself.

His conscience grumbled as it always did when he thought of the deceptions necessary in his undercover work; Dev reminded it that he had sworn an oath to defend the United States against all persons engaged in practices designed to undermine the country's economic sovereignty. This girl might be another bored society belle, but she was also clearly hiding something. And if that something was of a criminal nature, she might be in league with the Hotel Hustler himself, given the winsomeness of her charm.

Casually he stepped around Mrs. Van Eyck, placing himself within touching distance of Miss Pickford.

"Miss Pickford! Good afternoon." He doffed his straw boater and bowed, his smile deepening at her look of consternation. "What a stroke of good fortune to find you in this crush. I just arrived from London last night. Neville was overjoyed to learn my visit to Saratoga would coincide with yours. He planned to send you a telegram—did you receive it? Well, never mind, what matters is the special message for you, that he asked me to pass along in person." He leaned forward, adding in a dramatic whisper, "We should probably retire to somewhere more private. Since Mrs. Chudd is happily reading in the parlor, so much the better."

"How thrilling," Mrs. Van Eyck cooed, "to have something more…physical…than a telegram or letter bringing word from your beloved." Her eyes twinkled. "Do join me later, Miss Pickford, and share everything this handsome messenger imparts. Young couples in love liven things up. Brings back happy memories of myself and Mr. Van Eyck, three decades ago."

"I don't think…" Miss Pickford began as she fumbled to open a brightly colored Chinese fan. "I didn't receive a telegram."

"Well, it's doubtless waiting at the desk. We'll fetch it later." Devlin clasped her elbow in a display of seeming gallantry which also effectively edged Mrs. Van Eyck farther away. "Is this heat too much for you? Let me escort you over to that patch of shade under the elms."

"Yes, of course."

Beneath the flimsy lawn overblouse he could feel the tensile strength of her slender forearm. A twitch of puzzlement feathered the base of Devlin's neck. For an accomplished flirt and a liar to boot, at close quarters Miss Pickford struck him as...fresh, unspoiled, even. Untainted by the slight aura of dissipation that hovered around Saratoga. He could lose himself in those expressive dark brown eyes. Her bones were those of a finely bred Arabian instead of the massive draft horses he bred and trained at StoneHill.

Something didn't fit here.

Grimly he focused his attention back on the plump, perspiring Mrs. Van Eyck. "Forgive me for absconding with your friend. I wouldn't intrude except I'm planning to attend the races—the first is at one forty-five, I believe. Before that I'm to meet someone at Hathorn Spring, so have little time to spare. Miss Pickford? Shall we?"

Two spots of red now burned in the young lady's magnolia cheeks, but the tangled emotions swimming through her eyes jarred Devlin. He'd expected anger and possibly a show of outrage....

"I'll try to see you later, Mrs. Van Eyck," Miss Pickford promised, twisting her neck to address the older woman and in the process managing to discreetly free her arm. "Dear Neville is a dreadful tease. This past spring he sent a young fellow dressed like a medieval troubadour to my house. I was treated to a ballad—poorly sung, I'm afraid—about all of Neville's goings-on that week."

Her eyelashes fluttered and her lips curled in a smile as she moved the fan back and forth in front of her face, possibly to disguise a significant "tell": the corners of her eyes didn't crinkle, which told Devlin her smile, like Miss Pickford, was artificial.

"How droll," Mrs. Van Eyck offered after a pause.

"Yes, isn't it? Um... I'll speak with this gentleman, then how about if I meet you at the Congress Spring Pavilion? Say, in a quarter of an hour?"

Between the two of them, Mrs. Van Eyck didn't stand a chance. After a final sideways perusal of Devlin, she retreated.

"You're quite good," he began, "though might have been safer promising to meet her at—"

"I much prefer to converse with a gentleman if I know his name, especially when he claims to be acquainted with my fiancé." She stood still, fan now dangling forgotten from her wrist. One hand was planted on her hip, but the other had curled into a fist at her side.

So she wanted to prolong the game, did she? "Ah. How remiss of me. Devlin Stone, of StoneHill Farm, Virginia, at your service, Miss Pickford."

"I thought I detected a Southern drawl." For a moment she seemed to hesitate before tossing her head. A fine pair of amethyst earrings dangled in the sunlight. "Well? What is the message dear Neville requested you to deliver? You have a meeting with someone and races to attend, after all. You'd best get on with the delivery before you're late for your appointment."

"You've got me, ma'am." Devlin swept an astute appraisal over her person, noting how the pulse in her throat now fluttered faster than the second hand on his pocket watch. He wished he didn't admire her nerve as much as he did her creamy skin. "I've actually never met your dear Neville. I overheard your conversation with Mrs. Van Eyck, and couldn't resist the opportunity to meet a lovely lady."

"I doubt that very much, Mr. Stone." Humor flitted across her face—the second honest emotion she'd revealed. "Mrs. Van Eyck is devoted to her husband. She might be diverted by the dimples in your cheeks, but she would never dream of establishing a liaison with a strange man, no matter how attractive. Now if you'll excuse me, I did promise to meet her. I'll pass along your regrets."

She stepped back into a bar of sunlight while Devlin struggled to untangle the mess her wit, and her poise, had made of his mind. For the first time he noticed the scattering of faint pockmarks that marred the creamy complexion in several places. For some reason, after her magnificent charade the slight imperfections tilted his opinion in favor of charity instead of contempt.

Ruthlessly Dev squashed the emotion. "Before you leave, do you think you'll be running into Mr. Fane again soon? He's an attractive, personable fellow, isn't he? And one of the country's richest men. I wonder how your fiancé would feel, knowing of your interest in someone whose reputation with the ladies is ofttimes... less than gentlemanly?"

She gawked at him. "You know Edgar Fane?"

"I know of him. He scatters largesse wherever he goes. Perhaps that explains why he's always surrounded by a particular sort of woman."

"And what sort of man makes vile speculations about a woman he's only just met?" she whipped back. "Are you insulting, or threatening me, Mr. Stone?"

"Perhaps you should tell me, Miss Pickford?"

For a suspended moment he wondered if she planned to dig in her heels, or flee. The back of his neck itched like sunburn; he was ashamed of how he was baiting her. Yet he couldn't allow what might be the only lead in eleven months of fruitless investigation to vanish because the lead was a lovely liar struggling to hide her vulnerability.

Slowly a hint of color crept back over her cheeks. The dark eyes searched his, and Dev's own pulse quickened when her tongue darted out to moisten her lips. "Both," she whispered, and before he recovered from her unexpected honesty she vanished into the crowd.

This time, Devlin let her go.

Chapter Three

Theodora pushed her way through the crush of people strolling the Broadway. The energy that had fueled her encounter with Mr. Stone leaked away with each step until her feet barely lifted from the ground. A dozen yards from the Grand Union Hotel she stopped underneath the base of one of the elm trees shading the Broadway, needing a moment to collect herself. After several calming breaths, the spinning sensation receded; she fixed her gaze upon a fancy-goods storefront full of ladies' gloves while she thought about her reaction to the stranger.

How had this Mr. Stone known she was acting? His eyes, a mesmerizing blend of gray, slate blue and…and ice, had pierced every one of her painstakingly formulated masks. At the moment she should be prostrate with vertigo, her reaction to a bone-searing insecurity spawned early in her childhood. She kept this weakness relentlessly hidden from everyone but Mrs. Chudd, the widowed neighbor she'd hired at Grandfather's insistence to be her companion "while you work this mad scheme out of your system." Until the previous year, most of the attacks had disappeared altogether. Then Grandfather was arrested and spent a week in jail—for passing counterfeit money. The money Edgar Fane had paid him. The police and several Secret Service operatives had treated an innocent Charles Langston like a common criminal, but they hadn't even charged Edgar Fane, the lying, cheating snake.

Thea wasn't sure who she despised more, Edgar Fane or the sanctimonious Secret Service operatives with their closed minds and weak spines.

Edgar Fane was a villain. Thea had dedicated her life to proving his guilt, regardless of debilitating spells of vertigo. She owed that life to Grandfather, but would never enjoy it until she found a way to restore the twinkle in his eye and his wilted faith in God. For Thea, waiting for the Almighty to pursue vengeance was no longer an option.

Dizzy spells, however, might prove to be something of a conundrum. Certainly her first few brushes with Mr. Fane triggered the symptoms, probably because he'd ignored her. It was also turning out to be far more difficult than she imagined, projecting an attraction for a man she planned to skewer with the pitchfork of justice.

Devlin Stone claimed to know Edgar Fane. Perhaps…?

Perhaps she could jump off a cliff, as well. It might be less hazardous than pursuing Devlin Stone, who made her pulse flutter and caused a most unusual sensation in the region of her heart. Apparently Mr. Stone triggered a multitude of strange feelings, but not a single swirl of vertigo.

And he might be the only person able to help her.

Thea's hands clenched the Chinese fan. Mr. Stone's threat to expose her to her imaginary fiancé Neville could be discounted, but the threat itself would have to be dealt with. She'd learned Edgar Fane planned to leave Saratoga in three weeks. Less than a month…

Another swirl of dizziness batted her, a warning she would do well to heed.

So don't think about him, or Devlin Stone's unsubtle threats, Theodora. Think about how to persuade him to share everything he knows about Edgar Fane. Think about Charles Langston, and retribution. Think about flinging evidence at the Secret Service and humiliating them as they had humiliated her Grandfather and ruined his life.

But instead her mind reached back to the instant Mr. Stone had touched her. Strength, vitality and authority wrapped around Thea as securely as his fingers enclosed her arm. The impulse to confess everything had overwhelmed her senses, a terrifying prospect. Worse than the dreaded vertigo, she had been tempted to cling to a *stranger,* because…because unlike her reaction to Edgar Fane and despite all common sense, she had been drawn to Mr. Stone like penny nails to a powerful magnet.

There. She'd admitted the truth, to her conscience at least.

The whirling inside her head abruptly diminished.

She supposed she ought to be grateful. Regardless of Devlin Stone's too-perceptive gaze, apparently he only muddled her senses. If thoughts of him *lessened* the vertigo, she'd recite his name a hundred times a day.

Cautiously Thea straightened and headed for the hotel.

An hour later, dressed for her afternoon at the races, she left Mrs. Chudd reading a book and sipping fresh limeade. A spare woman with iron-gray hair, Mrs. Chudd was exactly the sort of chaperone Thea required: indifferent, and incurious. After confiding to her about the spells of vertigo, the woman had nodded once, then remarked that she wasn't a wet nurse but if called upon would do her duty. Today, her "Mind you use your parasol else you'll turn red as one of those Indians," constituted Mrs. Chudd's only gesture at chaperonage. At least this was Saratoga Springs, where guests discarded societal strictures like a too-tight corset.

After leaving a note of apology for the desk clerk to have delivered to Mrs. Van Eyck, Thea joined a dozen other guests in queue for one of the hotel wagons headed for the track. She felt awkward; there were those who disapproved of the entire horse-racing culture, denouncing the sport for its corruption and greed. Until she arrived at Saratoga, Thea had never paid attention one way or the other, though she remarked to someone at her dinner table how thrilling it would be to watch the powerful creatures thunder down the track at amazing speeds.

Today, however, was a hunting expedition, not a pleasure excursion. The tenor of her thoughts stirred up fresh guilt. After three weeks Thea could mostly block the insistent tug by remembering how her grandfather looked behind bars the only time she visited him in that foul hole of a cell. Voice cracking, fine tremors racking his stooped form, Charles begged her not to return. Because she saw that her presence hurt him beyond measure, Thea gave her promise.

Promises made to loved ones must be kept.

No matter how despicable her actions now, she would never break her word like her father with all his picture-postcard promises to come home, or abandon anyone at birth like her mother did Thea. Richard Langston and Hetty Pickford—what a legacy. Yet never once had her grandfather condemned their only child for the behavior of her parents.

Impatient with herself, Theodora glanced down at her blue-and-white costume, self-consciously running a finger over the perky red braid trimming the skirt and basque while she turned her mind to the afternoon ahead. A tingle of anticipation shot through her at the prospect of matching wits with Devlin Stone again.

She'd thought long and hard while she changed into her present costume. For some reason Mr. Stone had singled her out of a crowd of thousands of available, far more beautiful females. Based upon Thea's admittedly scant personal knowledge of romantic liaisons, all that was necessary to assure a gentleman's continued pursuit would be to indicate her willingness to be pursued. Very well, then. With a bit of pluck and a whole bucketful of luck, through encouraging Mr. Stone's interest in her, in turn she hoped to procure enough insight into Edgar Fane's habits to at last secure an entrée into the scoundrel's inner circle of friends. She refused to crawl home in shame and defeat.

Her tactics troubled Thea. If she ever blew the dust off her Bible and strove to establish a better communication with the Lord, she would doubtless spend many years on her knees, begging forgiveness for the sordidness of her present behavior. Even though he did not approve of her decision to pursue justice, Grandfather had understood her motives. Hopefully God would understand, as well, and help her achieve her goal. He was, after all, a God of justice. *If You help me now, perhaps I'll believe You're also a God of love.* If God helped her in this quest, perhaps she could also forgive Him for allowing her parents to abandon her, and an innocent man to be flung in jail.

But if she couldn't procure justice, and restore Charles Langston's faith, she saw no reason to waste time on her own.

As for Devlin Stone, she would ignore the prickle of attraction, maintain her distance with the laughing quips and smiling rebuffs that had thus far served her well with other flirtatious men. By the time Theodora Langst— The mental lapse stabbed her like a hatpin. For the rest of the way to the track she mentally repeated her assumed name—Theodora *Pickford,* Thea *Pickford...* Miss *Pickford*—and envisaged herself the privileged heiress whose beauty, grace and supreme self-confidence had won the love of a dashing Englishman. *Is Neville a baron, or an earl?* Inside her frilly lace gloves Thea's palms turned clammy; she gripped her lace parasol more tightly.

Her cause was just, her purpose noble, she reminded herself staunchly in a mantra repeated often these past weeks. The only person who would be hurt by her actions was the man who deserved it. Sometimes the end did justify the means.

It was ten minutes until post time when the load of passengers descended onto the velvet green lawns surrounding the racetrack. The crowd streaming into the grandstands looked to number in the thousands, not the hundred or so Thea had naively anticipated. Spotting Mr. Stone would be more difficult than she'd anticipated. Stalling, she opened her parasol and hoped she looked as though she expected her escort to appear any second. Beneath broad-trunked shade trees, jockeys fidgeted while trainers saddled the horses for the next race. Striped tents fluttered in a stray breeze, shading hundreds of race goers. Dust filmed the air. At one end of the sweeping slate-roofed grandstands she noticed a separate, open-sided structure full of odd-looking little stalls on stilts.

"What's going on over there?" she asked a passing gentleman studying a copy of the *Daily Saratogian*.

"Betting ring, ma'am. But that one's only for the gents. Ladies' betting is up on the top landing, rear of the grandstand. You a maiden filly, right? Well, you're in luck. Track was closed last year. But you can see for yourself the people have spoken, and the sport of kings is back at Saratoga. You go on up there, purchase yourself a ticket. Rensselaer looks good in the Travers. Good luck to you, miss."

"Thank you," Thea said faintly, staring after the man.

Older, shadowy emotions stirred inside, greasy splotches of childhood memories. One of the cards her father had sent to her years ago had been postmarked "Saratoga Springs." Now, though surrounded by faces full of excitement and nervous anticipation, for some reason she had to fight the urge to weep. In the distance a bell clanged several times, and the surge of humanity pressed upon her, sweeping her up in their rush to reach the stands.

Theodora, you dinglebrain, what were you thinking? She would never reach the stands, much less succeed in locating Devlin Stone in this sea of faces.

Abruptly she turned, elbowing her way through all

the bodies rushing in the opposite direction. Breathing hard, she at last reached a broad dirt avenue, and her gaze fixed upon the less-peopled stables to the southeast of the track. Perhaps over there she could snatch a moment or two of privacy, just enough to stiffen her spine again and set her to rights. She wasn't deserting the field of battle, nor abandoning her quest. She just needed to hush a few unpleasant voices from her childhood, and to come up with a more workable plan to locate Devlin Stone.

Chapter Four

Upon reaching the stable area Thea was disconcerted to find herself confronted by a stern-faced man, standing with folded arms under the boughs of a massive pine. At her approach he shoved back the rim of his bowler hat and looked her over.

"You an owner, miss? Not supposed to let race goers wander hereabouts unescorted."

"I'm… I'm looking for my escort, a Mr. Stone?"

She was taken aback when the suspicion on the man's face relaxed into friendliness. "Ah, he's been here for a bit. Nice feller, told me about his horse farm in Virginia. Sure has that Southern drawl, though." He tugged out a brightly patterned handkerchief and dabbed his sweaty forehead, then gestured toward the stables. "Go ahead, miss, but mind your step and your skirt. It's not as busy, now the racing's commenced. But you stay clear o' that aisle." He pointed. "Trainers are bringing out the horses for the next race, owners are jawing at the jockeys, the horses can be fractious. So don't go bothering them none, else you'll get us both in Dutch."

"Thank you. You're very kind. And I'll be very

careful." Flummoxed by her extraordinary luck, Thea smiled at the guard, closed her parasol and strolled with thudding heart toward the cool shadowed aisles in stables devoid of activity. Several grooms glanced over at her distractedly but nobody challenged her presence. By the time she reached a row of stalls near the back, the only person she had encountered was another groom, dozing on a fruit crate, his cap pulled over his eyes. All the stalls in this row were empty.

Earthy scents surrounded her, of hay and oats and leather and manure, all overlaid by the lazy heat of sunshine on old wood.

Gradually the knots in Thea's stomach unsnarled; she slipped down the cool, deserted aisle, then with more confidence approached the next row of stalls. A couple of stable boys touched their caps to her as she passed; some curious equine heads poked over stall doors, ears perked, nostrils whiffing. One horse, a chestnut with a white stripe down his forehead, nickered softly. Thea had never been around horses much, but after the tumultuous activity elsewhere, the tranquility here tugged her heart. Soon she found herself edging close enough to gingerly pat the chestnut's muzzle, which was softer than a fur muff. Warm air gusted from flared nostrils as the animal nudged her hand. Delighted, for a moment she savored the interaction, the unfamiliar scents swirling pleasantly around her. Then the horse retreated back into his stall, and with a lighter step Thea continued down the aisle. For the first time in her life she began to understand the compulsion to participate, even with only binoculars and betting tickets, in a sport where a rider harnessed himself to the horse and flew like the wind.

When she turned the next corner her gaze froze on the figure of a man standing a dozen paces away, his back to Thea. One of his arms draped companionably around a horse's neck, and Thea could hear the soft Southern cadences of his voice speaking to the animal. The pose struck her as almost intimate, and she found herself unable to shatter the peacefulness of the moment. Instead, drawn by a yearning that caught her even more off guard, Thea crept closer until she could hear Mr. Stone's words.

"…treating you like they should? You're a handsome fella, aren't you? For a Thoroughbred, that is. I'm used to something more substantial, say a Suffolk punch, or a Percheron? Magnificent horses, they are, and easily twice your size. But you'd put 'em to shame on a racetrack. Ah…easy, son. Touchy spot? Sorry. How about here, on the poll… Yeah, you like that, do you? That sweet spot between your ears, where the cranium meets the vertebrae."

Mesmerized, Thea watched the calm authority of his hands, deftly moving over every part of the racehorse he could reach from forehead to neck, moving only his arms. Never had she known a man could build such a connection with a beast that most likely weighed over a thousand pounds. Unlike the friendly but aloof horse that had allowed her brief pat before turning away, the horse with Mr. Stone had lowered his head over the stall door. The two of them looked as though they were, well, *talking* to each other.

Without warning, Thea's eyes stung, with a longing more forceful than the thirst for revenge that had dominated her life for nine agonizing months. What would it feel like to have a man lavish affection upon her, not merely a brief handclasp over her elbow? A man who communicated care and tenderness, like Mr. Stone with that horse? Plainly he loved the animals, and perhaps owned one or two himself. If so, he might be a man of some wealth.

Which meant, if she cozied up to Mr. Stone, he'd be justified in considering her as one more Saratoga sycophant, like all the women trailing along in Edgar Fane's wake.

Uncertainty glued Thea's feet to the ground.

One of the horses in a nearby stall snorted, then kicked the boards with his hoof. An involuntary gasp escaped before Thea could stifle it. Mr. Stone glanced casually around. Slowly he removed his arm from the horse's neck and turned to face her, the gentleness on his face hardening to—to stone.

"Miss Pickford. What a…surprise." Without looking away he gave the horse a final pat, then ambled down the aisle toward her. "I admit to chagrin. I…ah… wasn't prepared to see you again so soon, certainly not in this setting."

Thea squared her shoulders. "I didn't expect to find you in this setting either." He was taller than she remembered, his shoulders broader. Without the straw boater to soften his appearance, an aura of danger hovered around him now more than ever. Not the danger of a snake like Edgar Fane, but that of a thunderstorm— and she stood unprotected in an open field while lightning stabbed the sky. Thea focused on his hands—a stupid mistake because all she could remember was how they looked gently stroking a horse. "I have an important matter to discuss with you."

"Ah. Hmm." He seemed to hesitate. "Very well, I'm

not one to gainsay a lady determined to ignore her fiancé's existence—Miss Pickford? Are you all right?"

Unstrung by the bald reminder of the nonexistent
Neville, Thea almost backed into several stacked bales
of straw. "I'm perfectly all right," she said.

In the dim stable his light eyes bored into hers; he
lifted a hand to shove a lock of hair the rich color of
polished mahogany off his forehead. Despite herself,
Thea stiffened. Something flickered in his expression,
then without fuss he stepped back a pace or two and
folded his arms. "Are you a horse lover, Miss Pickford?"

"I've never been around them enough to know. But I
admire them, very much. A chestnut with a white strip
down his nose let me pat him for a second. I…you love
them, don't you?"

"Yes. More than just about anything else on this
earth. Most of the time, I prefer them to people." He
hesitated, then added matter-of-factly, "Don't be afraid,
Miss Pickford. I don't abuse horses, or women. Those
who do best keep out of my way, however. May I offer
an apology, for frightening you this morning?"

"I wasn't frightened, but an apology is definitely
called for," she agreed.

The lock of hair fell back over his forehead. He
brushed at it, and Thea stared, transfixed anew at the
long supple fingers, the tanned wrist almost twice the
size of hers. Why, that hand looked strong enough to
break a brick, yet a moment earlier his touch had transformed a high-strung Thoroughbred to a purring kitten.

Blinking, she reminded herself of her purpose in
hunting this man down. "You voiced several ungentlemanly accusations, which I'm willing to overlook because I—" The words faltered into awkward silence

until she added breathlessly, "Mr. Stone…you're staring at me."

"Merely returning the favor, Miss Pickford. I'm flattered. You're a lovely young woman, but I'm thinking your fiancé should conduct his courtship from a much shorter distance than the other side of an ocean."

Thea's parasol slid free and fell with a soft plop onto the packed dirt stable floor. Mortified, she bent to retrieve it, but Mr. Stone stepped forward and swooped it up instead, his fingers brushing hers as he returned the parasol. The jolt of sensation fried the air between them. "I would never dishonor my fiancé…" she began feebly, the once-facile lie now stumbling from her lips. "I merely need to ask you something, about someone else."

"Oh?"

As if in a dream Thea watched him idly stroke the side of his nose. The vivid image of that finger brushing *her* nose burned a fiery trail all the way to her toes. Hot color scorched her cheeks. Her grandfather was right: despite her sophisticated education and her acquaintance with numerous intellectual gentlemen, until today she had remained unblemished emotionally. A perfectly rolled and floured biscuit which had never seen the inside of an oven.

The friendly courtship she had enjoyed the previous summer with a neighbor's grandson by comparison now seemed a tepid thing, ending without fanfare when the young man returned to Boston. In Thea's opinion, romance between a man and a woman was vastly overrated.

This is not a romance, you limp-noodled ninnyhammer.

"Miss Pickford? You wanted to ask me about something, or someone?" Mr. Stone prompted.

"Oh. Yes, yes I did." Thoroughly rattled, Thea snatched a piece of straw from the bale of hay and distractedly wove it between her fingers. "I wanted to ask you about…about—you told Mrs. Van Eyck and me you planned to attend the races. It's, ah, past two o'clock…."

"So I did, and so it is." Mr. Stone's eyes narrowed, and for a moment he stared down at her without speaking. "I don't know what to do about you," he eventually murmured, his voice deep, the drawl warm and lazy. "You need to be more careful when you lie, and how you look at a man when your heart is promised elsewhere."

"Well, I'm not doing it on purpose," she blurted, stupidly. "As for telling lies, *you're* the one who pretended an acquaintance with my fiancé. How would you feel if I reported you to the local constable, or alerted—"

The words backed up in her throat when Mr. Stone took a single long stride toward her. The scents of starch and sweat and horse filled her nostrils. Before she could react, he plucked the straw from her fingers and skimmed it along the line of her clenched jaw. "No, you won't. You have too much to lose, don't you, to risk that sort of attention."

Stepping back, he sketched a brief bow, then swiveled on his heel and sauntered down the aisle, turned a corner and disappeared.

Thea remained motionless, one hand braced against the rough stable wall while she waited for the churning in her stomach to settle. After several moments she lifted her hand to the cheek the straw had touched. A tingle still quivered along her veins.

This bizarre physical attraction could be contained and ultimately controlled. But the absence of any signs of vertigo from their confrontation alarmed her profoundly. Such a reaction indicated a moral weakness in her character far worse to Thea than the facade designed to procure justice on behalf of her grandfather. A godly young lady of impeccable virtue should be outraged, or even nauseous with that vertigo—the latter her reaction on the four occasions when she had spoken to Edgar Fane.

Despite her sheltered upbringing, perhaps she had truly become her mother, whose acting skill was superseded only by her affinity for men.

The possibility cast a murky film over the summer afternoon, but Thea refused to abandon her purpose. Life offered choices, her grandfather told her frequently. She wasn't doomed to follow her mother's path; she would simply choose to avoid any further encounters with Devlin Stone. Another opportunity would arise to ingratiate herself with Edgar Fane, a man for whom she would never feel anything but disgust.

Stiffen your spine, Theodora, and get on with the task.

Chapter Five

With a theatrical flourish, Edgar Fane pulled the sheet covering his latest painting from the canvas. His appreciative audience—the fifty or so guests he had invited to join him aboard the *Alice* as the boat gently steamed across Saratoga Lake—applauded and lifted their champagne glasses to toast his artistic prowess.

The effort was not one of his better ones. He'd chosen a seascape—hence the unveiling on the steamer—but the colors were too bright, the people on the shore more reminiscent of paint smears. The frame, however, was a lovely antique gold.

He did like the frame, which he'd discovered in an antique store in Chicago. A satisfied tingle briefly tickled his insides.

"Who's the lucky recipient this time?" Richard Beekins gave his shoulder a congenial pat, wheezing noisily in Edgar's ear as he talked. "C'mon, be a good chap and tell your daddy's old friend."

Edgar gave the boozy fellow a smile, then used the excuse of setting aside the delicate champagne flute to turn away. "You know I never divulge privileged information. Everyone needs a secret or two in life. Besides, I need a gimmick to heighten the interest. We all know I'm no Michelangelo." He winked at Dahlia, his chosen dinner partner for the afternoon boating party. "Even my charming companion here, lovely lady though she may be, couldn't inveigle the name of the new owner."

Dahlia obediently pouted and fluttered her eyelashes. Diamonds twinkled in her ears, at the base of her throat and on almost every finger on both hands. "Darling Edgar, I haven't yet tried."

Bored with feminine fawning, Edgar downed another flute of champagne as he smiled his way among the guests until he reached the prow of the slender steamer. Dahlia fortunately had been detained by Richard Beekins. Propping his elbows on the narrow rail, Edgar contemplated the undulation of the water, how the sunlight danced over the ripples and whether or not he could capture the effect on canvas. Not that it mattered. His forays into painting provided a useful outlet, but he'd never intended to pursue the craft seriously. On the other hand, perhaps a studied dedication would offer an antidote to the ennui plaguing him the past few years.

"You're looking far too solemn." Cynthia Gorman's scent filled the air before the woman herself joined Edgar, close enough for the wind to blow her lawn skirts against his trousers. "You've been brooding most of the afternoon. What is it, Edgar?"

"Can't a man enjoy the sun on his head and the wind in his face for a minute or two?"

"Not Edgar Fane, apparently." Her laugh drifted pleasantly over the water. "When I spied you off by yourself for once, I grabbed the opportunity. You're the only member of your family I can stand being around for longer than a half hour, you know."

"Because I don't try and seduce you out of your fortune, or because I don't talk about mine?"

"My dear man, yours is the only seduction I might contemplate, but we both know that's never going to happen, so why don't you try me as a confidante? I can keep a secret."

Edgar's impatience erupted in a burst of laughter, which naturally offended Cynthia. He laid his hand against her heliotrope-scented cheek. "Don't," he murmured. "You know I love you dearly——"

"As you love all the other women in your harem..."

"Precisely. All a delight to the eyes, but I have no intention of confining my delight or confiding secrets to any of them. Thanks to my brothers and sister making more money and producing heirs, I am free to live— precisely as I please, unencumbered by familial obligation."

"Never alone, but always lonely."

Annoyed, Edgar straightened and stepped away. "My dear Cynthia, if I want a philosophical lecture I'll hunt down a mesmerist. The boat will be docking soon. I think it's time I made the announcement." He lifted his hand and brushed his knuckles against her jutting jaw. "Since we're such old friends, I will share one small secret with you." He waited until her eyes kindled with hope, then leaned to whisper into her ear, "You *won't* be the recipient of my latest work of art."

A loud burst of masculine guffaws echoed through the cut glass doors of the Casino's barroom. Half-empty glass of springwater in one hand, Devlin paced outside the entrance while he chewed over what to do next. Two of his suspects were here. Upstairs in the game room, Randolph Lunt had suffered heavy losses at the roulette table, and when he left off gambling to drown his sorrows Dev automatically followed; meanwhile, Joseph Scarborough was deep in a poker game with four other men. He looked to be on a winning streak and would likely stay in the game for a while. Back home, some of their wins, and many of the losses, would feed half the county for a year. Devlin sipped the now-lukewarm water while he fought the cynicism crusting, one barnacle at a time, over the idealism of his youth.

As for his remaining suspect, Edgar Fane—that slippery charmer had taken a party of guests out on the *Alice,* one of the steamers chugging around Saratoga Lake. They wouldn't return dockside until near sunset.

So Devlin paced, and pondered his options.

Moments later, across the room the narrow cut glass doors banged open, and Lunt shoved through. "Hey, you!" He headed toward Devlin. "Need change for a twenty. Help me out, won't you?"

"Let's see what I've got." Dev tugged out his wallet and made a show of leafing through the bills.

After handing him smaller bills Dev accepted the twenty in return, casually tucking it away with rock-steady hands, while inside his heart pounded like a kettledrum. When Lunt disappeared back through the doors, Dev exited the Casino and hurried down the street to his hotel room.

Thirty minutes after a thorough examination of what turned out to be a bona fide twenty-dollar bill, he headed back for the Park, his favorite sanctuary not only from the masses but his own foul mood.

Redesigned a quarter of a century earlier by Frederick Olmsted's firm, Congress Spring Park was a popular destination for guests and townsfolk alike. Meandering paths wove through neatly sculpted shrubbery and towering trees. Soft summer breezes carried the sound of the band playing hum-along tunes from a bandstand, built in the middle of a spring-fed pond at the center of the park.

Sunbeams turned the droplets of a fountain to twinkling crystal confetti. Steps slowing, Dev finally allowed the peace of the place to relax the knots in his muscles. The saw-toothed disappointment ebbed.

Most likely the soused Randolph Lunt was a dead end—a man who gambled away enough money to drive him to drink did not possess enough fortitude to be the Hotel Hustler.

That left Joseph Scarborough, Edgar Fane—and Miss Pickford, whose interest in Fane probably deserved closer examination, in light of her deceptions. By the time Devlin wound his way back through the pair of Corinthian columns flanking the entrance to the park he had settled upon a plan of sorts: shadow Miss Pickford for a few days, note who she saw and the circumstances, see if any pattern developed. He told himself this course of action was coldly professional, and had nothing to do with a pair of dark brown eyes or the longing expression he'd glimpsed when he first caught sight of her.

Nothing to do with the faint scent of lilacs or vivid blush when she looked at him and dropped her parasol.

Tranquil mood broken, Devlin headed for the lake to wait for Edgar Fane and his boating party to return. He could hunt down Miss Pickford tomorrow. After hiring a two-seater runabout, he drove the four miles at a leisurely clip, then left the horse contentedly munching a handful of oats beneath a shade tree. Dev wandered down toward the dock where several people were fishing, their poles stretched in ragged formation along the landing and the shore. Lake water lapped in lazy ripples, insects droned in the tall grasses and farther down the shoreline a pair of ducks took flight.

One of the anglers near the end of the landing was a woman, dressed in some sort of striped skirt, yellow overblouse and a floppy, wide-brimmed hat. Lake breezes stirred the blue-and-yellow ribbons tied around the crown and dangling provocatively down the woman's back. She was alone, the closest other fisherman a dozen yards away. When she half turned, Dev caught a glimpse of her face. The punch of disbelief—and elation—left him disoriented.

Theodora Pickford. Fishing alone, from the dock where Edgar Fane would shortly disembark?

Why should he be surprised? Dev shook his head. Though supposedly engaged to a supposedly beloved British aristocrat, the Jezebel had professed an interest in Devlin—and Edgar Fane—from the moment Dev met her.

On the other hand, he might be judging her too harshly. He wasn't in the best of humors, after all. And all right, he admitted to himself that the memory of their encounter in the barn burned in his brain like a brand.

His father, dead before Devlin's tenth birthday, would have thanked God for "arranging" this encounter, proclaiming it divine assistance. Dev however saw no reason to interpret Miss Pickford's presence here as anything other than deliberate design on *her* part, and luck on his. No divine intervention, no proof that God invested any interest in the species He'd created, and perhaps now regretted.

Absently Devlin kicked a pebble, his gaze on Theodora Pickford's distant silhouette. He was an independently wealthy man with an overdeveloped sense of responsibility and a restless soul. Two years earlier he'd gone to Washington looking for a half brother, and instead of returning home to StoneHill Farm, he'd become a Secret Service operative. On a good day, Devlin liked to think his path to the nation's capitol two years ago had been part of his destiny. That he had something to offer a world far beyond the boundaries of StoneHill, something grander, something...ordained. Something that kindled the internal jolt of satisfaction he felt when a herd of horses cantered over to greet him.

He'd never expected to experience that jolt just from looking at a woman who most likely he'd be arresting one day soon.

Chapter Six

He retraced his steps to his livery horse. Late-afternoon sunlight sheened the lake in gold and tinted streamers of wispy clouds a deep rose-pink. Steadily chugging toward the landing, the narrow-nosed steamer skimmed across the water, returning Miss Pickford's unwitting human catch to shore.

Perhaps he should warn Edgar Fane.

Instead Dev settled back against the tree trunk and watched. Sweat trickled down his temple; absently he swiped the droplets away, lifting his face to the light breeze, and waited. The *Alice* arrived at the landing and passengers swarmed onto the dock, their voices loud in the peaceful late afternoon. With scarcely a glance they streamed past Miss Pickford and the other anglers. Miss Pickford suddenly began a wild struggle with her fishing pole. Several passengers paused to observe, and over the swell of a dozen conversations Dev heard her breathless voice.

"I've been here for hours, and was about to give up. Oh—" Her upper body jerked, then steadied as she wrestled against the taut line. "No, no, don't help me.

It's very exciting, isn't it? I hope it's a largemouth bass. My grandfather is…" The rest of her words faded into the general babble.

A small crowd gathered, blocking Dev's view. He unhurriedly ducked beneath the gelding's neck to better monitor Fane's passage to shore, noting the instant the man's attention turned from the boat captain to Miss Pickford. *Poor fool,* Dev thought. Fane laughed and took a step toward the siren seducing him with her fishing antics, even as a shapely debutante decked out in a ridiculous mimicry of a sailor suit wrapped possessive fingers around his forearm.

Without warning, Miss Pickford emitted a cry of surprise, her arms stretching taut while she fought to haul in her catch, which suddenly soared out of the water in a graceful arc and landed wetly six inches from Edgar Fane's feet.

"I caught it!" she exclaimed, at last turning to face her spellbound audience. "Did you see? What kind of fish—oh." Even from twenty feet away Dev could read the emotions tumbling across her face—surprise, sheepishness, amusement…and guilt. "Why…it's a—a shoe! I've been fighting for ages, over a *shoe?*"

Laughter tittered through the group. Dev wandered closer.

"How embarrassing." Miss Pickford addressed Fane, a becoming shade of pink tinting her cheeks the same hue as the clouds. "I beg your pardon. Did my shoe ruin yours?"

The artful question, with its tint of good-natured humor, secured Edgar Fane's unswerving interest, Devlin noted. Miss Pickford had cast her lures with masterful expertise.

"Not at all." Fane leaned to pick up the "catch." "At least, not compared to this poor old thing."

"I suppose we could ask the cook at Briggs House if he's willing to try a fillet of sole?" Miss Pickford ventured, and the entire crowd burst into appreciative laughter.

"Ha! Not only a lovely angler, but a humorist, as well. I'm delighted to meet you, Miss—it is Miss, I hope?"

"Well…unofficially I do have a fiancé, but he's in Europe at the moment." After an appropriately timed pause she added, "My chaperone might not approve, but this is 1897, after all. Practically a new century, time to dispense with so many cumbersome formalities." And the chit had the audacity to offer her hand. "Miss Pickford. I'm very glad my catch didn't land in your face."

"Miss Pickford. Edgar Fane, at your service." He bowed, the gesture courteous but mocking. "Tell me, Miss Pickford, do you also bowl and don bloomers to ride a bicycle? Play tennis and golf? I'm intrigued by this new concept of femininity, unashamed to engage in all manner of outdoor sport. We must get together. Here's my card. Simpson? Where are you, man? Ah… this is Simpson, my personal secretary. Simpson, I'm hoping Miss Pickford will dine with me one evening this week. Can you check my schedule, and make arrangements? Miss Pickford? I look forward to sharing more of your exploits."

And with a final lingering perusal he left her with his secretary and joined the rest of his guests. They clattered down the landing and dispersed into various buggies and carriages, the secretary following a moment later. The pier was soon deserted save for Miss Pickford and a couple of other fishermen who steadfastly kept their backs to her. One of the trolleys that ran from the lake to the village clanged its pending arrival at the Briggs House hotel. Devlin's attention never diverted from the lone woman who stood at the end of the pier. She stared out over the lake, fishing pole drooping lifelessly in her hand. Nearby, the remaining anglers began gathering their equipment, likely intending to catch the last trolley.

Suddenly Miss Pickford leaned down, scooped up the shoe and heaved both it and the fishing pole into the lake. Then she whirled and marched down the landing, passing within a dozen paces of the tree where Devlin waited, a silent, cynical witness to her performance. Eschewing the trolley, she set out walking along the edge of the road back to town.

What kind of woman walked four miles when transportation was readily available? Certainly she'd hoped to secure a ride in Edgar Fane's private omnibus, but with that hope dashed she had nothing to gain now but blisters.

"Shortsighted a bit, weren't you?" Devlin commented aloud after she disappeared around a bend in the road. He climbed into the runabout. "Well, let's see what kind of line you'll try on me."

Ten minutes along the road, however, he still hadn't overtaken her. The sky was deepening to twilight, the trolley long gone and only three other horse-drawn conveyances and several bicyclists had passed; serve him right if Miss Pickford had accepted a ride in someone else's buggy. His report to headquarters would have to detail the account of how Operative Stone allowed both parties he'd been shadowing to slip through his fingers. Grimly he searched both sides of the road, slowing the horse to a plodding walk. Even so, in the gathering darkness he almost missed the flash of color behind a clump of bushes.

"Whoa…" he murmured, and set the brake, his gaze riveted to the bushes. There, another glimpse of creamy yellow, the same shade as the overblouse Miss Pickford had been wearing.

Then he heard a low moan.

Panting, Thea propped herself on her hands, but the motion triggered another bout of nausea; she retched, sides heaving, perspiration mingling with the tears that leaked from the corners of her eyes. Not since the night she'd visited Grandfather in that dreadful jail had she suffered from an attack this vicious. Stupid, stupid, *stupid* not to have realized what might happen if her little scheme to attract Edgar Fane worked.

Or more precisely, didn't work. The blackguard might have noticed her, but she hadn't garnered sufficient interest for an invitation to return to the hotel with the rest of his more favored guests.

Listen to yourself, Theodora. Her entire life now reflected the moral virtue of a…a vaudeville singer.

Which punishment in Dante's *Inferno* did she deserve, for becoming that which she most despised? The dizziness intensified, sucking her down, down into the depths. God would never forgive her, because she would never forgive herself.

"What the—" a man's voice exclaimed, and strong hands closed around her shoulders.

"Don't…" Thea managed before her stomach heaved again and she gagged.

"Easy. Shh…don't fight me, you'll make it worse."

The deep, now-familiar voice soothed, but humiliation scorched rational thought. Better a party of drunken fishermen had stumbled upon her than this man. "Mr. Stone..." Thea managed in a hoarse whisper, "please leave me alone. I'll...in a moment I'll be fine. I just need..." The effort to converse overwhelmed her. She could only close her eyes and allow those competent hands to do whatever they pleased.

A musky yet pleasant aroma drifted through her nostrils as he gently eased her back down on the warm earth. Instead of scratchy meadow grasses her cheek was cushioned by some sort of fabric. She tried to lift her hand, but flashing lights stabbed behind her closed eyelids. "Can't...please. Leave me alone."

"All right," Devlin Stone murmured. The air stirred vaguely, then stilled.

So. He'd listened, and obeyed. Life, Thea decided in utter misery, once again proved she was a worthless cast-aside, an inferior specimen of humanity nobody wanted. Both parents had abandoned her. Her chaperone ignored her. Edgar Fane gave her over to his *secretary.* And now Mr. Stone left her prostrate in the bushes, never mind that he'd only done what she requested.

Lord? If You care anything about me at all, let me die so I'm no longer a burden to my grandfather. Her quest for justice had failed. Her parody on the dock with Edgar Fane clung like a stench. No wonder Mr. Stone abandoned her, as well.

Chapter Seven

"Miss Pickford? You haven't passed out on me, have you?"

The calm voice penetrated her miasma, but Thea still started when a damp cloth passed over the back of her neck, then down her cheek. Next she felt his palm—warm, the fingertips slightly abraded—press against her forehead. "No fever. Eat anything today to cause a sickness in your belly?"

"Not…sick."

"Nor up to talking, either, hmm?" There was a sound of splashing, then he laid the freshly dampened cloth over her eyes. "I'm unbuttoning your sleeves at the wrists so I can bathe them, and your hands. Don't be alarmed, and don't fight me, all right?"

As if she could. Sighing a little, Thea allowed his skillful ministrations to lull her into a semicatatonic state, akin to floating on her back in one of the lakes scattered over Staten Island, drifting in the lazy current while the sun and water bound her in a lovely cocoon.

Time floated by, until she was able to take a deep breath without choking on the nausea. Hesitantly she opened her eyes. The whirling had abated. "Thank you," she breathed, and scraped up half a smile. "I'm better now." And saying it, she could feel the truth soaking into her pores. Edgar Fane made her sick; Devlin Stone made her feel safe.

Of the two, Mr. Stone probably posed more of a threat.

"Want to tell me what happened?" he asked eventually with the tone that caused a high-strung racehorse to rest its head against him.

For some moments Thea didn't answer. The vertigo had subsided, but humiliation still burned deep enough to smudge his Good Samaritan kindness into something less benign. A glance upward through the screen of her lashes intensified the uncertainty: he sat at ease beside her, one arm draped loosely across an upraised knee. A light wind stirred the fine linen of his pin-striped shirt. He was hatless today, and the wind brushed the lock of hair over his forehead, lending him the relaxed air of a man with nothing on his mind but a day at the lake. Yet, veiled in shadow, his gaze rested unwavering upon Theodora. She had the impression he would sit there, calmly waiting until Thea offered an explanation even if it took until darkness enfolded them like a blanket.

Who *was* Devlin Stone?

She had nothing to gain by telling him the truth, and everything to lose if she didn't. She might not understand his interest, but over the past several weeks she'd witnessed all manner of masculine conduct toward women and this man was no Edgar Fane. He could still be a charlatan, preying upon vulnerable women at resort hotels; from the first she'd sensed his contempt for her. But his present compassion contradicted every definition of a genuine cad. No man she'd ever known willingly nursed a sick woman.

On a more pragmatic note, the severity of this spell had robbed her of the strength to safely hike back to town. Whether the choice was wise or not, Mr. Stone remained her best hope. He might not be cruel, but something warned Thea he would leave her stranded if she wove another story about an English fiancé, or how much she loved to fish. "I…have dizzy spells." The words stuck in her throat. Clumsily she attempted to rise.

Without a word Mr. Stone wrapped a strong arm around her shoulders and eased her back against one of the outcropping of boulders beside the shrubs. "Here." He tucked his now-crumpled but still-damp handkerchief into her hand. "Wipe your face. It will help. Suck on this peppermint." He handed her the piece of candy. "Then you can tell me about these spells of yours."

"You've been very kind." The candy helped assuage the weakness. "If I told you I'd prefer not to talk about them?"

"I'd take you straight to a physician." He searched her face, then added without inflection, "Are you with child, Miss Pickford?"

"What?" She almost sputtered the peppermint into his face. "Did you say— Do you actually think— I told you I'm not married. Why would you ask such an insulting question?"

For the first time a glint of blue sparkled in his eyes, and that attractive dimple creased one of his cheeks. "Given your response, I withdraw the question. You may be a highly imaginative liar, but these days only an innocent would offer that answer to a man vulgar enough to broach the subject in the first place."

Well. Thea didn't know whether to be insulted or relieved. "You confuse me, Mr. Stone," she mumbled, ducking her head. "From the moment we first met, you've confused me. I know I'm a...a... I haven't been truthful. There's a reason. At the time it seemed the only way." She smoothed the crumpled handkerchief in her lap, folding it into a neat square, her fingers still clumsy with weakness. "I've been here at Saratoga Springs for almost a month. Until you, everybody believed everything I told them." It was difficult, but she made herself face him directly. "How did you know?"

"When I'm not indulging in the first pleasure holiday in a decade—" his smile deepened until dimples creased both cheeks "—I raise and train horses. Draft horses, to be specific, though we—my uncle and I— gentle the odd pleasure mount here and there. I've been around them all my life. Horses taught me a lot about observation, about sensing feelings, moods." He gave a short laugh. "When you're surrounded by creatures with hooves the size of a soup tureen, you'd better learn how to read them. Works the same with people. Although I prefer horses for the most part. They might bite or kick if frightened or provoked. But they don't lie."

Thea weathered the blow; it was justified. "I didn't think a harmless fabrication would hurt anyone, and it kept speculation about me to a minimum. It was the only way I could think of to attract..." Her voice trailed into silence.

"And when nothing worked, you got desperate."

Above them a burnt orange sky warned of encroaching night. Somewhere nearby, an insect commenced its ceaseless chirring. But between Thea and Devlin Stone silence thickened until each inhalation choked her lungs. "Desperate," she repeated, squeezing her hand until her fingers went numb. "Have you ever been desperate, Mr. Stone? About anything?"

"Yes. But never enough to cheat, or beg, or deceive."

"Then you've never been desperate, and faced with impossible choices." She paused. "Is that what you think of me?"

"I don't know what to think of you, Miss Pickford. Is that your real name, by the way?"

"What? Oh…well, no. It's actually my mother's maiden name." He slid the question in so neatly Thea answered before she realized it. But unless Mr. Stone frequented the tawdry depths of New York City's Bowery he would not associate her with Hetty Pickford. "Please don't ask for my real name. I don't want to lie to you anymore."

"Ah." Another one of those flicks of blue light came and went in his eyes. "We're in accord, then. I don't want to be lied to. Now, it's getting late. Is your companion—Mrs. Chudd? Is she likely to be concerned about your whereabouts?"

"Well, if I don't turn up by midnight, she'd notify the front desk at least."

"Not a very efficient companion."

"No. She's mostly for appearances. I'm supposed to be a wealthy heiress, engaged to an earl. A chaperone's expected. Mrs. Chudd's former employer just passed away. She said she'd always wanted to see upstate New York, but after we arrived she developed an aversion for crowds."

"I see." He rubbed his palms together. "All right,

then. What say we return to the village? Can you walk, Miss Pickford, or shall I carry you to my buggy?"

"I can walk," she answered too quickly, and in the sunset's glow she caught his ironic smile.

In her haste to scramble to her feet a wave of faintness almost contradicted her words. He put his hands on her waist to steady her, and though the courtesy was brief, almost impersonal, Thea's limbs turned to sand.

"Shall I carry you after all, then?" he offered after her first few steps.

"No. It's just a silly weakness, already passing." More a weakness of her mind than her limbs. "I could probably walk back to the village, but—"

"Don't be a goose, Miss Pickford. Pride's a useful commodity on occasion. This isn't one of them."

The sun slipped behind the mountains to the west as he handed her into his buggy. The contrast between this simple one-horse, two-seat runabout and Edgar Fane's waxed and gleaming omnibus harnessed to a team of four matched horses was as incongruous as the realization that, given a choice, Theodora much preferred the former. Confused, she watched Mr. Stone light the single carriage lamp, and give the horse an affectionate pat.

Who was this man?

Chapter Eight

She looked like a woebegone waif sitting beside him in the gathering darkness, smelling of peppermint and illness. Strands of hair hung limply around the pale oval of her face and dirt smeared over her yellow shirtwaist. The floppy hat rested forgotten on her lap. For the first mile Devlin fought a battle with his conscience. Fortunately Miss Pickford herself broached the subject.

"I don't suppose you'd consider forgetting every-thing you saw and heard," she said, her grimy hands smoothing in ceaseless circles over the equally grimy hat ribbons.

"Not a chance." He paused. "Especially the scene on the pier. Your staging and timing were impeccable, Miss Pickford. However, compared to Edgar Fane you're a very small minnow tempting a shark."

She groaned. "You saw that?"

"From start to finish. If it's any consolation, I think the tactic worked. Humor can be a powerful weapon in a woman's arsenal. The shoe definitely captured Fane's attention."

"Only for a moment. I wasn't expecting to be fobbed off on a personal secretary."

"A dinner invitation will be forthcoming, Miss Pickford. Count on it."

"That's what I'm afraid of."

She spoke so softly he barely caught the words, but a chill spiked down his spine. Snug cottages whose windows glowed with lights had begun to appear on either side of the road; in moments they'd be back in the village, and Dev would have to let her go. An opportunity would be forever lost. Off to the right, a grove of shade trees offered privacy and without a qualm he turned the horse off the road and into their concealing darkness.

"What are you doing?"

"Nothing sinister. I just want us to come to a better understanding of one another before I turn you over to Mrs. Chudd."

"There's no point. I don't think I can…" A long hesitation was followed by an unraveling sigh, then, "I promised myself I could do this, vowed I could ignore my conscience, and all the doubts. But it's not working. The attacks of dizziness…they're getting worse. Stronger." She turned to face him, the fuzzy light from the carriage lamp illuminating a face taut with misery. "You told me you knew of Edgar Fane. Could you… would you tell me everything you know, without asking why I continue to pursue this man?"

Her sincerity disarmed him; he didn't want to believe she was being honest with him, because it would corroborate his perception of her true character—and reinforce the dangerous attraction that intensified with every encounter. She was an admitted liar, with trouble and secrets stamped all over her face. Yet her vulnerability appealed to every one of his protective instincts.

Compassion might kill him yet....

"Horses are prey animals," Uncle Jay counseled often enough to annoy when Dev was growing up. *"Humans, now—we're predators. But that don't mean we never feel threatened, 'specially women. A mean woman, or a threatened woman, can kick you with words, trample your heart. After Sylvia and your mother, it's possible you may never trust another one. I don't look to forgive your intended myself—so can't blame you none for feeling the same. That don't mean all females deserve the scorn I hear in your voice these days. Regardless of their behavior, like horses a lady never deserves the back of your hand, or a fist. Always be a man instead of a two-legged mongrel, lad, so's you'll sleep at night."*

"How about we trade information?" he began, slowly. "You tell me about these 'spells,' and I'll tell you what I know about Edgar Fane."

In the darkness Dev heard her exhale a long wavering sigh. "My grandfather warned me about rogues and knaves. He never warned me about someone like you."

"Well, if I'm not a rogue or a knave, what does that leave?" *Keep it light,* he ordered himself. *Go gently. You can lead a horse to water, but if you want him to drink, feed him something salty to whet his thirst.* "Or perhaps I shouldn't ask?"

"Grandfather also warned me about men who think too much. Shakespeare had the way of it—such men *are* dangerous. I should be afraid of you. I don't trust you, but you've been...kind." A beat of silence hovered before she continued slowly, "Ever since I was a girl,

I've had occasional spells of vertigo. Sometimes they're debilitating. Since last year they seem to be worsening." Her voice thinned. "But there's no other course. I have to do this."

The last declaration was scarcely above a whisper. "What is it you have to do?" Dev prompted after a while. "Does it concern Edgar Fane?"

Her hands crushed the hat. "Yes."

"Ah." Since he wanted answers, not another episode of vertigo, he told her what he could. "Edgar Fane is a wealthy, likable fellow who enjoys the company of others, particularly attractive women. His father made a fortune, the older brother's expanding it and his other brother is marrying a French countess next year. From what I've gleaned, Edgar's decided his role is that of charming wastrel—one of those men your grandfather *would* have warned you about."

For a moment he silently studied her. "Is your family in dire financial straits, Miss—I can't continue to call you Miss Pickford, now can I? Will you tell me your name? I haven't personally met Mr. Fane, but I know enough to question certain aspects of his character. Of course, it doesn't seem fair to confide my observations unless you're equally candid." He paused. "For instance, when he asks you to dinner, how do I know whether you might decide to warn him about a certain Mr. Stone, and the rumors he's bandying about?"

This time she refused to rise to the bait. "Your observations about Mr. Fane must be highly salacious."

Night had fallen, covering them in a soft matte darkness. The carriage lamp threw out enough light to illuminate the intelligence glittering in the coffee–dark brown eyes. So. She had recovered. It was to be a battle of wits to the end, then. Strangely pleased, Devlin affected a shrug, then gathered up the reins and smoothly backed horse and buggy onto the road, all without saying a word.

She lasted until a block before the Grand Union Hotel. Garish electric lights strung on ugly poles shone down on crowds of laughing people. A loud burst of masculine laughter startled the livery horse; Dev automatically soothed the animal, then turned onto Broadway into a sea of gleaming carriages and buggies.

"You really do have a way with horses, Mr. Stone."

Dev pulled into a vacant spot a block from the Grand Union Hotel. "I love them," he replied simply, wondering at the undercurrent of longing in her voice. "If you treat horses with affection and respect, you'll earn their loyalty until they die. Yes, they're animals, and occasionally unpredictable. But if I had to choose between a horse and a human being for companionship, I'd stick with a horse."

"Then why are you here, at one of the most crowded hotel resorts in the world?"

Her astute question jabbed him square on the chin. He deflected it with some questions of his own. "Perhaps to rescue you from whatever harebrained scheme you've concocted? There's no titled duke, is there? Where did you get that ring? At a pawn shop?"

"The ring was my grandmother's," she retorted in a tone frosted with ice. The wobbly-kneed girl he'd ministered to had metamorphosed into the most dangerous of all species: an angry woman. "You made me want to trust you, and I'm ashamed of myself for that. Thank you for your kindness. I won't trouble you further. If we have the misfortune to meet again, I promise to ignore you. And for your information, Neville was an earl."

She made as if to leap from the cart. Dev grabbed her arm. "Sorry."

"You ought to be. Let me go."

"Not until you accept my apology." Beneath his fingers her arm tensed. In a soothing motion he slid his hand down to her wrist, keeping the grip gentle, yet unbreakable. "Besides, I would never abandon a lady I'd just rescued until she was safely home."

"Even if the lady wishes otherwise?"

"A dilemma, to be sure, Miss—what did you say your real name was again?"

"Lang—" Her lips pressed together.

A glaring beam from a nearby streetlight illuminated her face, allowing Devlin to witness the battle of emotions. *Lang...* Something tingled at the back of his neck, an elusive fragment of knowledge that vanished when her pursed lips softened in a *Mona Lisa* smile. She was disheveled, her attire wrinkled and soiled; dirt was smeared across one cheek. Yet that half smile somehow captured his heart and it swelled like a hot air balloon.

Panic skittered through him. "Ah. So it's Miss... Lang. Strange. Neither name really fits you." All the newly restored color leached from her complexion. *Insensitive clod,* he reprimanded himself. "I'll escort you to the lobby. Shall I have a bellhop fetch Mrs. Chudd to help you to your room?" He distracted her with verbal rambling while casually monitoring the pulse in her wrist. "How about if I call on you in the morning, say ten o'clock? I believe the band is scheduled to play a medley of popular tunes. Have you enjoyed the pleasures of Congress Springs Park?"

"Yes, I love the park. It's very peaceful, even with all the other people. Mr. Stone, I accept your apology. But I don't think it's wise for us to meet again. I don't want to encourage your false impressions of me, and I don't want to—could you please let go of my wrist?" She waited, her dark gaze unwavering, until Dev complied. The *Mona Lisa* smile flickered, then she passed her tongue over her lips and cleared her throat. "Thank you. I wish... I wish we'd met under different circumstances."

And before he could think of an appropriate response, she jumped out of the runabout and marched off toward the hotel. Though she garnered several strange looks from evening strollers, she sailed past with the regal poise of a duchess.

A man was in a wheelbarrow full of trouble when watching the back of a woman made his pulse rate spike and his fingers tingle.

Chapter Nine

The invitation from Edgar Fane arrived two days later. Thea read the lazy scrawl of words, with every breath a dull spike lodging deeper in her chest. So. Her wish had come true at last, but the fulfillment was tinged with the taste of gall: Dinner at Mr. Canfield's Casino was not the scenario she had envisioned.

The Casino might enjoy a reputation for first-class cuisine, and it might be patronized by the country's wealthiest and most powerful personages. But for Thea the dignified red brick building also housed a glittering palace of iniquity, a den of vice, preying upon weak minds with more money than common sense. From local gossip she'd learned that reformers had managed to close down the gambling there for a couple of years, but like the racecourse it had reopened for this summer's season.

She should have known a wretch like Edgar Fane would entertain guests at a gambling palace.

Her father loved gambling more than anything else on earth, including his family. He'd been playing roulette the night he'd met Thea's mother. After winning a small fortune, he convinced himself, and her, that together they'd change the course of each other's lives. In a way, he was right. The unwelcome appearance of a baby nine months later introduced an equally unwelcome dose of reality.

Her father dumped Theodora with a letter of apology on her grandparents' doorstep, then disappeared for three years. Only the infrequent postcards reassured the family that he was alive. Charles and Mathilda Langston loved her as their own; until she died Mathilda never gave up believing the prodigal son would see the error of his ways. But some of Thea's earliest lessons, learned snuggled in Grandfather's lap, included the evils of gambling.

Apparently she had shed that particular lesson along with her conscience. Life, she reminded herself defiantly, *was* an uncertain stew of happenstance.

So for thirty-six hours Thea suffered a Coney Island roller-coaster ride of elation, fear, guilt and determination. Now the time was at hand, and she would not, *would not* permit the shy, morally upstanding little girl she used to be to dominate her thoughts. Tonight she planned to practice every feminine wile she'd gleaned from years of reading literature and talking to many of the authors of it who enjoyed "rusticating" on Staten Island. By the end of the meal Edgar Fane would…he would—

Mrs. Chudd poked her head through the door to Thea's room. "Bellhop's here. A Mr. Simpson is waiting for you in the lobby," she announced in her flat nasal voice.

"Have the bellhop tell Mr. Simpson I'll be right down." Nerves cramped her stomach and chilled her skin. "Mrs. Chudd? Won't you come along? It would be more appropriate."

"Got no use for rich food." She skimmed a long look at Thea, her pale eyes briefly flickering with curiosity. "You been fine all month, ferdiddling on your own. So I'll stay here, same as usual." Jaw jutting, she nodded twice, started to turn away. "Not having a spell, are you?"

"No." Thea forced her lips to stretch in a rubbery smile, and beneath the satin-and-lace evening gown locked her knees. "I'm fine."

"Humph. Then I'll fetch my knitting, finish this sweater for my grandnephew. You might want to be careful what you eat."

"Ah, Miss Pickford. You're a vision to behold," Mr. Fane declared upon meeting her and Mr. Simpson at the entrance to the Casino's dining room. He himself looked very much the wealthy gentleman in his black evening suit and blinding white waistcoat. "Quite a dramatic change from the intrepid angler who reeled in a shoe." Mischievous brown eyes twinkled; to avoid looking at him Thea glanced around the crowded dining room.

"I've ordered us filet of sole for the entrée," he continued easily, a secret laugh embedded in the words. "I hope you approve."

Thea finally managed to tear her awestruck gaze away from the rows of stained glass ceiling panels, and the equally glittering rows of tables full of guests, all of them staring at Thea and Edgar Fane. *Either win him now, or justice will be denied forever.* She squared her shoulders, lifted a hand to lightly brush her grandmother's cameo brooch, a steadying touch to bolster her resolve. "I trust all the laces have been removed from my catch so they don't get caught between our teeth," she replied.

Mr. Fane threw back his head and laughed out loud. "I think I'm going to like you very much, Miss Pickford. Who knows? You might turn out to be the catch of the day."

"Mr. Fane, I might say the same about you."

He laughed again, then led her between rows of circular tables to the back of the room, where a party of ten—six ladies, four gentlemen—watched their approach with the intensity of a pack of jackals about to tear into the carcass. "I've asked some friends to join us," Mr. Fane explained. "Less…intimate, and safer for you at this stage of our acquaintance." With a flourishing bow he pulled out one of the empty chairs. A folded card with "Miss Pickford" written in formal script sent an oily shiver down Thea's spine. He gestured to the woman seated beside her place.

"This is a very dear friend, Mrs. Cynthia Gorman." As Thea gingerly sat down he leaned close enough for his breath to stir the fine hairs on the back of her neck. "If she takes a liking to you, you'll be able to learn anything about me good manners prohibit you from asking." He straightened. "Mrs. Gorman, Miss Theodora Pickford." Thea angled her head toward Mrs. Gorman, away from Edgar Fane.

"I asked Simpson to find out everything he could about *you*," Edgar next informed Thea without a shred of remorse. "I have to be careful, I'm afraid. Women can be fortune hunters, the same as men. Can't they, Mrs. Gorman?"

"As you can see, Edgar loves to torment, and call

it teasing," Cynthia said. With her long narrow face, worldly green eyes and golden hair, she reminded Thea of a beautiful but restless lioness. "I understand your fiancé is a British earl. Lovely engagement ring—antique, is it? I adore jewelry. We can talk about your fiancé and jewelry if you like, Miss Pickford. Or the charms of a season at Saratoga. Edgar of course will want to confine the conversation to himself. But whatever you do, please refrain from asking about his paintings."

"Paintings? I've heard he enjoys working with oils and watercolors. Why wouldn't I ask about them?" Thea returned, artfully lifting one eyebrow.

"Dearest Cynthia, is your nose still out of joint?" Edgar sat down on Thea's other side, and without a word the waiters began to serve crystal compotes full of fresh peaches, strawberries and grapes. "She wanted my latest work of art, but I gave it to a lonely old gentleman who owns a couple of quaint old bookstores in Baltimore. He was most appreciative."

"So appreciative he checked out of his room at the United States Hotel the next day," a round-cheeked man with a spade-shaped beard chimed in. "Last I heard, he was planning to auction your landscape to the highest bidder, to avoid the bank foreclosing on his stores."

"What must he be thinking?" Edgar popped a strawberry in his mouth and chewed it with unselfconscious enthusiasm. "I'm no Rembrandt. But if someone's foolish enough to spend their well-earned dollars on dabbling I give away for free, I'll not put a crimp in their style."

Everyone laughed, and as the rhythm of the courses moved in watchlike precision from fruit to oysters on a bed of crushed ice, to a delicate clear soup, Thea's nerves settled into quiet determination. Mrs. Gorman spent several moments deliberately prying, but when Thea remained charming but vague the other woman turned to the man seated on her right. Conversations swirled over and around them; Edgar Fane, she discovered reluctantly, made for a thoughtful, entertaining host. By the time the fish was served—and she laughed with everyone else when the waiter presented her with an exquisitely prepared filet of sole—Thea was almost enjoying herself. The vertigo remained in abeyance, and beneath the table her knees had finally quit shaking.

But she had not forgotten her mission.

Find a weakness. Find evidence. Expose Edgar Fane as a liar and a thief.

"Is Saratoga Springs your favorite destination for the summer season?" she asked Mr. Fane during a conversational lull.

"Certainly has been a wise choice this year," he replied, smiling at her. "When I heard the prim-mouthed do-gooders had failed in their attempts to keep the Casino closed, I decided to signal my support by spending the season here at Saratoga. I've rented a cottage a few blocks away. When not entertaining friends there, I invite them to superlative suppers here at the Casino, to help Mr. Canfield keep his coffers full." Something in the way he studied Thea set warning bells to clanging. "A lot of my friends enjoy the game room upstairs. In fact, several acquaintances have won and lost considerable fortunes. You look disapproving. Tell me your opinion toward gambling, Miss Pickford. Is it a tool of evil, or the engine that keeps not only Canfield Casino but this little community from sinking into oblivion?"

Thea took several sips of water, but her palms dampened inside the doeskin evening gloves. "I don't care much for gambling away monies someone else has earned by the sweat of honest labor. If those men lose a fortune they earned with their own hands, that's their choice. But men who gamble away food from the table or the roof over their children's heads are dangerously irresponsible."

"Mmm. A well-thought-out response. How about ladies, Miss Pickford? Are you aware that Mr. Canfield has altered the old restrictions and now allows ladies to indulge? Gave them their very own gambling room. There's now a betting ring at the racetrack for them, as well. I believe Cynthia actually won herself a tidy bundle a few days ago." Edgar picked up his wineglass and touched it to Thea's as though to let her know he'd noticed she hadn't taken a single sip. "So you pass judgment on *ladies,* for gambling food from the table and the roof from over their children's heads?"

"I'd say either gender is equally vulnerable to the risk of gambling, Mr. Fane."

"You snagged yourself one of those religious reformers, Fane!" Smirking, a needle-thin man with a monocle surveyed Thea. "Miss Pickford doubtless attends church every Sunday, praying for fire to rain down on the rest of us heathens."

"I don't have the right to pass judgment on anybody." Thea leveled the oaf a look that made him drop the monocle. "Neither, sir, do you. I was asked a direct question. I answered honestly. If my sense of right and wrong differs from yours, perhaps the matter would best be addressed someplace other than a dinner party."

Cynthia Gorman clapped her hands. "One for you, Miss Pickford. Geoffrey, stop needling her. Besides, if

I recall my distant childhood catechism, God Himself does not approve of gambling, which is why I only indulge once or twice a year."

Mr. Fane emitted a loud groan. "Cynthia, dear, must we introduce religion? Almost as taboo as politics, is it not?"

"You started it, *dear.* And controversy certainly livens things up a bit. Don't you get tired of trivial gossip, Edgar?" She made a moue, shrugged her shoulders. "Of course, none of it matters to me."

"Ah. Trivial gossip." Still smiling, Edgar turned to Thea. "She wounds me with words, Miss Pickford, though she's one of my oldest friends. Tell me, since you seem to be fearless as well as honest, do you think God will strike me dead because I'm one of those who enjoys gambling large sums of money I haven't earned?"

Chapter Ten

The clinking of glasses and the scrape of cutlery against china stilled. Once again all gazes fastened onto Thea, including the sideways flash of sympathy from a waiter removing her plate. "If you prefer honesty," she returned, picking her way through a mine shaft of volatile responses, "I'd have to say I agree with Mrs. Gorman about God's view of gambling. I can't quote a precise verse of scripture. On the other hand, I do recall a verse where Jesus instructs His disciples to *'Judge not, that ye not be judged.'*"

"Told you she was one of those reformers."

"Shh!" someone hissed, then added, "Let her be. Noose is already around her neck...."

"Jesus ate with sinners, didn't He?" A greyhound-thin woman sitting opposite Thea leaned over the table. "You think you're being Jesus, Miss Pickford, surrounded by so many evil people? Got to warn us about our wicked ways?"

"That's enough!" Edgar Fane half rose. "Miss Pickford is *my* guest."

Thea shivered a little at the possessive tone but managed a reassuring smile. "It's all right, Mr. Fane. Truly. I'm not offended. I've attended many dinner parties where the conversations broke every social rule in the book, and frankly, found them stimulating."

Mr. Fane sank back down into his chair. "Stimulating?" He shook his head, laughed. "You're…quite the lady, aren't you?" His hand came down over hers and briefly squeezed.

Quick as a terrified mouse who just realized the tickly feeling was a tom cat's whiskers, Thea whipped her hand away and thrust it out of sight beneath the table. For a moment the room shifted off balance…or was she tipping sideways?

For some reason an image of Devlin Stone popped into her head, auburn-tipped brown hair windblown over his forehead, lake-colored eyes intent as he washed her hands with a gentleness she'd never experienced from a man. "I was reared to be a lady," she murmured. "As for faith, I haven't talked much about God or Jesus with anyone lately. I haven't made up my mind what to think, until now." She lifted a stubborn chin and faced them all. "Now I see that most people, whether they call themselves Christian or heathen, are quick to judge, and slow to understand opposing viewpoints. I have compelling personal reasons that govern my views on gambling, but I ask forgiveness for any offense I caused in stating them."

"Dessert, miss?" the waiter's voice inquired at her elbow.

Startled, Thea glanced up. His face was expressionless, but admiration briefly lit his eyes. "Thank you," she said. The icy ball in her stomach thawed as the rest of the waitstaff efficiently drew attention away from her.

Another lady made some remark about the superb quality of the meal and queried if anyone planned to attend the concert at Convention Hall the following night. Someone else across from her responded, and the atmosphere smoothed into gaiety once more.

Later, while coffee was being served, Edgar Fane leaned over to Thea, his voice pitched so only she could hear. "I have obligations for the rest of the week, but I must see you again. Will you join me for a private dinner, next Tuesday night? Just the two of us this time?"

Another eddy of dizziness warned Thea to stall; she ignored it. She had survived an evening with Edgar Fane and his friends, so the worst of the attacks must be under control. "I'd be honored—as long as you fetch me yourself, and leave Mr. Simpson to whatever other duties he performs for you."

"Ah. Humor, principles and pride. Miss Pickford, I just might come to find you irresistible."

Panic leaped through her like a sword flashing in moonlight. "Then beware, Mr. Fane," she retorted, and tossed her head. "At the moment, I am not inclined to reciprocate."

Devlin loved rainy days. He could think better, more clearly, on days when rain drummed on the roof and splattered on the earth.

Or at least he could until Miss Pickford-Lang erupted into his life. Something about the elusive lady didn't fit, either her dogged pursuit of Edgar Fane, or the secrecy and lies. All clear markers of malfeasance, yet Devlin was ready to stake his reputation on her innocence.

Restless, he prowled the two-bedroom suite he'd rented in the Cottage Wing of the United States Hotel, alternatively casting glances through the windows at the rain and the writing table covered with documents, reports and reams of information he'd been analyzing for—he tugged out his pocket watch—for six tedious hours.

Dev wearily plowed a hand through his hair. *I could resign, turn the Hotel Hustler case over to somebody else.* Despite pouring heart, soul and a significant stash of his own money into this case, Operative Stone had precious little to show for his efforts.

The fleeting impulse to quit trampled him like stampeding hooves. Dev rolled his head to relax the knotted muscles in his neck and shoulders.

"You're such a sap," he muttered aloud. Then, jaw set, he picked up the daily report he'd been working on for the last few hours. *"...concluded the female Miss Lang, aka Pickford, in need of closer surveillance, due to unflagging interest in E. F. Will await instructions while maintaining present persona."*

Was it possible to sound more priggish? With a muffled imprecation Dev tossed the weekly report back on the heap of papers, snagged his umbrella from the stand by the door then strode from the room. Back in Virginia he never used the contraptions; here they offered a valuable aid to anonymity.

When he reached the entrance to Congress Park he realized it had been his destination all along—a place to satisfy his hunger for green spaces, for a patch of earth that retained at least a partial resemblance to nature as God created it. Dev paid for his ten-cent ticket, skirted the elaborate Arcade and the few visitors sipping hot coffee in one of the colonnade cafés and headed toward the center of the park. Due to the rain, pathways and lawns were deserted. He might have been tramping across a wooded meadow at StoneHill, except for the blurred outline of the music pavilion with its quaint domed roof. Weather permitting, the band played concerts there every afternoon. Today, happily, weather did not permit. Unable to resist the novelty of having the space to himself, Dev headed for the ramp over the pond.

Then between the decorative cast-iron posts, he spied a solitary figure seated in one of the band chairs. Disappointment ripped through Devlin. Confound it, was it too much to ask, a half hour of his own, without tripping over some—

The figure turned slightly and he stopped dead, his disbelieving gaze on the profile of the face that had haunted his dreams for weeks now.

Dev set the umbrella aside, a dangerous sense of jubilation coursing through his veins. "Seems I'm not the only one who enjoys a good rain. We seem to have cultivated a habit for unexpected meetings, Miss Lang."

Slowly she rose to face him. Hatless and gloveless, today she wore a narrow pin-striped shirtwaist and plain navy skirt, which gave her the look of a schoolteacher as opposed to a well-turned-out heiress. "If I'd known in time it was you beneath the umbrella, I would have left before you saw me," she said.

Not a chance, Devlin thought, though he nodded agreeably. "I experienced a similar reaction when I realized the gazebo was occupied. Since the rain's picking up anyway, we may as well allow ourselves to enjoy a bit of natural drama, together. Is that what you came out here to do? Enjoy the rain?"

A shawl was draped over the back of her chair; averting her gaze, Miss Lang wrapped it around her shoulders. "I suppose you think I'm even more of a peculiar sort of female than you already did, for seeking an isolated spot outside in the middle of a rainstorm."

"No more peculiar than a man after the same thing." He sensed her wariness and arranged a pair of the spindle-backed chairs where he could not only watch Miss Lang but prevent her from bolting across the ramp. "Mrs. Chudd's warm and dry in her room, I take it?" A wisp of a reciprocal smile fluttered before she nodded. "Good." He rubbed his palms together. "Then there's no reason we can't make the most of our opportunity to share what we've been up to this past week."

Between droning raindrops, turgid silence fell until Devlin plowed ahead. "I've only caught a glimpse of you once, outside a tearoom with several other ladies." And experienced far too much relief, because for the past several days he'd been shadowing Edgar Fane in an exhausting round of shopping, dining, solitary painting expeditions and noisy group excursions to every tourist attraction within ten miles. Not once had Miss Lang been part of his entourage.

"I didn't think you'd care to associate with a woman who makes a public fool of herself," she finally murmured.

"Oh, I don't know. I've seen a quite a bit of foolery over the years. Perhaps you don't care to associate with a man who's witnessed human behavior at its worst, and too often been unable to correct it?"

"Well, when you put it like that." Solemn-faced, she sat back down. "Your phrasing is intriguing. You sound like either a preacher or a policeman."

Fortunately a lifetime around horses and several years as a Secret Service operative had taught him not to betray strong emotion, particularly anger, fear—or surprise. "An intriguing analysis. Well, despite the unpleasant price you paid later, you were pretty entertaining the other day, there by the lake." He twitched a chair around and straddled it, propping his forearms over the back. "Was it worth being sick in the bushes? Did you receive your invitation?"

"Yes." A fleeting sideways glance. "Dinner at the Casino. I was offered, like bait to a bear, to a table full of his acquaintances."

Rage prickled his careful equanimity. "I'm sorry. Are you all right? Did the vertigo—"

"They made me angry. I didn't have a spell. The anger might have helped, but I've thought about it a lot ever since, and I think there's a more practical solution."

"And that is?" he asked when she seemed hesitant to continue.

"When you were a child, were you ever afraid of monsters hiding under the bed? And when you finally found the courage to check, you discovered your fear was the product of a too-vivid imagination?"

"So you no longer believe Edgar Fane is a monster."

"Let's just say I've come to understand that some monsters know how to disguise themselves more discreetly than others. His friends are mostly sycophants. A few tried to be kind. I can hold my own with them."

"Ah." This time they watched the rain in companionable silence. "Something's still troubling you," Dev eventually observed.

"Yes." Her shoulders lifted in a nervous shrug. "You really are very perceptive. Um…would you mind if I ask you something?" When he hummed a lazy sound of assent Miss Lang cleared her throat, fiddled with the ends of her shawl, then shared softly, "I don't know why, but for some reason it matters that you not think the worst of me. A month ago I didn't know you existed, but now…" She ran her finger over the chair finial, color staining her cheeks. "Never mind. This is silly. It must be the weather. Rainy days have always made me introspective. But that doesn't mean I should—"

"I feel the same way, about rainy days," Dev interrupted. Reaching down, he let his hand hover over hers for a moment, and when she didn't flinch away he gave her restless fingers a reassuring squeeze. "We have more in common than you realize, Miss Lang. Come now, tell me what's troubling you. Today I promise not to bite."

Chapter Eleven

Only a flicker of a smile appeared. "My last name isn't really Lang." Above the white collar of the shirtwaist her throat muscles stretched taut. "I would prefer to not reveal my surname right now. If you…could you call me Thea? That's my Christian name. I—it's unconventional, but here at Saratoga the unconventional seems to be the accepted standard of behavior. My name is really Theodora, but most times I prefer Thea. Theodora sounds too formal, when the man I'm talking to has… seen me at my worst."

In the muted, rain-drenched world her brown eyes had darkened to the color of wet pine bark. Automatically Dev registered the subtleties of her body that conveyed truth telling—slightly expanded pupils, crinkly eyes accompanying her shy smile, leaning slightly toward him—even as he filed away the revelation that she was afraid to tell him her last name. "Thea. It suits you. A strong name, and a deep one. Family name?"

"No."

He lifted an eyebrow. "Hmm. Touched one of those chords you don't want to play, did I? No, don't turn all tense on me... Thea. Yeah, that fits, much better than Miss Pickford, or Miss Lang. To even things up, call me Devlin. My grandmother was Irish. You may have noticed when the sun shines on my hair there's a wee bit o' red? But that's all the Irish heritage I received, besides the name. My grandmother died when I was two so I don't remember anything else about the woman responsible for naming me."

"Your parents didn't choose your name?"

"They couldn't agree, so they asked her to." He could hear the curtness in his own voice, but Thea merely nodded her head, that wistful aura hovering around her again, twisting his heartstrings. "What else did you want to ask me about?" he added quickly. Let it be Edgar Fane, or something about the vertigo. Or the weather, for crying out loud. Just—no prying questions where too much honesty might be demanded.

With this woman, he should have known better.

"Have you ever made one mistake," she said, the words emerging pensive and slow, "and no matter how hard you try to make up for it, the rest of your life crumbles a piece at a time, until you're left with nothing but wreckage?"

For a moment Dev scrambled for solid footing in a mental quicksand. "Everybody makes mistakes," he finally ventured. "It's the price we pay for being human. Some mistakes have lasting consequences, some pass into oblivion. I try not to dwell on mine more than I can help. I like to think I've done the best I can, to make a good life for myself." Fine words, from a man who an hour earlier had been halfway ready to hop aboard the first southbound train. "What mistake do you believe has destroyed your life, Thea?"

"Sometimes...being born?" A hollow laugh did little to ease the uncomfortable pall that descended between them. "I beg your pardon, Devlin. My grandfather scolds me about my propensity to talk before I think about how the words will sound aloud. It must be a family trait."

He barely heard the last sentence, since she'd mumbled it beneath her breath. "You've had some troubles, haven't you?" He kept his voice gentle. "This fiancé from England. He's a fabrication, right?" She nodded, but when she would have responded Dev shook his head. "It's all right. I've known almost from the first. You have your reasons, same as how you don't feel you can share your real surname. You asked me once if I'd ever been desperate. Are your parents trying to force you into a marriage you don't want? Is that why you came to Saratoga with a false name and a manufactured betrothal in your trunk, to chase after one of the country's wealthiest bachelors without looking...desperate?"

"If only it were that simple." Shifting on the chair, words abruptly burst forth in a passionate gush. "I'm not chasing Edgar Fane in hopes of a proposal. I despise him. He's a cad, and the only reason I'm 'chasing' him is because I want to find the evidence to stop him from ruining someone else's life. But nothing I've planned is turning out the way I expected. Nothing. Tuesday night is my last chance—he's leaving next week. One of his lady friends, a Mrs. Gorman, told me. And it's Sunday...." She stared through Devlin as though peering into a lake filled with monsters. "I don't know if I have the courage. I'm afraid I'll have an attack, I'm afraid I'll make a mistake and he'll know I'm a fraud, I'm—" her voice dropped to a broken whisper "—I'm afraid,

and I'm ashamed of it. But I have to do this. Have to…"
She pressed her lips together until they turned white.

The skin beneath her eyes looked bruised; above the tattoo of rain on the roof Devlin could hear the labored rasp of her breath. Without a qualm he mentally laid aside badge and credentials, and focused all his skill on coaxing back the woman who had faced down a crowd of bored sophisticates at the Casino.

"Don't be ashamed of fear," he said, leaning closer until their heads were inches apart. "It's an instinct, designed to protect you. If you're afraid to share a meal alone with Edgar Fane, perhaps you should heed those instincts, and call it off."

"I can't. I won't."

"Mmm. Which one, Thea?"

Some of the wildness dissipated, and the white slash of her mouth softened. "Won't. Grandfather tells me I'm more stubborn than an ink stain. My friends are kinder. They call it resolve. Mr. Stone—I mean, Devlin? Do you believe in God?"

What in the—? "You want to know if I believe in God?" Confound it, but her mind swished about like a horse's tail chasing off flies. She nodded. Dev sat back in the chair and studied on the question for a moment or two. "Well, yes, I suppose so. Most people do, I reckon. My dad was a praying man. But he died when I was six. I guess I've been looking ever since for what he found. Why do you ask, Thea?" There. That was better, him asking the questions. "This shame you're feeling. You think God's punishing you?"

"I don't know. I was sort of hoping you would. I used to say my prayers faithfully, at mealtimes and bedtimes, when I was a girl. But God never answered. When I was older, everyone I asked seemed to think God was whoever or whatever we created in our minds, as a way to cope with life. For a while I guess I came to believe them, except..."

"Except what?" Abruptly Devlin turned his chair back around and sat forward, his gaze never leaving Thea's face.

"Except my grandfather always believed God really was this omniscient Being, Someone who cared. Over the years we've attended many lectures by atheists, readings by naturalists or presentations by scientists, all of them trying to prove God doesn't exist. Or that we were all gods, ourselves. Grandfather always listened politely, always thanked them. Then on the way home he'd remind me that the greatest gift we enjoy as Americans is the right to believe whatever we choose to. He told me his choice was to place his faith in the God of the Bible, rather than human beings."

Incredible as the notion sounded, it was as though her words reached inside Devlin's own mind, releasing questions that had festered for years that he hadn't known how to ask. "And has he changed his mind?"

Shoulders slumping, she shook her head, started to speak, then her lips clamped back together.

"Lately I've been thinking about God more than I used to," he said, because those haunting eyes still begged for communion with another soul, and he wanted to be the person Thea communed with. He'd seen her at her worst, held her when she was too weak to stand. She'd allowed herself to be vulnerable with him.

Assuming for the moment God did exist, and did care, God would know this particular woman had stomped to dust all Dev's defenses against lying females.

"I was engaged once, years ago," he said. "Sylvia was a churchgoer. We attended services every Sunday for almost five years. Then she went to visit relatives in North Carolina, and I went to New York City. When I returned home to Virginia a few months later, Sylvia had eloped with a banker she met on the train."

"B-but you'd known each other for years. You were engaged." Her voice trailed away. "I'm sorry, Devlin. No wonder you didn't like me when we first met."

He managed a crooked smile. "It's a fact I'm not too fond of liars. Her being so religious, I couldn't understand how she could stab me in the back. For a long time I didn't have much use for God. Pretty silly, I guess, blaming God when it's a person who's at fault."

"You knew each other for *five years*."

Something inside Devlin relaxed. "Mmm. That's true. I'll put it this way. Back home, one of our neighbors owns an old plow horse, put to pasture years ago. I used to see old Betsy every time I drove to town, even stopped occasionally to give her a carrot. But that doesn't mean I'd walk up behind her and clap my hands. I can see what you're thinking. No, I'm not comparing Sylvia to a decrepit plow horse."

They shared a look of perfect understanding, and that unfamiliar sensation—soft, welcoming—uncurled even further. "You're a literal-minded soul, aren't you? Let's just say I knew Sylvia's outside, but I never saw her sick and afraid, never talked with her about God, or what went on inside her head." No weighty subjects like faith and fear. Good and evil. Hopes. Dreams. "In retrospect, even after 'knowing' her all those years I'd have to confess Sylvia and I never left the barn."

"I may be literal, but now you sound like a horseman. You wear a lot of hats, Devlin Stone." Her cheeks were flushed, her awkwardness charming. "See? I do know how to be metaphorical."

Unfortunately, her statement forced him to don his "professional" hat again. The woman seated beside him had not only lied to him, she was still hiding some monstrous secret; he knew little about her background, including her surname. She could still be a wanted criminal, even an accomplice of the Hotel Hustler, and Devlin Stone's profession as a Secret Service operative might be irrevocably compromised if he blindly accepted her innocence.

Yet Dev felt in his gut that he still understood Thea better than he ever had Sylvia. "Knowing" a woman must include more than the marriage bed. He swallowed hard as new truths tugged him completely out of the barn, beyond the pasture and into an unexplored forest: if he'd had to choose between the two women, Sylvia would have been left inside that barn.

But if the choice were between Thea and the Service?

Dev couldn't answer that question, so he shoved it deep out of sight.

Outside the gazebo, the rain abruptly dwindled to a misting shower. The air brightened, and a shaft of sunlight speared through the receding clouds, directly onto the chairs where Devlin and Thea sat.

Dev lifted his hand and watched the interplay of golden light transfuse the skin. "Do you think," he mused, watching the bar of light create a golden nimbus around her, "that after talking about Him so much, God might be trying to gain our attention here?"

Thea lifted her hand as well, holding it beside Devlin's, a slender-fingered, smaller and paler appendage bathed into transparency by sunlight. "If He is, I wonder what He's trying to tell us. I've been steeped in symbols and metaphors all my life. Frankly, I'm weary of them. I suppose I am a literal-minded soul. If the Almighty needs to send word to me, it will need to be something more tangible than a burning bush, or a sunbeam."

A warning chill brushed Dev's spine. "Have a care, Thea. That sounded more like a challenge than a request. My theology might be sketchy, but I don't think God responds well to demands."

Chapter Twelve

Thea sneaked sidelong peeks at Devlin as they strolled along the waterlogged path toward the entrance to the park. He moved with the unselfconscious power of a man comfortable enough in his own skin to not have to make an impression on others. Yet it was that unassuming confidence that had captivated her heart.

The tug drawing her to him strengthened every time they talked. She wanted to pursue their discourse about God; for months her hunger for meaningful conversation had remained unsatisfied because her thirst for justice was insatiable. But Devlin's caution about not tempting God, however well-intentioned, had effectively muzzled her mouth. For all of her life Thea had struggled with a feeling, however irrational, of inferiority. All right, so shaking a fist at God might result in eternal rejection. Until this moment, she hadn't really cared; the compulsion to avenge Grandfather had been her only solution to the ever-present memory of his gaunt face behind those iron bars.

Still, for a moment or two back in the gazebo Thea had almost yielded to the stronger-than-ever temptation to blurt out the entire sordid story to the only man other than Charles Langston who really *listened* to her.

"What is it?" His deep voice interrupted her melancholy; his warm hand pressed briefly at the small of her back, steadying her. "You're too quiet, and you look almost…" He halted on the path, stepping in front of her, his gaze searching her face, then lifting to scan the dripping shrubbery and trees. "I can't describe it," he finished slowly. "Not frightened, or angry, but something in between. It's a baffling expression. The first time I saw you, it was this expression that grabbed my attention."

Before she could frame an answer he shook his head and resumed walking. "It's Edgar Fane, isn't it? What has he done to you, Thea?"

"At the moment, he's done nothing. Devlin, I wish I could explain, but it wouldn't be fair to you. It means more than you can possibly understand, to have shared what I could, and that you…you've listened to me." She drew in a hard breath. "I'm having dinner with Edgar Fane tomorrow night because I have to, not because I want to. I'm telling you the truth, Devlin."

"You have to? Is he threatening you, Thea? Holding a gun to the head of someone you love?"

Shocked, before she could collect herself Thea laid a hand on his forearm. His head whipped around, scrutinizing her face with scorching intensity. Beneath her fingers and his damp tweed jacket, the muscles were hard as wrought iron fence posts. "Devlin—" her throat burned, and she passed her tongue around lips gone dry as dust "—I'm in no danger from Mr. Fane." It was the other way around, but she could not afford to confess. Not yet. "I'll explain, after Tuesday night. If you still want to hear."

Once again his hand covered hers, only unlike that

brief instant in the gazebo, this time the fingers crushed hers in a bruising grip. "I'll want to hear. But if he hurts you, Thea, he'll have to answer to me."

The light eyes had turned dark as charcoal, with diamond-bright chips hard enough to shatter a bone—or break a heart.

"You mustn't talk like that," she managed unsteadily. "I don't want you to make an enemy of this man. He... Devlin, his family is one of the most powerful in America. He could ruin you."

"And you're immune?"

"He thinks I'm just a pretty new toy. A novelty to entertain him, assuage the boredom. If I'm careful—and I have been—he'll have no reason to think anything else."

Devlin's nostrils flared, and for a moment Thea wondered if his dark glower would turn her to a pillar of salt. Then he released her and folded his arms across his chest. "You're lying," he snapped. "You despise the man, and you're afraid of him."

"I haven't had a spell. How can you *know?* Nobody else—"

"Your eyes. The way your chin tilts upward, how your nose crinkles when you talk about him. That's the contempt." Without warning his arm whipped out and he snagged her hand again, holding it up in front of her face. "Cold hands, which you twine together to try and control the fear. Listen to me, Thea!" A single tug brought her close enough to feel the heat of his body. "Whatever you feel compelled to do, it's not worth your reputation, or your self-respect. Remember the lake, and stay away from Edgar Fane."

"What would you know about it?" she flung back, stung. "Or is it...you still think I'm a—a floozy. I shared my heart with you, I actually trusted you enough, I believed you'd changed your mind about me." Her voice rose; biting her lip, she hurriedly glanced about the rain-soaked park.

"Great glory, woman!" Devlin Stone muttered. "You don't know anything."

Suddenly his free hand cupped her chin, tilting her head back. Rough-tipped fingers stroked down the line of her jaw, brushed over the pulse throbbing in her neck. "You don't know anything," he repeated in a growling undertone. Then he dipped his head and kissed her.

Thea gasped against his lips, closing her eyes as a firestorm of startled wonder consumed her. Her hands fumbled for purchase until they found Devlin's shoulders, muscles rippling with an entirely different strength from the day he'd found her helpless in the bushes. He'd offered her tenderness then, a pallid shadow of the intense response she'd unwittingly provoked now.

His mouth slid a breathy path beneath her jaw, then trailed fleeting kisses to her eyes, her forehead. Goose bumps raced over Thea's skin. A soft sound, somewhere between a laugh and a groan, blew into her ear. "You taste of rain, and flowers," he whispered, and pressed his lips against her temple. "And temptation."

Then his head lifted, his hands curved around her waist and he firmly set her at arms' length. In the golden mist rising from the saturated earth he loomed over Thea like an ancient Greek warrior in a gentleman's clothing. Emotion throbbed between them, beating time between each labored breath. Finally Devlin passed a hand around the back of his neck, and heaved an explosive sigh.

"I won't apologize, because I wouldn't mean it." A

crooked smile flickered. "Don't look like that. I might give in and kiss you again."

"All right. But I'm still eating dinner with Edgar Fane tomorrow night."

He groaned and flicked a glance heavenward. "Thea...is that why you think I kissed you? As a diversion? Seduction as the weapon of choice to bend you to my will?"

"Well, how would I know?" she threw back crossly. "Nobody's ever kissed me like that before. I mean, I'm not a naive schoolgirl, I've been courted by several gentlemen...." A blush burned. "See what you've done? You've rendered me a featherhead."

"That makes two of us. I've broken every rule in every book, so I may as well do a thorough job of it." Grabbing her hands again, he lifted them to his mouth and pressed a kiss against the knuckles. "Tomorrow night? I'll be watching as well as waiting, Thea. Don't worry. Neither you nor Edgar will see me. You're not alone anymore, all right?"

"There's something you're not telling me, isn't there?"

One dark eyebrow lifted. "Did you think you were the only one with secrets?" He gave her hands a final squeeze, then released them. "I'll be watching," he repeated, then swiveled and loped off between a hedge of boxwoods.

Thea stood in the middle of the deserted path, one hand fisted at her midriff in a vain attempt to calm her stuttering heart, the other pressed against her mouth, in an equally vain attempt to hold the warmth of his lips against hers.

Chapter Thirteen

"Take them into the room at the end of this hall," Edgar ordered the sweating laborers. "Carefully, my good fellows! The contents of those crates are invaluable to me." Chuckling to himself, he followed the two men down the rabbit warren hallways of the old house, noting the way they took care to lower the crates to avoid hitting the antique sconces on the walls.

After unpacking the crates, the laborer mopped his sweating brow and glanced at Edgar. "Where you want us to stack these frames, Mr. Fane?"

"Against the empty wall, to the right of the doorway. You'll see where I've rolled up the carpet and moved the furniture?"

"Yassir."

Unobservant dunderhead, Edgar thought. But then, most people were. After the workmen departed he rang for the butler. "Dodd? Please inform the housekeeper that I need a key for the door to the study down this hall. Tell her—what's her name again?"

"Mrs. Surrey, sir."

"Ah, yes. Tell Mrs. Surrey to instruct the housemaids to stay out of that room for now. I'll be gone for the night. If Simpson arrives tomorrow before I do, direct him to the morning-room office. I've left the correspondence on the desk there."

"As you wish, Mr. Fane."

An hour later, when the house was empty of everyone but Edgar, he strode down the narrow hallway and into the study. The frames had been stacked, most of them carefully, against the wall. Smiling in satisfaction, Edgar ran his fingers along heavily ornate gilt edges, polished cherry...ebonized wood that gleamed in the gaslight. *Which one?* he thought, in his mind's eye filling out the frame with a picture. A fruit study, perhaps for the cherry. An African village for the ebonized wood. Quietly amused, he turned off the wall lights and left, rubbing his hands together in anticipation.

Now he could focus all his attention on Tuesday evening, and the surprise he'd planned for Miss Pickford.

"Don't know why ya turned so particular," Mrs. Chudd grumped as she and Thea waited in the lobby for Mr. Fane's carriage. "M'rheumatism's acting up. And he better not serve shellfish. You know I don't eat shellfish. Gives me hives."

"You know quite well I can't go to a strange house, for a private dinner with a gentleman unknown to the family, without you," Thea repeated, not for the first time. "Some proprieties are common sense, even here in Saratoga Springs."

"Humph. No need to get on a high horse. I know my place." Her double chins quivered. "Your grandpapa ought to be 'shamed, agreeing to this twaddle." The heavy walking cane she'd produced to aid her with her "rheumatism" thunked dourly on the tiled floor. "But you needn't fret. My mouth won't be catching any flies."

By the time the shiny black coupé drew to a smooth halt in front of a large rambling house, Thea's nerves had dissolved into a gummy mess lodged beneath her breastbone. Light ripples of dizziness washed over her at odd moments, but she was able to ignore them, offering Mr. Fane a dazzling smile when he opened the carriage door himself to help her out.

"I appreciate your keeping our dinner engagement, since I was unable to obey my marching orders to pick you up myself." He greeted her with a bow. "An unavoidable telephone call. May I compliment you on your lovely costume? That shade of pink—mauve, I believe they call it—suits you."

His deft compliment flustered her. Evil villains weren't supposed to be so amenable. "Thank you. This is my companion, Mrs. Chudd."

"You are both welcome."

By the time dinner was served, Thea had almost relaxed enough to taste some of the food. Mr. Fane made no untoward remarks, instead offering almost courtly discourse devoid of sarcasm or scandal; after several attempts to include Mrs. Chudd in the conversation, however, he left her companion alone, giving Thea a conspiratorial wink.

"You say this house belongs to friends of your family," Thea ventured toward the end of the meal. She glanced around the cluttered dining room, suppressing a shudder. Pictures hung on every inch of wall space, and the massive table could have accommodated thirty guests. The walls were papered a dark red color that reminded her of calf's liver.

Edgar laughed. "Monstrous, isn't it? I believe the furniture in this room hasn't been moved in a hundred years. Don't worry, we'll have dessert in the morning room. It's one of my favorite spots, tucked away at the back of the house. Lots of windows, with a peaceful view of a pond, complete with ducks. The sun sets directly over it. I've been meaning to paint the scene. Perhaps," he added, idly tracing his index finger around the rim of his water glass, "you'll provide me with sufficient inspiration."

Thea almost choked, and hastily lifted her napkin to dab her mouth. Apparently the wolf had decided it was time to discard the sheep's clothing. "Everyone talks about your paintings—when you're not around, of course. But I've never seen one of your efforts. Does that mean you're a serious artist, or a dilettante, Mr. Fane?"

"When I decide, I'll let you know." Shifting, he scooted his chair a little closer to Thea's. "What about you, Miss Pickford? While pining for your English aristocrat, how do you entertain yourself, aside from reeling in gentlemen with your fishing pole?"

Thea wondered if this was how a fish felt, when the shiny bug gave way to a sharp hook. She laid the napkin by her plate, and ordered her face muscles to smile. "I enjoy fresh air and vigorous exercise, Mr. Fane, so I go for lots of walks. Back home I own a safety bicycle. I also enjoy meeting and talking with people." Always tell the truth whenever possible, she'd learned. Worming in a lie or two between made them more believable. "And I share everything I do, everyone I meet, with my Neville, in long weekly letters. We're thinking of spending every season in a different spa resort. How about you,

Mr. Fane? Do you have any preferences as to locale? I've heard Newport has become a fashionable destination, with first-class beaches. Have you ever been there?"

"Several times." Toying with his earlobe, he leaned closer and continued in a lowered voice, "If you plan to extend your season there, perhaps I could change my itinerary."

Shock almost made her jump. Boys had teased her, gentlemen had flirted, a few here at Saratoga had been a trifle forward. But Mr. Fane was neither a boy, a boor, nor she well knew, a gentleman. Given the circumstances, she should have anticipated such remarks.

"How flattering, Mr. Fane. But you're a little more forthright than I'm comfortable with, even with the presence of a chaperone."

"Agreed." He quit fiddling with his ear, studying her for a moment before he rose lithely to his feet. "I have just the solution. Mrs. Chudd? May I show you to the library? There's a comfortable chair, with a gout stool, which will be more comfortable for you. The Daubneys have wide and varied tastes. I daresay we can find you a good book to read while Miss Pickford and I stroll by the pond."

Chapter Fourteen

Moments later, her traitorous chaperone was happily ensconced with Tolstoy, her leg resting on the gout stool. Mr. Fane led Thea down several bisecting hallways into a large, airy room with wicker furniture and Boston ferns. Two paddle fans lazily moved the air. "Over here," he said. "We've missed most of the sunset, but there's still enough light to appreciate the view."

She approached warily; he had placed himself between a side table and a corner, leaving Thea little room. "Very serene," she agreed. And very isolated. "Um... I believe it's too dark for a walk."

"Possibly. I wouldn't want you to be nervous, so..." He took a step toward her, his mouth twitching when Thea stiffened. He reached past her and tugged the chain to a Tiffany floor lamp. "There you go. A bit of artificial light, to help you relax? Tell me, Miss Pickford, what really prompted an engaged lady to accept a private dinner invitation with a man like me?"

"A man like you? Heavens, Mr. Fane, have you crafted some nasty plot to drug the coffee, sell me to the Arabs? Or—" she darted around him, over to a floor globe situated between a revolving bookstand and a chair "—are you deliberately trying to fluster me?" With a flick of her wrist she set the globe awhirl and prayed her internal spinning would remain stationary for one more hour. She needed places, names—any clue, however oblique, to Edgar Fane's private life. A chink in his impenetrable armor. "I would like to know why one of the richest men in the country would ask a lady engaged to another man to have a private dinner with him."

"Irrepressibly impertinent. I think I like it." Mr. Fane ambled toward her, head cocked to the side and a brooding expression hiding his thoughts. "Would you believe me if I said loneliness?"

"No."

"Are you always this forthright, Miss Pickford?"

Her conscience winced, but Thea answered steadily enough. "I'm not going to hang on your every word, or offer flattering sobriquets in the hope you'll offer to drape me in jewels. On the other hand, I would like to understand the man hiding inside a crowd of hangers-on. Do you have a—a real job, Mr. Fane? Or do you merely enjoy spending the family fortune?" She stopped, biting her lip. "I beg your pardon. That *was* impertinent of me."

"You know, Miss Pickford… I wonder about you. I really do. I'm not sure you want to understand me as much as you want to—how shall I phrase it? Test the waters? See if I'm a better catch than your English earl?"

"I'm sorry an impulse to attract your attention led you to believe I could be that sort of woman."

"You already know I'm a wealthy man, Miss Pickford. Your fiancé might be an earl, but that doesn't mean he's well-heeled. I'm used to people who hope to benefit from my, I believe *largesse* is one of the press's favorite descriptions. Of course, many of them are the women who hope for a marriage proposal."

"I do not want to marry you, Mr. Fane."

For the first time a flicker of surprise cracked his set features. "You actually sound as though you mean that."

"Whatever else you believe or your secretary spy reports about me, you can count on my complete disregard for such an alliance." A stew of vicious emotions bubbled inside. She was a bat-brained idiot, to think she could pry information from a man sophisticated enough to convince bankers and government agencies of his innocence. "Mr. Fane, I think we should—"

"Well, well, well...what have I interrupted?" Cynthia Gorman emerged from the shadowed hall. Lifting a graceful hand, she flicked on an electric light switch, and green-gold light illuminated the morning room. "Forgive me, my dears. And here I thought *I* was the only woman to enjoy a cozy tryst with Edgar."

A flash of rage, quickly banked, darkened Mr. Fane's eyes but he recovered rapidly. "Cynthia, don't be more catty than you have to." He met the other woman in the middle of the room, effectively blocking her from Thea. "What are you doing here? I'll have that butler sacked."

"Oh, stop sputtering, darling. I told him I stopped by to fetch my parasol. I left it yesterday, in one of these private tucked-away rooms. The ones you like to hide people in. Forgive me, Miss Pickford. No offense intended. Edgar and I are forever teasing each other."

"None taken." Eyeing the doorway into the hall, Thea inched toward a sitting area behind Cynthia Gorman. "I should go anyway. My companion is elderly, and doesn't need to stay out too late."

Cynthia gave a peal of laughter. "The old woman in the library? She's snoring like an elephant with a cold. Please. I'll fetch my parasol, whisk myself out. Carry on with your evening together, and pretend you never saw me."

"I'm almost to a point where pretending won't be necessary," Mr. Fane said.

The caustic retort wiped the smile off Cynthia's face. "I've apologized. Nicely. Don't turn into an oaf, Edgar." Long, elegant fingers stroked down his sleeve. "I promise to be gone before you've taken a first sip of the coffee I smelled perking. Is it from those Jamaican beans you like so much? You'll enjoy it, Miss Pickford. Make sure you ask for some of the English biscuits to go with your brew. Mayhap it will remind you of your earl, loving you from afar." Smiling like a mischievous cat, she engulfed Thea in a quick hug, then disappeared in a froth of white lawn and lace.

"Ah, Cynthia. The air is rife with shiny knives when she doesn't get her way." Mr. Fane reached Thea's side. "You needn't glare at me accusingly. I did not invite her to be part of a ménage à trois."

"I beg your pardon? A what?"

Chagrin softened the thick ridges scoring his forehead; in all the weeks she'd been following him, Thea had never witnessed a display of such rancor. "Never mind," he said, but his smile looked forced. "I shouldn't have mentioned it. Let's have some of that coffee."

Her insides felt as though she were squeezing them through a wringer washing machine. Time was evaporating, the mood darkening, and she was…desperate.

Perhaps she could bait him with words, goad him into an unguarded response. "Only if you tell me why the son of one of the most influential men in the country spends most of his time doing…nothing useful. Along with healthy activities and socializing, like my companion I read a lot, Mr. Fane. Since arriving at Saratoga Springs I've discovered you're a favorite topic of conversation among people and newspaper articles, yet I still know very little about you. And your manner to Mrs. Gorman just now… I'm wondering if I made a mistake, accepting your dinner invitation." Invisible pressure against the side of her head gave an ominous push, and she surreptitiously gripped the curved back of a wicker chair.

"I was concerned her remarks had offended you. We've known each other for years, remember. Sometimes she abuses our friendship and I call her hand. Don't allow her jealousy to—"

"This has nothing to do with Mrs. Gorman. It's late, and I think I should leave. Can you direct me back to the library, please?"

"Are you all right, Miss Pickford?" Frown deepening, he studied her. "You're not acting like yourself." Slowly his hand closed around her elbow in a light grip, and it took the last of Thea's dwindling courage not to jerk away. "Very well. I'll take you to Mrs. Chudd."

Tension vibrated in the press of his fingers, and the way his gaze seemed to dart about every room they passed. Or perhaps she was superimposing her own nerves over his? He left Thea seated in the entry hall while he went to wake her companion and summon the driver; within moments he was handing her and a querulous Mrs. Chudd into the carriage.

"An interesting evening," he said, bowing over her fingers, which unforgivably trembled. "With an interesting woman. What a shame circumstances forbade the opportunity to get to know each other better. Mrs. Gorman has a lot to answer for."

All the way back to the hotel, with Mrs. Chudd glowering and silent on the opposite seat, Thea wondered at those parting words, and cursed herself for her ineptitude.

She hadn't even discovered Edgar Fane's pending destination, much less a crumb of condemnatory evidence.

The vertigo hit with the force of a nor'easter while she plaited her hair for bed.

"What are you doing here?" Edgar stalked across the room to Cynthia, who was sitting on a Turkish divan while she smoked one of his Cuban cigars. The affectation disgusted him, because whenever he smoked around her she taunted him about the filthy habit and vile odor.

"Saving you from yourself." She stubbed out the cigar and stood, idly waving the smoke away with her hand. "Why the interest in that girl, Edgar? You know she's only after your family fortune."

"You know less about her than I do." He went to stand over her, but Cynthia merely lifted her brow. Edgar took her chin in a forceful grip. "But I do know you, and this cat-and-the-empty-birdcage look. What have you been doing in my house, hmm? Tell me, my dear. I'm in no mood to play games this evening."

"Too bad." She shoved his hand away. "You play them so well. All right, I can tell you're in a beastly mood. I did forget my parasol, but I was at loose ends this evening so decided to prowl around this ridiculous pile of bricks while I waited for Miss Prim to decide whether or not to stay for coffee." A nasty smile curled her lips. "I found a locked door, in the opposite wing? And you know what they say about curiosity."

A sense of inevitability settled over Edgar, and he turned away from her until he could school his face to a polite mask. "I take it you charmed my soon-to-be-former housekeeper into unlocking the door?"

"Of course. I'm not stupid, my dear, and neither are you. I've wondered, for quite some time now, what you were doing with your many peregrinations from city to city, like Diogenes looking for the light. You're a very clever man, aren't you?"

"Yes. Why don't we go for a moonlit walk by the pond, and discuss the terms of your silence? It wouldn't do for Mrs. Surrey to overhear anything."

Cynthia tossed her head. "I don't mind filling in for Miss Pickford. But if you try to kiss me to seal the deal, tonight I might be inclined to bite first."

"You'll probably do more than that," Edgar replied, and tucked her hand through his crooked arm.

A thunderbolt of anticipation tightened his muscles, while every nerve tingled over the bold step he was about to take. How…fortuitous?…that Cynthia turned up earlier in the library. He'd grown tired of her possessiveness anyway, and had actually toyed with the idea of quelling it through a genuine pursuit of the intriguing Miss Pickford. On the other hand, he would still pursue Theodora, though the outcome for both women would be quite different from what they hoped.

"What are you smiling about?" Cynthia grumped

beside him. "Now *you* look like the cat by the empty birdcage."

Edgar patted her hand. "All in good time, my dear. All in good time."

Devlin waited until Thea and Mrs. Chudd entered the Grand Union Hotel before he stepped out of the shadows and followed them inside. *She'd looked pale, and drained, as though the evening had sucked color and life from her.* The open rotunda stretched all the way to the top floor; balconies on each level allowed guests to peer down into the lobby. Dev unfolded the newspaper he'd been carrying and leaned against one of the marble columns, watching with relief when the two women trudged along the second floor landing without glancing down. Just before they disappeared down a hallway Thea seemed to wobble, and one hand braced against the balcony railing until she recovered.

Moving rapidly, Dev mounted the staircase after them, gliding with soundless step to the corridor they had entered. A moment later he heard the sound of a key rattling in the lock, and a low murmur of voices.

For the moment, Thea was safe.

He padded to the end of the hall, where he discovered a small open parlor. Excellent. Relieved, Devlin stationed himself so he could see if anyone else followed Thea back to the hotel, or showed untoward interest in her hotel room. At a little past midnight a noisy family tromped back to a room two doors down from Thea's, and a half hour later the night watchman wandered past the parlor for the second time.

"Still here, eh?" Bald and potbellied, the guard

smiled sympathetically. "Fight with the missus? She lock you out of the room?"

Devlin yawned. "Worse. Insomnia," he said. "She snores."

Nodding, the watchman moved on. At two o'clock Dev concluded Thea was safely asleep. No suspicious strangers lurked outside her room. And if she'd suffered an attack of vertigo, she and Mrs. Chudd were handling it. For now, the need for vigilance was over.

Back in his own rooms, after writing his report Devlin passed the rest of a miserable night tormenting himself with images: Thea, dining with Edgar Fane; Thea falling ill and *Fane* holding her close, bathing her face with a cool cloth. Thea and Fane, laughing because the Hotel Hustler was not one man, but a team, and Devlin Stone had been duped by another woman. All her self-conscious ramblings had been designed to learn *his* soft spots, and fool that he was, Dev had handed her a cartful of them.

No. Call him arrogant, or duped, but he refused to believe Thea was a criminal, devoid of a conscience. He'd met enough of those over the past two years to tell the difference. Theodora was a woman in trouble, and she needed his help.

He hoped.

Chapter Fifteen

Dawn found him at the racecourse stables, helping the grooms ready their charges for the day. Over the past weeks his willingness to shovel manure, groom dust-coated hides and clean tack had earned him a free ticket to wander wherever he chose. Some of the owners even unbent enough to ask his advice, especially when one of the grooms announced that Mr. Stone had "the touch" with the creatures. Didn't matter that he owned and trained draft horses, not Thoroughbreds.

By the time the noon hour rolled around, the sanity of a sunny summer morning had dispelled some of the night goblins, and the physical exertion had cleansed his mind. He ate lunch with a pair of crinkle-eyed Irish lads, sifting through tidbits of possibly useful information, then wandered over toward the grandstands to catch a couple of races. Somewhere the ringer clanged the bell, signaling the minutes to post time, and Dev absently counted rings while he made his way through hurrying race goers. Thirty yards away from the betting ring a ruckus seemed to have erupted.

Dev wandered over to investigate. "What's going on?" he asked an onlooker.

"Fracas in the betting ring. Something about passing phony goods to the bookie. Someone fetched a copper. Just goes to show, don't it?"

"That it does. Thanks, friend." Without waiting to hear more Dev wove his way over to where avid witnesses circled the knot of red-faced, shouting men.

His big feet solidly planted on hundreds of discarded betting tickets, the policeman clamped a hand on one of the troublemakers' shoulders. When his call for order was ignored, he pulled out his billy club but achieved no noticeable effect, as all three men continued shouting threats and imprecations.

"…and if you don't release me this instant, the mayor will hear of this! I'm a guest and a law-abiding free citizen—"

"…know queer money when I sees it! Them hundred-dollar bills he tried to give me are bogus goods! Ask my sheet writer! He seen 'em, too!"

"Well, he paid me twenty-thousand dollars in bills that look just like those. If they're all fake, I want my money back—my real money, before they throw his carcass in the big house."

"I tell you, I have done nothing wrong. Officer, you are making a grave mistake here."

Every one of Dev's senses heightened when he caught a glimpse of the man in a neat gray suit and top hat being held by the policeman—Randolph Lunt.

After following him for weeks, Dev had been ready to scrub Lunt off the list, a discouraging admission, which did not bode well for his professional reputation. What a piece of luck, to happen along the very moment

Lunt made his move. Too bad he'd have to identify himself to the policeman as a U.S. Secret Service operative in order to verify fraudulent bills. Too soon, too public—too much of a risk.

More troubling, even if the bills in question proved to be counterfeit, at the moment the man could only be charged with passing bogus goods. With his connections, Lunt would be back on the street and out of sight before the ink dried on the order to release him. The previous autumn, a clever New York lawyer and an unimpressed judge had made mincemeat of the Service's case after Charles Langston was arrested on the same charge Lunt now faced. Langston claimed Edgar Fane had fleeced him, so Fane had been questioned, as well. But ultimately all charges were dropped for insufficient evidence. Langston and Fane walked, the case once more hit a dead end—and here Devlin stood, on the same precipice as his hapless fellow operatives in the City last fall.

Of course, if Lunt also had ties to the Hotel Hustler…

Not yet. The order whispered through him as clearly as though the words had been voiced aloud. Something—some blink of an instinct, something more forceful than a hunch, shut Devlin's mouth, held him poised and watchful, muscles bunched. A second thought crossed his mind that perhaps his presence here at this particular moment was something other than mere "luck."

Cautiously he inched around to better analyze Lunt's face and body movements. The man repeated his protestations of innocence, all without contractions, the timbre of his voice growing more elevated; his left hand was stuffed inside his pocket and bulging outward—all signs he was lying. Mr. Girard and the bookie, on the other hand, both radiated honest outrage.

"You're a liar, that's what you are!" Girard said, jabbing a finger toward Lunt's chest. "A cheat, and a liar."

"I won that money fair and square over at the Casino, not two hours ago," Lunt protested, his voice hoarse with outrage. "As for your libelous claim, Mr. Girard, I have paid you what was owed, and will see you in court, sir."

"Maybe, maybe not," the unflappable policeman returned. "Best all you gentlemen come with me. These here are serious charges, and I'll do my duty as I see it to keep all activities at this racetrack legal. Tully?"

"Yessir?" The bookie removed his flat cap and wiped his sweating forehead.

"Bring all them bills to police headquarters, every one of them. Right now, eh? We'll sort things out there, right and proper."

Two more policemen arrived, forming a wall of brass-buttoned resolve. Randolph Lunt, along with Tully, his sheet writer and Mr. Girard, were escorted from the betting ring and off the racecourse. Dev, unnoticed, followed them into the village, down Broadway to the stately brick Town Hall, which housed the jail and police headquarters. Pedestrians scattered out of the way, staring after the procession as the police ushered the three men up the steps and through the arched entryway into the building. On the opposite side of the street, Devlin paced as he waged an internal debate—telegraph headquarters? Reveal himself to the police? Or wait for that mysterious unseen Voice to give him further direction?

Either the God his father had believed in was revealing Himself to Dev in an unexpected manner, or lack of sleep had induced some form of cerebral delusion.

Nearby strollers were suddenly jostled aside by a woman who darted between them and passed Devlin with arms thrust skyward. Skirts and petticoats flared wide, she stumbled across the cobblestoned curb into the street, barely dodging a passing buggy in her erratic flight. "Help!" she cried brokenly. "Help! P—police! We need a policeman!"

A portly man had followed on her heels, but he stopped on the sidewalk, right beside Devlin. Breath sawed from his lungs, and his eyes stretched wide and unblinking in a darkly flushed face. One hand went to his chest.

"Easy," Devlin said. "Here, I've got you. Lean on this hitching post. Catch your breath."

The man shook his head violently, tried to speak and finally braced one shaking hand against the empty post. His white-eyed gaze latched onto Dev's at the same time his other hand grabbed Dev's sleeve. "Dead," he got out. "She's dead." Damp patches darkened the armpits of his blue blazer and large droplets of sweat rolled down his beet-red face. "A woman. Dead. Woodlawn Park. We found her, my wife and I...we found her, in some bushes. Out walking. I—we didn't know what to do, so we..." His lips turned an alarming blue tint. "We couldn't find...a policeman."

"Calm yourself, sir. Your wife's reached Town Hall. Catch your breath, hmm? I'll see that your wife is informed of your whereabouts, and promise her you'll join her soon. You, lad—" he caught the eye of a gangling young man wearing a cobbler's apron "—could you fetch this gentleman some water? Is there a place he could sit for a few moments, inside your shop? If you think it's necessary, go for a physician." He pressed the winded husband's shoulder in a final gesture of reassurance, then dashed across the street after the wife.

A dead woman in the park.

As he ran, a brief arrow of anxiety found its mark too close to his heart for comfort. For the first time in years a particular woman's well-being mattered, triggering irrational thoughts born both of too much knowledge—and too little. Surely, out of thousands of women who visited or lived in Saratoga Springs, surely the victim wasn't Thea. Devlin blanked the unwelcome conjecture from his brain.

But sure would help if he knew where she was at the moment.

Inside police headquarters, all attention had momentarily focused upon the two policemen with set faces who hovered over the distraught woman. Neither Lunt, Girard nor the bookie Tully and his helper were in sight.

A sergeant glanced up at Devlin's approach. "You the husband?"

"No. He's across the street, catching his breath. I told him I'd check on his wife, let her know he'll be along as soon as he can."

"I'll pass along the message." When the officer brusquely ordered Dev out of the way, he complied without protest. An unknown woman's death was after all none of his business. *It is not Thea, Stone. Concentrate on your own job, you tomfool chump.* Somewhere in this building Randolph Lunt was being held, and the charge against him *was* Devlin Stone's business. Thinking rapidly, he marked the presence of the Police Chief, whose double rows of buttons signifying his position gleamed dully against his uniform jacket. He was engaged in deep conversation with a gentleman dressed in a funereal three-piece black suit, probably a lawyer. They stood behind a waist-high railing, ignoring the furor taking place on the other side of the room. Dev waited until the black-suited man turned away to gather some papers off a desk, and the Chief set off toward the woman now quietly weeping into her handkerchief.

Decision made, Dev quietly moved to block his path. "Chief Blevins? My name is Devlin Stone. I'm an undercover operative with the United States Secret Service. I'll provide badge and credentials later. I know you have an unknown dead woman in a park, and a possible high-profile counterfeiter in your custody. Both require immediate investigation. I'd like to offer my assistance with Randolph Lunt. I witnessed most of the altercation at the racetrack, and am willing to testify under oath that Mr. Lunt was not telling the truth. With your permission, I can also determine whether or not the bills in question are bogus."

He paused for emphasis, then added, "But I need one request granted. It is imperative that my identity remain absolutely secret from everyone but you."

With an effort that threatened to crack his jawbone he managed to shut his mouth, before he included an *un*professional request for the identity of the murdered woman.

As soon as he could grab ten minutes, he'd verify Thea's whereabouts for himself.

She's fine, he repeated silently. *She's safe.*

Chapter Sixteen

Thea's latest spell of vertigo gave her no respite until lunchtime the next day. Mrs. Chudd ministered to her efficiently but without warmth, dosing her with cool sips of springwater or draping her face with damp, mint-scented cloths until Thea drifted off to sleep. When she woke, her companion silently helped her dress in a loose-fitting house gown and ordered a light brunch for them both.

"I'm better," Thea pronounced with relief when she managed to sit up enough to finish a bowl of soup by herself. Slowly she turned her head from side to side, smiling when the room did not dip and sway. "I think it's over."

"Humph. Bad one, this time."

"Yes, it was. But as you see, I'm quite recovered."

"Still planning to chase after that Mr. Fane?"

Thea laid her soupspoon down, stood and carefully walked over to the window, which overlooked the garden court. Near the center of the lawn, a group of children and their nannies were being arranged by a photographer for a group picture. Sunshine poured through the trees in golden streamers, birds flitted among the branches. A block away, a train whistle blew and on the piazza directly below, the hotel band warmed up its instruments. It was a lively, cheerfully *normal* scene, and bitterness coated Thea's throat like ashes. For the first time she couldn't banish a niggle of doubt about the ultimate nobility of her mission.

Devlin might be right: instead of making herself God's instrument of justice for Grandfather, she'd been challenging the Almighty of the universe to do something about Edgar Fane. On Thea's terms—not the Lord's.

"I don't know what to do about Edgar Fane," she said. Turning, she added slowly, "But I can't give up." Not yet, not now when she was finally making progress. "What did you think of him?"

Mrs. Chudd sniffed. "Too much teeth in his smile. Knows his manners, though. Not my business, but you weren't reared this way, missy."

"No, I wasn't. Times change. So do circumstances." Resolute once more, Thea headed toward the large armoire in the corner of her room and flung it open. "I think I'll go for a walk, clear my head. I don't need any further help, Mrs. Chudd. Perhaps we can dine al fresco for supper when I return."

With a short nod the woman departed into her own chamber. Moisture burned Thea's eyelids. More than anything, she would like to have buried her head in Mrs. Chudd's shoulder, given and received a hug and thanked her for her help. But Mrs. Chudd cared little for affectionate displays or words of praise, having rebuffed Thea sufficiently their first week at Saratoga to ensure the distance between them was firmly established.

Swallowing hard, she changed her attire and left the morbidly quiet room. As she wandered downstairs to the main level, she entertained a fledgling hope that Devlin would be waiting in the lobby. He'd promised to watch over her, whatever that entailed. Thoughts of him set her pulse to galloping like one of the racehorses. *Devlin*.

All right, these hopes were for giddy schoolgirls, but for an hour of her life she was going to be one. She had survived the disastrous dinner with Edgar Fane and the misery of a vertigo spell, and now she planned to savor every memory of the previous afternoon with Devlin. The words he'd spoken. The clasp of his hard hand. The creases in his cheeks when he smiled that smile.

Most of all…that kiss, and the heated warmth of his lips. Her palms tingled even now from the memory of his broad shoulders and strong arms, corded with muscles so unlike any of the pallid, intellectual young men she'd known back home on Staten Island. However, Devlin had awakened shrouded chambers of her heart not merely because of his masculine physique, but because he'd looked at her as though…as though she were someone precious, someone desirable.

Nobody had ever looked at Theodora the way Devlin Stone had, that afternoon in Congress Park. Many had praised Thea for her agile mind and her business acumen, her hostess skills and her cordiality. And if Charles Langston insisted on training his granddaughter to do so, why of course she could run a publishing company as well as any man, they told her.

Until Devlin, not a single gentleman ever thought to remark on her desirability as a woman.

Devlin thought she was *tempting*. Thea hugged the

word, and the incandescent memory of their kiss. After this walk she would address the consequences of her evening with Edgar Fane, analyze the few bits of information she'd gleaned, then decide the most judicious course to follow. But for one golden moment of time, she wanted to forget everything but the man who was dangerously close to capturing not only her imagination but her heart.

Late in the afternoon, she returned to the hotel, weary but refreshed in spirit. Devlin had not popped up at the Columbian Spring Pavilion to share a cup of water, or the Indian Encampment, where she'd peered at native beadwork, pawed at trinkets and souvenir glasses, watched tourists miss most of the shots at a target shoot. After a wistful hour, Thea bid the schoolgirl daydream farewell and simply embraced the freedom of enjoying herself. She didn't dwell on Devlin's absence or Edgar Fane's perfidies, or her doubts. For the first time in over a year, she dabbled without guilt in the trivialities of life.

Her heart, on the other hand, had been firmly leashed and muzzled. Thea Pickford was an illusion, a will-o'-the-wisp destined to die like the last of the summer roses. Charles Langston wasn't the only one who had lost everything. Courtesy of Edgar Fane, Theodora Langston had nothing to offer an honorable man like Devlin Stone. Her family's reputation was irreparably tarnished, her inheritance was gone, along with the small publishing company Grandfather had owned for half a century. The company Thea had been trained to run when he retired.

In fact, the next time she and Devlin crossed paths, if they ever did, it would be a kindness to confess the depth of her iniquities. He'd already suffered enough from the betrayal of his fiancée. *God…if only You kept Your promises like Grandfather used to believe, then I wouldn't be in this imbroglio.*

If only He would administer justice to Edgar Fane, and grant her a droplet of peace.

Somewhere a clock bonged the hour of five o'clock. Thea quickened her pace, aggravated with her inability to control this obstinate pining to believe in the God who loved humanity enough to sacrifice His Son for them. *Her present conduct precluded mercy.* So why appeal to the Almighty in the first place? He had never invested a presence in her life. From a theological perspective, her willful choice to hound Edgar Fane until he was behind bars pretty much guaranteed God would turn His back on Thea altogether. Certainly Jesus never stalked villains to proclaim their villainy.

But somebody had to do something about Fane. Thus far he spread his evil wherever he chose, claiming victims like wooden ducks at the shooting gallery in the Indian Encampment.

Evil. It was an old-fashioned word, difficult to apply to the debonair gentleman with his dark eyes and easy charisma—until Cynthia Gorman's interruption in the morning room. Shivery foreboding jigged down Theodora's spine. For over a year she had devoted every waking hour to a course of action, but not once had she seriously considered the possibility of personal danger. Then she'd glimpsed the look in Edgar's eyes when Cynthia walked out of the room, seen the banked eagerness of a wolf waiting for the opportunity to slake its killing hunger.

The next time Thea inveigled an invitation from the

man, she would armor herself with more than determination.

A policeman stopped her at the entrance to the Grand Union. Tall and gangly, with reddish sideburns showing beneath his policeman's helmet, he inquired curtly, "Miss Theodora… Pickford?"

"Yes? What is it, Officer?"

"Been waiting for over half an hour. You were to have returned by five."

Perplexed, Thea darted a glance behind him, into the hotel. "You've spoken to my companion, Mrs. Chudd? Has something happened to her?"

"No, miss. I need you to come with me to Police Headquarters, at Town Hall. Right now, if you please." He lifted a white-gloved hand. "It's right down the street."

"All right." Thea paused, then added firmly, "After you tell me why."

The policeman's face darkened. "Chief Blevins's orders." He glanced around at the curious gazes of passersby, then leaned down a bit, bringing a hand up to stroke his gingery red mustache at the same time he muttered out of the side of his mouth, "Miss, there's been an…incident. Your name has been introduced as a person of interest. I'd rather not say more, not here." He stepped back, somber and unflinching in his blue serge uniform and round policeman's helmet.

An incident? What did that mean? Obviously nothing good, or he wouldn't be so uncommunicative. "Very well." Thea thought about demanding that Mrs. Chudd be allowed to accompany her, but squelched the urge. Arguing with the police tended to achieve the opposite result one desired. "I do need to have a message sent to my chaperone so she won't worry."

"Already taken care of."

He gestured with his arm, and Thea fell into step a little ahead of him, uncertainty beating the air around her like thousands of bat wings. In her experience, the only reason for the police to demand your presence was because they believed you'd committed a crime.

By the time she and the impassive officer completed the two-block walk to Town Hall, uncertainty had metamorphosed into fear, and Thea could scarcely feel her feet inside her dust-coated walking boots. The stone lions guarding either side of the building looked as though they were about to pounce upon her, and she climbed the shallow steps on trembling legs. Heart racing, mouth dry, she suddenly realized in scalding clarity that this was how her grandfather must have felt when a New York City detective and two Secret Service operatives knocked on the door the previous autumn.

At the end of a long hallway the officer opened a door; Thea squared her shoulders as she entered a room crowded with sober black suits and blue serge uniforms, a rumpled clerk who gawked at her through wire-rimmed spectacles—and Edgar Fane.

A starburst of satisfaction spiked through Thea's fear. She inhaled a quick breath of relief, in her agitation completely forgetting the Theodora Pickford persona who knew nothing of Mr. Fane's perfidies. "You've arrested this man, then? You need me to testify? I'll be glad to tell you everything Mr. Fane—"

"My dear Miss Pickford," Mr. Fane interrupted, stepping in front of the speechless officer. The expression on Edgar's face belied the ice pick precision of his words. "More lies will only exacerbate your situation. You wove your web skillfully, and I'm deeply chagrined by my gullibility."

With the timing of a theater performer he waited until all gazes were riveted upon them. "I've abased myself before these officers of the law, honestly admitting my attraction for you. It's no secret I enjoy the company of ladies. But I have never misled a single one of them about my intentions, including you, Miss Pickford. Ah. Your look of shocked bewilderment is excellent, though a waste of time. Come now, let's be done with pretense. You worked so hard to gain my attention this past month, didn't you? Several acquaintances have remarked on your attempts. Well?"

"You're twisting the circumstances." Thea turned to the group of silent officials, but her tongue felt glued to the roof of her mouth. "He's…it's not what he's saying. I—I did try to attract him, yes. But—"

"But you discovered last night it was all for naught. If only I had known… Now my friend has paid too dear a price for your wicked schemes, for assumptions I never encouraged." His voice choked; he tugged a pristine silk handkerchief out and dabbed his temples.

"What are you talking about?" Thea cried, searching the grim faces gathered around her. "If anyone is guilty of deceit, it would be—"

Guilty of deceit. Further denials and charges died unvoiced. A chasm yawned at her feet; she tried without success to swallow a gelatinous lump threatening to choke her.

"You see?" Edgar Fane spread his arms in a gesture that triggered a groundswell of murmurs and foot-shuffling among the police officers. "Even now she seeks to spin her webs. Miss Pickford, or whatever your real name is, the game is up. If you'll confess at once to this heinous crime, and spare us all needless hours of suffering, I will in turn see that you are fairly treated."

"I've committed no crime." Her voice rose. "You're twisting everything around, just like…just like…"

"Silence!" A different policeman, older, with thinning gray hair neatly parted and authority stamped across his lined face, pointed an index finger at Thea. "You will have your day in court, Miss Pickford. For now, the magistrate deems probable cause, you are being charged on suspicion of murder and I am placing you under arrest."

Chapter Seventeen

"I'm under arrest?" Thea sputtered. "For—for *murder?*" The words made no sense, as if the man had spoken them backward, with all the syllables rearranged. She swept a loathing glance over Edgar Fane. "This is ridiculous. Based on the testimony of one person? Of *this* man?" Across a waist-high railing, the clerk busily wrote something onto a piece of paper. The scratching noise of the pen hurt her ears. A sensation of unreality infiltrated her skin until she felt disembodied and stripped of all emotion.

Then she saw the smug triumph hovering around Edgar's mouth. Temper flared to life. "What have you done to corroborate his charges? Who is the victim? Exactly when was I supposed to have committed the crime? And for goodness' sake, why have you allowed Mr. Fane to poison your minds? If a murder has been committed, *he's* the person you should be placing under arrest! Why don't you question him?"

"Miss Pickford, you will please show respect, and moderate your tone of voice. Legal counsel has been notified on your behalf, and will arrive shortly. But aggressive displays of temper cannot be tolerated." The authoritative policeman nodded once, and before Thea realized what was happening another policeman took her wrists and fastened them together with a pair of heavy metal handcuffs. "Mr. Fane is present because he identified the victim, and after apprising us of pertinent facts issued his complaint under oath. Due to the gravity of this case, Chief Blevins further ordered that every word spoken in this room be faithfully transcribed, including yours, Miss Pickford. Mr. Fane is well-known hereabouts. Over the years he and the rest of his family have established many friends in the village of Saratoga Springs. You, on the other hand, cannot offer such a history."

Thea's outrage fizzled into silence. Until last year, she had believed truth always protected innocence. Truth, ha! Truth was a multifaceted prism of many colors and multiple sides, not a windowpane. She stood mute, teeth grinding, while this gravel-voiced officer of the law recited Edgar Fane's distorted version of events.

"At approximately ten o'clock last night Mrs. Cynthia Gorman interrupted your evening together with Mr. Fane, at the Franklin Square residence occupied by him for the season. Mr. Fane grew alarmed by your irrational anger over her brief appearance to retrieve her parasol." He cast a baleful look at Thea. "A behavior corroborated just now by your tirade, in full view of this department. According to Mr. Fane, last night without cause or provocation you threatened Mrs. Gorman with dire consequences if she did not at once leave the dwelling where Mr. Fane currently resides."

"Lies!" Thea exclaimed. "Those are bald-faced lies! She stopped by to fetch her parasol, but it was Mr. Fane who was angry, not me. You should have seen *his* face. Wait—no." Cold chills racked her limbs. She felt as though she were fighting her way through a thicket of needle-pointed briars. "Are you telling me that Mrs. *Gorman* is the victim? Mrs. Gorman is…dead, and the man who committed the deed is standing right here in this room, yet *I'm* the one wearing handcuffs?"

The room erupted in a barrage of angry orders and accusations and shouts for silence. But it was Edgar Fane, the epitome of wealth, power and gentility in his dove-gray morning suit and silk tie, who finally restored a semblance of order.

"It's quite all right. I am not offended, gentlemen, and appreciate your spirited defense of public order." He gestured to Thea. "She is angry because she's been caught. She's afraid of the consequences. Over the years I've had plenty of experience with her sort, I'm sorry to say. The picture of innocence, but it's all the act of an unstable, desperate woman who took advantage of my trust. I almost feel pity for her, except Mrs. Gorman was like a member of our family."

Thea lunged forward. "You monster! You're a liar. A *liar!*"

Rough arms hauled her back, squeezing her elbows in a painful grip that took her breath away.

Another officer approached, double rows of buttons gleaming dully down his uniform. "One more display of histrionics and I'll add defamation of character and attempted assault to the charge of murder," he warned. "Do you understand?"

Chest heaving, Thea managed a nod. Abruptly her legs began to tremble and she swayed. The policeman holding her up shifted his grip until it supported, rather than restrained. "What about the defamation of my character?" she asked in a soft but clear voice.

A tornado of silence sucked all the air from the room.

Then Fane laughed. "You see why I was captivated by her? Impulsive, passionate. Cheeky, and courageous. I admired you, Miss Pickford, but you never should have allowed greed to blacken your soul beyond redemption."

Anger and a thirst for revenge had blackened her soul, not greed. But what did it matter now? "I didn't kill Mrs. Gorman," she stated dully. "You have no proof. I have a companion who can vouch for me. Why haven't you questioned her?"

"A companion who until last night never accompanied you anywhere," Mr. Fane murmured. "Chudd's her name. There is a possibility Miss Pickford hired this woman off the street—she's a sullen, unsuitable creature who deserted her charge immediately after dinner, by the way. In fact, Mrs. Gorman saw her in my library, where she was sound asleep. Such a woman's word is worthless." Shaking his head, he rocked a little on his feet before adding, "There's also the matter of Mrs. Gorman's jewelry, all of which is missing. Perhaps if we searched Miss Pickford's and this companion's rooms at her hotel?"

"The chaperone will be questioned, the room searched once a search warrant has been issued. Mr. Fane, with all due respect we must wait for—"

"Sorry." He smiled, that charming, oh-so-convincing smile to which not even police officers were immune. "I appreciate your duty, Chief Blevins, and in no way wish to trample upon it." Fingers steepled, he added lightly, "However, do not forget that I am the one who made a gift of her to you, saving this department time, expenditure of funds, correct? The need for manpower is already stretched to the limit at the height of the season, is it not? Mrs. Gorman's death is a terrible blow. I merely need to see for myself that Miss Pickford understands she cannot escape the consequences."

The chief cleared his throat. "I have allowed you license, Mr. Fane. But I cannot permit further badgering. Miss Pickford is entitled to legal counsel, and will have her day in court."

"Of course, of course. By the way, if money is an issue, I am willing to pay her legal fees. As you say, she is entitled—"

"I refuse to accept a nickel of financial assistance from that man, nor will I accept the services of any attorney he hires. Any money he offered would be as—" Barely in time Thea managed to choke back accusations concerning counterfeit money. Who would believe her?

She was innocent, yet about to be dumped in a jail cell. Just like Grandfather. Not fair. Not right. *Not right!* She longed to hurl the charge at every one of these blinded, unreceptive faces. Where was justice? Where was... God? No, why ask? She was the one who had turned her back on God.

"Could we let her sit?" the officer who had escorted her to police headquarters asked. "She looks a mite unsteady on her feet."

A chair was produced, and not unkindly, Thea was pressed down onto the hard wooden seat. Someone thrust a tin cup of water into her hand. Her teeth chattered against the rim, but she managed to choke down a sip.

And Edgar Fane watched, satisfaction stamped over his handsome face. "Not so confident now, are we?"

he said, the hard brown eyes boring into hers. "You believed Cynthia to be your competition, even though she went out of her way to treat you with kindness. Secretly you hated her—I witnessed it all, remember. Your hatred, and the fear when you finally realized the depth of my affection for her and that all your schemes had failed."

He surveyed the circle of stolid faces surrounding them. "I realize now I shouldn't have tried to befriend a young woman out of kindness, nor confided to her my true feelings for Mrs. Gorman. There's not a man among us who hasn't shuddered before the wrath of a woman scorned. Admit to your crime of passion, Miss Pickford, and let's be done."

Mutely Thea shook her head. Edgar leaned over her, his low voice an undertow that sucked her into a whirlpool of horror. "I'll never forget the sight of her lifeless body, and the marks on her neck," he said. "Paid some cutthroat to garrote her, right? Did you use some of the jewelry you stole from her body to pay him?"

"All right, Mr. Fane. That's enough, eh?"

Abruptly he swiveled on his heel and stalked away. "Almost, Officer. Almost enough. Chief Blevins, I appreciate your bending the rules. If there's any other paperwork you need me to sign, you know where to find me."

"You're leaving Thursday, for Boston?"

"The clerk already has the address where I can be reached. But first I'll make a trip down to New York City, where Mrs. Gorman's mother resides. Oh—one last thing. You'll want to talk to my secretary, Simpson, about the 'Pickford' name. He did some preliminary investigation on the girl and found some discrepancies, though regretfully I told him not to bother with a more in-depth search. She looked so innocent. Even now, it's hard to believe...."

Vaguely Thea listened to the steady tread of footsteps fading into the distance. She heard a door open and close. He was gone, but his taint still coated her in its deadly mist.

Edgar Fane was gone, and she had no one to blame but herself for the willful self-destruction that might end with her own neck in a hangman's noose.

Chapter Eighteen

It was a little past five o'clock. Devlin paced the train platform, checked his watch for the third time in five minutes and suppressed the need to kick the depot's brick wall. Fortunately from down the track the shriek of a whistle finally pierced the air and a moment later the train chugged to a hissing standstill by the covered platform. Shortly thereafter Dev greeted Operative Brian Flannery, from the New York City office. The operative grabbed a bulging Gladstone bag from the baggage cart and flipped the handler a quarter. On the short walk from the depot to the jail, Dev supplied details of the case Flannery hadn't heard via telegram and telephone.

"…and while I'm not prepared to say Lunt's the Hotel Hustler, he's definitely been passing bogus bills, mostly twenties and hundreds. Wish I'd been able to nab him earlier, but at least the timing finally worked out. He made a mistake. I happened to be in the vicinity."

"Better to be lucky than wise, my granny used to say."

Dev nodded, though he still wondered privately if

there was something other than coincidence at work here. His father once told him that God's ways were like the air—largely unseen, but always at work, even when a body didn't feel the current. "Police confiscated another two hundred thousand in counterfeit bills from Lunt's hotel room. I haven't interrogated him myself." He exchanged a rueful look with Flannery. "Chief Hazen agreed with my decision to identify myself only to the Chief of Police. Keep my cover intact. Chief Blevins secured a room for me in the basement of the Town Hall to examine the bills, and promised nobody would bother me, or know I was there." It had been a strange, lonely feeling, sequestered in a silent room while above and all around him people went about their business and, please, God, discovered the identity of the dead woman.

It was irrational, but until he could snatch a moment to talk to Thea…

"And?" Flannery asked impatiently.

Dev pinched the bridge of his nose. "Sorry. Long night, longer day. Over the past three hours I've examined about half the bills he tried to pass at the racetrack. Superb quality forgeries, but so far none of them bear the Hustler's mark. A couple with marred head vignettes, some where the Treasury seal is off a hair." He grimaced, flexed his stiff shoulders. "We're close, but not close enough. I haven't had enough experience to be able to tell where the paper came from, but even if Lunt's not the Hustler I can prove they're counterfeit, and that Lunt knew it."

Flannery swore cheerfully and clapped a freckled paw of a hand on Dev's shoulder. "You've done better than the rest of us, boyo. Uncanny, they tell me, after only a couple years' experience how you sniff out fakes and liars. This time we're that close. I feel it in me bones. Y'know, for someone who enjoys shoveling horse manure, you ought to look happier, not like a bloke on his way to a funeral."

Devlin's heart gave a quick flip. "Manure makes good fertilizer, and clean stalls make for healthy horses."

"You're a cipher, Devlin me boy. A regular cipher," Flannery said, sky-blue eyes alight with sympathy. "Say, you're not planning to up and quit over this Hustler business, are you?"

"No. I plan to get that boil on the Treasury's backside behind bars, whatever it takes, Brian." He smacked a fist against his open palm while he talked, hoping to relieve some of the internal pressure. "Arrogant peacock of a man. Those little clues he leaves on some of his work are nothing but jabs at the Service."

"Still on c-notes or tenners? Same mark, but never the same place?"

Dev gloomily nodded. "Before I came up here I spent a week examining two dozen different bogus bills recovered from the New York job so I'd at least know what to look for. I thought I'd come up with a good scheme, hunting in his own turf, so to speak, without draining the Treasury coffers. But unless Lunt ponies up some names..." There was little value in self-flagellation, so Devlin shut his mouth and shrugged his shoulders.

"Gotten a few stinging telegrams and a letter or two from Washington, hmm?"

Brian's easy sympathy soothed, lightening the yoke of too much responsibility and too few results. "I'm not the chief's favorite operative at the moment. He's wanting Lunt to be the Hustler, and I wish I could agree. But

I don't. The Hustler's too smart to be caught publicly in a lie, with the goods scattered for all to see."

They paused in front of the Town Hall, and Brian glanced at the two stone lions. "I like your guard dogs. We could use a pair of 'em downstate, somewhere in our little village."

For the first time in days, Devlin laughed. "I'm sure the architect would be flattered by the prospect." A noisy party of tourists was approaching; the two men exchanged looks. "I'll leave you here," Dev said in an undertone. "I have an errand to run. Good luck with Lunt."

"Aye. Don't you worry, lad. You might be the best at sniffing out a liar, but I'm the best at the art of non-violent, perfectly legal interrogation." With a wink and jaunty tip of his bowler, Brian Flannery strolled up the steps into the building.

The hands of the clock in the bell tower read seven minutes past six. *A quick quarter of an hour,* Devlin thought. That's all he would allow himself to focus on something other than a table piled with counterfeit bills. Long enough to make sure Thea had survived the aftermath of her evening with Edgar Fane. She'd be wondering where he was, because he'd promised to watch over her. A man ought to keep his promises...especially when the man's honor slipped its leash and he kissed an innocent woman without asking permission.

She'd kissed him back, melting against him, holding him with fervent abandon. And her eyes...dark, mysterious and luminous—the expression in those lovely eyes would be lodged forever in his head. A need he'd ignored for twenty-four interminable hours slammed into Dev. Need, mixed with that pinprick of fear. Inside the hotel, he bounded up the stairs two at a time.

Mrs. Chudd answered his knock, her countenance as welcoming as a hailstorm.

"I'm here to see Miss Lang."

"Wrong room." She started to close the door in his face.

"Wait. You are Mrs. Chudd?" As a precaution he planted a large booted foot in the doorway.

"Who's asking?" A tall, spare woman with mouse-brown hair and a formidable Roman nose, Thea's chaperone eyed the foot in the door, then favored Devlin with a disapproving scowl. "Your name?" she repeated, crossing her arms.

"My name is Devlin Stone, and I've had the pleasure of Miss Lang's company on several occasions these past weeks. Could I—"

"Don't see how, when you don't even know her name."

"Ah." Jaw muscles clenched, Dev fought for patience. However rude her manner, this woman was doing her best to protect Thea. "How about I stopped by to inquire about Miss Theodora Pickford?"

Relief flickered across her face before suspicion returned. "Police send you?"

The police? He felt mule-kicked, breath backed up in his lungs and ringing in his ears. "No, ma'am. I'm just a friend." He finally noticed the signs of strain in the lines on either side of Mrs. Chudd's mouth, and the beads of perspiration dotting her upper lip. "I'd like to think I'm a good friend, someone Miss Pickford trusts. Where is she? What's this about the police?" Foreboding stirred greasily in his gut. "Mrs. Chudd, I know Pickford isn't her true surname, and I know she had dinner last night with Edgar Fane. I know she hates him as much as she fears him. I want to help her, I promise. Just…let me see her. Please." *The police?*

For an interminable stretch of time Mrs. Chudd contemplated the floor, one bony-fingered hand rubbing circles over her elbow. Finally she lifted her head. "You wait here. I've got a note. I'll just fetch it and you can deal with the mess," she muttered, shaking her head. "Girl's got herself in trouble, I say, and only herself to blame."

Five minutes later Devlin left her standing open-mouthed in the doorway as he sprinted back down the hall.

A crowd had gathered outside the Town Hall, with a line meandering up onto the piazza. Most of the men wore black tie and tails, and the women's costumes were frothed-up creations of silk and lace with jewelry sprinkled from head to toe—something going on in the opera house on the upper floor, Devlin remembered, slowing his step and pasting a bland smile on his face to deflect curious eyes. Urgency pounded with a heavy fist but he sauntered, absently nodding as he made his way down the hall to police headquarters.

He opened the door.

Thea, her wrists handcuffed, was being led by a policeman toward the doorway to the cells.

If she focused on minutiae she could survive—the heavy weight of the handcuffs, the Wanted posters on the wall, the brass doorknob. A battered spittoon. Panic swelled when a large-knuckled hand closed over the knob and turned it. *They were going to put her in a cell, a dark cell devoid of light, like her grandfather.* He'd been a broken man ever since. No matter how hard Thea tried, she hadn't been able to piece him back together. If she couldn't help the only person in the world who loved her, how could she hope to help herself?

"This way, miss."

She jerked, staring up at the flushed freckled face. "Won't be so bad," he said. "See, I'm putting you on the end, in a cell by yourself. Only got two other inmates, see—and one o' them's being interrogated elsewhere." He paused, adding in a gruff rumble, "Sorry, miss."

"Not your fault." Her limbs might rattle like skeleton's bones but at least she managed to keep her voice free of tremors. "I am innocent, you know. I didn't kill her."

"Ha! They all say that!" the incarcerated man in the other cell called. He shook a fist through the bars. "What kind of copper are you, locking up a pretty little thing like that?"

"Shut yer trap, Girard, or I'll feed ya some brass knuckles."

Thea shuddered; a strange buzzing filled her ears. When the door clanged shut and locked her inside the cell, her mind went sheet-blank. She stood in the middle of the floor, terrified to move because if she moved everything would be real, she would understand that she'd just been arrested for murder and nobody…nobody on earth or in heaven was going to stand up for her. She had been efficiently erased from life. Hope? Hope had shriveled into a dry husk.

Devlin had made her a promise. Like every other person in her life except her grandfather, Devlin Stone had let her down. They had exchanged a kiss and she'd made the mistake of allowing herself to believe. To hope she was someone of value.

Now she knew the truth: Theodora Langston should never have been born. Her life was a mistake, created from a moment or two of carelessness, and nothing she had done her entire life could atone for that inconvenience.

Belief in someone or something—love, hope, purpose—hurt too much.

Each movement was an effort; like a mortally wounded animal, Thea crept to the darkest corner of the cell. Back pressed against the unforgiving wall, she huddled in the arid wasteland of her misery.

Chapter Nineteen

The door to the outer offices opened; Thea didn't bother to lift her head. A low rumbling of masculine voices ensued, followed by the scrape of hurried footsteps.

"Miss Pickford? Thea? For the love of Pete, man, how could you do this to her?" Keys rattled in the lock and the cell door swung open. "Thea? It's all right, now. You're free. Officer, stand back, please. Last thing she needs is crowding. Blast it all, she's shaking like a leaf." Unlike the anger-riddled words, warm hands closed gently around her arms, tugged her up, led her forward into the garish light and loud masculine voices. She winced away. The angry words softened to a coaxing drawl. "Shh, now. Don't struggle. I've come to take you out of here, Thea. Do you understand? The charges have been dropped. You're free."

Thea blinked slowly, lifted her head. A man's face swam above her, a blur of angles and planes with unruly locks of hair that reminded her of Devlin. *God? Help me, please?* Fear had finally tipped her mind into hallucinations. She didn't believe in dreams with happy endings. She couldn't....

Yet the hands propelling her forward didn't feel like a delusion. *Devlin?* Could this really be...? Somehow he had found her. He had kept his promise. The truth trickled through, dim but persistent. She tried to say his name, her voice a hoarse whisper. "D-Devlin?"

Somehow he heard. "Yes. It's Devlin." He shifted, wrapping one arm around her shoulders in a comforting grip. "I didn't know you were here until I talked to Mrs. Chudd. I'm sorry, Thea. But it's all right—you're all right." A husky note deepened his voice. "You're alive...."

"They think I killed Mrs. Gorman."

"Not anymore they don't. Here we go, that's it, through the door. I've got you, and I won't let go."

His hand closed over her fingers, which she belatedly realized had dug like frenzied claws into his forearm. "Sorry."

Devlin whispered something she didn't catch, because the Chief of Police suddenly loomed in front of her and reflexively Thea shrank against Devlin.

"Miss Pickford." Hands clasped behind his back, Chief Blevins regarded her in ponderous silence, then shook his head. "Mr. Stone has signed an affidavit. In it, he states that after your dinner with Mr. Fane, he observed Mr. Fane handing you and your companion into his carriage at approximately twenty minutes past ten. Mr. Stone followed the carriage back to the Grand Union Hotel, then followed you and your companion until both of you entered your room. At this point Mr. Stone kept watch in a small lounge with a view of your door. A private night security guard employed by the

Grand Union has corroborated Mr. Stone's presence there on two separate occasions as he made his rounds, until approximately 2:15 a.m. this morning."

"I don't understand." Thea passed her tongue around her rubbery lips. She'd doubted, when all along, unknown and unseen, Devlin had in fact been her bodyguard. Thinking hurt her head as well as her heart; sighing, she tried to focus on Chief Blevins. "I could have left my room, after two-fifteen."

A glimmer of some emotion lightened the police chief's tired eyes. "Yes, you could have. But not, I think, for the purpose of committing murder. The physician who examined Mrs. Gorman's remains has determined that death occurred well before midnight. You're free to go, Miss Pickford. I'm sure you and Mr. Stone wish to discuss his reasons for standing guard over you. Before you leave, however, please accept my profound apologies for your ordeal."

"Policemen don't apologize," she murmured.

Chief Blevins stiffened, but he answered equably, "This one does." His gaze shifted to Devlin. "You'll see to her care? When she's sufficiently recovered we might need to question her further about her last encounter with Mrs. Gorman." He paused, adding heavily, "But without Mr. Fane present. Try to understand, see. He and his family are well-known in these parts. Their generosity and affection for Saratoga has long been enjoyed by all. There was no reason to doubt the authenticity of Mr. Fane's shock, or his accusations. I allowed him to question this young woman against my better judgment. It won't happen again."

Tremors started inside Thea despite Devlin's comforting hold, which tightened further when she couldn't control the shakes. "Understood, Chief Blevins," he said. "We'll discuss it in more depth later. Right now, I'm taking Miss Pickford to her hotel room. Could someone provide a buggy?"

Moments later Devlin lifted her inside a run-down piano box buggy. Fervently Thea rubbed her fingers over the worn seat, inhaled the odor of old leather and stale perspiration, which smelled like a bouquet of roses because it meant she really was no longer in a cage. She was free. Safe.

Despite the mild summer night, after raising the top, Devlin tucked a scratchy woolen blanket around her, and only then did Thea realize she was still shivering. *Devlin came,* she repeated to herself over and over, struggling to believe the nightmare had ended. Struggling even more to comprehend that this man cared enough to bother.

He sprang into the seat beside her and lifted the reins. "Five minutes," he promised. "Mrs. Chudd can fetch some hot tea and toast. Can you hold on that much longer?"

"Yes. But I don't need tea or toast. I need to talk. It's just… I can't seem to stop shaking." A watery laugh trickled out, and she clutched the rough wool fabric, wishing it were his arm. "You came…you came for me."

"Would have a lot sooner, had I known." The buggy lurched into motion. "Thea… I really am sorry."

"Don't apologize. Please." She choked back tears. "I'm the one who needs to apologize to you, Devlin. I should have told you days ago who I am, and why I'm chasing Edgar Fane. But I was stubborn and foolhardy and…and afraid. If you knew who I was, if you knew my family, I was afraid you'd disappear. It's what I deserve, but I—I—"

"It's all right, sweetheart." With disarming swiftness he shifted in the seat and leaned to brush a kiss against her snarled hair. "Rest. Later you can tell me whatever you need to. I'm not going anywhere."

"You might change your mind, and I wouldn't blame you." Her voice broke at last but shock and relief and terror finally undermined the last of Thea's equanimity. "Devlin, I need to tell you the truth. The truth. Have you ever thought about truth? Is there a truth that stays the same, and no matter how a person twists and turns things about, the truth remains? Some of what Edgar told the police was true, but he—he twisted it into lies yet the police believed him. I told the police nothing but the truth, only they didn't believe me because I've told so many lies. Not because I wanted to deceive them, or all the people I've met here, or you. Most especially you. Devlin…" She covered her face with her hands. "God help me, I'm no different from Edgar Fane. Do you think God can forgive a liar? Can you?"

"Thea…" He spoke her name on a long, tired sigh. "For most of my life, I've hated liars. When my father died, my mother wanted to return to New York, but she also wanted me to appreciate my father's heritage—StoneHill Farm. She promised that if I waited in Virginia until I was eighteen, then I could come to New York, and choose for myself the life I wanted. She promised to write. Only I never heard from her again. Then there was Sylvia. After that, I pretty much funneled everything into a blind hatred for liars."

He pulled the buggy up in front of the hotel.

They were both lost souls, but knowing brought desolation, not comfort. "I don't want to go inside yet," Thea admitted. "I can't face other people, even Mrs. Chudd." Couldn't face the self-excoriation, couldn't face Mrs. Chudd's indifference that contrasted too sharply with Devlin's solicitousness. "I…can we walk? I need to feel—" Her mouth worked, but she couldn't explain the atavistic need to at least reassert her physical freedom, to know she could walk or run or skip anywhere she pleased without fear a policeman would haul her off to jail.

Penance, however, still shackled her mind. "I need to ask your forgiveness," she finally said, unable to look at him. "Even though I don't deserve it." After this night was over, he would vanish from her life because he hated liars.

"If you want to walk, we'll walk, sweet pea," Devlin drawled, the lazy Southern voice wrapping Thea up like a hug. His movements unhurried, he helped her down. "Sounds like we both have some millstones to lay down, hmm?"

They wound their way through the night, around guests enjoying their own perambulations, past the brightly lit restaurants and hotels where music from the nightly ritual of hops and dances drifted through opened windows. Eventually they reached a quiet residential street, where Thea could feel the cool night breeze on her face. Above them, a star-spangled sky and a fingernail moon dispelled much of the horror of the last hours.

"I'm ready now," she finally said. "I won't blubber all over you anymore, nor ask philosophical questions you don't want to answer."

"Mmm. How about if I find your tears and questions

irresistible, almost as much as I do you—no matter who you are? Which, by the by, I'd really like to know before I kiss you again."

Thea stopped dead in her tracks, her heart rhythm bumping painfully against her ribs. "You're going to kiss me again? Why? I'm a liar, just like Edgar. You hate liars."

"Absolutely we're going to share a kiss. As for the rest…well, you never let me answer your question."

"What question?"

He laughed, and before the sound died his head lowered, his warm breath gusting against her cheek just before he pressed a light kiss against her lips. "The philosophical one. Where I try to explain why I'm thinking that God wouldn't be God if He didn't forgive a liar, when Jesus reportedly forgave a murdering thief from the cross. If He could do that while dying in agony, well… I need to rethink my own attitude. Mostly I'm trying to change it because of you. While we're on the subject—don't ever compare yourself to Edgar Fane again. Unlike that double-tongued cur, you're not a liar by inclination, Theodora. I saw that, weeks ago. I just didn't understand the 'whys.'"

"I don't know anymore." The nearest streetlight was a block away. In the darkness, that brief kiss had taken on a life of its own. Thea wanted to lay her head against Devlin's sturdy shoulder and cling; she wanted to grab the lapels of his jacket and press her mouth against his for another kiss; more than anything, she wanted to be free of Theodora Pickford.

And she wanted to know if God could accept her as compassionately as Devlin.

Only one way to test them both…

Chapter Twenty

Resolution pushed through her in a furious gust. "My name is Theodora Langston. My mother's maiden name is Pickford. She's a vaudeville singer, and I have no idea whether or not she's still alive. I live on Staten Island with my paternal grandfather because my mother deserted my father a month after I was born. My father didn't know what to do with a baby, so he dumped me on Grandfather and left, too. His name is Richard, and he's a professional gambler now. Nothing matters to him but the next hand, or the next roll of the dice, certainly not his daughter. So you might say I understand better than most how you felt when your mother abandoned you."

"You might say that," Devlin responded after a prolonged tense moment. "So...your grandfather reared you? His name was Langston, I take it?"

"Yes. Charles Langston." Most men were awkward with female emotions, particularly dramatic displays of it. Thea shrugged aside his curt tone, her relief over finally sharing the truth filling her with giddiness. Confession apparently *was* good for the soul. *All right, Lord.*

I'll try. "My father used to send me souvenir cards from wherever he happened to be. Grandfather was ashamed of him, but never gave up hope that one day his son would return home." She chewed her lip a moment. "I did. The last card arrived two months after my tenth birthday. But at least I knew my grandfather loved me. Then Edgar Fane entered our lives."

"Ah. The serpent in the garden. Why didn't he recognize you here, Thea?"

He still spoke in that strange, carefully neutral tone, perhaps to calm her? Grateful, Thea struggled to emulate it. "He'd come to the island to visit one of his friends, met my grandfather at a lawn party. Grandfather liked him. *Everybody* always likes him. I never met him or I'd probably have been equally gullible. But I'd been trying to take over the reins of the publishing company Grandfather owned. I spent all my days in the City. The imprint was prestigious, but small. Times were bad—we still hadn't recovered from the Panic of '93 and Grandfather was concerned for my future."

Her voice wobbled, and without comment Devlin wrapped his hand around her forearm in a warm clasp. "There was the threat of bankruptcy. That we'd lose everything. There's no other family—Grandfather lost his wife and three other children in a ferry accident when I was three. Edgar Fane persuaded him to sell a piece of land Grandfather owned near Central Park—promised him top dollar. He also persuaded him to sell Porphyry Press. 'It will still be your company,' he promised. And he told Grandfather not to worry, he would take care of everything. His father is one of the richest men in America. Our lives, and our financial security, would be safe. We believed him!"

"His stock-in-trade," Devlin said. Shifting, his arm came around Thea's shoulders, a sturdy buffer despite the anger rife in his voice. "I understand, Thea. Try to relax."

"Not the worst!" she cried, twisting free of the comfort she craved but wouldn't accept. "You still don't understand the worst of it. Devlin, Edgar Fane is not just a criminal. He's *evil*. He paid Grandfather in cash, told him that way Grandfather would know the money was real. But it wasn't. It wasn't real!"

Arms wrapped around herself, she hurled each angry word. "He paid with counterfeit bills, and when Grandfather went to deposit the money the police and S-Secret Service arrested him. They arrested my grandfather and put him in jail. And now Edgar Fane has done the same thing to me and he's the one who's guilty. He's a filthy counterfeiter, and a liar. And if he's responsible for what happened to Mrs. Gorman then he's a murderer, too. I wanted to catch him, wanted justice! Why couldn't they see…" Her voice thickened, and in an outpouring of impotent rage she suddenly turned to pound her fists against Devlin's chest instead. "I loathe Edgar. *Hate him*. Him and the police and the Secret Service because they should have known. They should have known he was a liar. Nobody believed me, because I turned into a liar, too. I hate myself…."

"I believe you, Thea." Dev folded his hands over hers, stilling the blows, prying open the fists. "I believe you."

Thea continued to struggle, and Devlin reacted instinctively, stanching the anguished fury of words with his mouth. "I believe you," he whispered again and again against trembling lips, his voice hoarse. "I believe you.... I need you to believe in me." When at last she melted against him, her arms lifting to slide around his neck, Dev forgot about the danger, forgot about circumstances, forgot everything but the incendiary joy consuming him.

This woman was meant to be *his*.

He kissed her eyelids, tasting the bittersweet saltiness of her tears, her hot damp cheeks. Heard the soft gasps, felt the frantic need in her that met and matched his own.

In the darkness behind him the faint sound of clip-clopping hooves and the soft sputter of buggy wheels rolling along the street drifted into his ears. When the horse snorted, Devlin jerked his head up, then on a muffled groan yanked himself free of Thea's embrace and took two backward steps.

By the time the buggy rolled past, his head was almost clear enough to manage a single sentence. "I didn't mean to do that."

In the starlight he watched her blink rapidly, watched the incandescent softness freeze into a brittle woman with haunted eyes. "I didn't either," she said, but she touched her lips with fingers that trembled.

Watching her, Devlin inhaled a sobering breath of night air. "If I can keep my hands to myself, will you listen to me?" he asked. "It's important."

He felt like a man on a rack. For most of his life nothing, not even StoneHill, had filled that misshaped, ill-defined piece of Devlin that forever seemed to be... listening. Waiting. Searching for whatever it was that would fit itself into that misshapen piece, and make him whole.

Uncle J. told him more often than Dev cared to hear that likely the "feeling" would pester him the rest of his life. "You'll always have a home, and the horses, and I know you love 'em as much as a man can. It's a crying shame you lost your folks when your head weren't no higher than a Shire's knees. The thing is, lad, you can't spend your life looking for 'em."

And just when Dev thought he'd finally found the missing piece, he learned that the woman he'd passionately kissed was the granddaughter of Charles *Langston*.

When Thea learned Dev was an operative for the organization she hated probably as much as Edgar Fane, he would lose her as surely as the sun rose in the east. If he couldn't convince her to trust him now, and she ran for the sanctuary of Staten Island, she might unwittingly run into the arms of a murderer.

Thea wanted to know if God would forgive a liar.

Are You teaching me a lesson here? Or was this one of life's crueler ironies, that the woman with whom he was falling in love would never be able to return it?

Grimly he tried to think of a solution other than the perpetuation of his own lie by omission. Couldn't let her go—couldn't share his own deception. *Is there a truth that stays the same, and no matter how a person twists and turns things about, the truth remains?* Thea had asked. Dev didn't have an answer she'd like, but it was the only one he had to offer: he'd do whatever he had to, including withholding his identity as a Secret Service operative, to keep her alive.

Watching her, he ran a hand around the back of his head, then gave her a crooked smile. "Remember the first time we kissed, and I said you tasted of temptation?"

Solemnly she nodded.

"Well…now more than ever, I want to give in to it." He held his hand in front of her face to show her the tremor in his own fingers. "See? But I can't give in. I know I have a lot of flaws, but I wasn't raised that way, Thea. You're a lady, and you're in more trouble than I think you realize. I want to help, not take advantage of you."

"I'm the one who's been taking advantage of you. That first day, when I chased you down, I—I wanted to use you, to get close to Edgar Fane." She focused on some distant point over Dev's left ear. "I might have been a lady once, but not anymore. Perhaps I should try out for the stage."

"Don't be—" He swallowed the words then, impatient with them both, glared at her. "We'll discuss this, thoroughly, later. Right now we don't have the luxury of time. When Edgar Fane learns you've been released, do you think he's just going to dust you off like a piece of lint on his suit coat?"

"He's leaving day after tomorrow. He thinks I'm in jail. By this time next week he'll have forgotten I exist."

"Not likely. As I heard it, you more or less engaged in a slanging match in front of the entire Saratoga Springs Police force. Why did you do that, Thea? You believe him evil, then why provoke him?"

"I hadn't found another way to convince people who he really is. Why else would I risk my reputation and my future? It's imperative to find proof that will hold up in a court of law. Don't you see? At the very least, he's a counterfeiter, Devlin, and there's no telling how many other lives he's destroyed like he did my grandfather. But he may be guilty of worse. He said I hired someone to murder Cynthia. What if that's what *he's* done? We have to find out, Devlin. We have to."

Her voice had risen; quick as a blink Devlin covered her mouth with his hand. "Shh. Sounds carry at night." Touching her was a mistake. His palm felt branded by the imprint of her lips, and leashed desire strained to stifle further words with another kiss. In the blink of an eye his pale, defeated waif had once again transformed into a fire-breathing dragon. She was also using her agile brain and reaching the same conclusions as Devlin.

He was proud of her—and terrified for her. "Come over here, under this tree. The trunk should muffle some of our words, and we'll be better hidden from those houses." Once there, he planted both hands against the rough tree trunk, trapping Thea without touching her. "At this moment you have no evidence to prove he's a counterfeiter, and no proof other than instinct that he killed Mrs. Gorman, right?"

"No." A long sigh stirred the air. "Devlin… I'm not going to run away. Do you need to stand so close?"

"It's the best I can do, when I promised not to kiss you again." With a rueful half smile he dropped his arms. "Listen. We don't know everything that happened today, but while I was at the station, in between explaining why you couldn't have been party to a murder, I listened, analyzed reactions. I'm quite renowned for my observation skills, remember," he added, hoping to coax at least a small reciprocal smile before he had to whip up the fear again.

"I haven't thanked you, for saving me."

"Shh. I promised I'd be watching, didn't I?"

"Promises are usually only words."

"Not," Dev said, "for me. I spent a score of years, waiting for what turned out to be an empty promise, as empty as the word of the woman who was supposed to be my wife. I bear the scars of betrayal as much as you do, Theodora. So hear me when I tell you I don't make very many promises. But those I do—I keep."

Thea reached out and brushed light fingers over his bicep. Devlin twitched in surprise. "I'm sorry. I didn't mean to hurt your feelings," she said. "But I still need to thank you." And there came the smile, when he least expected it. "I'll listen now, and keep quiet. I believe you were bragging about your gift for reading people?"

Amazing, when he was terrified for her life and weighted with guilt, that she could make him feel lighter than a handful of sun-warmed hay. "Good with people, better with horses," he qualified. "Let's see, where was I? Oh, yes, while, ah, giving my deposition I…um… overheard Chief Blevins order one of his men to initiate a watch on Fane, but to be discreet about it. Do you understand the significance? The police were supplied with sworn testimony that legally required them to arrest you. But that doesn't mean they believed every word Fane told them, even though he's the son of Thaddeus Fane and could raise an almighty stink. They'll be risking their own livelihoods, maintaining surveillance."

"Even so, they won't stop him from leaving. He's guilty, Devlin."

Frustrated because she was right, he nonetheless pushed his point home. "You have to let the law do its job, Thea. It's an imperfect system, and yes, mistakes are made. But your one-woman crusade can also be perceived as vigilante justice."

"I don't want to hang him myself. I just want—"

She stopped. "It's not fair. I waited for months, but—" Again she stopped midsentence, once more wrapping her arms around herself in that heartbreaking posture of defensiveness and insecurity.

"You've accomplished more than you realize, but you must consider the consequences of your actions. What might Fane do to the woman who's out to prove him a liar, a cheat—and a murderer?"

"He doesn't know who I really am." The words emerged haltingly. "We never met on Staten Island, remember. To him, I'm just another avaricious skirt out to snare him for a husband. He believes the police didn't listen to me at all—he was gloating about it, Devlin. Why risk harming me when he's already beaten me?"

"When he learns you've been released—and he will—he won't feel victorious. He'll be enraged. Now we have an arrogant, angry man convinced he can do anything he wants. Anything. And the second killing will be easier."

Chapter Twenty-One

Unable to resist the need, Devlin unwrapped her arms from their protective shield. Urgently he rubbed his thumbs over her knuckles. "You can't stay here any longer. You're in too much danger. Yes, Fane is leaving Saratoga—but his absence makes for a good alibi. One evening you'll be strolling along—and the next morning your body will be found in the bushes. Wherever you go, Fane can have you followed. If you retreat to Staten Island he'll connect you to your grandfather in a heartbeat, and learn your real name. You've already discovered this man will stop at nothing to achieve his ends."

"I hadn't thought that far ahead," Thea admitted, her fingers nervously flexing in his.

"Mmm. You haven't been able to. I have." The possibilities frankly terrified him. "Thea… I don't want anything to happen to you." Nerves, hot and sharp as nails, blistered his spine. "Here's what I've come up with. I want you to come home with me, to StoneHill. Mrs. Chudd, too. And of course we'll arrange for your grandfather to come down. He and Uncle J. would have a grand old time together. My aunt loves to cook for crowds—it's one of her few vanities. And I'll introduce you to the most magnificent horses and the most beautiful piece of land on God's green earth. Most important of all, you'll be safe. Even with all his money and power Edgar Fane won't know how to find you. He won't even know where to look because he doesn't know I exist."

"I—I…what are you saying, Devlin? This is too much." In a frantic motion she tugged her hands free, then abruptly grabbed his again, clutching them with fierce strength. "You can't just sweep up my whole family and our problems and deposit us in the middle of your life. Despite what you say, what's to keep Fane and his band of hired henchmen from learning about you? Someone could follow *you* to StoneHill as easily as they could follow me to Staten Island."

"Chief Blevins has assured me today's events are vaulted within the walls of the Police Department. Nobody else will know I was there at all."

"I don't trust them." Shrouded in the night shadows beneath an old oak tree, all Dev could see was her poignant silhouette, resolute and alone.

"I know you don't. But I do. Trust *me,* Thea." He invested every ounce of confident authority he could muster into the words. "You and Mrs. Chudd will travel to Virginia in perfect anonymity."

"I think I could trust you, Devlin. I do. It's just…" She hesitated, then finished awkwardly, "Going to Virginia wouldn't be, well, proper."

Proper? *Proper?* She'd been arrested and tossed in jail; he'd jeopardized the entire Hotel Hustler operation for her sake and she was turning prudish? Hampered by the one secret he was honor bound to maintain, Dev's frustration got the better of him. "Ha! When have you ever been proper? If I were a wagering fellow, I'd bet your grandfather's had his hands full over the years."

"You'd lose." Her head drooped. "Growing up, I always tried too hard to make people like me. I tried, endlessly, to please them, especially Grandfather. I've spent my entire life atoning for the prodigal son who never returned home, and the tawdry actress daughter-in-law from the Bowery who never wanted me." A wavering catch-breath seared Devlin's ears. "I've never behaved like I have with you, not for my entire life. As for Fane, apparently I'm almost as good an actress as my mother. Now Grandfather might spend the rest of his life being ashamed of his only granddaughter."

"Sorry," Devlin said after a moment. "I'm a cad, I spoke out of turn. What you think about yourself—it's not true about the Theodora I've come to know. That woman is admirable. She's strong-minded, idealistic, principled— No, don't shake your head. You've been playing a part, yes. But from almost the moment we met, you tried to tell me as much of the truth as you felt you could." His mouth was dry as the dust on his boots, but he'd talk the rest of the night to undo the mess he'd made with his thoughtless words. "Let me finish telling you about this woman. She doesn't cower from her fear, she faces it head-on. She fights for what she believes. Your grandfather will be proud of that woman, Thea. He deserves the opportunity to meet her. Come to StoneHill. I can keep you safe—it's the only place where you'll *be* safe, until we—" he barely caught the slip "—until the authorities can deal with Fane."

To distract them both he gave in and slid his hands up her arms to her neck. Tenderly, he stroked the soft skin as he tipped her chin up with his thumbs. "I don't want to lose you, Thea," he whispered again.

"Devlin, please don't say things like that," she said, and faint starlight shone on fresh tears welling in her eyes. "You don't understand. I don't want to dream, to hope. It hurts too much."

Groaning, he cupped her face. "Do you think I don't know that? We're both of us two abandoned strays, fearful to trust an outstretched hand. But I'm willing to risk another smack, because it couldn't hurt worse than your ending up like Cynthia Gorman."

Her forearms rested lightly against his chest, her palm directly over his heart. "I agree I'm a threat to Edgar Fane. I know I can't stay here. But I can't let him walk away, free to destroy someone else's life. For me that would be an act of cowardice."

"We've talked the subject to death. *Stalking Edgar Fane is not your job.* Leave him to the authorities. They want him off the street every bit as much as you do. I know you've little use for them but the Secret Service's mandate is to track down counterfeiters, and—"

"I will not talk about the Secret Service!" Before he could react, she'd ripped herself away and walked several paces down the street before whirling back around. "I told you, you don't understand! How would you feel if your uncle went into town one day and didn't come back, because some officious lout from the U.S. government had had him tossed in jail? My grandfather is seventy-four years old! But until last November he'd been as strong as you or I, full of vigor and confidence. Now he's a broken man, and it's all because the Secret Service didn't care about the truth."

"Thea…" Dear God, it was more than a man could

take. Dev stood, every muscle taut, while the woman he'd fallen in love with verbally assailed the agency he'd sworn an oath to defend and serve. An agency he'd pledged his loyalty to, regardless of the personal cost. *God? I don't know what to do....*

"Devlin, forgive me." The words bridged the broken glass distance between them, but with every soft syllable, more shards punctured his heart. "You can't possibly understand what I'm talking about. You... I never believed a man like you existed. I'd give anything—almost—to accept your offer, and come to StoneHill. But I—I can't."

A man like him. Trapped, defensive, for the first time he could remember Devlin couldn't think his way out of a predicament. "Can't, or won't?" he repeated the question he'd tossed at her once before. Only this time the answer mattered, too much. "What will it do to your grandfather when he receives an impersonal visit from one of those operatives you despise, whose sad duty it is to explain how his stubborn, headstrong granddaughter got herself murdered? I can't follow after you indefinitely, like a shadow with strings, trying to protect you from yourself *and* Edgar Fane. I have a life, Thea, and people who depend on me. Horses who trust me to take care of them."

Except all of them had fended quite adequately for themselves without him.

Thea was not the only one with a choice to make. *If he told her he was a Secret Service operative, he'd have to turn in his badge.* The prospect no longer made him flinch, but the illumination smeared Devlin's spirit like soot.

"All right." The statement floated across on a sigh. "All right, Devlin."

"No, it's not all right. Nothing's right about this whole infernal situation."

"I'll come with you to StoneHill."

Devlin's jaw dropped. He shook his head. If a dozen rocks had rattled loose from his brain and rolled onto the ground he wouldn't have been more incredulous. "You'll…come? Just like that, you change your mind?"

"A woman," Thea replied with knife-edged sweetness, "who upon reflection doesn't change her mind, doesn't possess much of a mind at all. Although, given your response, I have to wonder if I'm losing mine altogether, agreeing to your quixotic proposition. I'm sure Mrs. Chudd will—mmph!"

He silenced her with a kiss.

Some things in life you learned to live with, some things you stood your ground. And some things you held on to, any way you could, regardless of consequences.

"And leave tips for all the household servants with Mrs. Surrey," Edgar instructed Simpson.

The secretary nodded his head while simultaneously slitting open the afternoon mail with an ivory-handled letter opener. "Unused frames were packed up this morning, except for one." Simpson finished opening letters and arranged them in a perfect stack, then glanced up at Edgar. "Do you have further instructions for that frame, sir?"

"We'll deal with it later." Tired of it all, he waved a dismissive hand. "Do you have our train tickets? Verified that one of the family's rolling stock has been added?"

"I have the tickets, and received confirmation while you ate lunch that your father himself arranged for The Wanderer to be made available."

"Good." Abruptly he dismissed his secretary to focus his attention on the Saratoga Springs Police Department, who had proved to be most cooperative.

He must remind Simpson to send along a memo to his parents, requesting them to send another expression of gratitude. Humming beneath his breath, he placed a call to headquarters. "Good afternoon, Chief Blevins," he said cordially some moments later. "My train leaves in a couple of hours. I won't have the opportunity to do so in person, but I wanted to thank you again for your handling of Miss Pickford's interrogation and subsequent arrest. I've had my secretary draw up a list of local attorneys, should the— What's that? I'm afraid we have a bad connection."

"...and the matter of Miss Pickford...you must understand...no longer at liberty...discuss..."

A moment later Edgar banged the telephone receiver down, kicked over a nearby spittoon, then stalked out into the hallway. A maid dusting furniture squealed in fright when he approached, ripped the dusting cloth from her hands and threw it across the room, then lifted her completely off her feet. "Get out of my way!" he snarled in her face. "And shut up."

"Mr. Fane," Simpson spoke somewhere behind him, "two Jockey Club members have arrived to wish you farewell. Dodd has seen them to the formal parlor in the south wing. Shall I inform them you'll join them in...a quarter of an hour?"

Edgar dropped the paralyzed maid, who gathered her skirts in bone-white fingers and fled for safety. A moment later a door slammed. Slowly Edgar turned around to his blank-faced secretary. "You're a good man, Simpson. How long have you served in your current position?"

"Three years and five months, sir."

"Find the maid. Extend my apologies. Offer a month's wages as compensation. Is that sufficient to retain your loyalty as well as your services?"

"Yes, Mr. Fane."

Edgar nodded. "I'll see the Jockey Club gentlemen. And Simpson? After you soothe the maid, I need you to run one final errand for me. It concerns Miss Pickford."

Chapter Twenty-Two

Thea spent much of her first week at StoneHill Farm in a daze. Forty-eight hours after their arrival, with no reports of strangers lurking in the area, Devlin decided Thea could safely wander the property on her own. She sensed his reluctance, but embraced the freedom to explore, especially since she seldom saw Devlin. He rose at dawn, and for the past three nights tramped back to the house after everyone else was in bed.

Both of them were determined—at least on the surface—to put Edgar Fane in the back of the larder. Devlin was utterly absorbed in taking control of the business of the farm once more. Whenever they did have a private moment or two it consisted mostly of a quick smile of apology on Devlin's part, a reassuring murmur on hers that she was perfectly fine, and for him to reacquaint himself with his horses. Much to her surprise, Thea was enjoying serene days, and the most restful sleep she'd experienced in months.

All right, yes. She missed Devlin, yearned for the solicitousness he'd offered at Saratoga and over their long trip south to Virginia. But she was pragmatic enough to know the difference between a summer season at a famous resort and the gritty essence of real life: Devlin was not a gentleman of leisure like Edgar Fane, but a horseman, trainer, breeder…. The more Thea learned about his life at StoneHill, the more she puzzled over why he'd hared off to Saratoga Springs Resort. When an opportunity arose, she planned to ask his true motivation for a summer sabbatical in upstate New York.

The dreamy little girl wanted to beg God's forgiveness and resurrect her faith in a loving heavenly Father, Who by divine design brought her and Devlin together.

The wiser woman was unwilling to lower her guard because, still lurking in a dark corner of that larder, the stubborn avenger refused to give up her quest for justice.

Most days Thea focused her time on exploring Stone-Hill. Devlin had not exaggerated the magnificence of his domain—the main house sat on the crest of a small hill surrounded by three thousand acres of prime bottomland and a view of the Blue Ridge Mountains that brought tears to her eyes, particularly at sunset. To the south, a sweeping panorama of blue sky, broad valley and hazy mountains made her feel paradoxically insignificant, yet able to breathe more deeply than she ever had in her life, secure on a tiny island in the Hudson River.

In green pastures, immense horses grazed in the shimmery heat of late summer. Hired workers gathered hay into towering stacks, while dragonflies and butterflies darted among late-summer wildflowers. Someone had planted hundreds of pink spider lilies and yellow black-eyed Susans around the dry stack stone walls which surrounded the dignified stone-and-brick house. Their sunny colors brightened the sultry air.

StoneHill charmed her with its storybook splendor; Thea stubbornly refused to fall completely in love with Devlin Stone, but she was utterly captivated by his home.

"Explore all you want," Devlin's Uncle Jeremiah told her in that slow cultured drawl that reminded her of Devlin, "but always wear boots and carry yourself a stout walking stick. Down here in Virginia, we got snakes. Mostly they'll leave you alone, but you have to watch out for the no-legged kind same as you do the two-legged. We got our share of both. Myself, I'd rather deal with a rattler."

Jeremiah possessed a dry wit along with his slow smile. Devlin was right about his uncle—when her grandfather finally arrived the following day, he would like Jeremiah, very much.

A clump of flowers peeking through the grasses at a bend in the creek beckoned. Thea swept her walking stick in front of her, then knelt on the damp earth beside the blossoms. "Look at you," she murmured, feathering her index finger over white-tipped petals, the center of which deepened to rich magenta-colored streaks. "So lovely, yet hidden away by this little creek." It seemed unfair, somehow, for God to have created such a stunning variety of flora most human eyes never beheld.

Apparently her soul still smarted, if she could hold a grudge against the Almighty for his placement of wildflowers.

"They're water willow, but still not as lovely as you." Devlin said behind her. "Here, now!" He lengthened his stride, grabbing her arm just before she tumbled backward into the creek. "Sorry I startled you."

"Well, I was having a private conversation with those flowers." Thea's gaze wandered over his cuffless and collarless lawn shirt, streaked with dirt smears. He looked as different from the urbane gentleman of Saratoga as a farm wagon from a barouche. "What are you doing here? I thought you had a yearling to train."

"I did. She behaved like a little lady, and I wanted to keep it that way. She's back frolicking in the pasture now, but she'll retain a positive memory of our time together."

"I'd like to watch, someday, unless... I'd be too much of a distraction."

"Well, you're a distraction no matter what."

They smiled at each other, and Thea realized only then how lonely she'd felt. "So you hunted me down because you were in need of a diversion?"

His smile deepened, forming the deep creases in his cheeks that never failed to weaken Thea's knees. "I'm headed to the hardware store. Ordered some new harness brackets a while back, and got word the shipment finally arrived. We've had too little time together, so I thought you might like to come along?"

"I suppose I can fit you into my crowded social calendar."

Sunlit sparkles danced through his eyes before they darkened to charcoal. "Do you have any idea how unique you are? I didn't realize until I walked into the barn, the night we arrived, how much I've missed this place, the horses. Thanks for understanding. For not..." He stopped, shaking his head.

"For not whining? Pouting? Making life miserable for you and everyone else?" Thea shrugged, though what she yearned to do was give him a comforting hug. "Of course, if you'd spirited me off to a rickety row house that leaked, with a curmudgeon of a housekeeper—"

"Bessie is a curmudgeon."

"But a lovable one. Believe it or not, she and Mrs. Chudd have formed a bizarre friendship. Bessie tempts her with Southern cooking, and Mrs. Chudd turns her nose up. Then they both cackle." She yielded to the temptation and brushed a dried clump of mud off his sleeve, just so she could touch him. "I'm at peace here, Devlin, I promise. StoneHill is even more breathtaking than your descriptions. Don't worry about me. I plan to savor every moment, including the few I can share with you." *Especially those,* she admitted silently.

As they walked back down the path, shoulders brushing, hands swinging inches apart, Thea sneaked sidelong glances, and told herself she was seven kinds of a fool to pretend their lives could last beyond an announcement of Edgar Fane's arrest.

"Something on your mind?" Devlin asked softly just before they left the woods. "The smile has left your eyes. You seem…preoccupied. Not afraid of going for an outing, are you? No dizziness?"

"I haven't been afraid since the train pulled out of Saratoga Springs, Devlin. Not a dizzy spell in sight."

"Good." His hand descended onto her arm, bringing her to a halt. "But I'm still sorry I haven't been able to keep you company, show you around. Once I catch up, I promise things will change."

"This is your home, your life. You love it, that's all. I don't know how you were able to leave it for so long." Or why…

The creases in his cheeks disappeared, and a shadow darkened his eyes. "I'm wondering the same thing," he said. "Human nature, I suppose, to not miss something until you don't have it anymore."

Abruptly he released her and resumed walking at a ground-eating pace. "We'd better hurry if we're going to make it to town and back before dark. Bessie's not shy about her feelings when someone's late for supper. And Mrs. Chudd's silences fill in the rest."

An hour later they rattled into the small community of Stuarts Crossing, a one-street assortment of aging brick buildings shaded by huge old trees. The hardware store was situated between two massive sycamores. A general store sat on the corner across the street, and a little past the hardware a post office had been built the previous year, Devlin told her. "We're on the map now," he said as he helped Thea down. "Bessie doesn't have to wait an extra week when she orders something from the Sears Roebuck catalog." He ran an affectionate hand over the sweating flanks of Dulcinea, the placid Percheron whose gray color just about matched Devlin's eyes. "I need to talk some business for a few moments, as well as pick up my order. Instead of perusing rows of tools, turpentine and nails, you might prefer Gilpen's Mercantile. We're not New York City here, but—"

"Neither," Thea interrupted him levelly, "am I."

A farm wagon rumbled past. Devlin stood, chagrin in his eyes and annoyance thinning his mouth. "I don't know what I'm going to do," he finally muttered half under his breath. "Thea…"

"You're going to take care of business," Thea told him, "and I'm going to go find a hostess gift for Bessie." With a firm nod and a hand wave, she hurried away before her resolve wilted like the sad row of asters drooping from twin flower boxes in front of the post office.

Chapter Twenty-Three

Devlin watched her stroll across the packed dirt-and-gravel roadway, his pride and his heart smarting. Didn't matter which hurt worse. How was a man supposed to accept spiritual guidance when life was a confounded mess? If God chose to soften his heart with an irresistible woman, He could at least have chosen one who didn't despise his current profession. If only—with an impatient swat at a hovering bee Devlin cut off the litany of "if onlys."

As soon as Thea disappeared inside the mercantile he grimly focused his gaze on the end of the street, and the dust-coated surrey slowly making its way toward him. Lawlor was late; Devlin had expected him to be waiting inside the hardware store. They could have shared their brief reconnoiter in relative privacy. Then he noticed two other men in the surrey with Lawlor. Fellow agents? They looked familiar. Devlin's jaw hardened. He went into the hardware to pay for the harness brackets.

Ten minutes later, after stacking a half-dozen boxes in the buggy, he straightened to scan the street. Conscious of the possibility of curious eyes, especially

Thea's, he noted the location of every person in sight. Footsteps scraped on the walk outside the Post Office, and without haste he strolled over under the shade of one of the sycamores to meet the trio of men. He never should have yielded to his need and invited Thea to accompany him to town.

Three pairs of narrowed eyes monitored his approach, but it was the gent wearing the navy striped suit, liberally coated with road dust, who stepped forward.

"Good afternoon. We're reporters from the Washington *Evening Star.* M'name's Lawlor. Other two gents are Mr. Wolfred and Mr. Amos. We're looking for a Devlin Stone, of StoneHill Farm?"

"Reporters, hmm? And why would three gentlemen of the press travel all this way to see a farmer?"

Amos, a slight young fellow with wire-rimmed spectacles and a severe case of acne, unwound the string from a portfolio and withdrew a newspaper. "P-perhaps this will explain." Splotches of red stained his cheeks as he held out the paper, but the mild brown eyes stayed steady on Devlin. "P-page eight, right column."

"So you know Stone's a farmer?" Lawlor said. "We'd appreciate your help in locating him, or his farm."

"You were the one who indicated he lived on a place called StoneHill *Farm.* Why are you looking for him?" Devlin countered without looking up from his perusal of the underlined article. "What does the murder of a society woman at Saratoga Springs Resort in upstate New York have to do with Devlin Stone?"

"Well, rumors are spreading thick and fast that Mr. Stone is a person of interest in this case." The third man, Wolfred, lifted a bushy black brow when Devlin made no comment. "He was seen at the Saratoga Springs police headquarters the same day the body was discovered, but then he disappeared. Police and an untold number of other private investigators from Boston to Richmond are eager to learn his whereabouts."

"I have an acquaintance in the D.C. Detective Bureau," Lawlor added casually. "When we…ah…discovered Devlin Stone was purportedly from the state of Virginia, only a day's train ride away from Washington, well, we thought we'd see what we could find out."

"So you're after a story, hoping to track down this man. Sell papers with whatever you discover?" Devlin folded the newspaper and tucked it under his arm. "I think you gentlemen have made a long trip for nothing."

"Maybe so." Wolfred pursed his lips, his index finger rubbing up and down his striped suspenders. "But there's another rumor floating south, one all three of us decided deserved closer investigation, as well. Has to do with one of the richest men in the whole blamed country, or at least the man's son—Edgar Fane?"

"Heard the name in passing," Devlin commented, every muscle in his body tensing when, from the corner of his eye, he watched Thea exit Gilpen's Mercantile. Her face lit up in a smile until she caught sight of the three men, who from her angle probably looked as though they'd surrounded Dev. His mind spun out a list of possible consequences of hastily spoken words on her part, none of them good.

Still he had to say something, anything, but even as he opened his mouth it was too late.

"Who on earth are these men, Lemuel?" Thea called in a Southern accent thick enough to suffocate a bull. Smiling prettily, she sashayed right up next to Devlin, and gave the others a blinding smile. "Y'all look like you've been drug through a plowed field. Come a long way?"

"Yes'm. We…ah, p-p-perhaps you know…" Amos's stutter trailed away as he darted quick looks at the two other men, then Devlin.

"We're looking for Mr. Devlin Stone. Do you know him?" Lawlor's blunt statement didn't faze Thea, who tipped her head to one side as though she were thinking hard.

"Name's familiar," she offered with an apologetic fluttering of her eyes. "Is he from hereabouts?"

The men exchanged looks, while Devlin struggled to keep his expression suitably noncommittal. "We think so," Lawlor finally admitted. "Heard he owned a horse farm."

"Well, if y'all don't know, then you must not be friends." Thea shrugged. "Sorry we can't help, but it's getting on for suppertime, so we best be heading for home." She nodded to the men, then turned to Devlin. "Don't stand there gawking. We need to go, Lem." She flashed the three flummoxed-looking men a final smile. "I hope you find Mr. Stone."

"If we don't, others might have better luck," Wolfred said. "All right, then. Let's go, boys. I don't much fancy taking this road back up the hill after dark." He touched the brim of his homburg. "Ma'am, sir."

The three men trudged past Devlin without further comment, though all of them slid heavy-lidded looks Thea's way as they piled into the surrey. Lawlor jumped into the driver's seat, then paused, fishing around inside his jacket. "One thing, Mr.—I'm sorry, I don't believe I ever caught your surname."

"Didn't give it," Devlin shot back, one hand lifting

to Thea's shoulder, gripping it with enough force that she pressed her lips together and kept silent. "Don't see the need. I don't much cotton to nosy reporters from Washington, or anywhere else, poking their noses in a man's life."

"Freedom of the press." Lawlor pulled out a small card and thrust it toward Devlin. "It's true enough, there's those who don't care overmuch for myself and my colleagues. But they still buy newspapers—and read every word. If you hear anything of interest about Mr. Stone, I'd appreciate it if you'd let me know. Address is right there on the card."

Devlin nodded. So. Three bodyguards would now be prowling the sylvan vales of northwestern Loudoun County, ears and eyes perked for anyone interested in Devlin as well as Thea. Deep in thought, he stood without speaking by her, though he softened his grip, surreptitiously stroking the taut tendon connecting her neck and shoulder. Only after the buggy turned onto the road that wound its way up to the turnpike did he look down at the amazing woman beside him. "A performance worthy of Miss Pickford. What made you pretend I wasn't Devlin Stone, Thea?"

"I could tell you were discomposed, and I didn't know if it was because those men were threatening you—or because you were scared I'd say something you didn't want them to hear." Eyes dark, she searched his face. "I thought you might not want them to know who either of us were. You say they were reporters? Are you in danger because of me, Devlin?"

"What," Dev managed when he could find his tongue, "made you think I was...ah...discomposed?"

"You're not the only one who notices things, Devlin

Stone. It's the way you held your shoulders, how your head was up and back—and there's an expression, actually it's more of a complete absence of expression, like you're trying very hard to keep any emotion from showing on your face. You looked at me like that, the day I stumbled over you in the Saratoga stables."

There was no help for it. Devlin slid his hand down to her wrist, tugging her until their noses bumped. "If we were anywhere but here," he murmured, the words low but gruff, "I'd have to kiss you." He rubbed the pad of his thumb in small caressing circles over the interplay of veins in her delicate wrist. "For now, this will have to do."

What he really needed to say, desperately, was that regardless of torturous inner conflicts he loved her. That with every passing hour he grew more convinced God really was more than a noncorporeal Being to say a blessing to before a meal, or to curse when disaster happened. That God, for whatever reason, had known exactly the sort of woman Devlin needed to open the rusted gate to his heart.

Sometimes a man had to trust without understanding.

Most people called it faith.

But the appearance of three of his fellow operatives made a declaration of love impossible right now, possibly forever. Devlin might submit to the need for God's will to supersede his own. But others were not so inclined, and Dev's personal decision could not alter an unpalatable truth.

Edgar Fane knew Devlin Stone's name—and planned to hunt him down.

If Fane succeeded, he would also find Thea.

Chapter Twenty-Four

Overnight the wind shifted to the northwest, sweeping in cooler temperatures and the deep azure skies of approaching fall. Hugging a shawl around her in the pleasantly cool morning air, Thea shifted from foot to foot, anticipation crawling over her like ants.

Today she would see her grandfather.

She was about to start toward the neat brick carriage house to fetch the carriage herself when the extended brougham rolled into view, pulled by two stately bay Holsteiners Devlin had imported from Germany. "I took a chance," he'd told Thea. "They're primarily coach horses, great bones and natural balance, yet mostly unknown in America." He grinned. "Uncle J. groused for months about the expense."

Nab pulled the team to a dignified halt at the front door. StoneHill's coachman and stable manager was dressed for the occasion in a hunter-green frock coat and top hat; when Thea told him he looked splendid a self-satisfied smile beamed from the coffee-colored face, still smooth as a river pebble even though he'd passed three score years the previous week.

"Mister Stone'll be along in a jiffy, miss," he said. "He's jawing with Jeremiah about Percy. Old boy's off his feed again, and you know Mr. Stone. Don't matter none that horse is older'n dirt, and if he takes a notion to pick at his feed a bit, why, leave him be, I say."

Oh, dear. Percy. Devlin and the Appalousey spotted horse had grown up together, and Devlin loved the animal with a devotion that moved Thea to tears.

"Nab, Mr. Stone doesn't need to accompany me." She buried the spur of disappointment deep, reminding herself that in a few short hours she would have all the company she needed. "Come on, let's swing back by the barn, and I'll insist."

Nab hopped down to hand her up into the carriage. "Miss Langston, you a mighty fine woman. The Lord took His time about it, but He finally gave Mr. Devlin what he's been missing for more years than I like to count."

Embarrassed, Thea busied herself with smoothing her skirt. "Thank you, Nab. But until the Lord sees fit to inform Mr. Devlin, I don't think I'll bring the matter up."

When they reached the stables, Nab darted inside. A short while later he returned with Devlin, who climbed inside the carriage, tossed jacket and homburg down on the seat beside him, then with a long sigh sat down across from Thea.

"Devlin, you don't need—"

"I'm coming with you," he cut across her protest. "I know you'd be safe with Nab, and are quite capable of traveling on your own. That's not the point. I'm coming because I want to be with you. Besides, it's the right thing to do, meeting your grandfather at the depot." He glanced down at himself and grimaced. "I did wash my hands and pick out the worst of the straw."

The odor of horse and hay and some stringent medicinal smell wrapped around Thea. Devlin's thick mahogany locks fell in haphazard disarray, and streaks of perspiration marked his temples. His blue shirt was wrinkled and streaked with dried horse saliva. But he'd cleaned up as best he could, just to be with her and show respect to her grandfather. The spiny knot in Thea's chest slowly dissolved. "Grandfather used to spend most of his days with printer's ink smeared on his face and shirt cuffs. Thank you, Devlin. Since you insisted on coming along, I'll confess how glad I am." She hesitated, adding hesitantly, "How's Percy?"

"Holding his own. Uncle J. and I have finally agreed it's either the sprained ligament that holds the ball of the femur in the hip socket, or a diseased stifle joint. I've placed a telephone call to a veterinary surgeon friend. I know Percy's past his prime, but I can't…" His eyes clouded over. "We've tethered him in his stall to restrict his movement. He's alert, no signs of sweating or agitation. I got him to eat a little more of his breakfast. He's not in severe pain. I'd know if he were, he'd tell me—" He stopped and momentarily closed his eyes. "You must think I'm a softheaded crackerbrain."

"I think—" Thea leaned across and took one large fist, still damp, in both her hands "—that you're the most compassionate man I've ever known, and you have a way with horses I've come to believe is a gift. I mean…oh, padiddle. Now I'm going to tear up."

She blinked rapidly, feeling silly until Devlin reached across and brushed away the welling tears with his thumb. Thea's breath backed up in her throat. While the carriage rattled down StoneHill's long drive, for a span of unmeasured time the two of them swayed with the movement in a silence fraught with feelings too fragile to be acknowledged.

But when Devlin's steady appraisal of her persisted, his eyes gone dark as a late-summer thunderstorm, the words finally broke free. "Devlin, you are…a very special man. And I think more than ever I want to believe what my grandfather used to believe, about God. You do have a gift where horses and people are concerned that can't be learned through studies, or thoughtful dissertations or reasoned thinking. I think God gave you this gift." She laughed, a soggy, self-conscious sound. "Now I'm the one who sounds like a crackerbrain. Grandfather would say I'm thinking too much. Probably talking too much, as well."

"Not for me." Without warning the carriage jolted, pitching Thea sideways. Before she blinked her startlement, Devlin's arms shot out and he grabbed her shoulders. But instead of settling her back against the seat he pulled her across the space separating them and into his embrace. "Never for me," he whispered hoarsely in her ear. "Thea, what you said, about God? What would you think if I told you I've been thinking, too? That maybe our meeting in Saratoga Springs wasn't happenstance, or fate, or luck?"

Crushed against the solid muscles of Devlin's chest, her heartbeat thumping in her ears, Thea wriggled her hands around his back until she could lay her head against him and hear the thunder of his heart. Incredulity fought against fear, and a lifetime of disillusionment. Was he sharing his feelings—or his faith?

Finally the weight of his arms gentled, but instead

of the kiss Thea secretly hungered for, he eased her back across the carriage, onto her own seat, then sat, elbows propped on his knees, his hands worrying his hair. "God," she heard him murmur, "what am I supposed to do?" Even as she sucked in air to offer something, anything, he lifted his head and gazed across the space separating them. "I can't tell you everything I want to—need to. Not today, not like this. I know it's not fair to you, but Thea? Will you be patient with me, for a little longer?"

In dawning wonder, Thea read in his eyes everything for some reason he wouldn't verbalize, and a wash of golden light seemed to flood her heart. For today, she decided, she could return to this man one of the gifts he had given her when he led her out of that jail cell into fresh air, and freedom. "Patience isn't my strong suit," she admitted, "but for you, Devlin, it's not difficult at all. Whatever you need to say to me can wait. After all, you did save my life. In some cultures, that means I'm bound to you, for the rest of it."

The lines of tension bracketing his mouth eased, and a slow smile spread across his face. "I like the sound of that," he said. "I like the sound of that very much, Theodora Langston."

Two weeks later, Thea and Charles Langston stood by the fence, watching Devlin work with Percy. The gallant old horse moved smoothly, with only a slight hitch in his black-spotted hindquarters. With each passing day, like the aging Appalousey stallion her grandfather had regained much of his former strength as well. Instead of the gaunt, defeated creature Thea had kissed farewell in June, he now stood tall and dignified. Courtesy of Bessie's cooking, he'd gained several pounds, and after the first two days had shed frock coat and bow ties altogether. He and Jeremiah acted more like long-lost brothers than two strangers.

StoneHill Farm, Thea decided, offered far more potent elixirs than all the springs in Saratoga.

"You love him very much, don't you, Taffy T?" Charles affectionately tugged a strand of hair that had slipped free of pins. Though now late September, a sultry summer haze still lay over the farm, and humidity had coiled the errant lock into a loose curl.

Absently Thea tucked it behind her ear. "So much it frightens me." Gaze fixed upon Devlin, she waited until the tremulousness that shadowed every waking hour subsided. "I think Devlin feels the same. But we haven't spoken the words." She laughed a little. "Do you see how wonderful he is with Percy? Infinite patience, gentleness—never a harsh word or sudden move? When Devlin and I are together, he treats me the same."

Charles snorted, then coughed to mask the ungentlemanly noise. "Can't think of a single woman I've known, including your grandmother, who wanted their man to treat them like his horse. That's a banal cliché straight out of Western pulp novels."

"Not when the man is Devlin." She glanced sideways. "On occasion he's displayed other emotions as well, Grandfather."

"Good." Beneath his neat iron-gray mustache the corners of Charles's mouth tipped upward. "I trust his intentions are as honorable toward you as they are toward his horses. I'm not sure I make as capable a chaperone as Mrs. Chudd, especially since I don't plan to give up my evenings playing chess with Jeremiah."

A deep chuckle rumbled in his chest—a sound Thea hadn't heard in months. "I beat him last night. Plan to do so again. All I have to do is bring up the War. So if you and Devlin want to slip out to enjoy the moonlight, have no fear of your grandfather interfering. Frankly, I'm enjoying the two of you trying to pretend you're not in the throes of a courtship."

A twinge of guilt nudged Thea. She had not confided *all* details of her sojourn in Saratoga. "Well…at least you're more agreeable to be around than Mrs. Chudd." Five days after Charles's arrival, Nab had driven her former chaperone off to the depot; she'd endured quite enough Southern cooking, she informed Thea, and too much Southern humidity. Her services hadn't been needed since their arrival at StoneHill anyway. "At any rate," Thea finished, "I don't need a chaperone. I am almost thirty years old, remember."

"Ha! Look more like a sweet young miss to me. Let's see what Master Stone has to say about it. He appears to be headed our way."

Heart racing, Thea nodded absently, unable to tear her gaze away from Devlin. Shirtsleeves rolled to reveal tanned forearms, thick hair gleaming in the morning sun, he flashed her a grin that oozed contentment. Halterless, Percy clopped along beside him, ears pricked forward, his speckled muzzle just brushing Devlin's shoulder.

"Your horse is certainly looking more lively than when I first arrived," Charles said to Devlin when they reached the fence. "You say you've had him since you were a boy?"

Devlin nodded. "My grandfather was out in the Oregon Territory back in '76, searching for land because he was afraid we were going to lose StoneHill. He saved a family of the Nez Perce tribe from slaughter, along with a half dozen of their spotted horses. In gratitude, they presented him with their best foal, a colt my granddad named Percy, in honor of the tribe."

"He grew up some." Uncomfortable around horses, Charles stepped back when Percy thrust an enquiring head through the fence rails. One striped hoof pawed the dirt—his way, Devlin had informed Thea, of demanding attention. "Based upon my very limited knowledge of horseflesh, he acts surprisingly vigorous for twenty-one years old."

"A whole lot of love and a little bit of—" Devlin hesitated "—what I used to call luck. These days I'm thinking I might call it something else." He stroked Percy's ebony withers, then ran his hand along the speckled rump. "Either way, he's been a faithful companion. It's a relief, seeing him improve daily."

"My granddaughter's perked up, as well." Charles winked at Devlin. "Does my heart good, seeing *her* daily improvements. She's needed to put this whole business with Edgar Fane behind. With that in mind—" he dropped a kiss on Thea's forehead "—I think I'll retire to a shady spot on your back veranda, and see if I can coax Bessie out of some of that apple strudel I smelled baking this morning."

Chapter Twenty-Five

"Subtle as an Appalousey's spots, isn't he?" Thea kept her gaze on one of the striped hooves, a characteristic of this particular breed. She seemed to be learning a lot about the equine species these days, she thought, scratching behind Percy's ear.

"I see where you inherited your predilection for speaking your mind. Well, since he's provided the opportunity, why don't you come along to the barn, help me get Percy settled. Then we'll go for a walk." His voice turned sober. "I've been thinking."

I never stop, Thea wanted to say, her pulse still settling after her grandfather's throwaway remark about Edgar Fane. But with a newfound patience—or was it the old fears?—she maintained her silence, and followed Devlin and Percy to the barn.

An hour later, they left the worn path toward the woodland to stroll alongside the two-foot high stone wall that for over half a century had marked the boundaries of StoneHill Farm. Tufts of Queen Anne's lace and bunches of goldenrod brushed their clothing as they passed, while a warm southern breeze caressed the distant treetops.

Then Devlin enfolded Thea's hand in his, and began to talk. "All my life, I've known this was home, and my responsibility," he said, trailing his fingertips over the wall as they walked. "Yet all my life, I've wondered who I might have been, if I'd followed in my grandfather's footsteps and headed west instead of going to college. Or if my mother had taken me back to New York City when she left after my father's death." The hand holding hers flexed, a restive movement quickly stilled. "These past weeks, I keep thinking that if she had, I might have met you earlier, before life got so complicated."

"Or we may never have met at all." Dread curled into a tight hot ball in her middle. "Devlin, if you brought me out here to tell me something unpleasant, I wish you'd go ahead and get it over with, particularly if you're trying to find a polite way to say my grandfather and I have trespassed on your hospitality too long. I've suffered through about all the suspense I can handle." Especially when a letter with a news clipping, freshly arrived with the morning mail, was now burning a hole in the pocket of her dress.

Devlin stopped and faced her directly. "I should have remembered. Your mind is prone to dark musings, and your imagination is stronger than a team of Percheron." When Thea opened her mouth to object, he kissed the tip of her nose, then cupped her cheek. "I love your mind, and have a healthy respect for your imagination. Which is why we're a perfect match. I can't hide what I feel any longer, Thea. Every day, those feelings dominate my day, no matter how hard I try to keep them stabled in the barn."

In one of the intimate gestures she'd grown to cherish he cupped her other cheek, holding her transfixed within a gentle cage. She could have broken free and run away—this man would never use force to bend her to his will, or trap her into listening to words she couldn't bear to hear. And because of it, she'd given him her heart as well as her trust.

"I can't hold the words inside any longer. Whenever you look at me," he finished in a ragged whisper, "I see the same feelings in your beautiful eyes. You dread suspense. So don't you think it's time we shared those feelings with each other?"

Thea swallowed hard. "Yes. No." He was close, too close. Her head swam; she twined her fingers to keep from touching him and losing the battle with inevitability.

Abruptly, the warm hands encasing her cheeks dropped away. She heard the rustle of his clothing, opened her eyes in a panic, to discover him standing a yard away, watching her. Thea suddenly discovered a costly mistake was easier to bear than the long-suffering kindness blazing forth from those eyes.

"I wish I were a horse," she blurted, almost as angry with him as she was with herself. "They don't need words. You know already by their responses how much they love you. You don't make demands of them they're incapable of meeting. You just care for them, and allow them to be...to be horses," she finished, adding grumpily, "Don't say it. I'm not a horse. Grandfather already reminded me."

"And here I am, hiding a specially made halter just for you underneath my shirt." His absurdity made her laugh, and Devlin's whole body seemed to relax. "I'm willing to do just about anything, you see, to keep you at StoneHill," he said. One long step brought him back to her side, close enough to count his eyelashes. "Since we're not horses, I suppose we're stuck with words. I've tried not to say them because I'm just as afraid as you are. What if your feelings are mired in gratitude? What if your heart is irrevocably tied to Staten Island?"

"It's not. They're not. It's just that—"

"Good. No more excuses, then. Close your eyes if you need to, but unstop your ears, and your heart." He watched her, the irises expanding in his pupils until the black completely crowded out the gray. "I love you, Theodora Langston. I love you, more than I can explain. If you tell me you could never be happy here at StoneHill Farm, I don't know if I'd survive."

Nerves roughened his voice, and Thea realized in misty-eyed astonishment that he was shaking. As though a warm gust of wind swept over the mountain and shoved her with an impatient hand, she took one faltering step, then threw herself against him, wrapping her own shaking arms around his back. "I love you, I love you, too," she choked out against the salty dampness of his neck. "And I don't want to go back to Staten Island. You'll never have to be afraid that I'll leave you like your mother. Or Sylvia." Helpless against the emotions buffeting them both, she pressed fervent kisses against his neck and jaw.

All of a sudden rough hands slid beneath her arms and Devlin lifted her completely off her feet. "Yes!" he shouted the affirmation, his gaze more open and joyous than Thea had ever seen. "Thank You, God!" He whirled her around, then his head lowered and he kissed her.

* * *

The Atlantic Ocean churned, white-capped waves crashing onto the cowering beaches. Storm clouds scudded across a sky the color of iron.

Edgar Fane stood on the widow's walk of the seaside mansion he'd bought off a bankrupt shipbuilder three years earlier. Face lifted to the spitting wind, he allowed the fury of nature to batter away his own fury until, chilled and damp from salt spray, he returned to his study.

Simpson had left the latest reports tidily stacked on his desk. A muscle jumped over Edgar's left eyebrow as he picked up the one that had arrived yesterday. Most of the private detectives he'd employed over the past two months were as stupid as tree stumps, not worth the energy it would require to have them tossed into the surf. But this last fellow, fired by Pinkerton National Detective Agency the previous year for his questionable interrogation methods, was a gift from the gods. He'd have Simpson pay Hiram Witticomb a bonus, this time with real money.

Though rage still hummed through Edgar, he forced himself to sit down, suppressing the urge to sweep the rest of the folders to the floor again, just to torment Simpson.

Perhaps it was time to pay his secretary another bonus, as well. After switching on the banker's lamp Edgar read through Witticomb's report, this time with his temper firmly in check.

…and after extensive interrogation of all ferryboat captains, have been unable to verify date when Charles Langston departed Staten Island. I have,

however, been able to verify the existence of a
son, CL's only remaining progeny, briefly married to a woman whose identity I will endeavor to
uncover by October 1. This union produced a female child, christened Theodora, as of this report
approximately 27–30 years of age. Unmarried.
Reared by CL, according to statements, having
been abandoned by parents at time of birth. Also,
according to three credible witnesses, in June of
this year above-mentioned granddaughter hired
as a chaperone one Irma Chudd, purpose and destination unknown, though witnesses speculate
either a) an elopement; or b) some form of travel
which necessitated the services of a proper companion. Description of granddaughter is as fol-
lows.

As Edgar reread the detailed notes his mind tor-
mented him with the mental image of Theodora *Pickford.* Witticomb's description of her couldn't be more
accurate had she been standing in front of the man when
he wrote it.

The chit had played Edgar for a fool, but she would
pay for her temerity. So would the man named Devlin
Stone, who had secured her release from Saratoga's jail,
then vanished, probably with Theodora.

A satisfied smile gradually soothed the jagged edges
of Edgar's anger; hands laced behind his head, he leaned
back and contemplated the final revelation Witticomb
had unearthed.

Name of CL's son is Richard. Lifelong estrange-
ment from father due to addiction to gambling.

Am at present following up on possible whereabouts of RL in Atlantic City, New Jersey.

"Every orphan dreams of a reunion with long-lost
relatives," Edgar mused aloud to the ceiling. "It will
be my pleasure to give you back your father, Theodora
Langston." But not for long…

This time, Edgar would also ensure that no pesky
lawyers or mysterious benefactors interfered. And an
impotent Secret Service would continue to flail after
shadow trails that led—nowhere.

As for Charles Langston, he'd always had a warm
spot for the old man. But Langston was too naive for
his own good. Another tidy moral lesson on life's disap-
pointments needed to be delivered. Edgar would allow
him to live out the remainder of his days, grieving for
his son and, when the time came, his granddaughter.

Chapter Twenty-Six

October arrived with a week of torrential rain, followed by skies blue enough to drown in, and air with an invigorating snap to it. Leaves lost their green luster, cloaking themselves instead in the first autumnal hues of the season. On a bright morning Devlin stood in the south pasture with Jeremiah, watching sunbeams dapple the hides of their small herd of Suffolk punch horses.

"Looking good, aren't they?" Jeremiah ruminated around a piece of straw he'd been chewing. "But I still miss the Clydesdales. They had...presence."

Stifling a smile, Devlin tucked his hands in the waistband of his trousers. They'd shared this conversation weekly for seven years. "Absolutely. But the country needs smaller horses for lighter loads, and logging." Starlight, one of the mares, wandered over; Dev fed her a carrot and idly ran his hand over her smooth chestnut belly and down her short sturdy forelegs. "At least nobody ever complains about leg feathers."

"Including me. Pain in the backside to keep clean."

They both laughed, then settled into companionable silence. Starlight wandered back over to the herd, and

Devlin allowed the freshness of the morning to settle his restless soul.

Then Jeremiah tossed aside the straw and looked him square in the eye. "Charles and myself had a long talk last night. He's wanting to know why there's no ring, and no talk of a wedding. He's also thinking it might be best if he and Thea returned to Staten Island while you make up your mind to ask the question."

The hairs at the back of Devlin's neck rose. For a week now he'd sensed a reticence in Thea, but he'd made the mistake of ignoring it. As a boy he poked sticks into anthills just to watch thousands of ants erupt in furious commotion, but he was long past the age where he invited turmoil. "That's probably just Charles's version. He's the one feeling restless. He's nervous around horses, so there's nothing much he can do around here except beat you at chess."

"He's turned into a gardener of sorts."

"So Thea tells me. She's tried her hand at hoeing and planting herself, when she's not helping out in the stables."

"Unlike Charles, she's a good instinct for horses, Dev. Amazing, when you study how things turned out with the pair of you. But something is plaguing her mind. Might be because the man she loves won't commit himself to her, for keeps."

The tranquil peace of the morning evaporated. "If I put a ring on her finger, I'll have to tell her I'm a Secret Service operative. When I do, I also want to be able to tell her I'm resigning. I can't do that yet, Uncle J."

"Confound it, boy, why ever not? You ought to have told her long ago, to my way of thinking. I've run myself to the bone these past couple of years, waiting while you chased after confidence men and worked the wanderlust out of your system. Now you're back home, with a good woman who won't up and skedaddle on you—"

"This has nothing to do with Sylvia and my mother."

"Bah! And the sky ain't blue today. Devlin, your place is here, and you know it. What's keeping you from sending in your resignation?"

Swiveling, Dev strode across the pasture, his thoughts black as Percy's ears. *Not much,* he wanted to yell. Just word from his "reporters" that a man's home in Philadelphia had been burglarized, and one of the stolen items was an Edgar Fane painting. Just that two days after the burglary, two Hotel Hustler C-notes surfaced in Steven Clarke's bank, though nobody knew who had deposited them so no charges were filed. Just that Fane still sought information about Devlin Stone so Dev had been "advised" to remain at StoneHill to avoid further jeopardizing the investigation. And the final gut-twisting news: an unscrupulous private detective now on retainer to Fane had bullied alarming tidbits about the Langston family out of local residents.

"Only a matter of time," Lawlor had warned him two days earlier, when Devlin was in Stuarts Crossing, "before he discovers your Miss Langston is the 'Miss Pickford' who was arrested in Saratoga Springs. Then, my friend, you'll both be frosted six ways to Sunday."

Devlin's choices might have put everyone and everything he loved in mortal danger, and his uncle wanted to know why he hadn't asked Theodora to be his wife?

Above him, the vast dome of an endless sky seemed to press down until he could hardly draw a deep breath; the soft outline of the mountains, worn to forested humps over tens of thousands of years, bore silent witness to pitiless reality—not even nature could halt time.

Over the past month Devlin had begun talking to God, cautious, stumbling efforts that left him feeling foolish, yet strangely at peace. The thought came to him now that maybe trust in God was akin to Devlin's love for his horses. The animals trusted a two-legged creature who didn't speak their language but nonetheless intuitively knew how to communicate with them, using as the foundation patience, gentleness and love. He understood their basic nature was different from his own, and he respected those differences.

All right, then. He'd try—no sense shying away from the word—he'd try some more praying, this very moment, before Jeremiah's questions provoked Devlin into losing his temper. *God? If You understand, You need to find a way to let me know what I should do. I've dug a hole here, but I can't come clean and confess right now. Especially to Thea.* God might know for sure what her response would be, but Devlin didn't. He was terrified she would bolt—straight into Edgar Fane. The burden was Devlin's alone, and his knees were buckling beneath its weight.

For some reason his eyes stung. A whisper of wind whirled around him, raising goose bumps on his flesh. Then it infiltrated the pores of his skin in a scalding rush, scrubbing raw the pretenses of pride in which he'd clothed himself. He was afraid, and ashamed, because he felt like a failure. A failure as an operative, a failure as a man, to not protect the woman he loved and the home that had been his legacy. Thea's possible reaction to his identity was not the true reason he had kept his mouth shut.

If his uncle weren't standing twenty feet away Devlin would have dropped to his knees. Instead he stood, hands fisted at his sides, and suffered through the agony of self-condemnation. Yet even amidst the worst of it, some nascent core in his spirit flickered to life, a paradoxical awareness of power and humility that built into a steady flame. Like an unschooled horse, yielding his will was neither swift, nor simple. But when the yielding achieved mutual harmony instead of brutal dominance, well, the possibilities shook his soul.

"Dev? Devlin! You all right, son?" Jeremiah's hand clamped down on his shoulder. "Confound it, should've kept my mouth shut. Bessie's right. Might as well plow a field with my tongue."

For a moment Devlin was unable to respond; he could hear his uncle's voice but could not see him clearly. It was as though Devlin had emerged from the bottom of a rushing stream and water still blinded his eyes.

"Aw…" Jeremiah's voice deteriorated into mumbles. He wrapped a sinewy arm around Devlin's shoulders. "Never mind. We'll work it through somehow. That's the important thing here, Dev. We're family. We'll work our way through it, together." Jeremiah glanced behind Devlin, in the direction of the barn. "Your sweetheart's headed this way, carrying a basket. After we help ourselves to whatever Bessie's cooked up, how about if I help Nab with the training this morning? Good. Glad you agreed without an argument."

Without a backward look he headed across the pasture toward Thea.

"What's happened?" she asked, the moment Jeremiah was out of earshot. "Here. Bessie made something called johnnycake. Eat while you talk, it won't offend me. Were you and your uncle having a disagreement?" Hastily she added, "If you were, of course you don't have to tell me if— Oh!"

"Best way I know to hush up idiotic notions," Devlin said when he finally ended the kiss.

"Only temporarily," she answered on a breathless laugh.

His gaze caressed her glowing face, the love inside him inextricably tangled with the need to protect. This morning she wore a practical tweed skirt and shapeless corduroy jacket. She'd plaited her hair in a haphazard braid; already errant strands dangled everywhere. But to Devlin she was the most beautiful woman in the world. Ambivalence finally conceded the battle. His decision was after all the only one he could make and still call himself a man.

A man who had called out to God, and God had answered.

Things would work out, Thea would understand when Dev was finally able to explain…. *She had to understand.*

The glow had faded from her cheeks. "Is something wrong with Starlight? One of the other mares?"

"The mares are all fine." He plucked the basket of yeasty buns off her arm, then threaded his fingers through hers. "Let's go sit under that oak over yonder. Seems like ages since we've had an opportunity to enjoy a solitary moment together."

The shadows lifted from her face. "I think everyone else at StoneHill agrees. Grandfather claimed a twisted knee, Bessie refused to let me help with the laundry and thrust this basket in my hands. When I asked one of the stable hands in the barn where you and Jeremiah were this morning, he pointed out this pasture, and winked. And you saw your uncle, practically galloping away from us."

"Then let's not disappoint them."

They reached the shelter of a towering black oak, and Devlin spread his jacket over fallen leaves and trampled-down grass. Thea sat, arranging her skirt in a graceful circle around her as Devlin sank beside her, the wicker basket between them. Thea handed him a bun. "We better eat all this johnnycake I brought so Bessie won't fuss." Then she added, her tone a shade too casual, "I've been needing to talk with you about something anyway."

Devlin returned his square of the hot bread uneaten to the basket. "You can't return to Staten Island. I won't let you go. If that's what you needed to talk about, you may as well save your breath."

One mink-brown eyebrow lifted. "Now whose imagination runs away with them? *If* I chose to leave, you couldn't stop me."

"Not by locking you in a room, no," Devlin agreed despite the anvil crushing his chest cavity. "You won't go, because I love you, and you love me. And I think it's time we made it official."

He removed Thea's half-eaten johnnycake so he could hold her unsteady hands in his. "There are probably more romantic places, and a dozen more romantic phrases. But when I look at you, surrounded by everything else I love, I no longer believe our meeting was an accident. I can't imagine not having you in my life, and I should have asked this question weeks ago." Briefly the crease appeared in his cheek. "But I was more afraid of the problems than the promises we'd just made to each other. So... Theodora Langston, will you marry me?"

Inside his, her hands stilled, then clung. She swallowed several times, opened her mouth, then chewed her bottom lip instead. For Devlin, the whole universe halted its rotation. He could hear the pulse pounding away in his ears, all sensation drained from his limbs into the rich earth and a dozen anvils now squeezed his chest while he waited for her answer.

"Are you sure you trust me enough not to run back to New York, like your mother?" A single tear overflowed. "We haven't talked about it, since we...since the day we confessed our feelings to each other. But sometimes I still see what looks like fear in your eyes. I love StoneHill almost as much as I love you. But I need to know you believe that," she finished, adding hoarsely, "Please ignore these tears."

Devlin shoved the basket out of the way and hauled the maddening woman into his arms, where she belonged. When she laid her head against his chest he pressed one hand against the silken softness of her hair, holding her there. "Whatever emotion you thought you saw had nothing to do with comparing you to my mother, or Sylvia," he promised thickly. "I *love you.* Marry me?"

"I've discovered I'm entranced with horses. I want to learn everything about them. I want to be your helpmeet there, not take over Bessie's domain."

"You can dress in dungarees and currycomb every horse every day. Bessie can remain queen of the kitchen." He wrapped her braid around his hand and tugged, tilting her head back until their lips were inches apart. "First you have to marry me. Then you can make all the demands you want."

A delicious smile curved her lips, the dark chocolate eyes turned dreamy. "I've always wanted to wear a pair of dungarees and ride a horse like Annie Oakley." Abruptly the arms she'd wrapped around his ribs squeezed, then her lips pressed against his. "Yes," she breathed. "I will marry you, Devlin Stone."

For a golden hour, they sat beneath the grand old oak and dreamed.

And Devlin believed love was enough.

Chapter Twenty-Seven

For Thea, October splattered over the Blue Ridge Mountains and StoneHill with a splendid lack of decorum. Days passed in a colorful blur, and most of the time she was able to ignore occasional twinges of anxiety. At night she fell into bed exhausted, her life full of newfound responsibilities and a sense of camaraderie she'd never before experienced. Devlin had given her the care of two horses—a dappled gray Percheron with intelligent eyes and a sweet disposition, and a mischievous Suffolk punch filly scarcely a year old. Under the careful eye of every stableman, including Devlin and Jeremiah, each day Thea gained confidence in her growing skills.

Bessie, however, also insisted on teaching her how to make some of her most famous recipes. "Because, miss, the day will come when you won't have me. You can hire a housekeeper, but a cook as good as me's hard to come by."

Her grandfather quit making plans to return to Staten Island, instead arranging for Mrs. Chudd to move permanently into their house until Charles decided whether or not to keep or sell. StoneHill, Thea mused fancifully, had become their Shangri-la, or perhaps El Dorado. At least, the pot of gold at the end of the rainbow.

Then another letter arrived, from her old friend who had married years earlier and moved to New Jersey. For months, Pamela had dutifully informed Thea whenever she heard a thread of gossip about Edgar Fane. In today's letter, however, she included some unsettling news, about:

> ...a private detective, hired by Mr. Fane to search for some woman who disappeared after she broke his heart in Saratoga Springs. I will try to discover her name, if you like. But I do wish you would quit blaming Mr. Fane for your circumstances, Theodora. Nobody thinks less of you due to your reduced situation.

Along with admonishments, almost every letter from Pamela also included an entreaty for Thea to come home where she belonged. Pamela believed she and her grandfather to be rusticating in some southern backwater nobody had ever heard of, until they recovered from the "troubles of last year." Thea had not confided otherwise. Risky enough, to be writing her at all. They had both attended Union Academy College for Women; of all her friends, Pamela was the only one Thea trusted to secretly send information concerning Edgar Fane, and to keep her correspondence with Thea—as well as StoneHill's address—a secret.

So many secrets.

Perhaps her friend was right. It was time to give up on her hopeless quest for justice and focus instead on a future with the man she loved. Edgar Fane was beyond reach, and she needed to leave retribution where it belonged—with God. Revenge, she had learned at too great a cost, ultimately harmed the person seeking it. That long-ago afternoon at the Saratoga Springs police station, trapped within her own web of lies, she had listened to Edgar Fane—and seen herself. Enlightenment produced a shame almost as debilitating as her brief sojourn in a cell.

Devlin had freed her from that jail, loved her and given her his heart. But only Thea could make the decision that would free her soul.

She and Devlin had shared much in the past weeks about the Lord's Presence in their lives. "He reminds me of how you used to talk to God, when I was a girl," she'd told Charles just this morning. "As if God cares about him, and even communicates with him. Devlin's *praying,* Grandfather."

"And how does a praying man for a husband strike you, Taffy T?"

"For some reason, that strikes me just fine. I think I've discovered a—a similar hunger. This past year, it's been dreadfully wearing, believing God is no more than an indifferent Creator, indifferent to human suffering. But…" But she'd been angry at God; she'd spurned Him to pursue her own course. She had abandoned Him.

Charles pinched the end of his nose, then gave her a sheepish smile. "There will always be 'buts.' Most of them can be turned into faith, instead of flaws." And patting her knee, he rose. "But for Edgar Fane's interference in our lives, you never would have met Devlin."

"That's what Devlin says."

"Snared yourself a wise man." Chuckling, he left to

go see how many autumn apples had fallen from the trees in StoneHill's orchard.

Now, as Thea stared down at the letter in her hands, she allowed a decision tugging at her for days to transform into certainty. She needed to release the past, along with her secret plans to pursue Edgar Fane. Nothing was worth the love of a man whose smile held the power of the sun whenever he looked at Thea. The man who had forgiven her own deceptions and seen beyond her flaws. To Devlin, she was beautiful. Worthy. Loved.

The way Jesus loved her.

All right, Lord. For months He'd been nagging her with wisps of remembered scripture, about His ways and His timing and His justice. *All right. I give up. Forgive my hard heart...restore the joy of salvation. Do as You will...* "But here's my final 'but,' Lord. Please, help me choose the right path?"

In a burst of energy she ripped Pamela's letter into confetti-sized pieces, and went to collect a couple of apples to feed her two horses.

Edgar strolled into Caruthers, a seedy gambling casino two blocks off Atlantic City's famous Boardwalk. Faded velvet draperies and crystal chandeliers were choked in a haze of cigar smoke. Ill-dressed patrons hunched around tables and roulette wheels, while aging ladies of pleasure pretended enjoyment in their duties.

Suppressing a shudder of distaste, Edgar walked over to a table near the center of the crowded room, where five men sat in a semicircle, playing blackjack against the house dealer. Only one player glanced up at Edgar's approach. The dealer shot a look toward the two bulky bodyguards who stood five paces behind Edgar, and kept his mouth shut.

"Good evening," Edgar said in his best Oxford-educated voice. "Is one of you Richard Langston?"

"Who wants to know?" a florid individual with squinty eyes demanded.

"Are you Mr. Langston?"

The man leaned back in his chair and jutted out his chin. "Any snoot who waltzes over and interrupts my concentration, he better be willing to give me *his* moniker before I answer a question."

"Now, Billy. No need to get testy." Rising, the only man who had acknowledged Edgar's presence adjusted his necktie and straightened his frayed cuffs. "I'm Richard Langston. What can I do for you, Mr....?"

"I'll explain everything." Edgar swept the room with an assessing look. "Is there somewhere we can enjoy a private discussion, Mr. Langston?"

"Mr. Langston owes the house two thousand dollars," the dealer said. "And house rules require him to stay until he wins the money back, or pays in cash before leaving the table."

"House'll have to wait its turn," the squint-eyed man said. "You ain't leaving my sight, Langston, unless you fork over the thousand you owe me."

"How 'bout my five hundred? Cripes, man, did you pay this bloke to help you wiggle out from paying up? You been begging me for two weeks now ta give ya more time."

"Gentlemen," Edgar interrupted the jackals. Behind him, the bodyguards stirred uneasily but, obeying explicit instructions, did not approach. Next, Edgar made a production of withdrawing a small leather-bound notepad and gold pen from his coat pocket. "Other than two thousand for the house, how much does Mr. Langston owe each of you?" He pointed his pen at the most belligerent of the group. "Starting with you. A thousand, wasn't it?"

While Richard Langston's complexion deepened to the hue of boiled tomatoes, Edgar wrote down responses and tallied his quarry's total losses: over seven thousand dollars. "Not a good season this year?" He clapped Langston's shoulder. "I can change that. Allow me." He drew out his calfskin bill book and to the riveted attention of the watchers, counted out bills onto the worn felt that covered the table. When he finished, he planted one palm firmly over the money. "Now, Mr. Langston, if these gentleman will write receipts to verify your gambling debts to them are paid in full, that should free you up to join me for a private discussion."

"What extortionist interest will you require, in turn for this generosity?" Langston looked him in the eye, but he was sweating.

Good. The man still clung to some remnants of intelligence. Shabby gentility combined with a weak mind and bad habits offered little challenge. "You're a gambling man, Mr. Langston. You decide."

To give him credit, Langston chewed through the proposition. Finally, after a lingering study of the other players and Edgar's watchful bodyguards, he turned to Edgar with a shrug. "As a gambling man, the odds strike me as more favorable toward an unknown benefactor than my known acquaintances." He paused, and a reckless grin spread over his face. "How about double or nothing? One round, just me and you?"

"No." Edgar scooped up the seven thousand dollars. "Now or not at all, Langston. Think carefully. I'm neither a fool, nor a gambler. Before I stepped foot in this establishment I learned enough to provide for my own protection." He delivered the coup de grâce. "I also learned I'm the only person willing to arrange for yours. At least one of the men at this table, along with that pudgy gentleman lounging at the bar—to whom you owe another two thousand from a poker game a week ago, correct?—and finally, the management of this place, all plan to deprive you of whatever monies you possess at the end of the evening. If your pockets are empty, most likely you'll pay with your life."

"I...see. It's possible you're in cahoots with them all, and this is an elaborate hoax. On the other hand, you might be telling the truth. I like the odds of the latter." Langston nodded once. "I accept your offer. Now... mind telling me who the devil you are?"

Without comment Edgar handed over his calling card. Richard Langston's smooth pale face drained of color; he blinked twice, then like a hound brought to heel without another word followed Edgar and the two bodyguards across the momentarily silent room, and out into the brisk salty air.

Chapter Twenty-Eight

❧

"Thought it better to deliver the news in person," Fred Lawlor finished. With a grunt of exertion he helped Devlin load the final sack of grain into the back of the farm wagon. "Sorry."

Devlin rotated his head to work the kinks out of his neck muscles. "We knew all along StoneHill was only a temporary refuge. Now that Fane's putting all the pieces together it makes sense, him using Thea's father to lure Thea out of hiding. It's also probable he hopes to catch me, as well. But his motivation's never been that of a spurned lover seeking retribution. I told you about Thea's suspicions about Mrs. Gorman's death? This would indicate her suspicions hold merit. For some reason, the blackguard had her murdered. Might even have done the deed himself."

A chill he couldn't ignore iced down his spine. "It's imperative to discover how Fane unearthed Richard Langston. He's trying to get rid of all witnesses who can implicate him in the Cynthia Gorman murder. Since he can't know what Thea's told me, I'm on that list as well. This is no longer about catching a counterfeiter…."

Lawlor glanced around to ensure nobody else was in earshot. "That's our assessment about Miss Langston, yes. We're not convinced of the threat to you personally. Appropriate actions are being evaluated in Washington. Devlin, you have to lay aside any personal feelings for this woman. Her protection, and securing proof that Fane is guilty of murder, is beyond our mandate, my friend."

"Obviously you don't understand something, Lawlor. This woman is going to be my wife. Nothing—*nothing*—is going to stop me from doing everything in my power to protect her. Have I made my position clear?"

"Completely." The other man lifted his hands in a placative gesture and backed away. "Take it easy, Devlin. I'm sorry. Until today we had no idea the two of you…you never mentioned… I—" He cursed under his breath, then offered a weak smile. "The one time I saw her, I should have guessed. Smart as a whip, isn't she? Pulled the wool right over our eyes, calling you by a fake name. Well, this will make for an interesting report tonight."

"No," Dev refuted, the word flat and final. "Until Edgar Fane is no longer a threat to Miss Langston, keep her name completely out of your daily reports. I've been working on my report for Chief Hazen, and will supply all mandated details. I'll also shoulder the consequences of flouting policy. Calm your conscience, all right?"

"Dev, I—"

"Subject's not open for discussion. I want to solve this case, now more than ever. But my first priority is my fiancée's safety." As long as he lived Devlin would never forget Thea's face when he led her out of the Saratoga jail. "All it would take is one careless word, and you know it. Give me your word, Fred, or Thea and I will disappear. Completely."

Lawlor's mouth thinned, but he quit arguing. "Much as it galls me to admit it, I see your point. You have my promise. If something changes, I'll do what I can to alert you. That's the best I can offer, Devlin."

"All right." Fred Lawlor was not a quick thinker, nor swift on his feet. But in the two years Dev had known him, Fred had kept his word. A careful, if pedantic Secret Service operative, he'd served honorably for fifteen years, and Dev also valued his insight. "Tell me the rest of why you came, then. I have to get back to StoneHill."

"Some of it's good news. A burglar arrested two days ago swears six ways to Sunday he was sent to Steven Clarke's residence in Philadelphia, not to rob the place, but to fetch counterfeit bills hidden in the Edgar Fane painting given to Clarke by Fane, just before they both left Saratoga. Fool of a burglar got too greedy and kept some of the bills for himself, along with half the Clarke's family silver. Bills recovered all bear the Hotel Hustler's mark. Operatives and police departments from Washington to Chicago are piecing evidence together to tie in the Hustler's work with paintings Edgar Fane donated to unsuspecting recipients. But…" He hesitated.

Ah, yes. Now for the bad news. "But we still need an operative to go in undercover," Dev finished for him. "The word of one no-name thief would never be sufficient to prosecute the son of Thaddeus Fane." He'd known ever since he heard about Thea's father what this personal visit from Lawlor was leading up to. "We've got to find some of those bills in Edgar's possession. It's possible Richard Langston's the next delivery boy."

"Won't be as workable as Saratoga. Jekyll Island is

an exclusive haven for America's millionaires, not a world-famous tourist destination." Scowling, Lawlor kicked the wagon wheel. "Plenty of other southern resorts where Fane could pass the winter. But no, he has to take himself and Richard Langston down to a blasted private island off the coast of Georgia."

"He needed someplace where Langston couldn't easily bolt," Devlin said thoughtfully, scanning the horizon.

Swollen clouds inched over the mountains to the west, blocking the sun. A gust of wind, smelling of rain, set the dead leaves heaped at the base of the two sycamores flanking the hardware store into a cyclonic frenzy. It was early November; back at StoneHill, he'd left a cheerful Thea swathed in one of Bessie's aprons, with Bessie barking instructions on how to make the best apple pie in the state of Virginia.

"I'll still be able to take care of my horses," Thea promised Devlin, waving flour-dusted fingers at him. "I might even squeeze in an hour to help Nab oil hooves. I plan to be an indispensable part of your life, Mr. Stone."

"You're indispensable, just by being you, Miss Langston."

Thea's face lit up like it did on those few occasions when he'd stolen a kiss. Over the past month his fiancée had flowered into full bloom, flitting between house, stables and Stuarts Crossing like a hummingbird. No more haunted shadows, no more vertigo spells, no more secretive, fleeting glances at Devlin when she thought he didn't notice. The insecure young woman who felt unworthy of love whisked through the days, radiant with confidence, soaking up life at StoneHill like a sponge. She and Bessie were planning a spring wedding, when dogwood blossoms covered the farm in drifts of white flowers. Edgar Fane, Thea had promised him three weeks earlier, had been exiled permanently from her life. "God gave me my very own miracle—the love of a wonderful man. What God brought together, I refuse to allow Edgar Fane to tear asunder."

Whirling abruptly away from Lawlor, Devlin slammed the wagon's tailgate shut and hooked the latches, his thoughts black as a crow's wing. He glanced over his shoulder. "The reason you delivered the news in person is because someone wants me to be that man on the inside."

Lawlor had the grace to look uncomfortable. "We know it's a fair risk. Obviously you can't go in under your real name this time. But he doesn't have a photograph, only vague, hearsay descriptions of Mr. Stone. You still have an advantage over all the other operatives, because you don't have to pretend to be a well-heeled gent."

"So did you bring along specific suggestions from Washington?"

"No. I was told to gauge your reaction, and hear what you had to offer. We're still doing research on Jekyll Island itself."

Devlin chose to interpret that as a compliment. "Give me twenty-four hours, Fred. I have a few ideas, but I need to think through them."

Resigned, his fellow operative shrugged back into his Norfolk jacket, donned his bowler and, using the wagon as a screen, handed over a thin sheaf of papers before climbing into his buggy. "That's everything we've collated since our last meeting, including the little we know about Richard Langston. It doesn't make for pretty reading, Devlin, especially since the man's Miss Langston's father."

On the twenty-minute drive back to StoneHill, Devlin chewed over his own strategy, and prayed his new-found trust in God would not be misplaced.

That evening, while Thea helped Bessie in the kitchen, and Jeremiah, muttering imprecations, retired to the study to do paperwork, Devlin asked Charles to join him in the parlor. "There's something I need to tell you," he said. "But you need to know up front that under no circumstances can you share this with Theodora."

"I've never been in the habit of keeping secrets from my granddaughter, Devlin."

"You will, once you understand that the repercussions from enlightenment might cost her her life."

Chapter Twenty-Nine

A week later, Thea joined Devlin in the family parlor for a rare moment alone with him. Despite Saratoga, or perhaps because of it, at StoneHill they practiced as much propriety as they both could muster. Cozy trysts in the parlor after everyone else had retired were avoided. Well, mostly. A giggle escaped as Thea sneaked down the hallway. A round harvest moon glazed the window-panes in a pearlescent sheen, and she blew the man-in-the-moon a kiss, her heart equally bright and swollen with love.

Devlin rose from the settee. "Sit here, across from me," he said. He gestured to the overstuffed chair her grandfather preferred, near the old-fashioned parlor stove, almost three yards away from the settee. "This is going to be hard enough…"

Laughing, Thea obeyed, wrapping herself up in her Scottish plaid shawl. But after he started talking, the bubbly urge to laugh fizzled and she squeezed her hands tightly together in the shawl's long fringes while she listened to her beloved regretfully inform her of a trip he had to make to Georgia. He would leave in two days.

"There's a breeder, near Savannah, with whom I've been corresponding for several years. He's given me first right of refusal on a yearling colt, a Holsteiner. If you and I were already married I could take you with me. Since we decided to wait until next spring to wed—"

"A decision I think I regret…"

"—and since I need to make this trip immediately, I'll make it as fast as possible. Thea, love… I don't want to go…." Finally his words lagged, the light eyes half-hidden behind the screen of his lashes.

"A 'have to' instead of a 'want to'?" Thea finished, hoping to lighten the mood. "As you know, I've learned a lot these past months, distinguishing between the two." The tips of his mouth barely lifted. Thea fought a brief internal skirmish, and switched tactics. "I'll miss you terribly, of course. But I know how much the Holsteiner breed means to you. I have to agree they're as… as elegant an example of horseflesh as I've ever seen. It's just, well, could you explain the urgency of traveling to Georgia right now? Bessie tells me this time of year the weather down here can turn nasty between the tick and tock of the clock." And Thanksgiving was less than two weeks away.

"Trains these days can handle bad weather." He heaved a sigh, flexing his shoulders as though they were weighed down with a sack of stones. "The breeder needs the money now, but I won't pay for any horse sight unseen, especially a Holsteiner. Thirty years ago, while America fought a nasty civil war, Europe struggled with turmoil of their own. The Holsteiner's reputation suffered from some poor breeding practices, and a resulting lack of quality. In this country there's very few stock I'd want to add to StoneHill, but this breeder in Georgia owns some of them. I don't want to lose the opportunity." Leaning forward, he searched her face, his gaze still cloudy. "You know I love horses. But do you have any idea how much I love you? I'd give my life for you, Thea."

"As I would you," she replied, suddenly understanding. Desertion and betrayal left lifelong scars. Proprieties be hanged, she rose to join him on the settee. The heavy velvet drapes had been pulled, exchanging moonlight for coziness. Intimacy, however, eluded them; the hissing parlor stove tossed wavering shadows about the room; on the side table the milk glass lamp cast a feverish glow over the furniture. A life-size portrait of Devlin's father stared down at her, his expression grave rather than kind. *Don't worry,* she promised Eli Stone, *it might take years, but one day he'll learn to trust me enough to travel in peace.* "I'll miss you," she told Devlin, "every hour of every day. But I will be here when you return."

"It's not that."

He looked so miserable she rushed the words. "And I promise not to weep, or slide into feeling unloved, or afraid. My faith in God has never been stronger, even when I was a child. I know you've postponed several other trips over the past month because you were concerned about—"

"I'll have words with Jeremiah."

"He knew I was fighting guilt about stifling your freedom, and offered good counsel." She nudged the tough, muscular shoulder with her own, love and admiration prickling her skin. "Jeremiah said you'd go when you were convinced I'd be safe, and not before, so there was no use pestering you, or fretting. So I didn't, and now you're ready. We're both ready." Softly she stroked his forearm. "I'll be waiting right here, for you to come home. Don't worry about me, Devlin. Go buy us a colt."

Devlin dropped his head in his hands. "God, help me," she thought he said in a throttled undertone.

Frowning, Thea ventured hesitantly, "Devlin? Do you want me to ask Grandfather to chaperone and the three of us will all go? We'd have a delightful excursion, traveling to Georgia together."

"Not this time, sweetheart. I can't." Abruptly he turned and with a hoarse groan wrapped his arms around her, pressing kisses against her hair, her forehead. "Thea… I love you. No matter how long it takes, I will come back to you. Believe in me, Thea."

Believe in him? "I do, I do. Devlin…you're going to see a man about a horse. If the weather holds and the trains run on time, you'll be home in a week, won't you?" Despite her resolve, uncertainty stirred. Thea stared down at her lap, trying to ignore an emotion she hadn't experienced since she'd given Edgar Fane's fate into the Lord's hands.

"I'll try," Devlin said after an uncomfortably long interval. "Don't hold me to a promise I might not be able to keep. We've both had too many of those in our lives." His fingers tightened. "Too many broken promises," he repeated, almost reverently caressing her cheekbones, the line of her jaw. His gaze, dark, intense, bored into Thea's. "But I can promise that no man will ever love you as much as I do. God as my witness, Thea, nobody but God Himself loves you more."

The single kiss Devlin pressed upon her lips tasted of

desperation as well as love, but Thea closed her mind to all the questions and held on to him with equal fervor.

Three days later she was in the barn with Jeremiah, helping Nab soothe an unhappy Suffolk punch gelding while Jeremiah examined the animal's mucous-crusted nostrils. Outside the wind whistled and roared, blowing up a Canadian cold snap, Nab warned everyone, "...'cuz my joints is aching something fierce. Whoa, boy, easy on now." He glanced at Thea. "You watch his hindquarters now, Miss Thea. He don't got a notion of how strong he is and how little you are. He just knows he's miserable."

"I don't like the look of this," Jeremiah said. "I'm pretty sure it's nothing but catarrh, but I'm not willing to risk a case of pneumonia, or strangles. Devlin will nail my hide to a tree in the back forty for sure if I don't call in the veterinarian, but I'll feel seven sorts of a fool if it turns out to be a simple cold."

"Do you want me to place a call on the telephone for you?" Thea asked. "Dr. O'Toole's information is in that ledger you keep in the harness room, isn't it?"

"Be a kindness if you did. Would you mind bringing back some leg bandages, as well? Might as well get the fellow as comfortable as possible while we wait."

Glad to have a task, Thea slipped away after giving Muggers's muscled withers a final pat. Moments later, however, she returned with bandages but the alarming report that the ledger was nowhere in the harness room. The oversize leather binder contained not only names and telephone exchanges, but also all the information on every single horse at StoneHill, from bloodlines to health histories. Due to its importance, the ledger was never removed from the harness room, where—until this moment—it resided on a small table situated below the wall telephone Devlin had installed six years earlier.

Jeremiah straightened, wiped his hands on his old dungarees and glared across at Nab. "I remember now. Confound the boy. Devlin himself took it up to the house before he left, to copy out all the bloodlines of our Holsteiners. In all the hubbub to get to the depot in time, looks like he forgot to bring the ledger back."

"I'll run up to the house and retrieve it," Thea volunteered. "I can make the call from the house telephone, then I'll bring the ledger back where it belongs."

"First thing when Devlin returns I'll string *his* hide to a tree," Jeremiah growled. "If you can't place your hand on it immediately, honey, try his desk. It's a mess, but I believe he stuffs telephone numbers in one of the cubbyholes. Come on, Nab, we may as well give this fella's legs a rubdown before we wrap 'em up."

Smiling, Thea stuffed her arms back into her coat and dashed outside into the wind. Once Devlin returned home, she'd have to poke a bit of fun at him over his extraordinary lapse. The evening before he left he certainly had been distracted, rushing around to prepare for a train trip that would probably, he grumbled, last twenty hours or more.

"I hope that Holsteiner colt is worth it," Thea said to him just before he'd ducked into the carriage, and a strange flicker came and went in his eyes.

"Sometimes it's hard to tell what's worth the trouble, until it's too late."

For the next quarter of an hour, while she and Bessie searched Devlin's bedroom and the study without success, Thea chewed over his portentous aside. "I'll

take the library," Bessie offered finally. "Your grandfather's dozed off reading a book on Middle Eastern
history, of all things, but I'll rouse him if we need another pair of eyes. You're Devlin's bride-to-be, so you
go paw through his desk. Won't even let me straighten
the papers on it when I clean, so mind you leave them
as mussed up as you find them." She paused with her
hand on the brass doorknob. "Year before last, when
Devlin was gone, Jeremiah lost a horse to pneumonia.
I don't want my man enduring that again. You find that
veterinarian's number, y'hear?"

She bustled off toward the library, and Thea returned
to the study, eyeing the massive walnut desk with trepidation. Full of drawers, cubbyholes and locked files,
strewn with books and papers, an adding machine and
several other contraptions, the thing hulked like a bad-
tempered grizzly disturbed in its hibernation. And the
ledger was nowhere in sight.

"After we're married," Thea announced to her absent
fiancé, "we're going to tame this beast."

When gingerly sifting through the mess on the felt-
covered desktop produced nothing, Thea knelt on the
floor to tug on one of the drawer pulls on the two ped-
estals—and discovered the entire drawer swung open
to disclose yet *more* cubbyholes and a stack of smaller
drawers, along with slots for files. The ledger would
have fit neatly in one of the file holders, except…it
wasn't there. Nor was it inside the opposite pedestal,
which also pivoted open. Aggravated, Thea blew hair
out of her eyes and glared at the upper half of the desk.
Behind the stacks of magazines and papers and letters
were more drawers and cubbyholes. The two center
drawers looked wide enough, and perhaps deep enough,

to hold the ledger. She pulled the bottom one open, in her frustration yanking a bit too hard. The entire drawer flew out, scattering the pile of letters, one of which slid inside the empty space behind the drawer.

When Thea reached to retrieve the envelope, her fingers brushed against what felt like a circular indentation in the wood. Mildly curious, she pressed against it, and with an almost inaudible snick, a hidden panel popped open. "Oh, how clever," Thea murmured, wondering if Devlin even knew of the secret drawer's existence. This desk, he'd shared, was one of the few things his mother had left behind at StoneHill, because his father had loved the intricate patterns of inlaid wood on the top and side panels. Completely diverted, Thea shoved aside the envelopes so she could pull the hidden box behind the panel completely out. Perhaps Devlin's mother had left behind something all those years ago—a note would be romantic, but even a haberdasher's bill with his mother's signature would give Devlin a piece of history he'd lost.

What Thea discovered was a sheaf of folded papers tied together with string, the bundle practically filling the bottom of the drawer. A thrill of excitement fluttered beneath her breastbone and her fingers eagerly untied the string. The papers fell open, and instead of a long-dead woman's script she recognized Devlin's distinctive handwriting. Unlike his hopelessly cluttered desk, his penmanship was neat, precise and eminently legible. Thea liked to tease him that he would have made an excellent schoolmaster on the strength of his letters alone.

Her gaze fell upon the words halfway down the first page—and Thea's world exploded in a haze of shock.

Chapter Thirty

"No. No…no…no!" The words blurred on the page, then sharpened into brutal clarity.

Richard Langston, estranged father to Miss Theodora Langston, has accompanied Edgar Fane to the Jekyll Island Club, located off the Georgia coast. Following instructions, I depart Paeonian Springs, Virginia, on the Washington & Old Dominion Railroad Friday, November 17, connecting with an Atlantic Coast Line Florida Special in Alexandria, for the purpose of going undercover at the Jekyll Island Club. As arranged with Club President Lanier, I will work under the moniker Daniel Smith as a seasonal stables employee. I hereby acknowledge receipt of two reports delivered to me personally by Operative Lawlor on Tuesday, November 14, which provided vital information pertaining to the Hotel Hustler case.

The rest of the words blurred. Thea shook her head, fought to breathe but there was no air, her lungs severed from a brain that continued to deny the evidence of her eyes. The bundle of papers slipped from her hands to fall with a soft rustle onto the desk. With the somnolence of a sleepwalker she stared down at them, at the condemnatory heading—*Daily Report of Agent. United States Secret Service.*

"God, You can't do this to me. It's a mistake. It can't be true." In a burst of frantic motion she pawed through the pages of the report, her heartbeat a concussive hammer against her rib cage.

Then she found what she was looking for—the signature.

Roaring filled her head and the neat inscription magnified, then receded down a dark tunnel. Thea stared at the name until the faintness passed, and hurt ignited in a conflagration of heat and red-tipped blackness. Devlin Stone, wealthy gentleman, horseman, breeder...the man to whom she had pledged her life, her love, *the man she had trusted with her whole heart*... Devlin Stone was an agent for the United States Secret Service. He could even have been one of the men who had her grandfather arrested a year ago.

"Thea? We found the ledger under a book in the library. Bessie sent me along to—" Charles's voice checked, and Thea heard him cross the room. "What's wrong?" He touched her shoulder as he peered down at the desk. "Heavens, what a mess. Well, I'll help you straighten things out a little. Devlin will never know." He reached to straighten the sheaf of reports, and went still. "Oh. Oh, my dear..."

All five of her senses felt as if they had been scraped over a washboard, leaving her raw, hypersensitive to every nuance. When she was able to speak, the words sounded strangely guttural. "You knew already. Devlin told you."

"Yes," he admitted. "He told me. Three nights before he left for Georgia. I gather there is some risk, what he's doing. He wanted me to know, because, well…" He hemmed and hawed, finally adding gently, "Thea, my dear, try to imagine how difficult this—"

"Does Jeremiah know? Bessie?"

In the lemony-yellow glow of a banker's lamp the lines on Charles's face deepened. "Yes," he admitted, his expression resigned. "Everyone knows. They also know how you feel, about the Service, and Edgar Fane. Taffy T…"

"Don't call me that again. The gullible little girl finally grew up." Like waves against rocky cliffs, the outrage of betrayal crashed over her. "You lied to me— *everyone* lied to me! How could you? How could Devlin?" She snatched up the first page of the report and thrust it beneath Charles's nose. "Did you know your son is part of this investigation? Your only living son, my *father?* The man who dumped his infant daughter and dragged the family name through the dirt of countless gambling halls is now in league with the very man who ruined you!"

Charles abruptly sank down into the office chair and covered his eyes with his hand. "I lost my son before you were born. As for his involvement with Edgar Fane, Devlin doesn't know what Richard is doing with, or for, him," he said, the words leaden. "Regrettably, if gambling money's included, I know Richard will do anything Edgar Fane demands. More troubling is Edgar's motivation for tracking him down at all. Devlin was disturbed enough to confide in me. He fears for your safety, and we both feared your reaction to the revelation that he's an operative for the Secret Service."

With every word, the hurt metamorphosed into anger. No, not anger—rage. A live monster with serrated teeth, beyond the scope of her experience. Not even her hatred of Edgar Fane or the news about her father matched the out-of-control emotions tearing through her, ripping open her heart, crushing preconceptions along with her bones. Devlin… Devlin. Eyes burning, she stared at her grandfather. "You feared my reaction?" Her tongue had difficulty forming the words. "So you both chose the coward's way out, hoping I'd— what? Never find out? Never discover that the two men I love most would rather lie to me than risk trusting me with the truth? While speaking our marriage vows to honor each other, would Devlin be breaking them with a secret life he refused to reveal?"

"Thea, the man's been torturing himself for weeks, waiting for a time and a way to explain, one which wouldn't precipitate this very sort of response. Try to understand from his perspective. You'd endured a horrific experience and spent your first weeks here wandering about like a shadow of yourself. And you've spent an entire year hating the Secret Service almost as much as you do Edgar Fane. You concocted a dangerous, implausible scheme, one which only by the grace of God didn't—"

"Don't you dare bring God into this!" A small metal postage-stamp box sat on top of a pile of bill receipts. Thea snatched it up, leveled a final scorching gaze upon her grandfather, then hurled the stamp box against the pine-paneled wall on the opposite side of the room. "That's what I think of yours and Devlin's avowals of faith in a loving God." Breathing hard, she stood, smothering in hurt darker than black tar until a strangled sob worked its way free. "After all these months together Devlin still didn't trust me enough to share the truth about his profession? Yes, I would have been upset, but why couldn't both of you have tried to understand how difficult the revelation would be for *me?* He says he loves me, he believed God brought us together until I believed, too. Ha! Jesus promised His truth would set us free, but Devlin never felt *free* to share it, did he? And you...you..." Blindly she shook her head. The rage withered. The hurt expanded. "No. It's me, isn't it?" She pressed a fist over her heart. "It's me. I'll always be the daughter of a gambler and a saloon singer. No matter how hard I try, I'm never enough to be worthy of *anyone's* love."

Charles heaved himself to his feet. "My dear, please. Don't. You know we both love you. We just wanted to do what we thought was best. For the first time in over a year you were happy. I promise I was going to tell you—Devlin planned to tell you himself, if he returns—" He stopped dead.

"What do you mean, *if* he returns?" Thea braced her palm on the desk. A film of perspiration broke out all over her skin, and an ominous wave of dizziness glazed her vision. "Grandfather? What else haven't you told me?"

He took her hand; never had he looked so old, not even on the night he'd been incarcerated. "Child, Devlin did not apprise me of what he plans to do. But I believe he's gone to this Jekyll Island alone, undercover, not only because he's honor bound to obey orders. Apparently the Service has been trying to learn the identity of this Hotel Hustler for years. Devlin is convinced now it's Edgar Fane, and proof is finally within their grasp. But Devlin also convinced his superiors that Fane needs to be more closely investigated for the murder of that woman in Saratoga. Now do you begin to understand? You are likely the last person to have seen Mrs. Gorman alive other than her killer. For the authorities to have a case against Edgar, your testimony is vital. Yet for the past three months, my dear, Devlin has fought tooth and nail to keep your presence at StoneHill a secret, insisting the Service secure evidence on the counterfeiting charges alone because the risk to you was too great. After hearing about Richard, I have wondered if Edgar Fane is trying to lure you out of hiding, using your father as the bait. A despicable tactic…" He faltered, the tendons in his throat quivering.

Thea pulled away, wrapping her arms around herself. "I don't care about my father." Under any other circumstances she would have been ashamed of the self-deception. "Fane's tactic won't work. Devlin should have told me. He should have allowed me the opportunity to make the decision." *If he died, she'd never forgive him, or herself.*

Charles inclined his head. "I agree with you. No matter what you think, Thea, I'm on your side, and told Devlin so at the time. But I will not condemn a godly man for following a noble course of action. He's gone to this Jekyll Island because he's honor bound to do his job. But I also believe even more strongly his primary motive is to protect you from a decidedly *un*godly man with enough money and power to hunt you down until he finds you. Thea? Are you hearing me?"

"Yes. I hear you saying it's acceptable for Devlin to protect me at the expense of his own life."

"I can appreciate how you might look at it that way." The lines crisscrossing his high forehead deepened to furrows. "Devlin loves you, and he's doing whatever is necessary to keep you safe. Alive. He's also a professional with a job to complete. Which means he's a man on a rack."

"He still lied to me about his true identity." Charles gave her a sharp glance but Thea stolidly averted her face. "I need to call Dr. O'Toole. Jeremiah's waiting."

"Bessie's taken the ledger to the barn. Theodora, Devlin's shared the best part of himself with you. His tactics might have proven faulty, but his motives are pure. I'll be honored to have him for my grandson-in-law. You don't want to believe anything but the worst right now, but after you've had a bit of time to recover from this conundrum I expect you to behave like the astute woman I reared you to be." He exhaled a wearied sigh. "These reports were never intended for your eyes, or mine. I don't know where you found them, but—"

"A secret drawer in his desk. It was by accident." Bitterness clogged her throat like gall. "Or perhaps it wasn't an 'accident' at all. Perhaps God wanted me to find them. Have a taste of Jesus' 'truth.'" She knew now what truth her grandfather believed, and likely the bitter taste would linger for a long time. "Of course, Jesus already knew better than to trust any man. Did you know that's in the Bible, Grandfather? How's that for truth?" With benumbed fingers she folded the reports up and tied them back together with the string, stuffed them inside the box and shoved everything back in its hiding place. "There. All gone, like they never existed."

She couldn't feel her feet, and shuffled backward one step, then two. "Sort of like me. Right now, I feel... invisible, as though my hopes and dreams, my heart, never existed. I finally believed what you wanted me to believe—that God should be Edgar Fane's judge, not me. I believed Devlin, that God had brought us together, had filled our hearts with love for each other, and Him. I was at peace. Until today. Tell me, Grandfather, what kind of God dangles peace in your face, then yanks it away? You want me to behave like a rational, intelligent human being, allow the man I love to hug his secrets, and perhaps die because of them. So what kind of God makes you give your heart to a man, then takes him away, perhaps forever? And what kind of man asks you to be his wife when he doesn't trust you enough to tell you who he really is?"

"Perhaps you need to reassess your understanding of the nature of God, Theodora? And the freedom human beings enjoy to make their own choices? You needn't look at me like that. I'm through lecturing, I promise—except for one final bit of counsel. Yes, I know you've not asked for it. One of the perks of old age is the prerogative to annoy loved ones with unsolicited advice. You're hurt right now, feeling betrayed. But be careful how you throw rocks at Devlin. The very nature of his profession demanded silence when you first met, the same way you demanded mine and Mrs. Chudd's when you played *your* dangerous game of deception."

A stronger blast of vertigo struck, making her stagger, but Thea lifted her chin and faced her grandfather down. "When I realized I was in love with Devlin, I confessed everything. For the past four months, I've been trying to relearn how to live a faith *you* seemed to have cast aside. Now I see why. It's impossible, isn't it, to believe God cares when everyone in your life betrays you?"

"Thea… I hadn't wanted to tell you this, but I believe you should know. You're not the only person Edgar Fane has been searching for all these months. He's also hunting for the Devlin Stone who secured a Miss Pickford's release from the Saratoga Springs jail. Devlin's undercover, but he's there alone, risking exposure for—"

"He shouldn't have gone alone! Does the Secret Service think so little of their operatives they sacrifice them like chess pieces? Excuse me, Grandfather. I'm not very good company right now. Perhaps by suppertime I'll be able to transform myself into that astute, understanding woman, and you'll be able to tolerate my company."

She walked out of the study without looking back; when she reached her bedroom she locked the door, then dragged down a pair of suitcases and began to pack.

Chapter Thirty-One

Jekyll Island, Georgia
Late November, 1897

Devlin finished raking the dirt floor of the new stables, then trod down the aisle between the forty-six completed stalls, absently patting one or two equine heads that nickered a greeting as he passed. Most of these stalls, purchased in advance by owners for their private use, were unoccupied; few Club owners arrived on Jekyll Island before January. Boatloads of staff, however, commenced arriving as early as October to prepare the land as well as the buildings for the season. Yet access to the island was so closely scrutinized Chief Hazen had had to secure special permission from the Club's new president in order for Devlin to go undercover.

Over the past days, in between studying the plain but elegant Queen Anne-styled clubhouse, and shadowing Edgar Fane on a couple of his painting expeditions, Dev played the stableman, and helped construction workers install cypress shingle siding on the almost-finished stable complex. Many of the longtime crew eyed him cautiously, but some of the Irish construction laborers could talk the ears off a mule; he'd learned quite a lot about this southern hideaway to some of America's most prominent millionaires.

Jekyll Island was no Saratoga Springs choked with grand hotels, shops and amusements, visited by tens of thousands every year. Instead, the tiny island across the sound from Brunswick had been purchased by a French family in the late eighteenth century. They built themselves a home where they raised cotton until the War Between the States erupted. Twenty years later the island was bought and a private, very exclusive club was established whose list of first members read like New York's social register.

Yankees, Devlin mused sourly to himself, were the ones with all the money after the War.

One of several tiny islands dotting the Georgia coast, on the eastern side Jekyll boasted a sandy beach facing the Atlantic, while a serene intermingling of marsh, creek and river on the western side framed stunning sunsets. In between, Spanish moss–veiled forest, open fields and shimmering ponds offered a winter paradise to those who paid handsomely for the privilege. Strangely to Devlin, the place was considered a *family* retreat, not a men's club. Activities consisted of benign pastimes like bicycle jaunts and carriage rides and hunting parties; in the evenings, instead of raucous festivities, owners enjoyed elegant dinners, followed by billiards, games of whist—and talking.

A safe haven for political and economic machinations perhaps, but hardly a hotbed of vice—until Edgar Fane chose to spread his poison here. Lost in thought, just outside the stable entrance Devlin absently picked up a hammer one of the workers had left behind and laid it on top of a stack of pine boards. It was late afternoon, and thin wisps of cloud smeared the deepening coral of the western sky. If it weren't for Richard Langston's presence, and the timing of Fane's visit, Dev would be enjoying the sunset at StoneHill, preparing the horses for winter and basking in Thea's love.

Lord? Keep her safe. Help me find the proof I need to bring this evil man to justice.

A chipmunk darted across the path, eyeballed Devlin with a bright reproachful look, as though a heavenly Voice were chiding him. *All right, Lord. You judge Fane's heart. Just help me find the proof so we'll know one way or another what to do with him here on earth. Justice, Lord—not vengeance. Due process of law.*

Perhaps he wasn't so different from Thea after all. Dev might cloak his thirst for justice beneath the mantle of the law, but he still planned to stay on this island until he could handcuff Edgar Fane and formally charge him with crimes against the United States government.

And stuff a few of his bogus bills down his silver-tongued throat.

Sorry again, Lord.

What Devlin wanted most, however, was to go home, to StoneHill. To Thea. She deserved complete honesty; he needed forgiveness and reconciliation. The restlessness that had led his feet into service for his country had come full circle, evolving to a profound reverence for the blessings God had provided. Home, his horses, his family and friends. Most of all, the woman he wanted to spend the rest of his life with.

Have to resolve this thing with Fane. Only God knew

for sure how fragile Thea's safety remained, with Edgar Fane still free.

One more request, Lord? Help her understand why I had to come here....

Fane normally arrived at Jekyll Island after New Year's Day. His decision to depart Atlantic City in the family yacht two months early—and only four days after the discovery of Hotel Hustler counterfeit bills in Philadelphia—offered the Service a rare opportunity, well worth the risk, especially after one of the baggage handlers who'd trundled cartloads of trunks to the clubhouse confirmed Richard Langston's presence with Fane.

"Pleasant gent—tipped me a fiver. But he din't look like he was that glad to be here. I ain't never seen him afore, neither, so's mayhap he allus looks like a lost hound dog. But I did hear Mr. Fane call him—what was it now? Linford? Lane? No—Langston, that's it!" He beamed a toothless smile at Dev, content with the quarter tip he'd just received.

Stable hands wouldn't be able to afford a fiver.

On one of Devlin's first nightly reconnoiters inside the slumbering clubhouse, he'd also verified the guest's name in the register: Richard Langston. Unfortunately, no opportunity had yet presented itself for Devlin to search their rooms. A ferryload of nonmember guests had arrived to spend the Thanksgiving holiday, with a bevy of curious children constantly underfoot. Servants and staff, some of whom lived on the Island year-round, knew everything about everyone, and they were everywhere. There was also the problem of the assistant superintendent, a dedicated and observant man, who would definitely question a stable hand's presence anywhere in the clubhouse other than the servants' dining hall. If Devlin did not succeed in breaking into Fane's chambers and finding some Hotel Hustler bills within the next twenty-four hours, he would be forced to telegraph Washington, using the telegraph room… which would mean his life as Daniel Smith, stableman, would be over.

Nobody could predict the consequences if Devlin were forced to reveal the Secret Service's suspicions concerning Edgar Fane. But after four days of futile undercover surveillance Devlin was desperate enough to risk a telegram, because the presence of Thea's father alarmed him on a visceral level impossible to ignore. He didn't dwell on issues of his own personal safety should Fane learn his real name.

"My good man, I need to hire a driver and buggy," a cultured voice spoke behind him. "But I can't seem to find anyone hereabouts."

Slowly Dev turned around—to face Edgar Fane himself. Behind him a colored servant carried an easel and a box of artist supplies. Dev hunched his shoulders and touched the brim of his old cloth cap. "Try the carriage room, down yonder," he said, exaggerating his drawl. He pointed, keeping his gaze respectfully averted. "It's a big 'un. This here's a brand-new stables. Forty-nine stalls when she's all finished, brand-new carriage room."

"Yes, I know that already. Imbecile." Fane swiveled on his boot heel and stalked off, muttering another imprecation about stupid cracker hicks and where on earth was all the help. The black man flashed Devlin a sympathetic white-toothed smile and a shrug before following after Edgar.

Very slowly Devlin's coiled muscles relaxed. Casually he stepped off the path, under the lengthening shadow of a palmetto, and flexed his cramping fingers while he watched. Moments later a shiny black buggy rolled out of the barn, one of the liveried drivers guiding the horse off down Shell Road until they disappeared into a stand of moss-draped oaks. Twenty minutes later Dev slipped inside the Clubhouse through the servants' dining room. Confidently he nodded to a cluster of chambermaids and some rough-looking men in dirt-smeared work clothes eating an early supper, then sauntered through the kitchen, snitching a piece of carrot from the chopping table and grinning at the flustered cook's helper.

He ducked inside the butler's pantry until the housekeeper marched past, her arms filled with unfolded napkins, then wandered down the quiet corridor, carefully peering inside the barbershop…reading room…card room, until he finally located his quarry—Richard Langston—disinterestedly shooting balls in the billiard room. He'd learned the first day not to think of Langston as Thea's father, or he'd go after the man like flies on horse dung.

Here at last was the opportunity he'd been waiting for through this interminable week: both men out of the rooms, and most of the guests with their younguns still outside enjoying the mild southern weather.

He would risk ten minutes.

Devlin darted up the U-shaped staircase to the chambers on the second floor, where Fane had rented two large rooms at the end. And discovered a chambermaid just unlocking the door to Fane's room, her cleaning supplies stacked on the floor at her feet.

Chapter Thirty-Two

Thea arrived in Waycross, Georgia, with her spine straight as an iron rod and the rest of her body throbbing with exhaustion. A rattling, swaying local railroad that lurched to a stop in every rural village it passed finally deposited her in Brunswick a little past one o'clock Friday afternoon, six days after Devlin left StoneHill. The hurt had solidified into a spiny lump, permanently lodged just below her breastbone. But from the moment she asked the station agent in Paeonian Springs to have someone return the horse and buggy to StoneHill, a steely calm had encased her with impenetrable armor. She'd left a letter for her grandfather, another for Bessie and Jeremiah, and packed herself enough food to last for two days.

In Washington, while she waited for a southbound train, she posted her letter to Devlin—in care of the United States Secret Service.

Standing on the depot platform, a shudder of memory caught her off guard and almost punctured her frozen calm. She didn't know which she feared most—that Fane would learn Devlin's identity and kill him or, if her bold plan succeeded and Devlin captured Fane before Fane killed her, she might never be able to forgive Devlin.

She didn't let herself dwell on either possibility. Right now, she couldn't afford emotion.

Emotions were as untrustworthy as people, especially when love and hate intertwined. She had failed in Saratoga Springs because her hatred toward Edgar Fane had blinded her to her own ineptitude. But fear for Devlin had hurled her south nearly a thousand miles to carry out a plan born of equal parts love, anger, hurt and defiance. She wanted to succeed where Devlin and the entire Secret Service had failed, wanted to hand over proof and humiliate them as well as Edgar Fane. Then…then….

She didn't know what "then" entailed, so she ruthlessly throttled the surge of emotion and set all her resources on accomplishing her purpose.

At the Brunswick dock she found her way barred by a group of Italian girls freshly arrived from the northeast on a Mallory steamer. Surrounded by piles of trunks and carpetbags, everyone in the group seemed to be talking at once, their escalating voices drawing stares, though nobody approached the tight little cluster. One of the group, a slight young girl, half turned, and Thea caught a glimpse of a frightened, tear-bright gaze beneath her cloth hat. Thea stepped closer, her mind scrambling to recall the Italian she'd learned over the years from two of the typesetters at Porphyry Press.

"Mi scusi, ma posso essere di servizio?" she said to the young girl, asking if she could be of any help. The girl responded in a stream of incomprehensibly rapid words. Thea set her carpetbag down and lifted her hands

in a calming gesture. "I don't understand. *Voi,* ah, speak English? *Qual è il problema?* What is the matter?"

A plump, middle-aged woman next to the young girl turned around, scrutinizing Thea with a blend of deference and desperation. "I speak English, *signora.* My name is Bertina, Bertina Giovanni. Please, a doctor is needed, but we do not know how to find, or pay. We have little money." Switching back to Italian, she spoke firmly and several women moved aside, allowing Thea to see a woman supine on the dock, her bandaged head in another woman's lap. Beneath the olive skin her complexion was chalk-white, her eyes closed.

"What happened?"

"On the ship, was yesterday, she fall, hit her head. There was a cut, but Carmella promise she is fine." She gestured to the hovering girl. "This is Maria, Carmella's sister. They are to be maids on the Island. They are new, this year. Now we are all afraid. We wait for the boat to take us across, and Carmella put her hand to her head, and then she fall down."

Slow tears leaked from Maria's eyes, and she silently pleaded with Thea, begging her to do something to help her sister. Thea finally clasped her hands and gave them a reassuring squeeze. "I will find a doctor. Um…*un medico.* Do not worry." After a quick scan of the dock, she addressed Bertina. "I'll be right back. Here—" hurriedly she unbuttoned her long coat and handed it over "—put this over Carmella, but don't move her. She might have a concussion."

"*Grazie, signora. Grazie.* You are a blessing sent from God. But…we have little money to—"

"I do," Thea interrupted. "Please do not worry. I'll be back, with a doctor, as soon as I can."

At the end of the dock she collared a barrel-chested

man propped against an empty wagon. After a brief conversation the man tossed aside his cigar, handed Thea up onto the board seat and hollered at his two mules. Moments later, they pulled up in front of a neat frame house on the edge of town. "Ol' Doc Merton'll fix ya'll right up, ma'am."

Less than half an hour had passed by the time she returned to the dock in the physician's buggy; a lanky man of few words but shrewd eyes, Dr. Merton examined Carmella, now conscious but groggy and confused, and concurred with Thea's diagnosis: concussion. She needed complete bed rest for at least a week. After a verbal skirmish conducted half in Italian, half in English, Thea arranged to have Carmella transported to the spare bedroom in Dr. Merton's house, where Carmella would be well tended by the doctor's housekeeper and Dr. Merton's wife. Thea paid the doctor in advance, adding an extra twenty dollars to ensure the Mertons suffered no financial hardship for their care of a stranger.

After Dr. Merton departed with Carmella, the other servants gathered around Theodora, their expressions an amalgam of awe, gratitude and confusion. Maria wept quietly into a large red handkerchief.

"Why you do this, for strangers?" Bertina asked, apparently the designated spokesman for the group. "For—servants. You are a lady."

"You needed help. I couldn't pass by, when I knew I might be of assistance," Thea stammered, suddenly awkward. These days, she didn't feel much like a "lady."

Heavy black eyebrows drew together over Bertina's forehead. "Yet…you travel alone?"

"I travel alone," Thea admitted. "I too am bound for Jekyll Island. It is very important to me. I—I cannot explain. *Mi perdoni.* Forgive me, I will leave you now, for I must arrange for transportation myself. I hope Carmella recovers soon."

"You are expected?"

Bertina's soft question halted Thea's retreat. "Yes, and no." Needles of shame stitched an ugly path across her conscience. Haltingly, because she no longer possessed the stomach to lie to anyone, ever again, she said, "There are...two men. One of them I believe is a very bad person. The other is—" the word stuck in her throat but she managed to force it out "—my fiancé. I don't know how to say...*mi innamorato?*" Color burned her cheeks. "He is in danger because he is a noble idiot. But it is my fault. I must go to him, to help."

Before Bertina could reply, Maria threw herself against the woman, sobbing and pleading, her words too thick for Thea to follow. For a moment Bertina allowed her to cry, then she set her away with a firm command to quiet herself. With a Gallic shrug she explained to Thea, "Maria is afraid Carmella will lose her position if she does not arrive today. She does not know these people. They have not met her or Carmella, so...she has no trust. I tell her I will explain to the boat captain, why we have one less number, that Carmella will still have her position when she is recover."

Abruptly she stopped speaking, her lips pursing as she looked first at Maria, then Thea. "Your *innamorato,* he is a member of the Club?"

"No, he's not a member," Thea confessed wretchedly. Her heart, which she had struggled to encase in ice, was awash in all the emotions she had tried to sever. Maria's wrenching tears, Carmella's bandaged head, her helplessness—suddenly all of Thea's hurt and rage against life seemed a paltry thing. The selfish tantrum-riddled reaction of a child. She focused her gaze on a small steamer chugging steadily toward the dock. "I will not bother you with my problems. You have enough of your own."

"*Signora,* I do not know how to say this. But you have shown kindness. I must do likewise. So I must say to you…is not allowed for visitors to come to Jekyll Island without invitation. Only members, their guests. Servants. The rules, they are to be followed." For another moment of prickling discomfort she studied Thea, then muttered something Italian beneath her breath. "Signora… I believe I have a way to help you, like you help Carmella. How long you stay on Island?"

"Not long. If I'm lucky, less than two days." *Luck has nothing to do with it,* she could almost hear Devlin's voice whispering in her ear. Like a snake, the quick bite of memory struck too fast, and she crammed a fist to her mouth to prevent an anguished cry.

"Signora, *scusi.* Please wait. I will talk to these girls."

Wait? She may as well wait until she crusted into a barnacle if she couldn't find a way to reach Jekyll Island. Her thoughts swarmed without direction, horseflies buzzing in her head.…

At StoneHill, the horses would be out in the pastures, their winter coats a patchwork quilt of dappled grays and bays…and in the paddock, Percy with his soot-spotted rump would watch the lane, black ears pricked, waiting for his beloved master to return. The animal walked now without a limp. He had completely recovered.

If she lost Devlin, Thea would never recover.

Tears scalded her aching throat. She was so intent upon controlling them that she scarcely noticed that all seven women had suddenly formed a circle around her again.

"Signora," Bertina said, "we have talked. We have agreed. To help you is the right thing to do. But we must be careful." Pausing, she watched Thea, gesturing the others to silence while Thea in dawning awareness examined each somber face.

"The boat captain expects eight of you, doesn't he?" she repeated slowly. "Not seven. He doesn't know Carmella. He doesn't know what happened."

Bertina nodded. "I have kept her papers, for safety." She glanced over her shoulder. The boat would arrive in less than five minutes. "You must be one of us, *signora*. This people, they no let you come if you not one of us. Here," she unpinned her own black cloth hat and held it out. "You cannot wear yours. Is too much like a lady."

"I don't want to cause trouble," Thea began, even as her pulse leaped with excitement—and resolve. She fumbled with her own stylish toque with its bird-of-paradise feather and ruthlessly stuffed it inside her suitcase. "I have no words...."

The other women commenced babbling in a stream of Italian and broken English, their gazes warm with sympathy. A lovely girl with thick dark hair and rosebud lips handed Thea a brightly patterned shawl, framing her sentences in slow, careful Italian so Thea could understand. "Do not be sad. You save Carmella. You follow your man to here to save him, no? This is why you come, all alone? We will help you."

"But you must not speak until we are safely to the servants' quarters," Bertina added drily. Then she grabbed Thea's shoulders and pressed a kiss on each burning cheek. "God is good," she pronounced. "God is good."

Chapter Thirty-Three

The Jekyll Island Club compound faced Jekyll Creek, on the island's western side. As the Howland steamed toward the wharf, Thea clutched the damp iron railing and tried not to panic. Five months earlier, she had spent weeks at one of the most famous grand resorts in the world, surrounded by entire blocks of hotels, choked with thousands of guests. Yet this serene, deserted-looking island with its collection of buildings intimidated rather than welcomed. Jekyll Island was private, for millionaires and their families, not a social watering hole for the masses. The owners had deliberately retained as much of its natural state as possible, so forests surrounded by pristine sandy beaches abounded with wildlife and birds and beautiful scenery. "*È como il Paradiso,*" one of the servants promised her as they chugged across the water. So Jekyll Island looked like Paradise?

Well, if Thea failed to find proof of Fane's perfidy this time, her fate would probably land her at the real pearly gates. *Lord? I know my sins number higher than grains of sand on the beach these past few days. Is it too late to ask You to forgive me?* Certainly her motives for haring off to this place were ignoble as well as heroic. She wanted to scream her hurt at Devlin, pummel his chest with her fists—but then she wanted to wrap him in her arms and feel the beat of his heart against her ear. *Please, God. I don't want him to give his life for me, not like this.*

Shivering a little in the ocean breeze, she studied the Clubhouse, which vaguely resembled a castle with lots of square windows and a round tower on one corner. The four-story building next to the club, Bertina told her, contained eight private apartments for members. Some owners had built large houses, most within walking distance of the Clubhouse, but they usually brought their own staff. There were also servants' quarters, gardens and stables. Paths of sand and crushed oyster shells, and roads wide enough for carriages wound their ways throughout the buildings and around the entire island.

"But be careful of the alligators when you go for a stroll," Bertina warned her. "Also to remember everyone knows everyone," she reminded her again as the steamer pulled up to the long wharf. "Unless they new, like Carmella and Maria, who are for to work in the clubhouse. You must be careful with the housekeeper, Miss Schuppan—she is, how you say? Particular. Yes." She nodded firmly. "*Signora*...you will be careful?"

The next morning, clad in plain black worsted skirts, over-starched white blouses and striped aprons, Theodora, Maria and two others from what Thea privately thought of as "her troupe," presented themselves to the housekeeper. A surprisingly young woman, Miss Schuppan inspected them with the thoroughness of a drill sergeant. After warning them her word was law, that slovenliness in either appearance or work would result in dismissal and that she expected the clubhouse to shine like the sun by the end of the month, Miss Schuppan turned them over to an assistant. Thea was assigned the task of sweeping hallways and public meeting rooms on the first floor.

At present only eight of the sixty guest rooms were occupied. The assistant, Mrs. Dexter, ticked them off her work-reddened fingers; when she spoke Edgar Fane's name, then his guest Mr. Langston, Thea jerked. Mrs. Dexter paused, a questioning look on her face.

"*Scusi, signora,*" Thea managed with what she hoped was a Bertina-like shrug.

After a narrow-eyed look, Mrs. Dexter continued speaking. "For those of you working on the second floor, where Mr. Fane is lodged, you may clean the rooms as usual but under no circumstances are you to bother the large steamer trunk in the corner. Mr. Fane has been most specific, and as you know, we pride ourselves on catering to every need of our members. So do not even dust the trunk, or mention to Mr. Fane that there is sufficient room to store it in the basement or attic." She paused. "Miss Schuppan was forced to dismiss a chambermaid yesterday, for making that suggestion to him. He was—most displeased. Do I make myself clear? Very good, then. Now let's be about our duties."

By midafternoon Thea had finished sweeping and with a pleased smile hovering around her thin lips, Mrs. Dexter told her to help with the dusting until four-thirty, when she could have a fifteen-minute break as a reward for her diligence. Armed with feather duster, a stack of cloths, a bottle of linseed-oil-and-vinegar furniture polish and Mrs. Dexter's advice: "and make sure you rub the polish, not smear it over the furniture," Thea walked into the card room, where a gentleman sat alone at one of the tables. He glanced up at her entrance, his dark brown eyes disinterested. Then the cards in his hands fell with a clumsy slither all over the table as the man leaped to his feet.

"Hetty?" he whispered hoarsely. He passed a shaking hand over his eyes, and slowly took a step toward Thea, who had frozen where she stood.

Tall and spare, dark hair streaked with gray at the temples, neatly combed and held in place by a touch of pomade, Richard Langston approached, color draining from his face with every step. A vein throbbed in his temple. He stopped less than a yard away, close enough for the scent of bergamot and cloves to flood Thea's nose. "Not Hetty," he said finally. "But...you're the spitting image of her... Theodora."

With preternatural calm she set aside the dusting materials, her gaze never wavering from his. "Father." She tested the word, found the syllables as foreign as the Italian she'd been practicing. "I'm afraid I don't consider that a compliment."

He inclined his head. "She lacked maternal instinct. But to me, once she was the most beautiful woman in the world." He half lifted a hand.

"Don't." A hot trickle of bile slid down her throat. Her automatic backward step was instinctive, and the heat spread. A daughter shouldn't feel this way about her father. "You left her. You left us all. You never tried to stay, not once."

"Is that what your grandfather told you? Well, part of it's true." Moving away, her father clasped his hands behind his back, his face now an expressionless mask. "I did leave—after your mother kicked me out along with the baby who had spoiled her figure. I didn't know what to do. I was only twenty, and knew nothing about babies. You can't appreciate it, I know, but I did you a favor, leaving you with family who would care for you."

"You're absolutely right. I can't appreciate being abandoned by both parents. At least Grandfather didn't dump me in an orphanage when the rest of that caring family perished in the Hudson. I was only three, but I remember them. Do you?"

A muscle twitched the corner of his mouth. "Hetty's dead, you know. Smallpox. After that ferry accident I did go back to her, Theodora. I was willing to try, but it was too late. I sent you cards for a while, but decided you were better off forgetting me. Seems like a lot of my life has been too little, too late."

"I don't care." The childish fantasy that one day her mother would appear and ask Thea's forgiveness shattered, one sliver at a time. The lovely Biblical parable would never happen; if forgiveness was to be granted, she would have to extend it to the man who had fathered, then rejected her. Grandfather had warned her many times she may as well carry a gravestone as a grudge. Both marked the spot where death held the upper hand.

Hate and hope could not coexist. "I used to wonder what kind of a person I would have been, if my parents had loved me. Then I stopped wondering, and thought of all the words I would throw in your faces if we ever met. Now… I don't want to care at all," she said thickly.

A flicker of pain glimmered in his eyes, quickly extinguished. "Then you shouldn't have come here, Theodora. Why did you?"

"Perhaps because until I saw you, I didn't want to believe what I'd learned—that you'd become another Edgar

Fane sycophant. Another lackey of the man who ruined our family. A man who continues to commit the same crimes against countless other innocent victims." When Richard merely continued to watch her with mournful basset hound eyes, Thea's outrage sparked. "Is the money he provides worth that much to you? In all your life have you ever considered anyone but yourself?"

"For the most part, no," Richard replied without a blink or a twitch. It was the face of a gambler—a poker face, Thea realized, and could have wept. "Mr. Fane hasn't chosen to enlighten me on the details of his life of crime," he continued evenly. "But I'm not here willingly, Theodora. If you won't believe anything else, will you at least believe that?"

For the second time his gaze searched behind Thea, through the open doorways on either side of a huge fireplace. "Which is why you need to leave, at once. Must I spell it out? I'm the bait," he confirmed, looking back at her. "This is a trap. For you, Theodora."

Bitterness coated his words, the same bitterness toward all of life that Thea had hurled at Grandfather in their last conversation. She flinched away from the comparison as though physically struck.

Richard didn't seem to notice. "Whatever you've done to him, this man is planning a nasty bit of revenge against you. You never should have crossed him. So please, Theodora. Leave now, before he returns from his bird hunting expedition."

"I'll leave—after I find proof to take to the Secret Service. You know precisely what I'm after, don't you... Mr. Langston? I'm pretty sure it's in his room, inside a locked trunk."

Chapter Thirty-Four

The poker face cracked at last. "*Mr. Langston,*" he repeated under his breath, shame and desperation blurring the chiseled features. For a taut moment he stood silently. "I suppose I deserve your repudiation, perhaps your hatred," he finally said. "If I thought it would do any good, I'd tell you I'm sorry." Watching her, he put a hand inside his silk waistcoat and withdrew two keys, one a skeleton key, the other a smaller brass key. "When Edgar and his assistant left this morning, he told me they'd return at sunset. I'm to finish hiding the last of the counterfeit bills inside the frames. They're hollow—he has them specially designed. Man's developed quite a little consortium for his secret life."

Thea nodded, her mind almost as numb as her heart. "He's the man the Secret Service calls the Hotel Hustler, isn't he? He gives his paintings away to other guests, then uses one of his minions to steal them and retrieve the money. I don't know what happens after that." She hadn't had the stomach to retrieve Devlin's report before she left StoneHill.

"I can tell you," Richard said, a muscle tensing in

his jaw. "By giving his paintings to guests, the bogus bills are circulated all over the country, far away from Fane. After the bills are recovered and distributed the frames are sold. From what I've seen his minions are so well paid they'd never snitch on him. Besides, he's Edgar Fane. So...poof. No evidence. The fellow's slicker than macassar oil."

And this was the man from whom she naively hoped to secure evidence on her own. What a stupid featherhead she'd been, not reading all the way through Devlin's reports. Thea grimly thrust aside the self-excoriation, the doubt.

"They've been trying to discover proof to arrest him. Well, I don't care if he is the son of one of the richest men in the country. I refuse to give up. There has to be a way and I'm going to figure it out." Now more than ever, because not only her life, but Devlin's, depended on it. Perhaps Richard could—

"How do you know all this, Theodora? Are you— don't tell me the Secret Service is using *you,* a young woman? I never thought a government-sanctioned organization could stoop so low. Vigilantes, that's what they are. A pack of baying hounds."

"You have no idea what those men do," Thea retorted hotly. For heaven's sake, no wonder Devlin had been afraid to confess his identity. So this is what spiritual scourging felt like—having all your pretenses whipped across your soul until it bled out. Well, she would try to atone for some of both hers and Richard's misconceptions.

"I've spent the last year reviling the Secret Service. But I was wrong. So are you. This organization you sneer at was formed to keep our country safe from fiends like Edgar Fane. These men choose to give up all hope of a normal life to…to perform a service for our country. Oh, excuse me. You wouldn't understand that, would you?" Uglier accusations pushed their way up. A single word—*forgive*—gave her the self-control to shove them aside.

"Those men put your grandfather in jail."

"Only because Edgar Fane paid him with counterfeit bills," Thea shot right back. "Fane's the villain here, not the Secret Service. So their operatives are human. Sometimes they make mistakes. And they have to live every day not only with the burden of their mistakes but with unjust accusations flung by people like you, and me, in order to bring cockroaches like Edgar Fane to justice. I've realized my error in judgment. Why can't you? You never should have agreed to help him, never!"

"If I refuse, he'll kill me, then find another way to get to you, Theodora."

"Don't you think I know that?" she hissed, belatedly realizing her voice had risen to a near shout. "But he won't have a chance if he's arrested. Now you will be, as well, for aiding and abetting a monster disguised as a man."

"I don't think it matters to me any longer," Richard said tonelessly. "Theodora… I don't have to tell you this, but I will. He's been using Porphyry Press. If you leave now, you'll be able to tell the Secret Service the location for the engraving plates, the ink and counterfeiting fiber paper from England." His mouth twisted. "He told me on the trip down, a smile on his face the whole time like he was merely sharing a joke. Well, the joke will be on him—if you leave now."

"You could have found a way to send out this information. There's a telegraph in the office. I don't see a guard with a gun, watching your every move. Club boats go and come all the time."

"I am watched, if I leave the clubhouse. I told you, you don't understand. He knows too much—I owe him." Beads of perspiration gathered on his brow. "I don't have a choice, Theodora."

"You always have a choice to do the right thing. But you never have made that one, have you?"

In a swift move he snagged her wrist. "Here." He dropped the two keys into the palm of her hand, then closed her fingers over them. His were damp and cold, yet steady as a rock. "The last of the Hustler bills are inside a cigar box in the trunk. I'll be along in twenty minutes, to stuff them in the frame before Fane returns. Either tonight or tomorrow he'll select one of the owners or guests to be the latest recipient of an Edgar Fane work of art. Then…" He stopped, exhaled a wearied sigh. "Every day I dragged the process out, hoping you'd show up. Wishing you wouldn't. This is your only opportunity. Take what you need and get out of here. Blast it, Theodora, don't look at me like that! He owns me now, I told you. But regardless of the sins I've committed, I don't want to see my daughter murdered."

My daughter. A single punch of dizziness shoved against the side of Thea's face. The two keys bit into her palm, and she couldn't seem to draw enough air into her lungs. She could deny him until the day she drew her last breath, but here was an example of irrefutable truth: she was the daughter of Richard Langston.

"Theodora? What's the matter with you? I told you, you don't have much time—hey!" His arm shot out and steadied her when she lurched sideways.

"Give me a second," she managed, closing her eyes, trying in vain to blot the memory of Edgar Fane, standing over her with gloating eyes while he described the sight of Cynthia Gorman's corpse. Trying as well to comprehend that the man in front of her had after thirty years acknowledged her existence. The vortex inside her darkened, increased in speed.

Not now, not now. After a year of thwarted plans she had been granted the means, and the opportunity to collect evidence against Edgar Fane. She needed to be Esther of the Bible, placed in a palace to save her people from an evil man; Samson, the mighty but flawed judge, who after his adulterous affair with Delilah had given his life to do the right thing.

All right, she was more like Samson than Esther. She hadn't honored God like she should, though after watching Devlin's transformation these past months she'd yearned to follow his example. *I want to honor You, now. I do. Search me and know my heart, Lord. Help me... I can't function with this vertigo. Only You can take this affliction from me.*

*Only You...*and she didn't deserve anything but the condemnation she'd shoveled over everyone and everything, including herself.

Richard's chilly hold on her arm tightened. "What's the matter with you?" he repeated. "Look, I gave you the keys and the information. I'm no good with fainting women. Don't do this missish swooning on me now."

Even before her father finished speaking, the vertigo vanished. Blinking in astonishment, Thea opened her eyes, slowly glanced to the left, then the right. No symptoms. *No symptoms.*

God had answered her prayer—instantly. She didn't

deserve His mercy, didn't deserve the grace or the miracle or His favor, yet He'd granted her plea anyway, from a love no human mind could fathom. The atheists and naturalists and scientists simply didn't understand the fundamental tenet of the Christian faith—Jesus' loving sacrifice of Himself on the cross. For everyone, including Theodora Langston…liar, hater, abandoned child, wounded woman.

Beside her, Richard swore, pacing the floor and darting her baffled looks. But the internal glow of transformation continued to flow unabated through Thea. She saw for the first time the flawed man too weak to accept responsibility for a baby—but strong enough now to offer her the way to escape.

"I didn't mean to scare you," she said, and briefly laid her hand over his wrist. "I have dizzy spells occasionally, particularly concerning Edgar Fane." Ten minutes ago she would have excoriated her father for his part in the lifelong secret affliction. "But I'm fine now. I'm fine… Father. I'm not really a delicate flower, you know."

"Good." They studied each other and a freshet of peace flowed between them. Then her father cleared his throat, strode over to one of the doorways and peered out into the hall. "Now go along, do what you've come to do. "

"I will. He's going to be arrested, very soon, then we'll both be free of him." *Thanks to You, Lord. All thanks to You.* Well…there was another father she needed to thank. After dropping the keys into her apron pocket, Thea gathered up the cleaning supplies and slipped beside Richard out into the hall. "Thank you for helping me," she murmured. "Perhaps later, we can talk?"

The poker expression returned. "I doubt we'll have an opportunity."

She paused. "We can make one." The blackened corner dirtying her soul for her entire life was gone like the vertigo, whisked away in an unexpected act of divine housekeeping. "I'm not going to let him win, Father. And you're going to stay alive."

The corners of his eyes crinkled; his shoulders straightened. Thea smiled at him, then set off for the stairs at the end of the hall.

Chapter Thirty-Five

His lips pressed into a thin slash, Devlin sent telegrams to Washington and Fred Lawlor, who had traveled down separately to monitor things across the Sound in Brunswick. Defeat was a dull ax, chopping away at Dev's neck. His only "success" thus far was his continued anonymity; when neither Mr. Grob, the Club superintendent, nor Miss Schuppan caught him inside the club office, he considered it mercy from God rather than proof of his own cleverness.

Task accomplished, he stepped back into the wide corridor, automatically noting a waiter entering the dining room, and at the other end of the hall a gentleman guest with his back to Devlin. The gentleman appeared to be speaking to an aproned cleaning woman whose face was blocked by his shoulders. None of them glanced Devlin's way.

He was still a shadow, unremarked upon and unknown.

A discomfiting squiggle crawled along the back of Devlin's neck. Pausing, he risked another glimpse down the corridor, where the cleaning woman was now walking away. Something about her posture—or was it the tilt of her head and the glimpse of brown hair?—reminded him of Thea. *Not again,* he thought morosely. Over the past week his pulse had spiked several times for the same reason. Annoyed with the propensity to imbue every woman he passed with Theodora's traits, Devlin headed for the doors leading to the piazza. He had risked his professional reputation and his future to ensure that his fiancée remained safely ensconced at StoneHill, almost a thousand miles away. Missing her was automatic, like breathing, both of which he ignored. He could wallow in loneliness later, because until he received a reply to either telegram Devlin Stone needed to hide behind the persona of an unremarkable stable hand named Daniel Smith.

It was a little past four in the afternoon; he exited the clubhouse onto the piazza and stood for a moment in the shadows, wrestling with the disquietude. No operative achieved sought-after results one hundred percent of the time; Devlin could accept his inability to secure proof that Edgar Fane was the Hotel Hustler. What he could not accept was his failure to protect the woman he loved. With Fane alive and free, Thea could never be safe, never stop wondering. The vertigo attacks, in abeyance for the past few months, might return.

When Devlin confessed his profession as an operative she might never forgive him.

She might repudiate him altogether.

Inevitably, Edgar Fane would discover her whereabouts.

I made the choice to trust You, Lord. But...do I have to lose the woman I love to prove my faith?

Luminous streaks of gold-and-orange-tipped red

painted the western sky, signaling the end of another day. From the direction of the marshes, he heard the plaintive honking of geese and, down Old Plantation Road, the distant voices of members, returning from their day's outing. As the sound of hooves and carriage wheels drew closer, Dev decided to head on over to the stables. Might yet hear something about Fane he could at least pass along to headquarters for the next operative assigned to the case.

A pair of buckboard carriages rolled into view, jammed with several women as well as men, most of them carrying shotguns. In the first carriage, tongues lolling, a pair of hunting dogs peered between the driver's legs. And behind the driver lounged Edgar Fane, looking smug and relaxed in his Norfolk jacket, yellow sweater and knee breeches. His personal assistant Simpson sat beside him. The carriages passed by, heading for the covered porch around the corner.

Instinct took over. Hands stuffed in his pockets, whistling a tune and shuffling his feet in the sandy soil, Dev leisurely followed. When he reached the hunting party, people were still mingling, talking about the day. Mr. Grob had joined the group, a deferential smile showing beneath his handlebar mustache. He congratulated the man who bagged an eight-point buck and a woman who had nabbed half a dozen quail, commiserated with those who had returned empty-handed, including it seemed Edgar Fane.

"I'm no good with guns," Edgar said with good-natured aplomb. "No doubt *un*masculine of me, but I prefer to potter with a paintbrush."

"I'm so dreadfully sorry to hear you're leaving us,"

one of the women gushed. "Next week, was it? And so soon after your arrival. You will return, I hope?"

"Alas, 'downward the voices of Duty call, to toil and be mixed with the main,'" Edgar responded, with a flourish kissing the back of her hand. "Incomparáble words from Sidney Lanier's poem, written for the marshes of this incomparable island sanctuary." He glanced at his expressionless secretary. "Simpson, that last painting I completed day before yesterday? I think you should present it to Mrs. Butler tonight after dinner."

"Yes, Mr. Fane," Simpson replied stolidly while Mrs. Butler squealed with delight.

Using the buckboard carriages for a screen, Dev maneuvered closer. After nodding to the colored driver standing beside the horse, he knelt to pretend to retie the laces of his work boots.

"…and sorry Mr. Langston couldn't join us today.…"

"…worse than I, at the sport of hunting…prefers taking risks with a deck of cards…likely still in the card room.…"

So the man Dev had glimpsed at the end of the hall had been Richard Langston, Thea's father. Apparently he was trusted enough, or cowed enough, to be left to his own devices while Edgar Fane enjoyed the island amenities. Dev filed both tidbits of information away.

The unwelcome news of Fane's apparently imminent departure would have to be investigated with—

"'Scuse me, suh? You be the new stableman what's got a dab hand with horses, right?"

Devlin's head whipped around to the driver, whose eyes flared in alarm. Dev offered a placatory smile. *Stay in character,* he reminded himself as he straightened. "I am," he said. "You're… Wiggins, isn't it?"

The driver nodded, pulling off his hat to run a hand over his head of kinky gray hair. "Would you mind looking at Brownie's right leg? He was favoring it just now. Might be nothin' but seeing as how you was walking by, thought I'd ask."

Dev throttled the frustration and approached the lightly sweating gelding harnessed on the right side of the team. After a rapid but thorough examination of all four legs, he showed Wiggins two fragments of oyster shell. "Likely these were the culprits —one was lodged in the central cleft of the foot on the right foreleg, but there was also a smaller piece in the left hind sole. The shoes are still properly nailed, so I don't think he'll suffer from lameness, but I'd let him rest for a day or two, just to be safe. Good man for noticing." With a final pat on Brownie's neck, he surveyed the dwindling crowd still clustered around Edgar Fane.

"Would you mind coming along to the stable with me?" Wiggins asked. "I can drive a carriage fine, but my knees give out on me when I have to stoop down." Anxiously he searched Devlin's set features. "You won't tell, will you? Me and the missus, we get to stay here year-round now, and I'd hate to be let go."

"Your secret's safe with me." Torn, Devlin hesitated, but Fane was already extricating himself from the group to "freshen up before dinner."

Suppressing a sigh, Dev told Wiggins he'd be glad to take care of Brownie.

Some ten minutes later, while gently cleaning the horse's feet with a hoof pick, the squiggle of unease he'd felt earlier returned to irritate his brain. He remembered the cleaning woman with more clarity, remembered her turning away from the man to walk toward the staircase. *It was the walk,* he abruptly realized. That walk…the first day he'd followed Thea down the steps of the Grand Union Hotel in Saratoga Springs, memorizing her unique blend of femininity and firm assurance… Would a servant, a cleaning woman hired to mop floors and dust furniture, walk like a woman of purpose, of power?

And why would Richard Langston converse with a servant at all? *What if Theodora weaseled the truth from her grandfather—and was playing another part?* If instead of a wealthy socialite with a titled fiancé, like Devlin she'd somehow slipped onto Jekyll Island in the guise of a servant?

Devlin had come to know his beloved and her propensity for impulsiveness very well indeed. For a fraught second he rested his forehead against Brownie's shoulder and absorbed what instinct already knew. He might have been within shouting distance of the woman whose courage far outweighed common sense. Never mind the wishes and elaborate schemes of the man desperate to keep her far away from Jekyll Island.

God, Thea's here, isn't she? And for some reason God hadn't alerted Devlin until now.

Urgency rolled through him, thundering its intensity; tail swishing, Brownie's skin quivered beneath Dev's hands. He automatically calmed the animal before obeying the insistent hum of warning.

Five minutes later he headed back to the clubhouse.

Thea heard the voices in the hallway. Fear exploded inside her stomach, but she managed to close and lock the trunk, stuff the last of the counterfeit bills in a hidden pocket of her skirt, then gather up her cleaning supplies. Several more bills were hidden beneath the rags at the bottom of the bucket. By the time Edgar appeared in the doorway, a scowl on his face and a shotgun balanced in the crook of his elbow, she was on the other side of the room, feather-dusting a lamp.

"What the devil are you doing here? The rooms were supposed to have been cleaned this morning."

"*Scusi, signore,*" Thea bobbed a clumsy curtsey and with her face averted, aimed her feet for the opened door. "*Io somo finito. Lascio.* I finish. Leave now."

Fingers slippery with fear, greasy nausea filling her throat, she had almost managed to gain the hallway when she sensed him looming behind her.

"One moment, girl."

Servants would never disobey such a command; if Thea ran, his suspicions would be aroused enough to chase after her. Yet if she obeyed his order, when he saw her face he would most certainly recognize Miss Pickford. *Into the lion's den,* Thea thought. Squaring her shoulders, she turned around.

"*You!*" Triumph flared in eyes gone hard and bright as polished black marbles. "So. My little plot worked. I thought it would, though you cut it close, my dear. Later, you'll have to share where you've been hiding all these months. For now, have you enjoyed the reunion with your long-lost father?"

Thea raised her chin. "What difference does it make? You never should have used him as bait. You might think you've outmaneuvered us all, but this time, Edgar Fane, you'll be the one in a jail cell. Not me, or my grandfather. Or my…my father." The bundle of rags wouldn't faze him, but if she threw the bucket, screamed to draw attention…

"Ah, then you have spoken to him. Sorry to have missed the exchange." He whipped out an arm, yanked the bucket out of her hand and tossed it through the doorway behind him. When the clatter ceased he resumed talking as calmly as though he'd plucked a dead leaf from his sleeve.

"Definitely didn't inherit your father's poker face, did you? Good thing I left my shotgun in the room. Of course, your weapon of choice is words. You verbally cut a man to the size of a mouse—one of your less-attractive traits, my dear Theodora." He made a tsk-ing sound and shook his head. "Poor Richard. Did you eviscerate him like you did me at Saratoga? I might feel sorry for him, except he handed you the keys to my kingdom. Too bad. I was going to let *him* go."

More voices echoed up the stairwell; seconds later a couple with three children crowded into view, a confusion of noise and movement with the children racing between Thea and Edgar, calling to one another while a flushed nanny scurried after them. The couple stopped to speak to Edgar, forcing his attention.

Thea dropped the rest of the cleaning supplies, gathered her skirts in fistfuls of fabric, and ran for her life down the staircase.

Chapter Thirty-Six

"Excuse me," Edgar explained urgently to the mystified Randolphs as Theodora whisked out of sight. "I must speak to Mr. Grob. I'm afraid I caught that cleaning woman trying to steal several personal articles from my room. She must be apprehended immediately, before she can hide what she stole."

He dashed down the stairs; fury and triumph throbbed to the beat of his racing footsteps. Based upon Theodora's expression of guilt and horror, Langston had double-crossed him. Likely his irritant of a daughter had stolen some of the bills, but her pathetic plan to outwit him was doomed to failure. Some of his work was probably at the bottom of that bucket. Some, but possibly not all. The wench had fled onto the piazza, and was scurrying down the path that led to the servant quarters.

She couldn't run far enough or fast enough to escape her inevitable fate, but blast it all, she'd just forced him to drastically hasten his plans.

Edgar found Simpson and Langston in the card room, talking in a corner while a threesome dealt cards at one of the tables on the other side of the room. "Simpson, one of the wagons from the hunting expedition was still under the porte cochere a moment ago. Go out there at once. Don't let the driver leave for the stable. I need that buggy, *now*."

He turned to Langston. "Wipe the smugness off your face. You gave her the keys, of course."

The older man stroked his sideburn for a second, then shrugged.

Only the presence of witnesses compelled Edgar to rein in his temper. "Deal yourself aces and eights, Langston, because you're a dead man."

"Everyone dies, Mr. Fane. Even you."

Edgar stepped close, keeping his back to the three card players. "I have men waiting on my yacht, with orders. It will be a pleasure having them carried out."

Langston's only reaction was a raised eyebrow. "You might be richer than Croesus, Fane. Like I said, every man has a day of reckoning. Perhaps mine's today. But yours, my friend, is just around the corner."

Edgar mouthed a vicious curse, swiveled on his boot and stormed out of the clubhouse. As soon as he caught Theodora and had her stashed safely aboard his yacht, everything else would fall back into place. He was prepared. He'd been prepared for her inevitable arrival, just as he'd been prepared for Richard Langston's belated streak of paternal instinct.

He had not expected Thea to sneak across to the island in the guise of the maid, however. Resourceful, he'd grant her that.

But like Cynthia, she'd made a big mistake, the last one of *her* life.

Outside, Simpson was arguing with the driver, who insisted the horses were too tired for another outing. In the distance, Edgar could just make out Theodora's dark skirted figure with the white splash of her shirtwaist, fleeing not in the direction of the servants' quarters but toward one of the roads that led into thick woodland. He had to capture her before she found a hiding place.

"I'm taking this vehicle." Unceremoniously he shoved the liveried driver aside. "Simpson," he bit out to the slack-jawed assistant, "see to that painting, and have Langston escorted to the yacht. He is not to be left unattended, do you hear?"

After grabbing the reins, he snatched the whip out of the holder and applied it to the two horses with the unleashed violence he longed to perpetrate against Richard Langston and his daughter. Half rearing in surprise, the animals leaped into motion and almost jerked Edgar over the dashboard. Cursing, he shook the reins, and finally the horses lumbered into a canter, careening headlong down the path where Theodora fled, the proverbial rabbit fleeing the hounds.

Dusk had fallen, the vivid colors of sunset a fading memory on the western horizon. Heedless of the crunching sound of the oyster shells, Devlin ran toward the clubhouse. At the bend in the road, just past the old duBignon house, a flash of movement distracted him. It was a person, a woman, running toward one of the roads that led into the island's interior—not a destination one would choose with night fast approaching. Denial and ice-edged terror streaked through Devlin, because he knew in his gut the woman was Thea. Knew she was that cleaning woman and Fane—

Panicked hooves thudded hard on the road behind him, coming from the direction of the clubhouse. Dev dropped to a crouch behind a shrub and watched while scarcely a dozen paces away, Edgar Fane drove past in an open buckboard carriage. White-eyed, their flanks wet with terror, the two horses who had been out on the hunting excursion all day had been pushed into a full gallop by Edgar's maniacal recklessness. His lips were stretched in a rictus of fury, and as he flew by Dev glimpsed murder blazing from his eyes.

Devlin would never reach Thea in time. *Dear God in heaven.* "Thea!" He roared her name as he sprinted after the buggy, an agonized cry of impotence swallowed up in trees that loomed like vultures over the road. "Thea, I'm coming! Watch out! *Thea...*"

A hundred yards down the road he watched her falter, glance over her shoulder, watched her throw herself to the side to avoid being trampled. Watched Edgar bring the horses to a snorting halt...watched him leap from the buckboard and manhandle Thea, kicking and punching, back up onto the seat beside him.

Sand and dirt and crushed shell from the churning wheels flew up close enough to spit in Devlin's face as the horses sped away beneath moss-draped live oaks and palmettos. The buggy disappeared from sight less than five seconds after Devlin arrived at the spot Thea had fallen. A deadly calmness settled over him. Calmness, clarity and determination. Running like a stag, he raced back to the stables in a diagonal dash through the undergrowth, burst into the courtyard and down the aisle to the stall where Lancer, a former Thoroughbred racehorse, was idly munching hay. "I need you, fella." His movements calm but swift, Devlin led the horse back down the aisle, stopping only long enough to grab a bridle. Then he mounted Lancer bareback and, once they left stable, kneed him into a canter.

Less than two minutes had elapsed since Edgar abducted Thea.

The horse's big muscled body surged into an effortless gallop at Dev's soft command. Balanced like a centaur, he funneled thirty years of rapport with equines into the task of winning the most important race of this horse's life—and prayed God would protect Theodora, for just a few more moments.

Chapter Thirty-Seven

Thea battered Edgar with fists and elbows, squirming every way she could to break either the iron bar of his arm around her shoulders, or the hand holding the reins, shouting at him all the while in a vain attempt to rattle his composure. The carriage swayed wildly, knocking both of them about on the seat, and at one point they swung almost completely off the path, the side wheels bouncing into a rut that rattled Thea's teeth. She didn't care, didn't cease yelling and struggling despite the certain knowledge that she was about to die.

She fought because she had heard Devlin, calling her name. *I love you,* she told him silently. She wanted to yell the words out, to answer the faint voice she'd heard just before Edgar tried to run her down. *I love you with all my heart. God? Please let him know I'm sorry...* She managed to wrest an arm free, and landed a solid punch to Edgar's jaw.

He mouthed a foul curse. The arm crushing her against his side shifted, squeezing her rib cage until she was light-headed from lack of oxygen and the dreadful certainty her ribs were about to crack and puncture a lung. Her efforts to escape grew wilder but lost force; abruptly the buckboard slewed to a halt. Edgar's hand closed around her throat and his face in the powder-gray gloaming loomed over her, an evil bird of prey poised for the kill.

"This ought to make you more manageable." She sensed movement, then something shiny appeared in her whirling vision. "Do you see this? Do you?" He spat the words and Thea managed a jerky nod. "A hunting knife is a useful thing, I'm told," he said. "This one fits in a man's pocket. It was a gift—from Cynthia. I've always appreciated irony. Let me think…where's the best place to—*be still!*" The command rasped out viciously. "Shut up and don't move another inch, or I promise I'll feed you to the alligators a piece at the time."

Amazing what passed through one's mind at the point of death. Thea stared up into the glittering dark eyes and silently thanked God that she could at least face them without the vertigo. That she felt no fear, only a ripping grief for Devlin, and a gritty determination to spit in Edgar Fane's eye.

"Devlin will hunt you down," she choked out, gasping when his fingers cruelly bore down against her windpipe. "He'll…find the evidence. Hotel Hustler…"

Pain suddenly exploded in her side, a spear of white-hot fire that stole the last of her breath.

"That ought to do it," Fane said, thrusting her away. "As for your pathetic Mr. Stone, he'll never find you. He's nothing but a gullible Southern gentleman who still believes in chivalry. When he learns the woman he rescued from jail is the daughter of a bawdy house singer and a gambler, he'll consider himself fortunate to be rid of you."

"The Secret Service…" The shock of pain had weakened her. She slumped, managed one last challenge. "They'll find you."

"Bah. Fools, the lot of them. They can't find their way across a street. Neither the Secret Service nor any other authority will be able to prove a thing. They never have. They never will. I'm Edgar Fane. It's quite delicious, you know, having all the power and wealth one desires."

Thea collapsed like a rag doll against the seat, her hands instinctively fluttering to the source of the pain in her left side. The white cotton shirtwaist blouse was wet, sticky with what dawned upon her in shock was blood. "You…stabbed me."

"You shouldn't have hit me. Here." He tugged out his handkerchief, pressed it with ungentle force against her side. "If you apply sufficient pressure, you should survive long enough to make it to my yacht." The carriage lurched back into motion. "If it's any consolation, after you and your father are disposed of, I've decided cold-blooded murder's not really my style. Frankly, I don't care much for blood, so if you don't mind, try not to bleed all over the buggy. As for the Hotel Hustler, I'd already decided it's time for him to retire, sail to the Fiji Islands. I plan to paint satisfying but mediocre art. The thrill's been gone for a long time. Tell me, did you hide some of my best work anywhere else other than the bucket? Perhaps somewhere upon your lovely person? Well, not so lovely now. But you were, Theodora. You were."

Pain and shock had weakened her resistance, but Thea smashed the heels of both hands over the handkerchief and pressed while she gritted her teeth, forcing her sluggish brain to ignore the dusting of regret in his voice and *think*. "Too many people know, this time. You're…no longer impervious."

"Remains to be seen, doesn't it? You'll never know, having tragically fallen overboard once we set out to sea." Suddenly his head lifted. Twisting, he looked behind them, then muttered a curse. Lifting the buggy whip, he slashed the horses' hides until their light canter erupted back into a frenzied gallop.

The buggy rocketed down the road. Winding curves with gigantic trees close enough for the Spanish moss to brush their heads flew by in a blur as twilight deepened toward night. Dizzy, depleted, Thea clamped her elbow against her side and wondered if the next bounce would propel her over the armrest. Then she heard it—a voice, calling out in the tropical wilderness of Jekyll Island. Devlin's voice.

Somehow Thea managed to turn, though an agony of pain sliced through her side. Her heart gave a leap of gladness. "Devlin." She tried to shout the name, but the word dribbled out in more of a whimper. Fane flicked her a single savage glance bristling with challenge. A taunting smile twisted his lips before he leaned forward to focus all his attention on the horses flying at the edge of control.

The sound of thundering hooves crescendoed off to her right, until the rolling rhythm filled her ears. Hope blossomed inside Thea's laboring heart and she managed to turn her head toward the sound. A horse's head appeared, mane flying, ears pricked forward, bright dark eyes focused on the two harnessed animals racing a few strides ahead. Then Devlin came into view, riding bareback, one long arm stretched out toward

Thea. Across the low armrest of the buckboard their gazes met.

"Take my hand, love," Devlin told her in a calm, commanding voice.

"Not a chance!" Fane shouted, and abruptly the buckboard swerved away, almost crashing into the underbrush before settling back into a shuddering path along the center of the road. "Catch me if you think you can!" he yelled over his shoulder.

Less than a hundred yards ahead, the road curved sharply to the left.

Thea stiffened her spine, never taking her gaze from the magnificent sight of Devlin riding a beautiful chestnut Thoroughbred as though he were part of the horse. Love and determination and—peace—washed over her. *I can do all things through Christ...soar on wings of eagles...walk on the heights with hind's feet...* Time stretched into a bright supple ribbon, wrapping Thea in an unearthly blend of strength and weightlessness. Grasping the wire arm rail, she pulled herself forward in the seat, watching the horse lengthen his stride until he and Devlin galloped less than a yard away alongside the carriage. Devlin had tied the reins together over the horse's neck and he was leaning, both arms now stretched toward her. Thea sucked in a deep breath, lifted her arms toward his, and as the ricocheting buckboard tossed her off balance and she toppled forward, Devlin's hands closed around her waist and lifted her out of the buckboard.

Chapter Thirty-Eight

Dev… Devlin. He had rescued her after all. Joy filled Thea's heart until pain from the knife puncture shrieked through her body. The joy and pain wrapped around her in blinding whorls of gold and scarlet. Sobbing, she drifted toward a fog of semiconsciousness while Devlin settled her sideways in front of him, his hard muscled arms on either side holding her in a safe protective cage.

"I've got you, love," his voice murmured in her ear. "You're safe, Thea."

He spoke to the horse, and a moment later the animal slowed to an easy walk, nostrils blowing hard but as quiescent as a purring kitten. Down the road, Fane and the buckboard carriage flew around the corner and out of sight. "Whoa, boy," Devlin said, bringing the horse to a standstill. He slipped to the ground, then reached to haul Thea down.

"You crazy little fool! You almost died!" His voice broke and he abruptly wrapped her in a smothering embrace, his arms shaking. "Thea… Thea… Thank You, God. You're alive. Lord, thank You…"

"Amen," Thea breathed waveringly before her legs

collapsed beneath her. "Devlin…sorry. Had to come. Found out your secret." His face turned gray as the Spanish moss and she tried to lift her hand to soothe him. "Don't care. Love you…"

"Thea, I wanted to tell you, but I didn't know how. I—hey! What's this?" He grabbed her hand and stared. "This is blood. Did that monster hurt you?"

"'fraid so." She could feel herself sliding back down a slippery slope into darkness. "Knife. Left side. Then he gave me a handkerchief. He doesn't like blood…."

Before she finished the sentence Devlin had her stretched out on the path, his jacket under her head while he ripped open her shirtwaist with scant ceremony. "I see it. All right, sweetheart, you're all right. It's actually not too bad, only a couple of inches deep. Still bleeding a bit but it's starting to clot. You'll need stitches but—you'll live."

A single shuddering breath escaped before he shrugged out of his shirt, then tugged a flannel undershirt over his head. In a few swift tugs he ripped off the three-quarter sleeves and tied them together. After folding the shirt into a wad he carefully covered the wound, then used the tied-together sleeves to wrap around Thea's side to hold the makeshift bandage in place. Edgar's blood-soaked handkerchief was hurled into the undergrowth.

Then he was covering Thea's face with desperate kisses. "Don't ever do this to me again. I love you. I never should have kept my profession a secret. I never want to keep sec—"

A loud scream ripped the air, then was silenced with the abruptness of a snuffed candle. A pall of stunned, absolute silence quivered in the twilight.

Devlin sprang to his feet, standing literally over Thea in a protective stance that moved her to tears. Yet his reaction awakened in her a longing wide and deep as the ocean to cover *his* face with kisses. When he knelt beside her once more, she fumbled for his hand, holding it against her wet cheek. "Go find out what happened," she told him. "I'll be fine."

Devlin shook his head. "I'm not leaving you alone in the darkness. If I hold you, can you stay on the horse?"

"Absolutely. I'll even ride astride. The pain's much better."

"Liar." He covered her mouth in one brief, hard kiss, then stroked his index finger down her cheek. "I love you for your bravery. But no more secrets or lies between us, all right?"

"All right. But I do feel much better. You're here."

Gently, he lifted her into his arms, settled her on the horse. After mounting with a breathtaking display of masculine strength, they set off down the road at a smooth, controlled canter. When they reached the bend in the road Devlin pulled the horse to a walk, and used the shadows of a thick grove of live oak to conceal their presence as much as possible.

A dozen yards into the bend, they saw the two livery horses standing near the side of the road, heads drooped, sides heaving, globs of white foam coating their flanks. The empty buckboard carriage was tipped sideways over the branches of a fallen tree which protruded halfway across the road.

Edgar Fane was nowhere in sight.

"Can you stay on the horse by yourself?" Devlin began urgently, just as the sound of a low groan reached their ears, followed by a garbled string of illegible words, then silence.

Thea passed her tongue around lips gone numb and sand dry. "Be careful. Please. He still has the knife."

"I'll be careful. Thea…"

"Don't worry about me, Devlin. I've discovered I've a knack for horses. Lancer and me, we'll be fine."

The stormy blue-gray eyes lit up for a moment, then he melted into the shadows, using the screen of the buckboard to shield him from sight. Thea sat still, basking in the afterglow of that expression. She might be sitting astride a lathered horse, her side might be on fire and shivers still racking her body, but nothing could dim the wonder of this moment. Devlin was here, alive. She was very much alive despite Edgar Fane's evil intentions.

Amazing, how love could transform a knife wound to a pinprick.

Devlin returned quickly. "It's not a trap. Thea…" He paused, then added simply, "Fane was thrown from the buggy. He broke his neck. Right now, he only has a few moments to live. He asked for you."

"He—what?" She couldn't absorb the words, couldn't grasp their significance.

"Hold on to Lancer's mane, love. I'll take you to him. It'll be faster if I don't try to carry you myself."

Fane lay without moving in a patch of dry weeds, his head twisted at an unnatural angle, inches away from the trunk of the fallen tree. The last beam of burnt-orange light streamed over his body in macabre illumination. Silently Devlin lifted Thea into his arms and carried her over; she knelt beside Edgar.

His eyes were open, watching Devlin. He spoke

with difficulty. "Not just... Southern farmer. Secret Service?"

Dev nodded. "But I'm also a Southern farmer."

"Would have made a good jockey. Looks like... you win...this race, after all, Stone." The opaque gaze drifted over Thea. "Will she live?"

"Yes," Thea answered. "God willing, for a very long time. Long enough to learn how to forgive you, I hope."

"Ah." A rattling breath struggled to escape from his throat. "Always did like...straightforward women." A strange baffled look drifted across his face. "Can't feel anything. Can't move...tell Simpson...sorry, about Cynthia. I was wro—" The final confession sighed out unfinished as Edgar Fane breathed his last.

Chapter Thirty-Nine

Clean, milk-white skies and mild winter sunshine greeted Thea the next morning. Stitched up and sore, her body squawked in protest the entire walk to the clubhouse from the infirmary, where the compound doctor had insisted she spend the night. Thea didn't mind the discomfort; she and Devlin were both alive, and safe. *Thank You, Lord.* The grateful prayer winged upward with surprising naturalness.

When she opened the door to the office, the first voice she heard was her father's. "One villain dead, the other captured. You've certainly earned a gold star for your 'Secret Service,' Operative Stone."

"That's one way of looking at it." Devlin's back was to Thea and she couldn't see his expression, but he responded to the light sarcasm in a deceptively lazy Southern drawl.

Another Secret Service operative, the "reporter" Mr. Lawlor, lounged against a desk. No difficulty reading the contempt in his expression, she thought sadly. But then, her father deserved it. Neither the Club superintendent nor Miss Schuppan were anywhere in sight. Feeling like a trespasser herself, Thea awkwardly cleared her throat. "Good morning," she said.

Devlin swiftly turned and started toward her. "Thea! We didn't expect you much before noon."

He said something else but she didn't hear because she had just seen the handcuffs around her father's wrists. For an instant time telescoped backward, and she felt the cold heavy manacles around her own wrists. Remembered the hopelessness inside that barren cell. *Every member of her family...* Blindly she focused on Devlin.

He reached her side in two long steps, filling her vision, calming her senses. "You're still pale. Did you sleep? Did the doctor give permission for you to leave?" The intensity of his loving perusal mitigated the churning in Thea's stomach. His anxiety made her want to wrap him in a hug.

And yet, her father's hands were shackled together. "I slept. The doctor grumbled but gave in. I'm stiff. Sore. Grateful to be alive... Devlin? Why is Richard...why is my father handcuffed?"

"Mr. Langston," Mr. Lawlor said, answering for Devlin, "is under arrest for aiding and abetting a notorious counterfeiter guilty of abduction and committing bodily harm, who may or may not also be guilty of the crime of murder." For some reason he scowled at Devlin, then walked over to stand with folded arms in front of the door.

"Don't fret, Theodora," Richard said. "It was inevitable from the moment I followed Edgar out the door of an Atlantic City casino. The arm of the law is long and unrelenting. Unfortunately, so was Edgar Fane. At least I'm still alive." A corner of his mouth curved. "As are you."

And Edgar Fane lay covered in a shroud on his yacht. The men who would have killed Richard and tossed Thea overboard had been taken to the jail in Brunswick. Fane's crimes were at an end…but their consequences still remained. For a painful moment she studied the man who for almost a quarter of a century had pretended she didn't exist.

And yet… "Devlin, my father also aided and abetted *me,* knowingly put himself at risk so I could secure the evidence—for you. For the Secret Service. Doesn't that count for something? Must he be treated like a criminal?"

Deep lines furrowed Devlin's forehead, and shadows smudged the blue-gray eyes. But he allowed Thea to speak, not interrupting or defending himself. Suddenly she realized with a sharp internal click that she'd fallen back into the same toxic trap that had poisoned her spirit for much of her life. Her father had never escaped. With God's grace leveraging some spiritual muscle, Thea could.

"I'm sorry," she said. She darted a glance at the impassive Mr. Lawlor, then stretched up and right there in front of the Lord and everyone else pressed a repentant kiss to Devlin's cheek. Beneath her lips the muscles in the hard cheekbone jerked once, then stilled. "I'm sorry." She breathed the apology again, into his ear, and stepped back. "You're right. You're upholding the law, and I know it's also the right thing to do. It was just…"

"You don't have to apologize. I understand." Softly he brushed her clenched knuckles. "Mr. Lawlor?" he said without looking away from Thea. "Can we have a moment, please?"

"Why am I not surprised? Come along, Langston. You and me'll—"

"Leave Mr. Langston here, Fred."

"Oh, all right." The other operative winked at Thea—*winked*. "You're the boss." He sauntered out, quietly shutting the door behind him.

"My dear man," Richard began, "if you're needing to assert your power over my daughter by ogling her in front of me…"

He hushed up fast when Devlin whirled around and leveled a look that could fry an egg. "You lost your rights as a father a long time ago, Langston. And this woman is going to be my wife. You will treat her with respect. I don't want to regret what I'm about to do."

He turned back to Thea, his tone altering to the deep warm syrup drawl that flowed over Thea in a healing balm. "Your father abandoned you, robbing you of self-confidence. A year ago, another man robbed you of your inheritance, and your grandfather of his self-respect. Then the Secret Service, albeit unintentionally, robbed him of his reputation."

He paused, searching Thea's face, regret carved like old scars in his own. "Not even God can change the past. He can only help us heal from it. But I can try to make some sort of reparation, by giving you a choice. Theodora, nobody outside the Service—except for you—knows your father was forced to become one of Fane's accomplices. Fane's dead. Simpson has sworn in an affidavit that Richard Langston was threatened with death for refusal to comply with Fane's demands, and was used with ill will as a tethered goat to lure an innocent woman to her own demise. To everyone else on Jekyll Island, Mr. Langston was just another guest. Last night, I sent another telegram to the head of the Service. His reply came fifteen minutes ago. Mr. Lawlor and I have been granted the authority to determine Richard Langston's fate. We've decided to pass that determination along...to you."

Disbelief wrapped Thea in barbed wire suspense. Slowly she sank down into Mr. Grob's desk chair. "What are you saying, Devlin?" she managed through stiff lips.

With easy masculine grace Devlin knelt in front of her. "I'm saying your father's fate rests entirely in your hands. I can't undo what operatives up in New York did to your grandfather last year. But Fred and I agreed we can balance the scales here, perhaps a little bit. Say the word, dear heart, and your father walks, free to choose the course of his own life."

Blindly, she reached out, and his hands closed around hers, warm and strong and sure. "What he did was still wrong. He could have approached the Secret Service before leaving Atlantic City. He could have appealed to someone here."

"He could have turned you over to Fane," Devlin murmured. "But he gave you the keys, which allowed you to collect the evidence we needed—knowing the gesture would probably cost him his life. So. Judgment or grace, Theodora? The choice is yours."

Thea looked over Devlin's sturdy shoulder to her father, who stood in profile gazing out the window, his face expressionless, his posture relaxed. The shackles holding his wrists together might have been a figment of Thea's imagination. *What am I supposed to do here,*

Lord? What? When she stirred, Devlin helped her to her feet, tucked a tendril of dangling hair behind her ear, then stepped aside so she could approach the man who had given her life, yet who she knew in her heart still wanted nothing to do with her.

"If you're free, what will you do?"

"If he decides to take up counterfeiting as well as gambling for a profession," Devlin put in smoothly, "he'll be hunted down without mercy."

Richard shrugged. "I'm too old to pretend in the game of life any longer, Theodora. Fane did teach me something, though. In the future, I won't gamble with money I don't have; and haven't legitimately won. As for the rest, Operative Stone, your warning is duly noted." The chains rattled as he made a restless move with his hands. "Charles did a good job with you, Theodora. You might look like your mother, but you're nothing like her at all." He laughed a light, bitter laugh. "An upstanding professional government agent with a heart wins over a professional gambler without one, every time. Though in my opinion, any man willing to toss away his career for a woman is gambling more than he ought."

Chapter Forty

"Toss away his career?" Thea retorted furiously. "Is that a taunt, or a threat? Never mind, it doesn't matter. Since that's your attitude, you can go straight to jail. And I won't regret one bit being the one who sent you there. I will not allow Devlin to ruin his career because of a poor decision on my part and poor judgment on yours."

Devlin joined her and touched her shoulder. "Thea, it's not a threat. We've had a long talk with your father. There's something I haven't had a chance to tell you."

Richard shook his head ruefully, admiration sparking behind the shuttered expression. "Let her be," he said. "Fierce in her defense of you, isn't she, Operative Stone? I could envy you that, but what's the point? Deal the cards, Theodora. Freedom or jail, whatever hand I draw, it's up to me to play. No obligations on your part either way."

"I know," Thea admitted. "I learned that lesson from you a long time ago. But lately I've learned a few others, as well." Moisture gummed her throat as she struggled, the words halting and hoarse, to set both of them free.

"Thank you, for what you did, yesterday. For caring enough to try to save my life. I...don't want you to go to jail, not for this. Let him go, Devlin." She glanced up, and his smile erased any lingering doubt. "I want you to let him go. I believe in my heart it's the right choice."

"I agree," he said, and tugged a key out of his vest pocket to remove Richard's handcuffs. Then he held out his right hand. "You'll always be welcome at StoneHill Farm. But the only games we play there are chess and dominoes."

Richard stared at the outstretched arm, then with another shrug shook hands. "I've seen my share of grifters and green goods. Maybe we can work something out." His shoulders squared as he lifted his chin and looked straight at Thea. "I haven't been a good father, but I want you to know—I've never cheated. Not once." After a final glance he strode across the room toward the door.

Two betraying tears rolled silently down Thea's cheeks. "Father?"

He stiffened but turned, hand on the doorknob. "Yes, Theodora?"

"Every now and then...send Grandfather and me a postcard?"

The poker face crumbled suddenly, and for one fleeting second she glimpsed the shadow of a weak, vulnerable young man trapped between responsibility, and a compulsion that refused to relent. "I'll try," he promised. "I'll try...daughter."

With a firm click, the door shut behind him.

Thea closed her eyes. So this was what it felt like, to see someone through the eyes of Jesus. When Devlin carefully drew her into his arms, she laid her head against his chest. "Thank you," she said after several long moments, soaking up the love, the kindness, the exquisite compassion of this man God had brought into her life. "I love you with all my heart, Devlin. But… your career? What will happen? I know you have to write a report. You have to be honest. You have to, or I'll never forgive myself. No, wait. You'll do the right thing, no matter what I do or don't do." She listened to the steady rhythm of his heartbeat, and was content. "I'm learning…."

Devlin chuckled, then led her over to a table, picked up a sheet of paper and handed it to her. "Before I came down to Jekyll Island, I visited the man who persuaded me to join the Service, Micah MacKenzie. We had a long talk. Then I went into Washington and talked with the Chief. I've resigned, Theodora. As of this morning, it's official. Operative Lawlor has taken over to tie up the loose ends, your father being the final thread. You and I can go home."

A long, cleansing breath ruffled Thea's hair. "Home," he repeated. "For three years God allowed me to wander in the desert of deceitful, greedy souls and dirty cities full of crime. I like to think that, in my wanderings, I at least honored Him by serving my country. But StoneHill is my promised land, and I don't ever want to leave it again." Searching her face, he lifted his hands to tenderly cup her cheeks. "I want to marry you, and raise horses and babies with you. On our way back to Virginia, I want to stop by that breeder and hopefully buy a Holsteiner colt."

His eyes closed, then opened, dark now with desperation. "But what I need more than anything, Thea, is to know you forgive me for hurting you. For not telling you months ago I was part of an organization you hated. If you can forgive your father enough to give him his freedom...?"

"Devlin..." Wincing a little, she carefully wrapped her arms around his waist and hugged him close again, inhaling the wonderful scent of soap, starch and the most dear man in the world. "Of course I forgive you. What woman could resist a dashing hero who rides to her rescue?" Then she balled her fist and punched him hard enough in the ribs to surprise a whoof of discomfort from Devlin and an internal screech from the wound in her side. "But don't you ever do anything that dangerous again, do you hear? I came down here to find proof and save you from Edgar Fane myself. If he'd discovered you, he would have killed you."

"Looks like we saved each other, and God administered divine justice to Edgar Fane." He rested his head against her hair, his palms warm against her back. In all her life, Thea had never felt so protected. So at peace.

"Devlin?"

"Hmm?"

"If I told you that I believe God's looking down on us right now and smiling, would you think I was an emotional mush head?"

"No, sweetheart. Because I sense Him, too. As warm and real as the fire burning in the fireplace."

"Fires in fireplaces burn out...."

"Ours won't." Devlin pressed a gentle kiss to her eyelids, forehead, then each cheek. "Because we'll work to keep it alive, every day, for the rest of our lives."

Theodora gave herself over to the embrace of her beloved, and with a yielding internal recklessness, finally abandoned everything else to God.

* * * * *

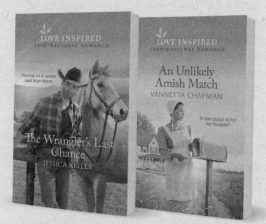